ALSO BY SARA SLIGAR

Take Me Apart

VANTAGE POINT

VANTAGE POINT

SARA SLIGAR

MCD | FARRAR, STRAUS AND GIROUX NEW YORK

MCD
Farrar, Straus and Giroux
120 Broadway, New York 10271

Printed in the United States of America
First edition, 2025

Title page and chapter opener art by YIK2007 / Shutterstock.com.

Library of Congress Cataloging-in-Publication Data
Names: Sligar, Sara, 1989– author.
Title: Vantage point / Sara Sligar.
Description: First edition. | New York : MCD / Farrar, Straus and Giroux, 2025.
Identifiers: LCCN 2024024400 | ISBN 9780374282295 (hardcover)
Subjects: LCGFT: Thrillers (Fiction) | Gothic fiction. | Novels.
Classification: LCC PS3619.L56 V36 2025 | DDC 813/.6—dc23/eng/20240607
LC record available at https://lccn.loc.gov/2024024400

Designed by Abby Kagan

Our books may be purchased in bulk for promotional, educational, or business
use. Please contact your local bookseller or the Macmillan Corporate and Premium
Sales Department at 1-800-221-7945, extension 5442, or by email at
MacmillanSpecialMarkets@macmillan.com.

www.mcdbooks.com • www.fsgbooks.com
Follow us on social media at @mcdbooks and @fsgbooks

10 9 8 7 6 5 4 3 2 1

To Laura and Chris

How imperfectly acquainted were we with the condition and designs of the beings that surrounded us?

—CHARLES BROCKDEN BROWN, *WIELAND*, 1798

VANTAGE POINT

PROLOGUE

Drowning doesn't look how I thought it would.

And I've imagined it often, over the years.

I imagined giant waves. Hands pink from the cold. White spits of foam. I imagined water as green as envy, or as gray as unplated steel.

I imagined what an onlooker would see.

In fact, drowning is colorless. It's blind. It's darkness crowding out your vision. Your eyes blurring with water.

Even so, I won't let go. I grapple for arms, shoulders, legs, anything I can hold on to.

I've got you! I shout.

I can't understand the reply.

Then there's a sharp kick, and I'm alone.

When I open my mouth, water comes in. When I try to spit it out, I swallow more. *I'm coming*, I say—I try to say. The water presses ruthlessly down my throat, pushing oxygen aside. I can't see. I don't know if my eyes are closed, or if I'm underwater. It doesn't matter. What matters is the burn in my chest, my slackening limbs, the water filling my lungs.

In the end, death is a thing you feel.

I've lived on this sound for so long. I've seen it in summer and winter. I've seen it smooth as glass and striped with waves. I've jumped into it, swum in it, trailed my fingers through it on hot days. From the shore, it looks like nothing. It looks as shallow as a lake. Like you could walk straight across. Underneath, reality: a chasm of water, two hundred feet deep, cold and unkind.

The underneath is what drowns you.

Surfaces tell you nothing.

Surfaces lie.

1

CLARA

March 31

The thermostat is fucking with me. For months, the display has insisted that the conference room is a pleasant sixty-eight even though it feels more like the steam room in a Russian banya. I've only been in here ten minutes and sweat is already soaking my shirt. Today's guest (beneficiary? panderer?) is an old friend of Teddy's, a blond guy named Conrad Gaffney, and as he sets up his presentation, my brother leans over to ask me quietly whether I remembered to call down to facilities management about the furnace.

"Yes, of course I did," I hiss. "I told you. They're holding a grudge."

"They're not holding a grudge," Teddy whispers back.

"They are. They're trying to sweat us out. Like bedbugs." At his skeptical look, I add, "You have to call down. They'll listen to you."

"They'll listen to you, too. If you speak with authority."

I want to roll my eyes, but that would be unprofessional, so I grit my teeth and flip to a new page of my legal pad. When Teddy told me he wanted me to take over as director of the Wieland Fund for Community Investment, I told him he was making a mistake. I can't even keep a houseplant alive without our gardener's help. It isn't my fault Teddy decided to embarrass himself on the national stage with a run for a Senate seat and no longer has time for philanthropy. It maybe *is* my fault that a few weeks into this role, I accidentally started a feud with the facilities manager of the Brenner Science Center, where WFCI leases office space. Now here we are, five months later, hearing pitches in what has essentially become a sauna with whiteboards and task chairs.

At the front of the room, Conrad pulls up a deck so plain that at first I think he's accidentally opened a PowerPoint template instead of his intended slideshow. He claps his hands once, like *Gather 'round*, even though it's only Teddy and me in the room and we're already seated. I roll my chair a few inches away from Teddy's and assume a virtuous expression.

I've met Conrad before. His parents used to be summer people, and he was one of those interchangeable sailing-lessons kids who were always stumbling around the docks in orange life vests. Most summer kids vanished from our lives as soon as they aged out of family vacations, but Conrad and Teddy eventually ended up in the same class at Harvard, even roomed together a couple years. I think that's why Teddy felt obligated to invite him to pitch WFCI, even though Conrad's work experience is limited to a few failed crypto start-ups with names like Jaggr and PeskBall. He hasn't grown up to be interesting. He has a firm handshake and a pseudo-hipster undercut. His hobbies are probably rock climbing and grilling meat. I've dated a thousand men like him, back when I still dated men.

Not that personal mediocrity automatically disqualifies him from receiving a grant. But if Teddy actually thought the project was a contender, he would have told me to bring in Allan, the chief scientific officer, and the rest of the team. He wouldn't have scheduled this meeting on a weekend afternoon, right before the annual opening of Cicero's Fish House. Teddy invited Conrad to pitch as a favor, and I'm pretending to have organized it, also as a favor. So the world goes round.

I do my best to pay attention. Conrad's pitch is, essentially: National parks, digitized. He's an avid rock climber (nailed it) and studied business and computer science at Harvard (I was wondering when he'd drop the H-bomb), and the combination of those interests led him to create an immersive virtual reality platform that people can use in their own homes to have the 3D experience of communing with nature. All they need is his company's unique projector string and access to their library of simulations, and they can visit Yosemite while the pasta's boiling on the stove. Because marveling at the Half Dome is everyone's top priority when dinner's running late.

"Can we see it in action?" Teddy asks.

"I'm not really set up to do that today," Conrad says. None of these people ever say what they really mean, but I'm fluent in bullshit. He means the technology isn't ready. "But soon."

"Soon" in bullshit means maybe in, like, a decade. If we double their funding.

Conrad shows us an unimpressive prototype, a spool of cord that looks like cheap Christmas lights, and I doodle a fern leaf in the margins of my page. The loops make it look more like handwriting from afar. Teddy looks at me askance and I turn the leaf's stem into the words *patent pending*.

When the presentation finally limps to an end and I shake Conrad's hand goodbye, his grip is looser, his shoulders tighter. Somehow he's sensed that it's a wash.

"It's a really neat project," I say, trying to soften the awkwardness. "And it's nice to meet you. I mean, see you again. It's been a while."

He returns the smile, slightly strained. He wants to get out of here as much as I do. "Nice to see you, too."

As Teddy walks him to the elevator, I collapse back into the nearest chair. It's hot as fuck. I peel my shirt away from where it's stuck to my front and try to use it to fan myself, to no avail.

The screen has flipped back to its usual screensaver, a colorful topographic map of the island, a repeating WFCI logo in the background. I could draw the silhouette of this island in my sleep. It's shaped almost like a circle, except that the sound runs right through the center, coming up from the south and going more than halfway across before ending abruptly, as if someone was sawing through flesh and stopped when their blade hit bone. So instead of a circle, the island is more like a hoofprint, a balsam leaf, its edges fringed with coves and inlets. Every Locust Harbor boutique sells a million souvenirs printed with that outline. Sweatshirts, dog tags, lampshades, throw pillows. The silhouette is cartoonish, cute, inviting.

And misleading. Millions of years ago, glaciers formed this island, slowly scraping away at the granite, pressing down until it gave way. They left wreckage in their wake, gulches and cliffs, shorn rocks, mountains that jut from the sea. This place is the work of slow violence, and the topographic map shows those battles. Red claw marks where the mountains were dragged southward by melting ice. Marigold hills, yellow valleys. And at the southern end of the sound, where land and sea meet in noncommittal green, and the ground parts like a curtain onto open ocean, you can see the telltale protrusion of Vantage Point—our home.

Teddy comes back in and takes the seat next to me, a casual sprawl.

"Well?" I ask. "Do you think we should give him the grant?"

"What do *you* think? You're the director now."

"Ha." But he waits for an answer. "I don't know," I hedge. "It doesn't seem far enough along. And even if the technology was perfect, and he could actually create the feeling of visiting a place from inside the home, would that be good for the island? People wouldn't come here anymore. And everyone would be out of a job."

Teddy pretends to give me a noogie. "See? You're good at this."

"What, poking holes in people's dreams?"

"Taking care of WFCI."

I pull back and smooth down my hair. "I'm only here until you let me start a foundation for the study of British punk rock."

Inside, I'm preening. It's nice to joke around with Teddy again—we haven't gotten a lot of one-on-one time the past couple months. It's even nicer to know he thinks I can run WFCI; I'm helping him. He trusts me. I've been working a long time on that.

"Should I wait a few days to let Conrad know?" I ask. "So he thinks we debated it more?"

"No, I'll tell him in person."

"I don't mind telling him, if you want to preserve your friendship or whatever."

"Don't worry. I'm going to say it was your idea anyway."

"Ha, ha."

Teddy messes with my hair again as he stands. "I'm going to grab my jacket out of my office—"

"*My* office."

"Your office," he corrects himself. "Then Cicero's? I'm starving."

2

CLARA

March 31

Forget groundhogs, equinoxes, religious holidays. On our island, spring starts the day Cicero's Fish House plugs in their deep fryer. By the time Teddy and I get there, the deck is packed. Half the draft beer list is already crossed out. Every available surface overflows with empty pitchers and crumpled napkins. Empty fish crates litter the side yard like hunks of marble.

Jess has claimed our usual table, but we've barely hugged hello before Teddy's swarmed by a group of middle-aged men. Ernie Gluck wants to report Millie Powell for illegal clamming. Teddy tells him that's a task for the island police. Max Lisle wants to ask when the town council will repaint the crosswalks in Locust Harbor. Teddy reminds him that he stepped down as mayor last month, so Max needs to talk to Dale Simonson. Joe Michaud, who owns the hardware store in Chaumont, wants Teddy to hire him to install security cameras around Vantage Point.

"As protection," Joe explains.

"From what? I feel safe on this island. I feel secure." Teddy grins. "Unless you know something I don't."

"Faded crosswalks are a safety threat," Max says.

"So are clam poachers," Ernie says.

"I don't think cameras would help with either of those," I point out.

Joe peers down the length of the table. "What do you think, Jess? How do you feel about some cameras around your place?"

Wedged up against the railing, she nods thoughtfully. "Your system definitely sounds top-of-the-line." Jess is good at finding answers that satisfy everyone.

Sure enough, Joe raises his hands in triumph, even though she's committed to nothing. "There you go, Teddy. Happy wife, happy life."

Teddy shakes his head. Before he has to reply, a frazzled server arrives at the end of our table, struggling under the weight of an overloaded tray of food and beer.

"Here we go!" she announces, out of breath. My stomach goes tight. I didn't even notice Teddy placing the order.

"Okay, that's our cue." Joe slaps the table and gets up. As he shepherds Max and Ernie away, he points a finger at Teddy. "But think about it, yeah?"

"Absolutely," Teddy promises.

By the time the men have squeezed their way back into the crowd, the tray is wobbling in the server's hands. When she tries to shift the weight to her left arm to distribute the food, beer sloshes at the pitcher's

lip. Teddy leaps up and takes the whole tray from her, moving it gal-
lantly out of reach, so all she can do is stand there and wring her hands
as he passes the baskets down to us. Cheeseburgers, lobster rolls, fries.
Way too much food for three people.

"Thanks, Mr. Wieland," she says, her tone a mixture of gratitude
and embarrassment.

I recognize her now: Lisa Cicero, the owner's daughter. Last time
I saw her, she was in braces. Now the braces are off, and her hair is
striped with box highlights. Under her jacket, she's knotted her
T-shirt at the waist to reveal a slice of stomach spotty with cold.

Jess gives her a warm smile. "Lisa, how are you? How's school?"

Lisa wipes her forehead with the back of her arm. "Oh, it's good.
I mean, I'm taking this semester off. There was, um, an administrative issue? But I'm going back in the fall."

"I bet your parents are glad you're here to help out."

"Yeah," she says with wan enthusiasm. "Well, I'm looking forward
to the May Day party."

"Us too. We can't wait," Jess says.

The fries pass under my nose, golden-white, wilted with fat.

To Teddy, Lisa adds, "I'm excited about the primary, too. I regis-
tered just so I could vote for you."

"Really? I'm honored." He sets down the last basket with a flourish
and hands back the empty tray, adding a wink for good measure.
"Thanks for helping us out."

She blushes and clutches the dull black circle to her stomach like
a shield. "Sure. Let me know if you need anything else?"

When she's scurried out of earshot, I lean over the table and whisper, "She looks so different! Last time I saw her, she was, like, twelve.
Now she's in college?"

"*Was* in college," Teddy corrects. He removes a hamburger's top
bun and arranges the onion with military precision. "Sounds like she
got suspended."

"What are you talking about?" Jess asks.

"She said there was an 'administrative issue.'"

"I think she meant a problem with the tuition."

"She'd have said that."

"Uh, no," Jess says, "I don't think she would have told the Wielands she couldn't afford a semester of college."

He shrugs. "If you say so." As he lifts the burger to his mouth, he nods at me, then at the food baskets. "Want anything?" Trying to sound casual; failing.

"Maybe in a second," I say in an equally pleasant voice.

"You need to eat something."

My lips tighten. "I will."

Jess tries to redirect us. "I don't think security cameras are a bad idea," she announces. "They could at least show us how the raccoons keep opening the latch on the trash can."

"I don't want people thinking I don't feel safe on my island," Teddy says.

"*Your* island?" she teases. "You own the whole thing now?"

He waves his hand. "You know what I mean."

She gives me a smile that's supposed to be triumphant—*Look, I changed the subject*—but it only makes me feel worse, incapable and pathetic. I didn't need her to jump in.

And her ploy doesn't even work, because as soon as Teddy finishes his next bite, he pokes a basket of fries toward me with his elbow. "Eat something. You're hungry."

I narrow my eyes. "Stop telling me to eat."

"I will when you eat," he says.

"Okay, okay, okay." Jess pushes Teddy's arm back to his side of the table. "Let's all relax."

Teddy is relaxed. I'm the one who's wound up. It's almost magical, the way he manages to push all my buttons without batting an eye. I was doing a good job of not thinking too much about the food on the table, and now the thoughts are surging back: how much I have to eat to get him off my case, whether I could take one fry and chew it and store it inside my cheek and spit it out when they're not looking, or if I should just eat a handful, and if so how long is the bathroom line, and is it loud enough inside that people wouldn't hear me puke, and then I'm thinking about how the purge would feel, how beautiful and free.

I stand up. The table seems to have changed shape and grown tentacles since I sat down: my knees knock against its underside, a bolt of bright pain, and my feet tangle under the bench.

"Clara." Teddy doesn't bother hiding his exasperation.

"I'm just going to have a smoke."

I kick myself free of the bench and stagger back into the crowd.

On the other end of the deck, a set of rickety wooden steps leads down to a stretch of rocks and the battered shed where the Ciceros store dry goods. I unhook the NO ENTRY rope and step gingerly down to the landing. It's just past high tide, and the sea spray has made the wood's top layer mushy and slick.

I arrange myself against the railing and rummage through my pockets until I find a half-finished joint and a lighter. When Teddy announced his candidacy, his obnoxious campaign manager gave me a cute soliloquy about "increased scrutiny" and how maybe I shouldn't do things like have rampant casual sex or do drugs in public. Jess was there, too, but I was obviously the lecture's target. I asked Mike if he counted pot as a drug and he said obviously. I said it wasn't obvious at all, it's legal now. He said, "Still, it's not a good look." Jess nudged my foot under the table, and I reluctantly agreed.

I take a big, deep drag. Smoke hums in my mouth. I hold it there for a second, feel it soak into my palate.

Before me, the harbor has quieted for the evening. This time of year, the lobstermen can dock on the slips, so the outer moorings are mostly empty. Numbered white buoys hold spots for the summer boats that have been jacked up on blocks in Jim Hobart's dry-storage lot or sailed down to the Caribbean for the winter, swallows heading south. The few remaining boats look small and lost. Their hulls rest in the water like open eggshells. I picture myself swimming to one—arm over arm, through the freezing water. Climbing aboard. Sailing away.

Then I exhale, fogging the view.

The planks under my feet wobble. Someone's coming down the stairs, and I don't even have to look to see who.

"Hey." The landing isn't big, but Jess slides in next to me, bumps my hip with her own. "You okay?"

I make an irritated gesture. "He needs to stop telling me to eat."

"I know." She zips her coat up against the wind, loops her dark hair over her shoulder to keep it from blowing in her face. The cold has put a flush on her cheekbones, paled the rest of her skin. "You know it's because he cares."

"Well, it makes me want to eat less."

"I know."

"Can you tell him that?"

"*You* can tell him."

I pull a face. "But what's the point of my best friend getting together with my brother if she can't do my dirty work for me?"

She snorts. "You're right. I forgot my whole marriage was a long con to help you avoid confrontation."

The weed has started to loosen the knot in my throat. I offer her the joint. She shakes her head, as I knew she would, the same way I knew she would follow me down here. Jess has been my best friend since we were nine. Her choices come to me as easily as my own.

"I just want him to give me more credit," I explain.

"It's an adjustment." We both know she's not talking only about WFCI. "Plus, he has a lot on his mind lately."

She's right, of course. Still, I miss being able to talk to her without having her argue his side.

"Come over tomorrow night," I say abruptly. "Let's do a girls' night. I'll finally watch that Hallmark Christmas movie."

She raises a perfectly tweezed eyebrow. "I think you missed the season by a couple months. Anyway, I can't. We have some events in Brunswick tomorrow, I don't know what time we'll be back."

I frown. "Tomorrow's April first."

"Yes, I know."

"So you probably shouldn't be traveling."

"You want us to stay home all month?"

"Kind of." I'm only half joking. We've had this discussion before.

"The campaign doesn't stop for superstitions," she says in her pragmatic way. She doesn't stop for superstitions, either. She squeezes my shoulder. "But we'll do a movie night soon. I'm going to go back up now."

"I'll be there in a sec."

The stairs shake again as she mounts them. It's March, so the staircase stays intact, but tomorrow is April: The month a shake portends a splintering. The month a scratch in the skin means tetanus, and a long drive ends in a ditch, and a single misstep becomes a long fall. Six hours left before the odds turn against us.

I know I shouldn't think like that. But with a history like mine, it's impossible not to.

I stub out the joint and squint across the sound. With the fog rolling in, Vantage Point is almost obscured. I can just barely see the peak of the big house's roof, the railing of the balcony off my parents' bedroom. I was born in that room. A home birth, before they were trendy. My mother always said the first thing she saw after she pushed me from her body was the surface of the water in the sound, so bright in the morning light that in her exhausted haze she could have sworn the trench was filled top to bottom with diamonds.

She held me in her arms, sticky with vernix, and told my father she had received a sign. For months they had been planning to name me after a distant relative. Now she had changed her mind.

She wanted to call me Clara. Clear, bright. An omen of an easy life.

My dad shrugged. *Sure.*

Secretly, he thought it was pointless. My last name was already Wieland.

That was a kind of omen, too.

Wieland curse

The **Wieland curse** is a series of deaths and calamities involving descendants of the American steel tycoon <u>Thomas Edward Wieland Sr.</u>

Notable events attributed to the curse have included stabbings, drownings, poisonings, yacht fires, suicides, collisions, disappearances, and more.

Most of these incidents have taken place during the month of April. Some historians therefore claim that the curse was the inspiration for the line "April is the cruellest month" in <u>T. S. Eliot</u>'s modernist poem <u>The Waste Land</u>.

In a 1972 interview, actress <u>Olivia Tew</u> blamed her sensational divorce from financier Richard Wieland-Smythe on the curse, stating, "I could have put up with the philandering, the smoking, the gambling, the lies . . . but I could not bear the feeling of the curse hanging over my head, an axe waiting to fall."

3

JESS

April 1

This afternoon's campaign event is at Brunswick High School, which
is different from Friday afternoon's event at Harpswell High School,
which is different from Friday morning's event at the Harpswell diner,
which is in turn different from tomorrow morning's event at a diner in
Sheffield. I am wearing a burgundy skirt-suit and matching heels,
which is different from yesterday's navy skirt-suit and matching heels, and
also different from tomorrow's cobalt skirt-suit and matching heels.
Sometimes when the stylist sends me the week's clothes, I wonder if
I could wear the exact same garment every day and ask the news

outlets to change the color in Photoshop before they publish the images. Select, fill selection. Copy, paste.

The events could be copy-pasted, too. The populations change, as do the refreshments. In Cape Elizabeth, there was brand-name bottled water and the attendees had salon highlights. In Farmington, we drank Diet Coke out of plastic cups and the hair colors came from a box. But the rallies themselves are all basically the same. A place, a crowd, a speech. A permanent state of déjà vu.

Today's backstage is a maze of high school theater paraphernalia: clunky set pieces, painter's tape blocking marks, ancient sound equipment. Beyond the curtain, the people in the auditorium are getting restless. We were supposed to go on half an hour ago.

"Hold still," Phoebe whispers. Phoebe is a speechwriter, but by virtue of her gender, has also become the person responsible for making sure I am presentable before any event. She makes sure my hair has no flyaways, my pantyhose have no ladders, my underwear line is not visible, my bra straps are safely tucked away, and generally sweeps away all other telltale signs that I am a normal human woman. The first time she looked me over, I was offended, because I take my appearance very seriously. But it's true there are always angles I can't see, like now, when she plucks a stray hair off the back of my jacket.

Another minute ticks by, then another. The temperature rises another few degrees. The buzzing voices still sound upbeat, but soon they will want to get home to dinner, off to their night classes, on with their lives. It could happen any minute. Sentiment turns on a dime.

My bladder pinches again, more insistently. The A/V guy is still huddled by the control panel with the most tech-savvy campaign staffer, frantically flipping through a thick instruction manual. In the opposite corner, Teddy's patient smile is slipping as the high school principal drones on about the junior class's average SAT scores. Phoebe keeps adjusting the waist of my skirt an inch to the left, an inch to the right, trying to center the zipper. The more nervous she gets about the delay, the harder she tugs, and I have to bite back a yelp as the skirt's inner hook scrapes across my back.

"Can't we do it without a mic?" I ask Phoebe, trying to edge subtly out of her grasp. "Teddy can talk loud."

She shakes her head. Her fingers stay tight on my waistband. "The acoustics are really bad."

We've had this conversation four times already today, but I don't know what else to talk to her about. With all the dead time on the campaign trail, shuttling between cars and hotels, I've been working on making a taxonomy of all the different ways people react to Wielands. Phoebe is Type C: the Clam. She will converse as much as you want if it's related to her job, but the prospect of speaking to me about anything personal paralyzes her with fear. Mostly, I don't mind. Right now, I'm bored, I have to pee, my copy-pasted heels hurt like hell, and I've been pushed around all day like Barbie in her Dream Car.

I peek at Teddy over the costume rack. He's wearing chinos and a fleece quarter-zip, because research says voters prefer their women to look pretty and their men to look approachable. His campaign quarter-zips are identical to his usual quarter-zips, except that these ones are ironed and lint-rolled and can only be washed four times before they're quietly donated to a nearby charity. Too much longer and they start to look dingy on TV.

He catches my eye and smiles sideways at me, and warmth uncurls in my stomach. Anyone else might think it's just another smile. Teddy is impossibly, unfairly handsome, handsome enough to silence a room when he enters, even if he weren't so recognizable. Women unbutton their shirts for him, slip him their phone numbers; after every meet-and-greet, he pulls fistfuls of paper from his pockets. But I know things about Teddy they'll never know—like this secret smile, a little more crooked, a little more dimpled, a smile that is mine and mine alone.

A chant starts up in the auditorium. *WIELAND! WIELAND!* Teddy turns toward the noise. *WIELAND WIELAND WIELAND*— over and over, until my last name doesn't even sound like a word anymore, but like a meaningless sequence of sounds, an alien distress call. Phoebe is so flustered she yanks my skirt almost halfway around my waist, and my patience disappears.

"Phoebe," I whisper in a measured voice, "I have to run to the ladies' room."

She freezes. "Right now?"

I gently disengage her hands from my body. *Please, a moment alone.* "Yes."

"It can't wait?"

"I'll be fast," I promise.

She looks around in panic for Mike, Teddy's campaign manager, who is marching toward the sound system with his phone pressed to his ear. Phoebe winces and waves over a woman with a long frizzy braid. A guide. I suppress a groan.

"*Fast,*" Phoebe reminds me as she hands me off. Then she remembers who I am and adds, "Please?"

The venue coordinator hurries me through a maze of cords and cameras and out the heavy metal doors, the bar handle depressing with a loud thunk. We are in a narrow hall lined with green lockers. The fluorescent lights are blinding. The door whooshes shut behind us, muffling the chant.

"I feel like I'm back in high school, begging for a hall pass," I joke.

"Oh, no, you don't need a hall pass," my escort trills. "Actually, we got rid of hall passes last year, because we had a student with Crohn's disease whose parents lobbied the school board and now instead students are supposed to—"

Type D: the Chatterer. I put on my most attentive face. The typology isn't only for my own amusement. You have to know how to interact with other people. Mike is always going on about how we need to make personal connections with everyone we meet. *You especially,*

Jess, he said last week, with the sort of brutal honesty that only mothers and campaign managers can get away with, *you can come across a little aloof.*

I said, *I think that's just my face.*

He said, *Okay, well, get it under control.*

What I do right now to control my face is I imagine what this woman will say tomorrow, when people ask if she met Teddy: *I met his wife, and she's so down-to-earth.* I like "down-to-earth" because people only ever use it for people they think are better than them. "Down-to-earth" means you would be allowed to be be a bitch if you wanted to, but you are a good person, so you try to be nice.

"—*love* him," she's saying. "As a candidate. He's such a great guy. I mean, even aside from being so cute."

I'm pretty sure she's talking about Teddy, although I doubt they've ever met and under normal circumstances it would be weird to talk about someone to his own wife this way. I've gotten used to people name-dropping my own husband to me, total strangers talking about him as if he were a close personal friend.

"You're so lucky," she finishes.

"Thanks." I see the sign for the women's room at the end of the hall. We're close, maybe thirty seconds. I hope she doesn't follow me in. What if I fart and then this total stranger hears it and tells people I fart when I pee? What if that becomes my thing? The brilliant senator and his wife who farts when she pees.

"I remember when you got married," says Type D.

I want to say *That makes one of us,* but I don't know if she would realize it's a joke. "That's nice."

"Actually, my cousin went to elementary school with you."

I start paying more attention. "Your cousin's from the island?"

"No, Kattinocket."

My foot lands wrong. My ankle twists under me. I stumble a few steps, like a panicked bird, catching myself with one hand on a locker. "*Shit,*" I say, forgetting myself.

"Oh my god!" Type D rushes forward. "Are you okay?"

"Yes. Yes! Sorry." I pin my smile back on. "Just slipped. I'm fine."

She retreats, but not far, holding her hands a few inches away from me like a parent watching their child take their first steps. The surprise has made my bladder clench tighter, and I move forward steadily, trying not to limp. The restroom is twenty feet away, ten, five. We're almost at the door when Type D's walkie-talkie squeals. The sound system is working again, and I'm wanted onstage.

Two hours later, after the speech has been given and the hands shaken and the babies held, another staff member ushers Teddy and me through the school's cavernous kitchen, past an announcement for an active shooter drill next Monday, and out onto the stairs by the loading dock. The town car loiters outside, along with a few photographers and some fans who figured out the exit plan. I wait in the background while Teddy works his way down the line. He has perfected his handshake: firm and inviting, while also communicating that he needs to move on, so keep your comments concise.

At the end of the line, he opens the car door for me and I slide in, sitting on the seat first and then pivoting my knees inside, the way my etiquette teacher taught me, and he slips in after me, and finally we are alone.

"Whew," he says, with a comical grimace.

He leans in to kiss me. He smells like cedarwood and sage, from the same artisanal soap he's used since puberty. Underneath it, a faint whiff of deodorant, and then, finally, sweat and warmth, a long day, uniquely Teddy. I could crawl inside that smell.

"I'm exhausted," I murmur against his mouth.

"Me too."

His hand closes over my thigh, automatic and possessive, his thumb settling in the crease behind my knee. The pantyhose block most of the sensation. Before the campaign, I hadn't worn pantyhose in years. Political wives and church ladies must be keeping the whole pantyhose industry afloat.

"Your speech was great," I say. "After they fixed the sound."

"I told Phoebe we have to work on the last section. It needs to end with a bang."

"You have a few days to figure it out."

"Yeah, that's true." He frowns in thought.

I press my nose to his neck. "I was talking to this school administrator inside and—"

The car door across from us opens, and I jerk upright. Mike gets in.

"Uh, hi," I say.

Teddy says, "Mike's going to ride back with us, so we can go over the week's schedule."

"Sorry, Jess," Mike says.

I manage a weak smile as the car starts to move. Mike has been with the campaign since the beginning—since before Teddy, even. The DNC recruited him first. On the surface, there is nothing special about Mike. He's a nice, slightly loud guy with a generic face, generic wire-rimmed glasses, and a generic family back in Arlington. His wardrobe comes exclusively from the Ralph Lauren section of Saks. His only memorable attribute is his hair, which he wears swept back from his forehead with so much product you can still see the marks the comb left in it, like the shiny grooves of a record. Everything else about Mike is forgettable, which is how he likes it.

The problem between Mike and me isn't personal. It's that our interests are fundamentally opposed. I want Teddy to stress less, sleep more, say no to more things. Mike wants him to say yes to as many things as possible. Mike wants me everywhere for the visuals and wants me nowhere because I am inconvenient. I am always introducing new problems, such as needing to pee, but everyone has to be nice to me, because I'm sleeping with their boss. If Mike had his way, he would probably run this entire campaign as if Teddy were single; but married people poll better.

"Here, let's switch places," I tell Teddy, so they can sit across from each other. I clamber over his lap. Teddy's hands clasp my hips to help me move, and my skirt rides up my thighs. In another world, it could have been sexual, but Mike's presence is the ultimate boner-killer.

When I'm settled on the other side of the car, Teddy says, "What were you saying about the school administrator?"

"She's cousins with someone I went to school with in Kattinocket."

"Oh?" Teddy's voice drops in concern. He knows I don't like talking about the place. "You remember them?"

"Probably not. I didn't ask the name."

"Kattinocket?" Mike says from the other side of the car. For a split second, I forgot he was here. "I thought you went to elementary school on the island."

"I moved in fourth grade."

"We have a town hall there in a couple weeks," Mike says.

I glance at Teddy. "You do?"

"You don't have to come," Teddy assures me. He raises his hand to the nape of my neck, rubs at the knot of tension there. "It's only one day. I asked them not to schedule you for it."

I am both touched that he thought of that and slightly annoyed that he didn't ask. But he's right: I wouldn't have wanted to go.

Mike says, "It would be great if you could make it, though. If you're from there."

The car rumbles up the ramp to the highway. I drum my fingers against the pebbled leather of the door handle and make myself sound flippant: "I don't know. I haven't been back in years." *Ever.* "I doubt anyone remembers me."

"Obviously this person's cousin does. You could even introduce Teddy. I've told you before, you're a valuable surrogate."

What a strange word, *surrogate.* Until this campaign, I heard it only in connection with pregnancy. Friends would spoon through an alphabet soup of abbreviations, IUI and IVF, and then find the word *surrogate*, arranged expensively at the bottom of the bowl. Last year, Teddy's cousins chartered a private plane to fly them ten thousand miles to a military air base because their baby was stuck in the womb of a woman stuck in a country stuck in a war. Now *surrogate* has another meaning, and the meaning is me. The campaign has filled me ripe and fertile with Teddy's message. I am an extra body, an extra voice. A copy. A stand-in.

"I'll think about it," I say.

"It's only a couple hours awa—"

"She said she'll think about it," Teddy interrupts. I squeeze his hand gratefully.

Mike lets the topic go. "So, Ted. Can we go over the channel 6 appearance? They changed the format a little."

The ride back to the island is slower than usual. We've entered roadwork season, the short window between when the ground thaws and when the tourists descend. The bulldozers at least are something new to look at. Otherwise, the view is so familiar it's like running laps around a track. Dense forest alternates with strip malls, the parking lots dotted with puddles of melted snow. In the past, I've found that life as a Wieland gets easier after April, when the stories about the curse dry up and the crackpots move on, and then summer hits and life in Maine gets easier, too, as everything reopens and everyone's mood improves. I've been assuming this summer will be the same. Only now, as we pass a motel with a sign that says GRAND REOPENING, does it occur to me that the arrival of summer might actually make things worse. Teddy has only been on the trail since November, right after Senator McBay announced his surprise retirement. We haven't dealt with the extra events, the longer days, the bigger audiences, the bumper-to-bumper Saturday traffic.

I should have anticipated this Kattinocket thing, the same way I should have expected that Teddy would end up running for Senate. I was surprised by that, too. Teddy's young, and he's never held a political office higher than mayor of a ten-thousand-person island. But I forgot the crucial detail, that his last name is Wieland. There are towns, banks, and schools with that name. A bridge in Queens. A skyscraper in Boston. *Gryllus wielandis*, a species of cricket. Steak Wieland, a tender cut of beef taken from below the cow's eye. Of course the DNC would come to him as soon as they got news of McBay's retirement. And of course the campaign would ask things of me I don't want to give.

It's fully dark by the time we make it back to the island. We drop Mike at the apartment he's renting, then the driver turns away from the lights of the town, toward Vantage Point. Teddy puts his phone away and takes my hand again.

"Hi," he says.

"Hi," I say.

I lean my cheek against his shoulder. "I really don't want to go to Kattinocket."

"I know. I told Mike no."

"He'll ask again."

"I'll tell him no again."

The more Teddy reassures me, the more unreasonable I feel. It's only a day trip, another copy-pasted rally. Would it really be that bad? Well, yes, it would be. I would have to be there, after I've worked so hard to get away.

When we reach our property, the car slows to rumble through the open gates, which are spread like dark wings against the night. The headlights catch the narrow trunks of the birch trees, the lumpy shapes of moss along the forest floor.

It takes another five minutes to reach our actual house. Vantage Point covers more than a hundred acres. When Teddy and Clara's great-great-grandfather started developing the property, he had a long list of demands. Formal gardens, informal gardens, tennis court, swimming pool, guesthouse, stables, deep-water dock, artist's studio, canoe shed, servants' quarters, and a separate building for cleaning the house's many rugs and textiles, so he wouldn't have to smell the lye.

It was a big ask. Ambrose had first seen the property from the ocean, with the mist hovering over the virgin pines, and what looked gentle from the sea was fierce up close. Granite bedrock, steep slopes, and loose soil. The land resisted being tamed. Construction took fifteen years. The pièce de résistance was the big house, designed by Frederick Lincoln Savage, the architect responsible for all the most glamorous summer cottages of the 1920s. Legend has it that Ambrose hired Savage with the instructions: *Whatever you usually make, I want more.* Half the house was torn down in the 1960s, to minimize the upkeep, but what remains is still an architectural monster. Twelve bedrooms, fourteen bathrooms, gable windows with scalloped siding, a wraparound deck, finials carved with the family seal.

Now, when the car turns down the driveway and triggers the security lights, the house emerges from the woods like an angry, spitting animal being dragged forward by its collar.

A Savage house in more ways than one.

As I'm unbuckling my seat belt, a chime comes from the seat pocket in front of me. My phone. As I reach for it, a *ding* in a lower octave comes from Teddy's phone on the seat next to him. This isn't unusual. Service is spotty on the island because of the mountains, and we often get a cluster of notifications as soon as we get back in Wi-Fi range.

But the chimes keep coming. One from Teddy's phone, another from mine, back and forth, until both phones are dinging and dinging and dinging like a deranged orchestra.

"What the—?" Teddy mutters, only to be cut off by his phone ringing in his hand. He shows me the screen. Mike, already.

As soon as he answers, Mike starts shouting, a flurry of static.

"—called five times—"

"Slow down. We just got home. I have to get closer to the router." He slides over to get out the opposite door. Through the tinted window,

I watch him jog up the front steps, holding his phone away from his ear as Mike keeps shouting.

I glance down at my own screen. Four texts from Mike, others from the comms director, from a college friend, from the family lawyer, even one from my mother. They all must have come in within the last ten minutes. I open the first one, which is from Teddy and Clara's cousin Felicity.

Felicity Bayer-Wieland: *Just saw!! Clara's not answering. Are you with her? Is she okay?*

Fear shears down my spine.

I type: *I haven't talked to her today. What's going on?*

A dot-dot-dot appears. I go back to my messages. None from Clara. The lawyer's text says: *Reaching out to chat. Have messaged Clara and Teddy as well. Regards.* My college friend says: *Oh my god!!!* My mother says: *Call me when you get a chance.* The fear moves outward, across my back, down my arms.

Another notification. Felicity again. This time, all she's sent is a link to a video. The preview image makes my throat go dry. I fumble for the door handle. My fingers are clumsy. It takes me a few tries to get it open. I trip out of the car and sprint after Teddy, up our driveway and into the house.

4

CLARA

April 1

I learn about the video from a guy I used to party with, someone I barely know.

He texts me out of the blue, while I'm on my sofa watching a reality show where people have sex with their spouses' best friends as an "experiment," and when I see his name pop up, I figure he's too broke to get his own drugs and wants to see if I'm in the city so he can bum some from me. But his message says: *shit Clara just saw, so sorry*

I say: *. . . saw what?*

He says: *the video?*

I say: *What video?*

He says: *oh shit*
I say: *What???*
He sends the link.

The video begins with a girl sitting on a bed. The first thing I notice—the first thing anyone would notice—is that she is very, very skinny. There are divots between her ribs and shadows around her collarbone and hips. Her breasts are flat coins. Her legs are landscapes of bone and ligament. Her joints are bulbs. There are other contexts (well-lit, draped in a designer dress) where her body might be considered ideal. Here, it's obvious that she's sick. Her eyes are dull, sunken in their sockets. Her limbs hang oddly, as if she can't summon the energy to hold herself up. Her legs are spread apart. Spread for the camera. She is a skeleton with a vulva.

I press play, which is more a reflex than a conscious decision. The girl shakes out her hair. It's well-cut but lank and unwashed. She looks straight at the camera and moves her legs farther apart. Her waxed pubic bone gleams. She touches herself.

"Ready," she slurs.

From out of frame, a man surges up the bed. We can't see his face. Average build, short hair. Big cock, which he grips and, without further ado, shoves inside her.

He pulls her down the bed, closer to the camera, angling her so we can see him stretching her, pounding her. Her face comes farther into view. Her knife of a jawbone, the holes of her eyes. Her arm falls open. My stomach crawls up my throat. Below the crook of her elbow, there's a black swoop of ink: the Wieland family seal.

My tattoo.

It's me.

My body goes hot, then cold. I feel like I'm going to puke, and then I feel like I want to.

Because this is—it's *me*, and I don't remember any of it.

On-screen, the guy is still fucking her. Fucking me. In and out, in and out. I want to tell the director that the video could use some editing. We get the point. And yet it continues, on and on, brutal, unavoidable. At last, with only a few seconds left in the video, the guy pulls out and comes on my face.

Then it ends.

It was one minute and fifty-nine seconds long.

I stare at the final, frozen frame. My vacant face. In the real world, my face is hot and flushed. The room is wobbling. I hear a high-pitched whistling noise, like a tire leaking air. After a second, I realize it's coming from me.

I have a sex tape.

Look, there are plenty of things in my life I don't remember. I challenge you to find any former party girl not familiar with the morning-after Scroll of Shame. You can't make a thirty-hour-rave omelet without scrambling a few brain cells. And that's not even counting my bad habit of starving myself literally almost to death. Years of bad decisions have worn down the fabric of my memory, even rubbed some spots clean through.

But I thought I knew where all the blank spots were. Even when I was blacking out more often, I always heard about my transgressions soon after the fact. Evidence surfaced within a day or two, a week at most. I didn't know my mind was still keeping secrets from me. I didn't know the tapestry was still coming undone.

I'm not sure if it's denial or masochism that makes me lift my thumb—the only muscle in my body I can move—and press the play button a second time. I watch the video again, willing myself to remember.

This isn't the first time it's taken me a moment to recognize my-self. Every time someone tags me in a photo, there's a split second where I can't find myself in the image. I couldn't be the tall girl, or the girl with brown hair, or the girl in the blue coat. That's not my nose, that's not my smile. They must have tagged me by mistake.

Then something snaps into place, and I see that this person in the middle is me, yes, of course—or rather, she's my body. She's the thing people mistake for me.

This time, nothing's snapping into place. I mean, I know it's me. I understand that. I see the details: My eyes, the right one a little crooked. The freckles on the bridge of my nose. The indent in my chin, a scar from when I was seven and wanted to touch the bottom of the pool's deep end, and I grabbed the edge and levered myself half out of the water, intending to use the momentum to shoot myself all the way back down, but when I released I didn't push back far enough. I caught my chin on the edge. Blood everywhere, thin and watery, mixing with chlorine, and for the rest of my life, this small indentation.

It's all there. But as hard as I scour my brain, I can't recognize anything else. Not the guy, not the room.

I watch it again. Where was it filmed? I can't see much of the hotel room. The bed is nondescript. Full or maybe queen. The headboard is wood. The sheets are polyester satin, thin and shiny like a drugstore Halloween costume. On the wall, a corner of a framed museum poster, a smattering of pointillist dots.

I watch it again. I can't say when it was taken. During one of my worst episodes, obviously, but there were a few of those. It must have been after I got the W tattoo (nineteen) and before I got any other tattoos (twenty-eight: the Sagittarius constellation on my shoulder blade; thirty: birds flying over my ribs). That doesn't help much.

I watch it again. The girl doesn't seem so skinny anymore. I notice new things: a swell of fat beneath the belly button, a fold in the neck. Little failures. What is sick in another person is a mistake in me. *We have to hold ourselves to higher standards*, my dad used to say.

The threads of my memory shiver and break.

I watch it again, I watch it again. I watch it until my hands are shaking so hard the screen blurs. I watch it again. The screen darkens: an incoming call. My cousin Felicity, who only ever calls to gossip. I decline. A banner descends at the top of my screen, a new text message, a different cousin. I watch the video again. Another call comes in. Another banner, another text. Another. Another.

I drop the phone. It lands on the rug with a muffled thud. The video keeps playing. *Ready. More! Harder!* The texts keep coming, an endless scroll of pity, the notifications nesting together on the screen.

When Teddy and Jess burst in, the phone's still on the floor and I'm still on the sofa, head in my hands, staring through my fingers at the screen. I'm up to thirty-four unread text threads, all received in the past ten minutes or so. Thirty-four text threads means thirty-four people I know have seen me naked, at my sickest, getting fucked by a random man in a cheap hotel. Thirty-four acquaintances know what my pussy looks like. And if they've seen it, then so have others, many others. An unfathomable number.

"Hey, Clara," Teddy says with fake cheer. He doesn't know if I know. He's preparing to break the news. "Something hap—"

I cut him off. "I saw it."

"Shit." His expression softens. "How are you doing?"

"Amazing. Incredible. Favorite day ever."

In the foyer, Jess quietly closes the front door. No one bothers locking their doors around here, especially this time of year. The biggest risk is high school kids breaking into empty vacation houses to throw parties—and, I guess, your older brother marching in when he learns your sex tape has gone viral.

Teddy braces his hands on his hips, a superhero planning a counterattack. "It's okay. We're going to fix this."

I look at him through my fingers. "How?"

"We'll get it taken down."

"Everyone's already seen it."

"Not everyone," Jess says, but her voice is more uncertain than I'd like. She sits next to me, landing with a dull thunk that Teddy would usually comment on—he hates the sofa, says it feels like a concrete slab. Today he barely notices the sound. He's in repair mode. He's used to being in this mode, with me.

"I already called Pierce," he says. One of our family lawyers, who's worked for our family since before I was born. Pierce wears a bow tie and suspenders and signs his emails "Best regards." I doubt he knows anything about sex tapes. I bet he's never even said the word *sex* aloud. Then again, these sweet, unassuming old guys usually have some borderline-illegal fetish, so who knows. "He's getting his team on the line and calling us back. He wants to get in touch with someone who knows more about revenge porn."

I flinch. Revenge porn. What an awful term. *Revenge* suggests I did something to deserve it. *Porn* makes it sound voluntary, performative. And reminds me of the people watching it. The people who might take pleasure in it.

Jess rubs my back. Her hand is warm and light. I thought I was numb; now I feel hypersensitive, can feel each thread in my shirt dragging across my skin as she moves her hand in circles over my spine. Sheer pantyhose stretch across her thigh, limn her kneecaps in nylon. She and Teddy must have come straight from a campaign event. Maybe the video interrupted the event. Maybe everyone in the audience learned about the video all at once, the murmurs growing louder and louder until they couldn't even hear Teddy speaking anymore. Maybe I ruined another thing.

Teddy starts pacing across the rug, which is patterned with tigers. Every time he turns to go back the way he came, his foot lands on a tiger's snarling head. "Pierce said it would help if you typed up the details about the video. Who's the guy, where was it taken, when was it taken."

Jess reaches down to pick up my phone from under the coffee

table. The screen is still crowded with notifications. She pretends not to notice, swiping to pull up a blank note before handing it to me.

Remember something, Clara. Anything. Get it together.

But all I can think about is how long I watched the video before I realized it was me.

"Does Pierce have to know all that?" I ask.

Teddy frowns. "I mean—he said it would help."

The cursor blinks. On, off. On, off.

In, out.

Would Teddy be surprised if I told him I didn't remember? He knows the things doctors said, about memory formation, about neurological damage. But I always tried not to let on how much I didn't remember, and experience has made me a decent liar. Teddy might be shocked to learn that there could be a whole night, a whole person, a whole place, a whole video I still don't remember. I hope he would be shocked. It would be worse if he already suspected I'm only half here—if he said all those nice things yesterday, acted like he was proud of me taking over WFCI, while at the back of his mind he was waiting for this other shoe to drop.

I put down the phone. "Can we take a quick break from the problem-solving? I'm not feeling very well."

Teddy opens his mouth, but Jess beats him to it. "Sure," she says brightly, with a warning look in his direction. "Do you want anything to drink? Tea? Water?"

"Chloroform?"

She nods serenely. "I'll see what you have."

When she's gone, Teddy looks at me warily. He knows I'm evading.

On the coffee table between us is a three-foot-tall flower arrangement, which arrived today from our grandmother Celeste. She always sends the most heinous bouquets to commemorate our parents' deaths, and every year they arrive earlier and earlier, as if she's trying to beat us in a perverted etiquette arms race. The anniversary is weeks away, by which time Celeste will undoubtedly be on a yacht in the Mediterranean somewhere, doing a song and dance about how her son wouldn't have wanted her to mourn.

"Clara—"

"I know. Give me a minute."

With a sigh, Teddy starts another lap around the rug, past the ironic greyhound statue by the fireplace. His hair is lit in pink from the vintage neon sign from a lesbian bar called THE WET THIGH. Before I moved in, the guesthouse was all toile wallpaper and colonial detail. Eventually, Jess made me hire a designer to help it feel more like me. Nothing completely irreversible, nothing you can see from the outside. Nothing that would make my mom roll over in her grave. Toucan-patterned wallpaper in the downstairs bathroom, magenta built-ins in the office. This uncomfortable sofa that looks like a deflated hot-air balloon. I approved everything. It isn't the designer's fault that two years later it still feels more like a place I *would* live than like the place I do.

"Look, Clara," Teddy finally says, and I'm impressed he managed to do two whole laps before speaking, "I know it's a lot to process, but we need to act quickly."

A buzzing noise starts in my brain. "I know."

"Even if it's hard to talk about. There's no judgment. But you have to tell us what happened. Like this guy, did you know him already? Before this happened? Did you know he was filming? Did he trick—"

"Oh my god, Teddy, stop." I drop the phone again and press my hands over my ears. It doesn't stop the buzzing. "Please."

I want answers to all these questions, too. Who is the guy? Who put it online? Why now? The answers must be in me somewhere, slid into some little fold in my brain. I want to take my head and shake it until the right memory falls out.

I'm still slumped forward over my knees, my hands over my ears, when Jess returns. I've known her so long I can read her mind. She's wondering what happened, why we're arranged in these positions.

She's thinking: *Teddy pushed too hard, but Clara provoked him.* She sets down a mug of tea in my line of sight.

"Hey," she begins, probably about to soothe one of us. "How's it going?"

"It's not," Teddy says.

Behind him, a large framed certificate hangs over the mantel—the deed of trust from when my great-great-grandfather donated eleven thousand acres of land to the National Parks. Woodrow Wilson's signature is at the bottom, and Ambrose Wieland's is next to it. Him, a national park; me, a sex tape. All us Wielands create such illustrious things.

Headlights flare through the window. I sit upright. "Who's that?"

"Relax. It's just Mike," Teddy says.

Under the circumstances, it takes me a second to place the name. "Your *campaign manager*? Why'd you call him?"

"He knows how to handle crises."

He moves toward the door. I want to cry out *no* and lock down my house like a fortress. We have us three, we don't need anyone else. We can't trust anyone else. He could welcome in a monster, a vampire with ragged teeth, a box of sins. But fear freezes my throat, and by the time I croak out any kind of noise, Teddy is already opening the door.

"Long time no see," Jess says lightly when Mike enters.

"Hey." He turns to me. I've removed my hands from my face, which is progress. "I saw the news. I'm so sorry."

"Why? You didn't release it, did you?"

"Still." There's a pitying look in his eyes, the facial equivalent of the texts streaming in, and I know that he's watched the video. For research purposes only, I'm sure. "I don't mean to interrupt. I'm just here to help."

"Clara's putting together a list of details for our lawyers," Teddy says.

Mike nods. "That's a great idea. Do you know where the video came from?"

"No," I say. "I don't know who posted it."

"I imagine the guy in the video is a good guess," Teddy says. He raises his eyebrows at my phone as if to say *Go on, write down the name.*

But Mike's here now, too. If I couldn't tell the truth to my own brother and my best friend, I certainly can't tell it to a guy who looks like he gets his hair product applied by the wax machine at a Hoboken car wash.

Teddy's phone rings. It's Pierce, calling back with his IT guy on the line. Teddy puts it on speaker and places it on the coffee table so everyone can hear. "I've been doing some digging into where the video was first posted," the IT guy says. "It looks like someone programmed a bot to post the video to various specialized forums. An ophthalmology forum was first at 7:08 p.m., then one about Ford F150s, one for slash fiction, one called NeedleNuts—"

"NeedleNuts?" Jess repeats.

"It's for knitters. The bot chooses the forums randomly, they aren't relevant." Whenever he says the word *bot*, I imagine a small robot vacuum working its way along a baseboard. "We're contacting the different forums, but even if we get the video deleted from those sites, the bot will keep posting it to others. We can't issue cease and desists to the entire internet. And the video's already reached the more mainstream social media."

"From the same bot?" Teddy asks.

"No. Real people are sharing it now."

"So I'm fucked," I say. "Literally and figuratively."

No one disagrees.

Teddy addresses the phone. "Pierce? Can we do anything else about getting it taken down? From a legal standpoint?"

There's a click on the line, and then Pierce's voice. "Maine has revenge porn laws, so posting a video like that without Clara's consent is a state crime. Statute 17-A, section 511-A. We can write up cease and desists to the websites hosting it. It's just very hard with this stuff to contain the spread."

"Can we go after the people reposting it?"

"Not everyone, realistically. The first poster, maybe, if we can fig-ure out who that is."

Teddy lets out an exasperated noise. "That's ridiculous. These people are harassing her. We should be able to stop them."

Another voice comes on. "Mr. Wieland? Ms. Wieland? This is Vishal. I'm one of Pierce's associates." With a lurch of my stomach, I realize I have no idea how many other people are on this conference call. They must all have the video open on their laptop. Maybe they ordered popcorn. They're making a night of it. I wonder if they cringed when they watched the video, or if they got hard.

Vishal continues, "The person who first posted it is probably the person who filmed it. If Ms. Wieland didn't know it was being filmed, that would be invasion of privacy. Possibly stalking. Can you tell us more about the circumstances of the sex act? Where it took place, for example? Did you know it was being filmed? Were you sober?"

I twist my necklace around my fingers. "Does it really matter?"

"Well, yes. If you want to report a crime, the authorities are going to need to know the details," Pierce says.

I imagine myself in an interrogation room, like the ones on TV, my own face reflected in the one-way mirror. *Tell us the story from the beginning*, they'd say.

And I'd say, *I can only tell you how it ends.*

Another twist of the necklace. "And if I don't want to report a crime?"

Teddy has been staring down at the phone, but now he looks up in consternation. "What are you talking about? You have to report it."

It's all happening too fast. There's Teddy and Jess and Mike and Pierce and Vishal and God knows how many other people waiting for me to answer. And then off in the background, across the world, an even larger number watching the video, more and more every minute.

If I could have a moment alone, just one moment—

"I need to think," I tell the phone.

Irritated, Teddy pinches the bridge of his nose. "Pierce, we'll call you back. Keep working on getting it taken down from online."

"It's going to be slow going."

"Do your best," Teddy says, in his tone of voice that means *Get it done.*

He ends the call and addresses me, slightly more gently. "What's going on?"

I turn the mug around in my hands. My fingerprints stick to the glossy surface. Cloudy ovals. Each whorl perfectly defined. When I was little, I thought all families shared fingerprints. I assumed mine and Teddy's would be identical, since we look so much alike. I was crushed when our nanny explained that everyone has their own. I had liked the idea that he and I would be the same in this way. Exactly alike, according to our hands.

But we aren't alike. Teddy would never end up in this situation. If he's ever blacked out, it was probably exactly once, a few too many beers at a tailgate in college, just enough to be able to tell a perfect, relatable story if the topic ever comes up.

"The guy in the video didn't post it," I say, even though of course I have no idea. "I don't want to send a bunch of cops to his door when he didn't do anything wrong."

"What are you talking about, he didn't do anything wrong? He took advantage of you. Having sex with someone who's so out of it is rape."

The word sucks up all the air in the room. "Don't call it that."

"Anyone can see you weren't well," he insists.

The heat on my throat climbs up my cheeks and scalp. Is he right? Does me not remembering the sex mean that I didn't consent? But then there I am in the video, saying *Ready.* I've consented to lots of sex. Certainly rougher sex than that. How humiliating, to have been raped and not know.

Meanwhile, my phone keeps lighting up. Seventy-two texts now. Seventy-three.

In the corner, Mike clears his throat. "Look, we don't need to resolve the question of an investigation tonight. What we do need to do is figure out what we want to say about the video. Teddy should make some kind of statement by tomorrow. I would propose it says something like the video is a long time ago, it's private, it was released without Clara's consent. We pivot to some related policy initiative. Just short and sweet."

"Sweet?" Jess says.

"You know what I mean," Mike says.

Duh me. Of course Mike isn't here just because he "knows about crises." He's here because this video might impact the campaign. I would have realized it earlier, if I hadn't been so focused on trying to remember.

"In terms of what to say publicly," Mike is saying to Teddy, "I think we make one very quick statement, and then you shift the conversation to policy. I'll tell Phoebe to pull together some language about revenge porn, privacy, women's rights."

"Oh yeah, women's constitutional right to get railed in private," I remark tonelessly. Mike flicks an annoyed glance in my direction.

Jess has sat up a little straighter, which gives me room to tilt my phone at an angle where she can't see it and open my Instagram: 99+ notifications. I've gained two thousand followers in the last hour. These kind, gentle souls have thoughtfully annotated any picture I'm in.

On a photo of me with my cousin Brent at a fundraiser, someone has commented: *slut slut slut slut slut*

On my most recent photo, someone else has written: *She looks good here. Fatter*

There are comments on my older photos, too. On a picture of me right after I got out of Marien, a woman wearing Mickey Mouse ears in her profile picture announces, with several emojis: *If you're a young*

girl seeing this photo, I want you to know that THIS IS NOT BEAUTY!
Beauty is loving yourself and being true to yourself. NOT STARVING
YOURSELF INTO A SKELETON!

Below that, a debate is raging:

Would anyone actually fuck Clara Wieland?? Be honest

Reply: *Yea I would. Skinny girls are really tight*

Reply: *I would if she paid me & u kno she has the money*

Reply: *It would be like fucking a bag of nails*

"Clara." Jess has caught me. She takes the phone out of my hand
and turns off the screen. "Don't read the comments."

"I wasn't."

She doesn't dignify that with an answer. My hand feels empty
without my phone. Ten years ago, people were constantly losing their
phones, leaving them in cabs or at restaurants. No one does that anymore. It would be like leaving behind a limb.

But Jess won't give it back. She turns away and listens like a dutiful
student while Teddy and Mike brainstorm solutions. They come up
with bullet points for the statement, which Mike will hand off to their
comms team to draft. Jess and Teddy are supposed to leave again
Wednesday for five days of political dick-sucking. Teddy asks me if I
want them to cancel, and Mike gives me a hard little look, so I say no.
Go ahead. Go do normal-people things while I deal with this cluster-
fuck. Anyway, I know that if they stayed, Teddy would keep hounding
me about who this guy is, keep telling me I should call the police.

That's rape. Anyone can see.

I pull at the necklace again, harder. No, it isn't anyone *can* see.
Anyone *has* seen. Everyone has seen. That's what upsets me, more
than the sex itself. I almost don't care if I was raped. Which surely isn't
the right way to feel. I should feel violated, and I do, but by the video,
not by the sex, which I don't even remember.

In Jess's lap, my phone lights up again with another message from
Felicity, and this time I notice something new on the screen—not

the messages, but the time and the date, which I had temporarily forgotten.

I suppress a giddy, panicked laugh.

April 1.

Right on time.

Deaths attributed to the Wieland curse

Thomas Edward Wieland Sr.

On April 6, 1902, self-made steel tycoon <u>Thomas "Senior" Edward Wieland Sr.</u> was giving a group of politicians a tour of his newly built steel mill in <u>Harrisburg, Pennsylvania</u>. The tour was intended to showcase his latest innovation: <u>steel rollers</u> that used a <u>reversing electric drive</u> to speed up the process of flattening ingots into beams.

Senior, at that time the richest man in the country, was known for showmanship on his tours, often wading into the workers' ranks to demonstrate his hands-on approach. On this occasion, when the group reached the new rolling machines, he seized the tongs from the worker and took over the task of feeding <u>metal stock</u> into the rollers. On his third attempt, he failed to release the tongs in a timely manner and was pulled into the rollers by the arm.

A minute later, his body came out the other end compacted into an inch-thick slab of skin and muscle, the precise size and shape of a standard <u>steel beam</u>—the very item that had first made him a millionaire.

5

JESS

April 2

"I went to see Clara this morning," Teddy calls out, then immediately turns on the shower.

Inside our walk-in closet, I narrow my eyes. He has a habit of starting a conversation, jumping into the shower mid-monologue, and then resuming his comments six minutes later, right where he left off. I've gotten used to this habit over the years, but he doesn't usually end on such a cliff-hanger. I turn away from my outfit options and go into the bathroom, watching him through the shower's glass door.

I raise my voice to be heard over the water. "How was she?"

"Okay, I think. She said she didn't sleep much."

"I'm not surprised. Was she up reading the comments?"

"I told her to ignore them."

"Yeah, well."

He tilts his head into the spray, slicks back his hair. "Apparently people keep editing Wikipedia to say her job is *whore*."

"How creative."

"She still wouldn't say who the guy in the video was. Or agree to call the police."

"She's overwhelmed."

"Doing nothing's only going to make it worse."

"It hasn't even been twenty-four hours."

"Well, and then the window closes."

"That's for missing persons, Teddy. And it's a myth."

He lathers his arms, his chest. "I don't understand why she won't *do* something."

I don't bother explaining anxiety to Teddy. There's no point. His world is black and white. If he decides to do something, he does it. If he sees a problem, he fixes it. If he doesn't see the problem, it doesn't exist.

I check my phone to see if Clara's returned any of my earlier calls, but she hasn't. I check my calendar. We leave tomorrow, five days on the road, and then Teddy wants to have Conrad over for drinks when we get back. *Something low-key,* he said. Hosting is always low-key for Teddy, because he doesn't do anything to prepare. To be fair, Teddy tells me I shouldn't prepare, either. I should leave it all to Stephanie. She's the housekeeper; that's her job.

But I didn't grow up having guests over. My mother and I were always moving between apartments, sometimes to places with nosy neighbors or strict landlords, usually to places with yellowed linoleum, leaky toilets, inconsistent heating. Letting someone in was a disruption of our routine. To me, it seemed like tempting fate. The same way a rusty nail through the skin might carry infection, an outsider might bring judgment, theft, bills, eviction.

So even now, before we host someone, I like to have everything in place. I have a whole checklist to get through. Fresh towels in the bathroom, clean countertops, unsmudged glasses, full decanters, Teddy's stupid boots *under* the entryway bench, not beside it, and his coats on the mudroom pegs. Teddy teases me about these routines. One time I almost left a dirty casserole dish in the sink before a dinner party, and he pretended to stagger back in horror. Of course, I can see how it would be funny to him. He'd never take a mistake personally. If something were out of place, no one would think it was his fault.

But that's next week. Right now: Clara.

"I'll go talk to her before we leave," I tell Teddy.

"Yeah?" he asks, sounding more upbeat. The glass door is fogging at the edges. He uses his finger to draw a heart in the condensation, then *T+J*, although from my side the *J* looks backward. Even through the steam, his smile is nearly blinding. "Thanks, babe."

Water tracks down his hip, over the cut of muscle. The campaign has destroyed our sex life. Nothing kills libido faster than a 5:00 a.m. wake-up call. I miss his hands on me, the ravaged way he says my name when he's inside me.

"You need company in there?" I ask, unbuttoning my shirt.

"I wish." The smile turns regretful as he reaches to turn off the shower. "But we're already running late."

6

JESS

Twenty-three years ago

I didn't set out to become a Wieland. I know from the outside it might seem like I planned it all, like I walked into my fourth-grade classroom with my sights trained on Clara, the closest access point to a beautiful life. But it wasn't like that. My motives were pure.

My mother and I had recently moved to the island from Katti-nocket so she could take a hotel housekeeping job that had become available last-minute when the previous cleaner was T-boned by a drunk driver with six weeks left in the high season. My mother had never lived independently before, and she was a mess, depressed and overwhelmed. I did most of the chores, because when she got home from a shift at the hotel, the last thing she wanted was to look at a mop and bucket. I spent the summer in our small apartment, watching one of two channels on the tiny TV that had come nailed into the wall, or sometimes, if my mother had a lot of rooms to turn over, helping her wipe down counters and fold sheets into tight triangles. By the time the school year started, all I wanted was a friend.

On the first day of school, after the painful few minutes where I was forced to stand at the front of the room while the teacher instructed the class to *be nice* and *welcome our new student with open arms*—has it ever actually made any new student feel better to hear their peers being commanded into kindness?—we were told to split into pairs to make posters about our summer vacations. Kids began partnering off immediately; they all knew their usual configurations. Even then, I was generally good in a crisis, but the stakes were so high: I had already figured out who was everyone's least favorite, the surly kid who had spent my introduction eating gum off the bottom of his shoe, and I was sure that if I were paired with him now, I would be stuck forever on the lowest rung of the grade-school hierarchy.

Then I felt a tap on my shoulder. I turned and saw a slight girl with light brown hair and a stripe of freckles across her nose. She was wearing a blue tank top that, for reasons I couldn't immediately specify, struck me as unbearably cool.

"Want to be my partner? I have gel pens."

It took me a second to get my tongue untied. "Okay."

She brought over the gel pens and poured them out on my desk. They scattered everywhere, pink and purple, green and gold. I caught a blue one before it fell off the edge.

"What's your name?" I asked.

"Clara Wieland," she said, surprised, as if everyone knew it, which I guess they must have.

The first step was listing what we had done on our vacations. Initially it seemed like we didn't have many points of overlap. Clara had been out on her family's boat, she said, and played tennis and sailed. I said I had mostly watched TV, and she said she was jealous, because her parents would only let her and her brother watch two hours a week during the summer and he was older so he usually got to choose the show. I told her about *Judge Judy*. She thought it sounded like the greatest show in the world. That was a favorite phrase of hers. Everything—the color red, S Club 7, pastrami sandwiches—was the greatest in the world. I quickly ran out of other activities to add to our list, but it didn't matter; she had an infinite number and was happy to share. She had touched a starfish. She had played chess. She had caught a firefly and watched it glow in her hands.

She glowed, too, I thought: she shone and sparkled. It was impossible not to notice how the other kids looked at her, how they held up their posters for her to admire, or called across the room to ask her the name of that song she liked. But I was the one she had chosen. We complemented each other. I organized the list, told her what to draw first. She drew the outlines, and I colored them in. When she got distracted and skipped ahead, I pulled her back on track. When we were done, our poster was perfect, brighter than everyone else's, a glittering blast of color.

It was that easy. After that, Clara and I were inseparable. I went to her house almost every day after school. We played board games and braided friendship bracelets. We cut pictures for collages out of brand-new magazines she bought expressly for this purpose. We ran wild through the woods of Vantage Point, over soft green blankets of moss and well-kept trails. We played witches among the birch trees, with a rock as our cauldron. We got our periods and compared notes. We ranked our peers by hotness, niceness, intellect. We moaned to each other about being misunderstood.

I was good for Clara, I overheard Mrs. Wieland say once. I focused her, I calmed her down. I was glad to hear I was returning the favor. Because Clara was good for me, too. That seemed too obvious to bother saying aloud.

I didn't bother with other friends. What was the point? Clara and I knew each other perfectly, fully. We didn't need anyone else. I was at an age when I still thought being wholly understood was good, and possible; when it seemed entirely reasonable that a person might know you better than you knew yourself.

But Clara's days in public school were numbered. Mr. and Mrs. Wieland had always planned to keep their children on the island through middle school, then send them to the Halpern School in New Hampshire, the institution of choice for generations of Wielands. Cousins and aunts and uncles had streaked across square green lawns, cheated off one another's exams, and lost their virginities on the dining hall roof. It was their birthright. Teddy left first, when Clara and I were starting sixth grade; three years later, it was Clara's turn.

When she left for Halpern, it was almost like I started a new life, too, even though at the public high school I was surrounded by classmates I had known for years. I hadn't realized how much time I spent with Clara until she was gone. I had relied on her humor to hide my shyness, her status to hide my desperation, and without her, I felt constantly both invisible and exposed. I should have reached out to other girls, tried to find common interests; but I worried that I might change too much, and that when Clara returned she would notice the change and think I was a try-hard. To a Wieland, I sensed, a try-hard was the worst thing someone could be.

In March of our freshman year, lonely and bored, I took Clara up on her offer to visit her at Halpern for one weekend of my spring break. Mrs. Wieland insisted on sending me in a town car. It was a five-hour drive, farther than I'd ever traveled in my life, and when Clara greeted me outside her dorm, a red brick building with imposing white columns, I felt as disoriented as if I had just been thrown from a mechanical bull.

Clara wrapped me in a tight, squealing hug.

"I missed you," I said into the side of her neck.

Another, tighter squeeze. "I missed you, too."

I had seen photos of Halpern before—her acceptance packet had come with a forty-page glossy booklet, full of photos of students lounging in piles of colorful leaves, presumably talking through some deep philosophical question. In real life, it was even more impressive, every building power-washed to a bright gleam, the lawns unnaturally green, even in March. I didn't say so aloud. I suspected the beauty was something that was supposed to go unacknowledged, that commenting on it might violate some cardinal rule of wealth.

Clara had three roommates, tall girls with shiny hair who paired pearl earrings with baggy school-issue sweats. I disliked the roommates. I especially disliked their reactions to jokes: instead of laughing, they would simply say "That's funny" in a flat, unyielding voice. The four of them did everything together, moving around the campus like an eight-armed being, or preschool children on a walking rope. I cringed at this assumed camaraderie, but I envied it, too.

At dinner, I ate with deliberate slowness while the roommates complained about the food. It seemed fine to me. One of their complaints seemed to be the rigidity of the schedule, although I thought the idea sounded comforting. Veggie burgers on Tuesdays. Chicken piccata on Wednesdays. Every day, you knew exactly what you'd be getting.

One of the roommates—I couldn't tell them apart—moved her fork between us. "So how'd you two become friends?"

The way she said it made it sound like *How could such an abomination occur?*

Clara didn't seem to notice. "We were in fourth grade," she said cheerfully. "Jess had just moved to the island. She was super shy. We had to partner up to make posters about our summers and I picked her to be my partner."

One by one, her roommates nodded and said, "That's funny."

I didn't think it was a funny story. I felt the way Clara had told it hadn't done it justice. There was nothing objectively inaccurate about her version. I *had* been shy. She *had* picked me to be her partner. It just came across differently, made me seem weaker than I thought I had been, more like a charity case. I wasn't sure whether that was how she really saw it, or whether she had shaped it a certain way for her audience, and I wasn't sure which would be worse—that she believed it, or that she would change something between us for their benefit.

That night, the roommates and Clara and I dressed up in spandex miniskirts and shearling-lined boots. I borrowed a pair of Clara's. With Halpern-branded miniature flashlights, we shivered our way over to the copse of woods where upperclassmen would go when they wanted to get wasted. Teddy hadn't exactly invited us, but he also didn't yell at us when we arrived. A dozen or so people were standing by a shitty little gas stove fire, passing around Smirnoff handles bought with fake IDs. Others were rooting through a pile of half-opened beer cases. Still others were off in the shadows, trying to feel each other up without freezing off any important parts.

"Just like home," I said, pulling my coat tighter around myself against the chill.

Clara plucked two PBRs from a dented box. "How so?"

"Ryan Bollen and his friends hold parties in the woods all the time." I stopped myself before adding *Rich people don't have dibs on getting drunk in the middle of nowhere*. It was the kind of comment Clara might have appreciated before Halpern. I wasn't sure about now.

Clara knew everyone at the party, of course; or rather, they knew her, which was even better. She flitted easily between Teddy's friends. Some treated her like their own younger sister, and some flirted relentlessly. Some did both. At first, I followed her around like a shadow, but I thought maybe that was irritating, so I slowly melted farther and farther back, and drank faster and faster, until after an hour or two, I was sitting at the base of a tree, too drunk to stand.

"Jess?" Clara crouched down in front of me. "Are you okay?"

I tried to look composed. "I'm fine. Just need a minute."

"Drink this." She twisted the cap off a water bottle and handed it to me. I took a sip and tried to give it back to her. She shook her head. "Keep going."

I made a face. Privately, I was impressed. She knew exactly how to handle someone being drunk. I wasn't sure if I was behind where I should be for my age or if she was ahead. That was the problem of having Clara Wieland as a benchmark. She did everything on her own schedule. I wanted to crawl inside her body, know all the things she knew.

I drank the water.

She smiled at me. In the shadows cast by a nearby camping lantern, her mouth was fuller than usual, her dimple a dark comma. "I thought you said people back home do this all the time."

"People do," I said. "I don't."

"Why not?"

Even if I were sober, I wouldn't have explained what high school was like now that she had gone. Instead, I held up the water bottle. "I finished."

"Good girl."

I let her help me up. She was taller than me, and less fragile than she later became, so she could support me okay. When we were standing, she looked down at my boots, which were actually hers. I looked down, too, and wailed.

"Oh my god. I'm so sorry."

I bent over to wipe off the vomit, but Clara stopped me, hauling me back upright. "It's okay. They're just shoes." She linked her arm through mine. "Come on, let's get you home."

"That's too far."

"No, it's only five minutes," she said, and I realized by *home* she meant the dorm.

The woods truly were identical to the woods back on the island. The same tangles of roots and tall thin trees growing in parallel. The same squish of moss. When the lanterns from the party faded away, we turned on our flashlights and aimed them at the ground. The beams strobed across the path, bouncing as we walked, catching on stones and broken roots.

"Is this the way we came?" I asked.

"A detour. I don't want to run into campus security."

We were used to walking in the woods at night, but not in short skirts. We shivered. Our knees knocked. My legs grew colder and colder until it felt like the top layer of skin was separating from the muscle. Her arm through mine felt like the only source of heat.

Clara said, "I'm really glad you came to visit."

"Really?"

"Yes, really! Of course. Are you glad you came?"

"Yes." Emboldened by the alcohol, I added, "I don't know if your friends like me very much."

"Sure they do." Her foot hit a puddle and sprayed mud on my bare calf. "Anyway, who cares? I wouldn't really call them my friends."

"You introduced them as your friends."

"Well, of course," she said, as if this made perfect sense. "But they're not my friends the way you're my friend, you know?"

"Oh." I was so pleased I forgot to look where I was going. I tripped on a rock and fell forward. My reflexes were too slow; my arms didn't extend. Then, in that split second of weightlessness, a hand closed around my arm and yanked me back.

"Careful!" Clara said.

"I think I'm drunk."

She laughed. "I *know* you're drunk."

I hugged myself and tilted my head back to look at the sky. The night was purple, clouded. No North Star. My emotions seemed to ooze into one another, mixing into a gelatinous mass. I had thought being drunk would be more fun.

"I think you should apply to transfer here," Clara said.

I was still looking at the sky. "I did."

"You applied?"

"This year." I had forged my mother's signature to do it, submitted all the financial aid forms on my own. "I got in."

She took me by the shoulders, which forced my gaze back down. "You're coming here?" Her excitement was incandescent.

"No, no," I said, laughing and not laughing at the same time. I hadn't intended to tell Clara any of this. "I got a partial scholarship."

"So you're coming!"

"No, I mean, I *only* got a partial scholarship. So I can't come."

She scoffed. "Of course you can come."

"Clara, I can't."

"Money shouldn't be the thing stopping you."

"It's okay." I was used to money being a thing that stopped me. But this was probably the first time Clara had experienced it. I didn't want to have to comfort her through this loss of innocence.

After a couple seconds of silence, she kicked a pebble. "My parents could help out."

But there had been that hesitation. Clara was extravagant and generous by nature, but sometimes she unexpectedly shut down, held herself back; a protective impulse, from growing up in a position where people wanted to use her. Was that what she thought of me now? Had she paused because she thought I was asking for money? Or had she paused because she knew I wouldn't like the idea? I didn't like it at all. I hated it. I didn't want the Wielands to pay for my education. Or did I?

I was disappointed by the pause, and I wasn't sure if I was disappointed because she was questioning our friendship, or because I couldn't take her up on her offer.

"No," I said.

"A loan, or whatever."

"No, Clara."

She didn't press further. Oddly, I was disappointed by that, too.

We resumed walking in silence. The mood had shifted. I felt suddenly very tired. It had been much longer than the five minutes Clara promised, and the woods around us looked the same as they ever had. I suspected that she didn't know where we were, but didn't want to admit that she had gotten us lost. Halpern's grounds were huge, the woods extending halfway around the lake. It was land that would never be used, they only saved it so no one would obstruct their view. We could be walking in circles for hours. I'd give her a few more minutes, and then I'd have us retrace our steps. I'd get us back on track.

Dried grass scratched at my boots, little claws. Clara and I had never had uncomfortable silences before. I thought about the thing she had said at dinner, and then how earlier tonight I had held back my joke. I had the horrible sense that something was changing between us, and she might not even know it. Even as we walked arm in arm, clutching each other tight, there was a distance between us I couldn't cross.

What would come next for us? I had always assumed we would be together forever. But now Clara had left. She had moved on. She had friends, opportunities, two parents who loved her. She was flighty and overly optimistic, but she could afford to be. As for me . . .

The truth was, I didn't know who I was without Clara. I felt as if she had taken my sense of myself with her when she went away, and kept forgetting to give it back. She had always been the bright light. The shining one. I was a mirror ball, and without anything to reflect, indistinguishable from the darkness around.

"Here we are!" Clara chirped.

I blinked. We had reached campus without me realizing it. I recognized the narrow diagonal paths that crossed her quad, dotted with yellow pools of light, and the columns of her dorm, illuminated from below. The ground beneath my feet was asphalt now. All along, Clara had known where we were going. I was the only one who had been confused.

Deaths attributed to the Wieland curse

Matthew Thomas Wieland

Matthew Thomas Wieland was a Boston financier and the youngest son of Thomas Edward Wieland Sr. On April 6, 1912, the tenth anniversary of his father's death, Matthew took advantage of his wife and son's absence from town to pay a surprise visit to his mistress Polly Parks at her row house in the North End. When he arrived, he found Parks in bed with his business rival Dimitri Hungerford. A fight broke out, during which Hungerford stabbed Matthew through the eye with a candlestick. Matthew bled to death in the lane outside.

A historic plaque commemorating Matthew now hangs over the Starbucks at 27 North Margin Street.

Delphine Lafayette Wieland and James Lafayette Wieland

Matthew's wife, Delphine, and eleven-year-old son, James, were on holiday in Ireland when they received news of his death. They immediately booked return passage on the maiden voyage of a brand-new ship: the *Titanic*.

When the pulley lowering their lifeboat snapped, Delphine was crushed against the side of the ship "like a spider under a shoe," in the words of eyewitness Madeline Kent. James fell forty feet into the ocean and drowned.

7

CLARA

April 3

"I was out for a jog, I thought I'd pop by," Jess says in a rush as soon as I answer the door.

I lift an eyebrow. She's a runner, sure, and she's outfitted in her usual sleek thermal leggings and neon shoes, but her cheeks are barely even pink.

Ever since Teddy showed up unannounced yesterday, I've figured another welfare check-in was coming. At least Jess knocks.

"What a happy coincidence." I gesture extravagantly inside: *After you.*

The video has been online for thirty-nine hours. I didn't mean to keep count. But Pierce's IT guy mentioned the exact minute the bot first posted the video, 7:08 p.m., and later that night I happened to glance at the wall clock at 9:08, and I thought, in the nasal voice of a cartoon narrator, *Two hours later.* Once I started the tally, I couldn't stop. One hash mark, then another, black scratches crowding out everything else in my mind. It would probably be easier to lose track of the hours if I could sleep more than forty minutes at a time. The past two nights, every time I finally drifted off, I snapped awake again, fresh from a nightmare where the whole internet has seen me getting fucked violently by a stranger in a cheap motel. I'd roll over and see the soft glow of the clock on my nightstand, the minutes always sliding irreversibly toward :08, and I'd remember that it wasn't a dream at all.

Jess and I go into the living room, which is admittedly a disaster. I've spent most of the last two days on the sofa, and the coffee table is a sweep of half-drunk water glasses, empty vape cartridges, and piles of coins. In the grips of insomnia last night, I decided to sort all my loose change, but I never got around to placing them in separate jars.

"Wasn't Stephanie supposed to come this morning?" Jess asks, about the mess.

"I told her to take a couple days off. I wanted some privacy," I add, pointedly.

"I'll be out of your hair in two minutes." She nudges a wadded-up tissue off a sofa cushion and sits in its place. "How are you doing?"

I give her a look.

"Okay, stupid question," she admits. "You haven't been answering my texts."

"I'm a little afraid of my phone right now."

The whole device is a train wreck of notifications. The comments sections on all my social media accounts resemble those word games where you change one letter at a time to get from DRAWER to SHOVEL:

Do people actually think ur hot
you'd be hot if you ate something

Eat shit and die
gross as shit
you look like dog shit
what a dog
what a bitch
kill yourself bitch

Ta-da, SHOVEL. Now hit me over the head with it and put me out of my misery.

When people jump in to defend me, it only sends the original insult back up to the top of my notifications:

@joemo13: I went to college with @clarawieland and she slept with the whole soccer team. men's and women's

@rejeanie: @joemo13 @clarawieland Who cares who she sleeps with, this is the 21st century? don't slut shame

@truebadour: @rejeanie @joemo13 @clarawieland so you agree she's a slut LOL

@champiori: @joemo13 @clarawieland how much you think she paid them to sleep with her? $100k each?

@joemo13: @champiori @clarawieland I'd do it for $200k

@champiori: @joemo13 @clarawieland $300k and a house in the Hamptons and that's my final offer

I've been trying to stop reading them. Really, I have. It's like my thumb works on reflex, opening the apps without my conscious decision. If I read one single comment, it's game over. I tell myself I'll keep reading until I find a supportive one—but then as soon as I find it, I scroll right past. It's only the cruel ones that make me feel something: a tiny burn of satisfaction, confirmation. Look, I was right, I'm trash. I'm a monster. I'm a blight.

Some comments stick with me because they're so graphic.

Some just stick.

"Maybe you should get a new phone and only give the new number to Teddy and me. Then you don't have to worry about all the other stuff," Jess says.

"Sure, maybe." I know I'll never get around to it. Executive function is already hard enough when I'm not the world's laughingstock. Right now, managing two phone numbers sounds like scaling Mount Everest.

Celeste's flower arrangement has shed a few clumps of seeds onto the coffee table, and Jess leans forward and uses a cupped hand to sweep them into a neat pile like a server at a restaurant. Nervous cleaning. Without meeting my eyes, she says, "I talked to Teddy."

"I figured."

It's hard to concentrate on what she's saying. My brain keeps fritzing to the comments. *Wonder what her family thinks. Usually the Wielands are so private.*

"Clara, I really think you should talk to the police."

"I don't want to file a rape complaint," I say automatically.

"Okay, fine. But you could ask them to investigate the video as revenge porn."

"You know what the sentence is for sharing revenge porn? A two-thousand-dollar fine and a year in jail. That's not worth my time."

She sits back. "But they'd be able to find out who released the video."

I snort. "You have more faith in Bobby Ouelette's skills than I do." Bobby is an island cop best known for drinking too much at last year's benefit for the whaling museum and accidentally lacerating himself with a nineteenth-century harpoon.

"I'm sure Bobby Ouelette would not be in charge of the investigation."

I shake my head. "It doesn't matter who released the video. It's already out there. The damage is done."

"Exactly. So what's the harm in talking to the police?"

I groan. She's like a dog with a bone, and my brain is melting. There's no way around it. "Jess, I can't."

"You can."

The words come out of me in a bitter rush. "No, I mean I *can't*. I don't know who that guy is. I don't remember him. I don't remember taking that video."

She frowns. "You mean you blacked it out?"

"I guess so."

"Completely?"

"Completely."

"But"—she's already shaking her head—"you knew when it was from."

My stomach dips. "I guessed, based on my tattoos."

"And you said you were sure the guy hadn't done it."

"Well, I lied."

As soon as she understands what I'm saying, her face goes perfectly blank.

When I first met Jess, I assumed her shyness came from fear. But she's simply private, self-contained. She carries herself in a suitcase, packed and ready to go. The more I got to know her, the more she settled in. She took out her sense of humor, her fierceness. She unfolded her secrets and ironed them flat.

It's a little unsettling to realize that she can still lock herself away from me when she wants to.

"Why didn't you say any of this the other night?" she asks quietly.

I throw my hands up. "Because it's embarrassing! The video's embarrassing, not remembering it is embarrassing, the whole thing is embarrassing."

"No, it's not," says Jess, who would probably be embarrassed by a photo with so much as a bra strap slipping out. "It's human."

"Sweating is human. Shitting is human. Forgetting you made a sex tape is not human."

"You're being very hard on yourself."

"Haven't you heard? That's my brand."

She doesn't laugh. "This is why you need to call the police."

"And tell them I forgot an entire person I had sex with? Tell them my brain is so permanently fucked up I don't even know when it happened?"

Her poker face wobbles. She pulls off her fleece headband and plays with it, looping it into a figure eight over her wrist, sliding it off, looping it again as she tries to come up with a tactful response that reassures me without being an outright lie. I don't envy her. It's a delicate rhetorical task to explain how she, a good and normal person, could be best friends with someone so cataclysmically broken.

Then her hands go still and she narrows her eyes, as if something has just occurred to her. "Clara, if you don't remember the video, how do you know it even happened?"

"There's a video of it—in case you haven't heard."

"But how do you know the video's not a deepfake? Someone could have put your face on someone else's body."

Deepfake. A door swings open inside me, a cold rush of air. But I've watched the video so many times. There's no way I wouldn't have noticed it was fake.

"You can see my tattoo," I say.

"They could have added that."

I think about that moment where I first saw the video, when I watched it for twenty seconds without realizing it was me. I blamed my confusion on my fried neurons. But what if that first instinct was right? What if the body everyone on the internet hates isn't my body, and the world hasn't seen me have sex? What if the reason I don't remember the man or the room is because they don't exist?

If that were true, it would mean I'm not crazy.

Or—that I'm crazy in a different way.

Because you have to be a little crazy, not to recognize yourself.

"Let's watch it again," Jess says when I hesitate. "I'll help. We can see if we notice anything off."

Again. Meaning she's watched it before. I figured she had, of course. Even so, I certainly don't want to *watch* her watch it. I don't want us to squint together at the details of my naked body, whether or not it's mine. I don't want to feel her body stiffen as she tries not to wince, or see her blink the pity from her eyes.

And what if I go through all that, only for us to decide it *is* me? Why get my hopes up when the easiest explanation is already in front of us? I am, after all, the kind of person to whom this could have happened.

A commenter from Kentucky, a mom of two I stalked for a solid twenty minutes: *Humiliatinggggg.*

"The video's real," I say. "I would know if it wasn't me."

"But if you—"

"It's me, okay? I know what my tits look like," I snap.

Jess gives me a mildly affronted look.

"Sorry," I mutter. "I know you're trying to help." As usual.

She twitches her shoulders, shaking it off, then checks her watch. "I should get going."

"Oh, right. You have to finish your 'run.'" I add air quotes with my fingers, trying to lighten the mood.

Her smile doesn't reach her eyes. "We're leaving this afternoon and not back until Sunday. Can you let me know if you need me to come back earlier?"

"You're just looking for an excuse to get out of donor lunches."

"Maybe a little." She starts putting her headband back on. "But also, I mean it. Let me know. And start answering our texts!"

"I will," I say. "On one condition."

"Yes?"

"Don't tell Teddy I don't remember the video. I want to be the one to tell him."

Jess freezes, the headband looped around her neck, her hands pulling the fabric taut. "I can't keep it a secret."

"Just for a little while. Until I figure out what to say."

"When will that be?"

"Soon." When she looks uncertain, I amend: "*Very* soon."

"Clara—"

"If you hold off, I'll answer you every time you text."

One second passes, then two. It isn't hard to read her expression anymore. She's pissed, probably counting to ten before she retorts. Jess has always taken the phrase *think before you speak* very literally. It was wrong of me to ask. But I've barely slept for two days. I'm running on caffeine and fear. The idea of Teddy banging down my door to talk about the video again—the idea of another strategy session, another conversation about everything I've done wrong—

Finally, Jess looks away. "Fine. But you better tell him very, *very* soon."

Her mouth twists to the side as she says it: she's annoyed with herself for giving in. If I were a better friend, I'd feel guilty about putting her in that position. Instead, relief rises in my chest like a balloon.

"Very soon," I agree.

8

CLARA

April 3

As soon as Jess jogs back down my driveway, I go to the kitchen table, where my laptop is parked next to several dirty coffee mugs. The cursor is blinking in the search bar. I've been googling a lot, the past two days. I googled *how to find out who posted a video* and found a "premium electronic tracing service," which charged me $29.99 and then emailed me a typo-riddled report with the stunning revelation that the video was posted by a human being somewhere in the world. I googled random things in the video (*brown sheets, striped wallpaper, French art poster*) until I found similar versions at various online stores, and then for some perverse reason I ordered them all. I goo-gled *how to get rid of a sex tape* and fell down rabbit holes about re-venge porn cases, women who lost jobs over leaked sex tapes, women whose press interviews stalled when their "eyes glistened with tears," women who built their leaked videos into promising porn careers.

This time, I type: *deepfakes.*

I've heard the term before, in action movies and news articles. Stories of other people being fooled. The word sounds so technical and speculative. A trendy problem. A novelty. Now, the internet tells me they've been around almost since photographs were invented. Stalin would execute cabinet members and then have them painted out of photographs, replacing their faces with extensions of the background—shining water, another comrade's suit—until a photo of eight people became a photo of three, separated by yards of flat curtains.

When computers got in on the game, deepfakes really took off. Image manipulation became standard. Photoshop, CGI, filters. The biggest step forward came with machine learning. Programmers taught the computers to compete: one computer tries to make a deep-fake good enough to fool the other; when it fails, the other computer learns from the failure and makes an even better one. Back and forth, back and forth, getting more and more convincing.

So now software can devour huge numbers of files and spit back out a video of your mother sucking someone's dick, a photo of your friend shooting someone in the head, a call with your son's voice begging you to wire money. You don't even need to know much about computers to do it. There are apps that let you make your own deepfakes in twenty seconds (ten seconds with the premium sub-scription!). Children can do it—and have. My searches keep turning up clickbait titles like *How a deepfake ruined a high-schooler's life,* or *Clever students convince principal the superintendent has called a snow day!*

There are other results, too. There's an actor suing a studio for using his likeness to create a stand-in. There's a deepfake of that same actor calling himself a turd. There's a Spanish reality show where they show contestants fake videos of their partners cheating, and make them guess if it's really them. The person who guesses correctly wins a hundred thousand euros. There's a case where a guy used a deepfake to create an alibi for his wife's murder. There's a guy whose defense against child porn charges is that the children in his videos aren't real.

My heart is going a thousand beats a minute. I type in *how to know if a video is a deepfake*. There are sixty-five million results. The most popular article says that the signs of a deepfake are: Blurry edges. Sharp edges. Inconsistent lightning. Unusually consistent lighting. Smooth lines. Jagged lines.

Pay close attention to the teeth, it says: those are difficult to fake. I touch my tongue to the point of my canine. But I have veneers. My real teeth are already fake.

I watch the video again, and this time I try to imagine it as a grid, look at it in parts. In this square, labia. In this square, a toe. Knee, navel, chin. Is that my tongue? Is that my anklebone? I don't know. Maybe. Maybe my nipples are a little pinker, or less pink. Maybe my fingers are longer, or not. The most I can say for sure is that everything is plausible.

When Jess first said the word *deepfake*, it felt like a door opening in a dark maze. Now it turns out the door only leads to another maze, maybe a worse maze. Take a left and I'm the idiot who got duped by a fake of myself. Take a right and half the country has seen my vagina. Which I still think is maybe marginally worse than them seeing a vagina they think is mine, although maybe not as bad as the thought of someone going through so much trouble to make them think that.

The deepfakes everyone on the internet loves are the ones that show people doing things they'd never actually do. A president saying *fuck,* a movie star clipping her toenails in public—what hilarious jokes. The videos make the unlikely real. And at the same time, the unlikeliness is how you know it's fake. But my video doesn't show me doing anything out of character. It shows me doing something I definitely could have done. The only joke is me.

I shut the laptop. The light outside has changed. It's well past lunch. My stomach gurgles and begs, my hunger a creature inside me. I'm supposed to shush it now, with a nutritious meal, portioned according to my many pamphlets. But its noises are so familiar, so identifiably my own. So much more manageable than what's happening online. I'll eat something later. For now, I let the creature roar.

The first thing the police would ask: *How could you not know?*

I'm not sure when it became pathological to be the way I am. At Halpern, all the girls seemed alienated from their bodies. Surprised by their own mood swings, furious at their zits. Everyone was always looking at their profile in the mirror, the curve of their stomach. *Ugh, is that me? Ugh, is that my stomach?* We'd turn to each other for help. *Does this make my ass look big?* Everyone needed a second opinion. Everyone was a stranger to themselves.

And then at some point it changed. They veered onto a new course, while I kept going, trudging forward into the blizzard. One day I looked up and saw that I was alone. And the snow had covered the footprints behind me; I couldn't see how to return.

So I kept walking. I cleaved my body from me. I made it my student. I picked apart its hideousness, congratulated it on the revelation of each new rib. What is yours is not you. There was my body, and then there was *me,* an open blister hidden beyond anyone's reach, even my own.

So no, I don't have any idea what the real me looks like: in my wildest dreams, I don't look like anything at all.

✦

Around 9:00 p.m., I go to roll a joint and realize I've run out of pot. I text Drew Kelly, which I know to be a bad idea; he's known around the island for dealing pills and heroin, and having him come to the house is risky. But weed is the only thing stopping my heart from jumping out of my chest, and I trust Drew more than a concierge service. When we were teenagers, I gave him his first blowjob, and he's been loyal ever since.

When I open the door to him, his face dips in pity. You know things aren't going great for you when even your dealer is relieved he's not in your shoes.

"Rough week, huh, man?" He hands me a paper bag. "I threw in some new stuff, too."

"Wow, samples. You're getting fancy, Drew."

"I meant as a gift. Since you're having a bad week." He looks injured. "Samples? What do you think this is, Costco?"

When he's gone, I stand by my window and light one of the new pre-rolls. I smoke until my eyes are dry from the pot and not the screen. My knees become jellied. The glass is clean and streakless, only a few stray drops of water at the corners as proof of the earlier rain. Outside, the moon casts the edge of the woods in tarry shadow.

I'm thinking about the video, of course. More specifically, about my tattoos. First the W one, which I feel is to blame for most of the situation. If I didn't have this big shining brand on my arm, I doubt enough people would have recognized me for the video to take off. I'm not especially interesting-looking. Brown hair, a long nose. Probably, once leaked, the video would have gone nowhere, another anonymous girl lost in the infinite void of the internet, buried under layers of more exciting porn. But I monogrammed my body. I made myself easy to find.

Then I think about the other tattoos, the missing ones. When I first watched the video, I assumed their absence signaled how old I was when the video was filmed. It occurs to me now that if the video is a deepfake, it makes sense that the other tattoos are missing. The W is splashed across my arm in plenty of photographs, but the others are in places I usually keep covered. It would be hard to find enough images to make a convincing likeness, especially if the person has never actually seen me naked. The person who made the video might not know those tattoos exist.

So that isn't proof, either. It's only another thing that can be seen two ways.

I'm looking out at the yard without really seeing it when suddenly there's a flash of movement, a dark shape jumping across my vision. I can't tell if it's past the window or inside it or inside my head. I only register the motion, and the way I reflexively shrink away from it. I make a noise, a scream's precursor, a squeaky inhalation: my hands come up to protect my face, my shoulders bow. The stub of the joint falls to the floor.

Not again—not again—

When I blink, it's gone. The lawn is still and quiet. A black expanse. A breeze sweeps through the trees, twitching bare branches, shaking down needles. I'm shaking, too. I'm remembering the last time I saw that shadow, years ago, the day my world fell apart.

Sweat breaks out on my forehead. It's been too long, I tell myself, it wouldn't happen again. But then there's that rhythm beating beneath my ribs: April. April. April.

The wall clock says 11:08. Hour fifty-two.

I press my palm to the glass, toward the melting black line of the woods.

Deaths attributed to the Wieland curse

Gerald Hamming-Wieland

Financier and amateur ornithologist Gerald Hamming-Wieland, the son of Thomas Edward Wieland Sr.'s only daughter Ellen Wieland, became addicted to opium after an injury sustained in pursuit of the black-thighed puffleg (Eriocnemis derbyi) in Ecuador in 1931. On April 14, 1933, he attempted to drive under the influence of the drug and crashed his car into the front of the Brookline Marionette Theater in Brookline, Massachusetts. The impact dislodged a row of marquee lights that fell on his head, killing him instantly.

At the time of the accident, the theater was hosting an experimental performance called *The Stringer Family Special*. After Gerald's death, the show's popularity soared. It became one of the most successful marionette shows ever produced.

Mirabella "Peanut" Wieland

Mirabella "Peanut" Wieland, Ambrose Wieland's youngest daughter, starred in two Hollywood films (*Catch a Woman* and *Money Can't Buy Me*) before her untimely death in April 1951. While filming a new movie on location near Yellowstone National Park, Peanut had a confrontation with the director over her costume for an upcoming scene. To calm herself down, she walked into the woods to smoke a cigarette. When several hours passed and she had not returned, a search party was sent out. They found her remains in a clearing. Bite marks and deep claw scratches suggested she had been attacked by a grizzly bear. Most of her face was missing. Her remaining fingers reportedly still held a cigarette, burned down to a stub.

9

JESS

April 6

When Clara said she wanted to be the one to tell Teddy she didn't remember the video, a part of me was proud of her. It seemed like a sign of maturity, even generosity, that she didn't want to make me the messenger.

On the fourth day of our trip, I finally have to accept that I've been played.

It comes to me in the hallway of a recording studio on K Street, where we've just finished up an interview for a podcast about cyberbullying. Mike has a new plan to transform Teddy into a leader on women's rights and internet law, and it's in full swing. He's rustled up support from the Maine chapter of Planned Parenthood and the National Organization for Women—plus an endorsement from a Portland pastor, to emphasize Teddy's own moral rectitude. Phoebe's been feeding Teddy talking points about revenge porn, and two sound bites have already gone viral. Just now, the podcast host claimed that Clara's video was released as payback for Teddy's tireless advocacy for internet privacy, even though I know for a fact that until last week, the most Teddy knew about internet privacy was that there was an incognito browser option.

The podcast went well, and Mike is beside himself with joy. As we head to the elevator bank, I can practically see him adding this to his mental database of strategic moves for future campaigns. *Release an embarrassing video of a candidate family member, pivot to outrage.*

I check my phone again. Since we left the island, I've sent Clara a constant stream of texts. All softballs: *how you doing today?* or: *did Paul come cut down that branch?* or: *how's work?* Nineteen messages.

She's replied to three.

This morning, I sent what I considered the nuclear option. *Remember we agreed you were going to answer my texts??*

That was six hours ago. Still no response.

"Have you heard from Clara today?" I ask Teddy quietly.

He shakes his head. "But she must be okay. Last night you said she's been viewing your stories. So it's just Clara being Clara." He sounds vaguely annoyed but not particularly surprised.

He's right. The flakiness is normal for her. It's only because she and I made our bargain that the phone's blank screen comes as such an insult. I check my Instagram. Sure enough, in the time since I sent the message, she's liked Phoebe's post from our visit to the science fair. So she has time to watch a video of Teddy making paper airplanes with fourth graders but not to type out a simple text telling us she's okay. What is she doing on social media, anyway? I told her to stop reading the comments.

"I wonder who the guy is," Teddy says. That's what he keeps fixating on: finding out the guy's identity, convincing Clara to file a police report. Actions he can take. "She cares so much about protecting him. Do you think it could be someone from Marien? Someone she met there. You know, a real addict. Maybe she doesn't want to report him because he has too many strikes."

It isn't the first time he's floated me one of his ideas about who the guy might be. Each time he presents a possibility (her neighbor in New York, an obsessed ex, a stranger), I recall Clara's anguished admission. *I have no idea who it is.* If she isn't going to keep her end of our deal, then why should I keep mine? But if I tell Teddy now, he'll be pissed I didn't tell him right away. Maybe that's what Clara has been banking on. The bargain was just a way of buying time. Making sure I agreed for a little while, because the longer I kept her secret, the harder it would be to divulge it.

She wasn't being mature. She was creating a loophole.

Which leaves me stuck here, evaluating my husband's theories about the identity of a guy who might not even exist.

So it turns out there is something worse than being the messenger, after all.

Teddy invites his friend Conrad for drinks the same day we get back, because God forbid we have an evening to ourselves for once. We stop by Clara's on our way home from the airport, intending to check on her. Her car is in the driveway, as is her bike. All the curtains are drawn. We knock twice, but she doesn't answer. Teddy wants to open the door, but I put a hand on his arm to stop him.

"She doesn't want to talk to us right now." I omit the second part of my thought, which is that I also don't especially want to talk to her.

Conrad arrives at six on the dot. It feels a little overeager. I've barely gotten through my checklist. His haircut screams luxury condo on Canal Street, but he's dressed the part of a Mainer, in Bean boots and red flannel. The giveaway is that his coat is a Burberry trench, much flashier than anyone around here would wear. He presents me with a bottle of wine, which good manners says I'm not supposed to open unless he tells us that he wants us to try it or that we should pair it with a specific food. When I married Teddy, I hired an etiquette instructor to teach me rules like that. I took a class on wine, too, and I became adept at recognizing whether a wine is expensive, although I still don't know how to tell if it's good.

The wine Conrad's brought is Hungarian—my weakness, as far as estimates go. It could be very cheap or very valuable, and the fact that I can't tell irritates me immediately.

Teddy's still going through his call sheet, so I lead Conrad to the wet bar and place his bottle ceremoniously on the counter. I gesture, Vanna White–style, at the row of jewel-colored liquor bottles, the gentle blue glow of the wine fridge. "What do you want? We have Cab Franc, Sancerre, or we can bring something up from the cellar. Allagash, there's an IPA Teddy likes. Or obviously any cocktail. This is an interesting gin, if you like a martini—"

"Cab Franc is great. Thanks."

Teddy's voice drifts from the next room over: "I completely agree. Universal pet insurance is at the top of my list of priorities . . ."

I pull a face at Conrad as I wedge the wine opener into the cork. "Sorry. He'll be done soon."

"There's no rush. I know you're really busy with the campaign. I appreciate you making time."

"Of course. We're so happy you could come." The point of the wine opener slips, gouging out a fleck of cork. "Crap. Sorry."

I start over. This time the cork breaks in half.

"Want me to try?" Conrad holds out his hands.

Embarrassed, I pass over the bottle and opener. I'm on a first-name basis with minor royalty, Oscar winners, Nobel laureates. But I still get nervous around people like Conrad—the former summer people, the ones I probably scooped ice cream for, the ones whose beds I might have cleaned, the ones who knew me as part of the faceless, polo-shirted mass of waiters and tour guides that revolves around them, tending to their every need. I prefer to meet people as Jess Wieland. I like to have a clean slate.

Conrad gets the bottle open within seconds, the cork releasing with a quiet pop.

I smile placidly. "So, how's your visit been so far?"

"Great. I mean, I've been trapped inside working for a lot of it. And then yesterday it rained. But I've gotten to see some of the usual stuff. Falcon Lake, sunrise from the top of Granlac, et cetera. It's incredible seeing it without anyone around."

"It's definitely a different scene than in the summer." Heartened by the reminder that he's an outsider here, I add generously, "If you're staying for a while, you should come for May Day."

He closes the corkscrew, hands it back. "What's May Day?"

"On May first, we open up the property so locals can come in, wander around, see the gardens. We have some music and drinks. It's a tradition Teddy's parents started, to share the property with people who live around here."

"Huh. I never heard of it."

"Well, you were a summer person."

"Guilty as charged. I'm going to be gone by May first, though."

"This year we're doing it a few days early, because of Teddy's travel schedule. I'll send you the details." I don't add that Clara's still bent out of shape about the date change. She thinks holding it in April is bad luck. Everything in April is bad luck, if you ask her.

Not that I can ask her anything, when she doesn't even answer my messages.

Teddy strides into the room with his hands lifted in the air, as if showing us he's unarmed.

"All done!" He kisses me on the cheek. "I'm all done, I promise. No more calls. Conrad, man, how you doing? Jess got you something to drink?"

We sit outside by the firepit, where the Adirondack chairs are arranged in a semicircle overlooking the yard. The whole house was built around this view: woods on either side, and the infinite sprawl of grass that fades into cattails, then rocks, and then over the edge into a scrape of ocean, pink fog drawn tight across the opposite shore of the sound. Conrad looks impressed. Good.

"How's the campaign going?" he asks Teddy after we're settled in.

"Good! Poll numbers are looking good. It keeps us busy. Jess and I have been running all over the state—"

"And beyond," I interject.

"—but we love it."

I take a long sip of my wine. I've had this conversation so many times, I could put my head down and go to sleep and still respond to my cues at the right time. A nod here, a wry comment there. Scrunch my nose at Teddy to show how in love we are.

"How does it work if you win?" Conrad asks. "Do you move to Washington? Or do you go back and forth?"

Teddy rolls his beer bottle between his hands. "We'd get a place down there, for sure. But when the Senate isn't in session, people go back to their districts."

"So what are you going to do in Washington?"

It takes me a moment to realize Conrad is talking to me. "Oh! Um."

I'm drawing a blank. I can't remember anyone ever asking me that before. I've thought about it, of course, although I haven't come up with any answers, certainly none that have been Phoebe-approved. When I look over at Teddy for help, he's watching me with interest, as if the question has never occurred to him, either. It may not have. That thought depresses me more than I expect. Teddy and I spend so much time talking about what he would do as a senator, we haven't talked at all about what I would do as a senator's wife.

Clara sometimes jokes that there are two tiers to the Wieland family. Blue and black. Blue means they have a whole Wikipedia article to themselves, footnotes and everything. Black means their name is in plain text, no links, lucky they're even mentioned.

"You're blue, I guess," I said when she first told me this, figuring all the core members of the family must be blue.

She laughed. "No. Teddy is. I'm red. You know, like a placeholder. They're waiting for me to do something someday. But I haven't done anything worth writing about yet."

After I married Teddy, my name showed up on the list, too. It was in black, of course. Not blue, not red. I don't need a placeholder. I've already achieved the impossible: getting my name on the page at all.

No one expects me to do anything else.

Conrad's still waiting for my response.

"Let's not jinx it," I improvise. "We still have to make it through the primaries."

"Fair enough." His smile is faintly sympathetic, as if he knows what I'm thinking, which undoes whatever goodwill I was starting to have. "And how's Clara holding up? With . . . everything."

Teddy's smile fades. "She's doing okay," he says carefully.

"I assume you're going to slap whoever leaked it with a massive lawsuit, right? Or criminal action."

"Ideally." After a beat, he admits, "Clara doesn't want to call the police."

"What? Why not?"

"She doesn't want to get the guy in the video in trouble." Teddy scrubs his hand over his face. "I don't know why she cares what happens to him. I mean, it can't be a good memory."

Or a memory at all.

I finish my glass of wine in a single gulp.

"Hey, guys!" comes a shout from the yard. We turn just as Clara rounds the side of the house on her bicycle, wobbling over the muddy grass until her momentum dies and she jumps off at the last possible second. The bike falls to the side, the front wheel spinning slowly to a halt.

Teddy gives me a curious look: *Did you know she was coming?* I shake my head minutely.

She climbs the steps like her joints are paining her. My stomach sinks. She looks even worse than she did when I saw her the other day. Her hair is lank. Her enormous coat swallows her from chin to knees. Her expression is oddly fixed and uneven, smiling in some parts, frowning in others. A cubist painting of a face.

"Hey," Teddy says cautiously. "How are you?"

"Amazing. I'm amazing." Immediately I know that she's stoned, and probably also already drunk. Her vowels are drowsy, her consonants violently overpronounced. The whites of her eyes are pink.

"Hi, bro." She pats the top of Teddy's head. "Hi, Conrad!" Clara comes around the circle, then stops behind Conrad's chair and flings her arms around him, hugging him over the top of his chair. He starts in surprise, but he can't move far. Her arms are tight around his neck.

Confused, he pats her elbow, which is nestled over his jugular. "Hi, Clara."

She keeps hugging him, nuzzles her face down toward his neck as if she's smelling him. Over the fabric of her sleeve, Conrad's panicked eyes dart to me, then to Teddy. I am mortified.

"Clara," Teddy begins.

She releases Conrad as suddenly as she embraced him. As if nothing happened, she comes over to the table next to me, where the open wine bottle is sitting with my glass. She picks it up, glances at the label. "Bleh."

She heads for the sliding doors. Teddy gives me a look, and I jump up.

"I'll come, too," I say.

Inside, she makes a beeline for the bar and picks up the bottle on the counter.

"That's the one"—I begin, but she's already tearing off the foil—
"Conrad brought," I finish, more quietly.

"Great. I like this importer." She opens the bottle expertly, a single twist of the corkscrew. "So how was yesterday's event? Where were
you again?"

"D.C. and Augusta." I add evenly, "You didn't answer any of my
texts."

"Yes, I did."

"Okay, you didn't answer *most* of my texts."

For several seconds, the only sound in the room is a steady glug as
she pours her wine into a handblown glass—past the standard pour
line, then higher still. I can't tell whether she's not answering because
she's drunk or because she's avoiding my question. Irritation pulls all
my muscles taut. Irritated at myself, mainly, for expecting something
different.

"I went into Axe Harbor today," she says, seemingly out of
nowhere.

"Okay." I'm not sure why this is news. Axe Harbor is only five
minutes down the road; we drive through it to get anywhere on the
island.

She sets the bottle down too hard on the counter. "Linda-May was
at the deli. I ordered coffee. She put milk in it. She knows I take it
black."

"Okay—?"

"The way she was looking at me . . . I can't even describe it. It was
horrible. She was pitying me."

"You don't know that."

Clara gives me a withering glance. "I know what pity looks like."
She threads her fingers around the stem of her wineglass. "And then
Sadie Michaud was there with her daughter Laura—"

"Lola."

"Lola. The kid tried to talk to me, and Sadie came up and guided
her away, like I might infect her. Like if little Lola comes too close,

she might grow up to be a bulimic who likes rough sex and shows the whole internet her vagina."

I wince. "Well, who cares about Sadie Michaud?"

"And the other night"—Clara's hand flattens on the counter, knuckles going white—"I saw something. A shadow."

I feel vaguely nauseated. "A shadow," I repeat.

"Like the one I saw when—" She breaks off, unable to finish the sentence. But I know what she means.

"It's a coincidence," I say.

"I *saw* it."

I make my voice as soft as I can. "Were you high?"

"No! Well, yes. But only a little." She pushes her sleeve up to scratch her arm. There are red marks running up and down it, over her tattoo, like she's been scratching it for a while. "It wasn't the pot. I don't hallucinate on pot."

"What else could it be?"

She gives me a look.

"It wasn't that," I say.

"How do you know?"

I throw up my hands. "Because *curses don't exist!*"

It comes out harsher than I intended. All my annoyance about the missing texts, and the stupid secret, and her general behavior, and now the fucking *curse*, spilling out in that one phrase.

Clara stops scratching.

"Sorry," I say more softly. "I didn't mean it like that." Too late. I can tell from her face that she's stung. I rub my forehead. I have to get myself under control. "When are you going to tell Teddy you don't remember the video? He keeps talking about it, and I don't like keeping it secret."

Her lips flatten. "Soon."

"How soon?"

"Soon soon." She snatches up the bottle with one hand and grabs my wrist with the other, tugging me away from the bar. "Let's go join the boys!" she says with almost violent cheer.

Out on the deck, the sun has dropped almost fully behind the hills. The maples lining the yard are still mostly bare, and the shadows from their branches fork across the grass like cracks through an old mirror. Clara drops sideways into an empty chair and tucks her feet up beside her. She's smiling again, peppy. I have whiplash. I try to sit upright, stay vigilant for whatever comes out of Clara's mouth next, but the chair's slope makes it impossible. I slump back, defeated.

Teddy and Conrad are chatting about some girl from their college class who's dating an NBA player. Small talk. A gimme conversation. Teddy's posture is relaxed, as if he's forgotten about Clara altogether. But I see how his eyes dart toward her every time she lifts her glass.

When Conrad says, "I heard they met because she slid into his DMs," Clara sees her opening.

"DMs!" she crows. "I get DMs."

"Yeah?" Conrad asks politely.

"These days? Sure. Hundreds a day." She puts down her glass to tick items off on her fingers. "DMs telling me to kill myself. DMs telling me I'm a dirty dyke cunt who got what's coming to her. DMs asking me to promote a detox skinny tummy tea because I'm such an *inspiration*. DMs saying pictures of me should come with a content warning. DMs saying they want to burn me alive and fuck my rotting corpse until it crinkles like a burned marshmallow."

I almost spit out my wine. "Oh my god, Clara."

"That's a direct quote." She turns to Teddy. "And before you say—*go to the police*—I asked Pierce. The threats are perfectly legal as long as they don't give a time or place. So," she says, her voice high and mocking, "I just have to wait for the trolls to let me know when it's time for s'mores."

There is a long, long moment when all I can hear is the wind rushing through the trees, a sound like fabric rubbing. Even Teddy seems temporarily speechless.

Our shock seems to satisfy her, because she settles back in her seat and lifts her glass to her mouth, smiling to herself. I can no longer tell how much of Clara's drunkenness is real and how much is a performance, but I suspect that she's making a scene of herself intentionally, and I can't fathom why.

"I'm so sorry you're dealing with that," Conrad manages. "That's horrible."

I wish he hadn't come. I hate that someone is here, witnessing this. His presence makes me see us all through the most unflattering lens—Clara's performative chuckle, Teddy's hands tight on his chair, my foot bouncing restlessly. I see us the way an outsider might. The way a paparazzo might, if they were hiding in the woods.

"See that boat?" Clara asks Conrad. She points down the slope toward the dock, where the *Transformation* is finally out of winter storage.

"I do," Conrad says. "It's yours?"

"Used to be our dad's," Teddy says, finally gathering himself. "An '85 Blackfin. We try to keep it as close as possible to original condition. Kind of a bitch to get parts for. When the cushions faded, the guys had to go to three antiques fairs before they found the right fabric. It's a lot of work, but—"

"Jess and I stole it once," Clara announces.

Teddy and I freeze.

Conrad looks confused. "Stole the boat? Doesn't it belong to you?"

"I mean, we drove it when we weren't supposed to." She leans forward conspiratorially. "It was right after my parents' funeral."

"Clara," Teddy says in warning.

My heart ticks like a bomb.

She swirls the wine in her glass. "Jess and I took a bottle of bourbon my dad had been saving. I mean, he wasn't going to drink it himself, right? Ha! We went down to drink it on the boat. Then one thing led to another, and we decided to take the boat out. We drove it into—"

"Drove is an overstatement," I interrupt. "We forgot to raise the anchor."

"No, we—" But then Teddy gives her another look, harder this time, and her brain finally catches up with her mouth. She stops talking and fills her mouth with wine.

Because of course, we didn't forget to raise the anchor. The anchor wasn't down at all; the boat was docked, and we cast off just fine. Blind drunk, hasty, stumbling to the wheel. We hit the gas in the low-wake zone, zigzagged over the waves. There was a lone kayaker at the mouth of the sound. We turned later than we should have, a sharp C that sent the boat tilting to one side, and our heavy wake made the kayak bounce up and down like a seesaw. The man in the kayak shouted, then capsized. Behind us, a horn blared. Blue lights flashed. The Coast Guard drew even with us. One officer raised a megaphone. *Stop the engine!* My whole future flashed before my eyes: an arrest, a DUI, no chance of college scholarships, cleaning toilets with my mother for the rest of my life.

That's what would have happened, had we been anyone else.

But by the time the officers had fished the man out of the water and boarded our boat, their faces were already embarrassed, apologetic. They knew the *Transformation*. They knew who we were. "Girls, can we take you back home? We need to talk to your parents." Clara let out a dry laugh, and the officer reddened, realizing his mistake. "Or . . . whoever's in charge."

Clara's grandmother was still recovering upstairs, so *whoever* turned out to be Teddy. The officers let us go into the house alone to bring him outside, so that the lingering guests wouldn't see them. We convened by the side of the house, not far from the deck we're sitting on now. Teddy looked at Clara and me (our eyes bloodshot, swaying as we stood), then at the empty whiskey bottle in the officer's hand.

"Are you sure they're under the influence?" Teddy asked with a straight face. Nineteen years old, in his funeral suit. "It's been a very emotional day. Did you do a Breathalyzer?"

"Not yet," the officers admitted.

Teddy paused. A tiny, nuanced pause. A pause beyond his years. "Do you think you need to?"

The officers looked at Clara and me.

They looked at the empty whiskey bottle they had found in our cup holder.

They looked at Teddy, and at the house behind him.

Slowly, in unison, they shook their heads.

My future, restored.

The story probably wouldn't shock Conrad. He went to Harvard: he probably knows a hundred wealthy kids with unprosecuted DUIs. But that's a lot of stock to put in *probably*. All it takes is one retelling. One unsympathetic listener, and Teddy becomes the candidate who talked his sister out of a DUI. I become the drunk-driving wife. I imagine the headlines, and my gut turns sour.

"Crap, forgot to turn this on," Teddy says, louder than necessary. He points a remote at the firepit. There's a quiet whoosh of gas, like a sharp inhale, and a row of blue flames as the ring ignites. Conrad is immediately distracted, as men tend to be when something catches fire, and he and Teddy start talking about where the firepit's from, how many burners it has, how often we go through a case of propane—as if Teddy, not the gardener, is the one who replaces the tank. As night falls, Clara stays quiet, thank god. I force my body to relax, muscle by muscle, until the only tension left is a rigid knot around my spine, which tightens every time I think about Clara's recklessness: how close we came to this outsider having a piece of us, knowing something only we should know.

When we start to say our goodbyes, Clara hops on her bike and takes off before anyone can insist on giving her a ride. I call after her to turn on her back light. It will only take her a couple minutes to get home, and the road is private; still, I worry as the red light bobs and weaves through the darkness. Conrad thanks us effusively, which seems sincere but under the circumstances only compounds my embarrassment. He goes the other direction, in a sleek gray sedan that looks like a hundred other premium rental cars and not at all like any car an actual islander would drive.

Teddy and I clear the empty bottles and the cheese board with its last couple grapes, smears of chèvre, a damp fold of soppressata with its polka dots of translucent fat. He is methodically scraping everything into the trash when I come in with the last wineglasses, the stems threaded through my fingers. I flip them upside down easily, a remnant of all my years bartending, and rinse them in the sink.

"Well," I say lightly, "that was interesting."

Teddy lets out a one-syllable laugh. He has scraped the marble board clean, but the cabinet for the trash can is still pulled wide open. He stares down into it. "I can't believe Clara."

"I know."

"She was high. And drunk. Why would she come over when she's like that? When she knows someone else is here?"

"I don't think she thought about it very much."

"She almost told him about the DUI."

"I know."

"Imagine the headlines. 'Teddy Wieland covers up DUI.'"

"I know."

He's started loading the dishwasher, slotting the dishes into the racks wherever they fit, not caring whether they face the same direction or not. "Saying that right in front of someone. Now, of all times. Right when Mike's finally managed to fix things."

"Mike the miracle worker," I mutter.

Teddy rests a bowl between two plates. "What's your problem with Mike?"

I straighten. "I don't have a problem with Mike."

"He's been doing a great job."

"I never said he wasn't."

"Then what is it?"

"Nothing."

"I know it's not nothing."

"It's just . . ." I drag out the sound.

Teddy picks up a bowl and rubs his eyes with the back of his free hand. "Jess. We've been on the road for days. I have fourteen events next week and ten more calls to make tonight. My sister's apparently on the verge of yet another breakdown. Can you please just tell me whatever you're trying to tell me? I can't guess what you're thinking."

I'm supposed to agree. Of course I shouldn't make him guess. Of course I shouldn't expect him to know, magically, what I want. But is it really such an insane expectation? After all, I know what he wants. I know what he believes, what he dreads, what he needs. More than that, I know why. I know why he forces food on Clara, why he doesn't go on diving boards, why he said yes so quickly to the Senate run. I know these things, and not because he sat me down and explained them to me, but because I pay attention. I observe and draw conclusions, and then I take those conclusions and push them outward, so that I might consider what else in his life that reason might affect. For example: he avoids diving boards because they're slippery, he says, and I conclude it reminds him of how his parents died, and I conclude therefore he will also want the outdoor stairs to have nonslip treads, and he will want his shoes to be replaced before they lose traction, and he will want to be warned before Stephanie waxes the floors. I consider the whole chain reaction. I anticipate him. I work at knowing him. Is it so much to ask, that he might work at knowing me?

I say, "When Conrad asked what I wanted to do, you changed the subject."

"What does that have to do with Mike?"

"It's just—of course Mike's doing a great job. But he forgets that we're humans. Things have been moving so fast. You and I haven't actually talked about what I would do in Washington."

"Well, what do you want to do?"

"I don't know."

"It'll be a good time to start a family. Like we've been talking about."

"We haven't talked about it in months."

"We talked about it just yesterday, for that podcast."

"Talking about it in interviews doesn't count." Because when you're a thirty-five-year-old childless political candidate in a swing state, the only acceptable answer to *Are you planning to start a family?* is *Yes, definitely.*

"You're saying you've changed your mind about kids?" Teddy asks in disbelief.

"No! I didn't say that. I just meant—we haven't *talked* about it."

"Okay, let's talk about it."

"Not right *now*, Teddy."

He runs his finger over his forehead, like he's warding off a headache. "It's not like you won't be busy in D.C. There will be a lot of events to go to. Luncheons. Charities."

"So, wife stuff."

"You *are* my wife."

"I know, but you're talking about me doing stuff only related to you."

"Isn't that what you've been doing the last two years?"

I flinch. "That's mean."

"How is it mean? It's true. You quit your job when we got married."

"You *told* me to quit my job!"

He looks incredulous. "So you want to go back to batch-killing mice for science experiments? Be my guest." He closes the dishwasher and punches the start button a little too hard. "I'm going to go make my calls."

Everyone has arguments, I remind myself when he's gone back to his study. *You just don't get to see anyone else's.*

I stop the dishwasher, which has finished its initial phase and moved on to the one that sounds like someone smacking a baseball through water. When the water has drained enough to unlock the door, I open the machine's well and drop in the detergent pod Teddy forgot.

Deaths attributed to the Wieland curse

Elizabeth Harper Wieland Crosby

In April 1954, several branches of the Wieland family gathered to celebrate Stanley Wieland's fortieth birthday at the Vantage Point estate in eastern Maine. The multiday festivities culminated in a polo tournament. Stanley, an avid equestrian, competed on his prized gelding Butter Biscuit, a retired racehorse known for winning the 1951 Preakness. In the tournament's final round, Butter Biscuit unexpectedly reared and threw Stanley, fracturing his spine and paralyzing him from the waist down. Butter Biscuit then charged into the crowd of spectators, causing pandemonium. Eight-year-old Elizabeth Harper Wieland Crosby was caught under the horse's hooves and trampled to death.

The Vantage Point stables were demolished shortly after the tragedy, and the horses were relocated to the Saugerties estate of politician Timothy Kurtz-Wieland, best known for his involvement in the Rum Wilter pay-to-play scandal of 1964.

10

CLARA

Sixteen years ago

I can't remember when I learned about the family curse. It wasn't an event. No one ever came out and said *Clara, the world thinks our family's doomed*. The curse was a story I grew up with. I always knew its contours and its consequences. It was a thought before I could think, a word before I could talk. A scar before I was born.

My parents didn't discuss it. They didn't need to. It was there every April, a month full of days when my mom snapped more easily, and my dad barely spoke, and the air in our house was humid with sorrow. It was there at the funerals we attended, with the cousins I only ever saw dressed in black. For a while, I thought it was normal. In second grade, we did an oral history project where we were supposed to come up with three interview questions to ask someone about their family. My questions were: *What color is your dad's plane? Does your mom dye her hair? What month are you afraid of?* Gradually, through covert looks and teachers' tactful interventions, I pieced together that not every family had a plane and not every family had a curse. My family was special. Something in our blood had predestined us for tragedy.

In the outside world, talk of the curse waxes and wanes. You might hear about it in a conspiracy rant alongside 9/11 truther theories, or once in a while some uncle's assistant's boyfriend decides to write a tell-all memoir that is usually half made-up. If the curse hasn't struck recently, though, most people don't give it much thought. Then, surprise, there's another death, a disappearance, a coma, and for a short time the curse floods back into the American imagination, and the name Wieland once more becomes synonymous with a dark, twisted thing, an uncanny fate.

If you're normal.

If you're a Wieland, the curse never really goes away.

My sophomore year of high school, the curse was in a dry spell. Five years without a family tragedy. The only direct mention I heard was when our social studies substitute teacher put on *Jeopardy!* and the curse showed up as a four-hundred-dollar answer in the category "American Myths." She was so flustered she unplugged the TV and we had to have silent reading for the rest of the period. I rolled my eyes. It reminded me of the containment measures my parents would take during the weeks after a family member died, when the curse conspiracies were in full swing. They'd confiscate the family computer, turn us away from tabloid racks when we were out and about. After the really big scandals, we'd take a trip somewhere. When a plane carrying three cousins disappeared over the Bermuda Triangle, we went on a monthlong private safari in Botswana, communing with rhinoceroses and pangolins, far from any newsstand. At sixteen, I was sure I could see through these protections. It wasn't until several months after the *Jeopardy!* incident that I learned how sheltered I had been.

Because of Halpern's January term, our spring break always landed in April, which meant I always spent it at home, since my dad refused to travel that month if he didn't have to. Teddy was away at college. It was the first school break I had been home without him, and I was frustrated by the extra attention from my parents. My mom kept following me around the house, kissing me on the forehead at unexpected moments and telling me to comb my hair and interrogating me about my "boyfriends," because I hadn't told her I also liked girls, and my dad kept asking me to do things with him that he really wanted to do with Teddy, like go golfing or build his ships-in-bottles. Of course, if I had known what would happen next, I would have tolerated a hundred probing questions. I would have reconstructed a thousand schooners.

My second night home, I skipped dinner with my parents to see a movie with Jess, and in return I promised I would join them the next day on their morning walk. They had two usual routes, but their favorite was a loop around the property, down through the woods to the granite cliffs at the southern tip, then up the sea path, over to the Axe Harbor beach and back along the main road. The walk took an hour or more, and they always started at exactly 8:00 a.m. I was barely awake by the time we set out, and I slumped along twenty feet behind them, crabby and tired, dragging my boots noisily through the mud.

"Isn't this beautiful?" my mom asked.

I grunted in reply.

"It's great exercise," my dad informed me. "Did you know? Since we started, we've lost twenty-five pounds!"

I did know. Ever since they'd started the routine, they bragged about their collective weight loss to anyone unlucky enough to come in earshot. Now that I had been at Halpern almost two years, though, surrounded day and night by other self-conscious teens, the number sounded a little different. I calculated how much I would weigh if I lost twenty-five pounds. Did my dad think I needed to lose weight?

After twenty minutes of walking, we reached the cliffs. The woods thinned out, and the trail turned into a patch of gravel and then a sheet of granite that dropped off unevenly into the water. From the ocean, the cliffs looked like a pile of stacked blocks. Jenga played by gods.

My dad stopped and turned to me. "This view is why your great-great-grandfather bought this property in the first place."

I rolled my eyes. "Yeah, I know."

"It's a defensible position." He made a sweeping gesture. "That's why Ambrose chose the name Vantage Point. When you stand here, you can see in every direction. East, south, west."

"Unless they're coming from behind you," I said.

It was my dad's turn to roll his eyes. But I had heard everything he was saying a million times. He was always going on and on about family history, our birthright, *responsibility*. Teddy seemed to be into the lectures. I wasn't. My dad was always leaving important parts out. For example, he didn't mention what I knew to be true, which was that the reason Ambrose wanted a "defensible position" was because by the time he was looking for a property to buy, several members of his family had died off in strange ways. He had become paranoid, which was probably why he eventually hanged himself from one of the elm trees in the backyard. April 29, just under the curse's deadline.

While my dad was reciting his sanitized version of the story, my mom had stepped off the trail and onto the plateau. She was edging her way toward what we called the fireworks hole, a sheer cliff with a cavern tucked underneath. When the tide was right and a wave rushed inside, the pressure forced all the air out of the cavern at once, with a bang like a grenade going off, and water erupted upward in a white fan. If you caught it at the right time, it was beautiful.

"Be careful," my dad called out.

The wind blew her curls against her face. From the direction of the hole, there was a rumble, then a boom and a small spray of water. "It won't go off for another half hour," she said.

She came back toward us, and I thought she was done, but instead she pulled a little digital camera out of her pocket and held it out to my dad. "Take a photo of me and Clara on the cliffs."

I groaned. "I don't want to take a photo. I'm wearing sweatpants."

"You're always wearing sweatpants."

I took the camera from her instead. "I'll take one of you two."

"We don't need another photo of us."

"Well, you're not getting one of me."

She sighed. "At least put the loop around your wrist so you don't drop it."

They arranged themselves on the ledge with some argument, as my dad nagged my mom to avoid the black moss. There was another rumble from the hole.

I raised the camera to take the picture. The tiny digital screen pixelated their figures and heightened the colors of their outfits. Their smiles were stiff.

I pressed the button. The camera made its fake shutter noise. *Cha-ching.* My dad started toward me. I shook my head. "Let me get a better one. Look happy."

"Hurry up," my dad said with mock impatience. "Some of us have places to be."

They posed again. I raised the camera again. But before I could press the button, something strobed across my vision: a dark shadow, moving fast, like a diving bird.

I cried out and recoiled instantly, throwing my hands up to protect my face. The camera banged my chin.

My mom lunged forward, a maternal instinct. Her boots slipped on the moss. Her arms windmilled. My dad reached for her—too late. She slid backward and over the edge into the hole.

"Eleanor!" my dad shouted.

I froze in my hunched posture. The shadow was gone. There was no bird. I stared in horror at the empty rock next to my dad, the place where my mom had disappeared.

From over the ledge came a scream.

Stunned, I took a step forward, but my dad held up a hand. "No, Clara! Stay there!"

I stopped. He carefully got down on his knees and lay on his stomach, his head extended over the hole, his arm outstretched. "Grab my hand!" he called down.

It's fine, I remember thinking. She's okay. I've seen this movie before: she'll be pulled to safety at the last moment. It didn't matter that I heard the water sliding back out through the rocks, a sound like someone sucking air through their teeth. It didn't matter what I knew to be true—about how this hole worked, the physics of water, our family's fate. Even then, I believed everything would be okay.

The wave was huge, thirty feet high and thunderous. There was a split second when my dad tried to crawl in reverse, the toes of his boots clawing at the rock. But he was too slow. As the water fell back down from the sky, it grabbed him and dragged him into the hole.

And then the water was gone, and my parents were gone, and the ledge was empty, the wet rock shining in the sun.

The nature of waves is that they return.

I heard the loud whoosh of the water sucking out through the rocks, then a lull as the water gathered force: a half second when it was quiet enough for me to hear them scream. And then the water rushed forward, the air hit the cavern with a percussive bang, and another tower of spray. A whoosh, a scream, a bang. I've done the math. It can't have taken me longer than sixty seconds to scramble around to the rocks on the other side of the hole, which would have left time for only three of these cycles. And yet I remember an infinite number. Infinite waves, infinite screams. Sometimes I dream that I am still on those rocks, hurrying to reach them, and I wake in a sweat, my limbs moving, my hands clutching for thin air.

If my unconscious is especially cruel, I will dream the rest of the scene. It comes as colored squares, light refracted in a kaleidoscope. Green jacket. Brown hair. Pink water. Blue jeans, my mom's, on unmoving legs. My dad surfaces with a gurgling shout. He splashes, looking for something—a handhold—me. The whites of his eyes, wheeling. He shouts my name, at least I think it's my name but it's hard to tell because the water is rushing in again, and he is pinned in the cavern, and the water buoys him up, and I cover my ears and screw my eyes shut but I am too late. I have already heard the sound his head makes as it slams against the rock, a wet thunk, like a dropped melon. I have already seen his head turn from a part into an object, the fruit and its separated rind.

It took the police eighteen hours to pull my parents' bodies free of the rocks. The current had shoved them under the cave, trapping their legs in an underwater crevice, and there was only a short window between each tide during which the climbers could work. They had to wait through two full circuits before they could pry the flesh from the rocks and belay the bodies up on yellow rescue boards. As we waited, a swarm of people began to descend on the house: Teddy, the lawyers, the business managers, the assistants, the cousins.

Detectives, too, who questioned me about what had happened. Teddy sat next to me, and Pierce stood in the background, ears pricked for any inquiries he perceived as dangerous. But the police were gentle. WFCI had paid for half their station remodel, which included an infrared sauna. Mostly they wanted to know about what I had seen. Could it have been a bird? A plane? A falling leaf? I didn't know. Anything seemed possible, in this new impossible world. Did I have a history of epilepsy? Eye floaters? Hallucinations?

When I began to crumble, Teddy put his arm around my shoulders. "That's enough," he told the detectives in a hard voice. "I think you got what you were looking for."

Our loving Nana Celeste descended the following day in a swirl of cashmere and Ambien. Thanks to her, it was two weeks before we could bury our parents. She wanted an open casket, so she flew in a mortician who was renowned for his work restoring drowned corpses—he did a good business with the Russian Mafia—and it took him that long to drain the bodies and reconstruct their faces to an acceptable standard.

It was disconcerting how little changed at Vantage Point in those two weeks. Aside from Celeste's arrival, everything marched forward the same way it always had. The linens were washed on Tuesdays and Fridays, and the bathrooms were deep-cleaned on Saturdays. The mud the investigators had tracked in along the hallway was swiftly mopped up. The many sympathy flowers were placed neatly in our dad's study. Rosa, our housekeeper at the time, moved away the traces of our parents' day-to-day, so we wouldn't stumble across our dad's shoes when looking for our own boots. The groundskeeper parked their cars in the garage so they wouldn't be out in the rain. Our parents were whisked away so quickly it was hard to believe they had ever even lived there, much less been in charge.

Celeste spent most of that time rotating her jewelry boxes in and out of the wall safe in our dad's study and going through rooms to make sure our mom hadn't stolen any of her Dresden figurines. One day, she swanned out to the shops and brought home a thick stack of newspapers and tabloids, which she dropped dramatically on the dining table.

"Can you believe this?" She ripped one open and showed us the headline. *WIELAND COUPLE DEAD IN TRAGIC ACCIDENT.* She tossed it aside and took out another. *FAMILY CURSE? WIELAND SCION FALLS TO DEATH WITH WIFE.*

"It's morbid," Celeste declared. "Who buys these?"

Teddy eyed the stack, a whole newsstand's worth. "No idea," he said dryly.

I fanned out the papers. Within hours of the accident, boats had started lining up for their turn to motor past the scene with binoculars or 600mm superzooms or dinky disposable cameras. Here was the fruit of their labors. Below each headline was a grainy image of the cliffs at low tide, each one a little different but fundamentally the same. The best photos got a stripe of police tape in the background, or a neon dot of a rescuer clambering over the scene.

I ran my fingers over one of the images, which showed a Coast Guard boat stationed in front of the rocks. Behind it, the inlet was a dark line, the pool barely concealed by the angle of the rocks.

"There are lots of that kind of cliff on the island," I said. "I could take a picture of other cliffs and send them in and no one would know the difference. We could trick them."

Celeste looked at me like I was stupid, which to be fair, she thought I was. "What good would that do? They'd still think they were looking. That's what's offensive."

"But you want to have an open casket," Teddy said.

"That's different," she replied. "Those people are *friends*. These people are vultures."

I thought the coverage would let up quickly. But the photographers were still there the next day, and the next. The articles became increasingly outlandish. The details of the deaths had leaked, and now the newspapers implied that I had distracted my mom on purpose, or even that I had pushed her. They dug up a still from a beach volleyball game the previous year where I collided with another player, so readers could see my violent side. They published an old photo of my parents arguing at a fundraiser, and another of a body—who could even say whose body?—being rolled into the morgue. They published a photo of Celeste and Teddy walking out of the funeral home, their faces tight with grief. They would have put the autopsy photos there if they could have.

I started to question Celeste's metaphor. Yes, like vultures, the paparazzi preyed on our dead. But even vultures filled up, were sated. The cameras could eat forever. They could swallow you whole.

The funeral was awful, of course. Everyone kept talking about how it was such a *beautiful service,* which I found perverse. Celeste kept hitting my back with her purse to make me stand up straight. Every time I made eye contact with someone in the pews, they folded their faces like origami to prove that they were sad. After the origami face, they cringed away, like if they looked at me too long, they would be the next to die.

By the time we got back to the house for the reception, my nerves were shot. While we were at the service, the caterers had set up a massive buffet in the dining room. So many trays of our parents' favorite foods: shrimp toasts, mushroom tarts, cheesecakes. All their favorite foods were beige. Jess, who had hardly left my side since the accident, filled a plate of food for me, and I picked at it in the corner while people came up to say they were sorry and what a lovely eulogy Teddy had given and, oh, had there been any news about the reading of the will?

I was accepting unsolicited spiritual guidance from the pastor, to whom God had granted the divine gift of halitosis, when we heard a shriek from the other side of the room. It was Celeste. She was bent over double by the buffet in her black Chanel suit, clutching her stomach. She had shown almost no emotion the entire day, so at first I thought she was having a medical episode. Then she stood up and smacked the side of a tray of mushroom tarts.

"They're *soggy!*" she wailed. "They're soggy. That's not how he likes them. I mean, liked them—" It went on and on like that, screams going up and down in volume and pitch. Just when I thought she was petering out, she whirled on me. "Did you do it?" she demanded. "Did you order them this way?"

"N-no," I stammered. I had no idea who had ordered the catering. The pastor stepped to the side. Even the man of God was eager to get away from me.

"It's your fault. The whole thing's your fault," Celeste hissed.

"Okay, okay." Teddy came out of the crowd and took her arm. One of our aunts took her other arm. They guided her away from the table and half carried her upstairs.

Whispers broke out.

I marched over to the table and picked up the tray of tarts. I took them to the kitchen, where I dumped them in the trash. Then I decided that wasn't enough, and I took them out of the trash and put them down the garbage disposal. The blades churned and sucked. Mush spit from the hole. I wanted to stick my whole hand down in there. Then my arm, and the rest of my body. Until I was bloody chunks, liquid tissue. Until I had flushed my whole self clean away.

A hand reached over and turned off the disposal switch. Jess. The night before, we had painted our nails a matching shade of dark red. I didn't turn away from the sink, because I was crying too hard. She put her arms around me.

"She didn't mean it."

"I didn't order the catering," I sobbed.

"I know. Shh, I know."

I let her hold me. I closed my eyes, and I thought I saw a stripe across my vision, an afterimage of what I had seen on the cliffs. That was nothing new. It had been there the past two weeks, every time I closed my eyes.

"She was right," I mumbled into Jess's damp shoulder. "It was my fault."

She hugged me closer. "No, it wasn't."

"I saw the thing. I screamed."

"Anyone would scream."

"What did I see?" I asked. Somehow, I was crying again. "What was it?"

"I don't know," Jess said.

"The curse," I said. I hadn't been able to voice it to anyone else— not the police, not Teddy. It seemed too ludicrous to say aloud. A statement I couldn't walk back.

"No," Jess said patiently. "Not that."

The only people who take teenage girls seriously are other teen-age girls.

I don't remember whose idea it was to steal the boat. I remember what it was like to shoot across the waves, the prow of the *Transformation* lifting high into the air. We flew like eagles. Dark water raced beneath us, a churn of black and shine. I watched it, and imagined it was the barrier between worlds and my parents were on the other side. Right there, just below the surface. If I jumped off the boat, I thought, clean into the icy water, I could join them. It had only been two weeks. They couldn't have gotten far.

But Jess was with me, and Teddy was back on land. So I held on to the railing and faced into the wind. The curse had come for me, and it had left me alive. That was punishment enough, for now.

11

CLARA

April 8

Sixteen years later, the trail to the cliffs is still narrow and brown, still matted with mud and twigs despite the gardeners' efforts. Under the spruce trees, the light is wet and milky, stuck in a limbo state between night and day. The only sounds are a few rustling leaves, a birdcall, and my footsteps on the dirt. The closer I get to the rocks, the heavier the air becomes, like I'm pressing through a thick substance.

Teddy and I used to make special plans for the anniversary of our parents' deaths. It felt important to choose the perfect activity. Something meaningful or traditional or adventurous. We've had many years to experiment, and we've tried it all. We've visited our parents' graves, helped at a soup kitchen, flown to the Maldives. One year I convinced Teddy to do shrooms and then go on our mom's favorite hike. It's the only time I've seen him tripping. We ended up lying flat on our bellies at the summit for hours, watching ants ferry crumbs along the edge of a boulder while the sun boiled us red. The next day, we watched gladiator movies in the dark while we slathered ourselves in buckets of aloe, our raw bodies sticking to the leather sofa in glistening eucalyptus-scented circles.

Our experiments were never successful. Nothing ever undid what happened. Nothing ever brought them back to life. Over the past few years, our plans have gotten less elaborate. This year, we haven't planned anything at all. The Day is a wound we have to clean, and it doesn't matter if we do it with salt or peroxide. It'll hurt either way.

When I step onto the plateau on top of the cliffs, the wind seems to rip clean through my layers, like a pair of scissors neatly clipping the fabric away. I tuck my chin into my coat collar and scan the cliffs. The view is an empty gradient, pink and yellow stone sliding into gray fog. There are seagulls resting on ledges, and in the water the dark blot of a seal coming up for air. Otherwise, I'm all alone.

The cliffs look exactly the same as they did that day. Sixteen years are nothing to these rocks—a blink, a sneeze, a single heartbeat. For me, it's half my life. I've been alive without my parents for as long as I was alive with them. My grief is old enough to drive. In Europe, it can order a drink.

I tell myself these things to try to wrap my mind around the length of time, but there's no making sense of it. Sixteen years seems too long and too short. Sixteen years is nothing. And it's forever.

I'm used to setting my grief away from me, putting it on a high shelf somewhere inside my mind to rest until an earthquake comes for it, a vibration shuddering the shelf and sending everything tumbling to the floor. Now I reach up and take down my sadness, turn it over. I note its shape, its sheen; I wipe off the dust and study it, and it is heavy in my hands.

I sidle up to the edge of the hole and peer over the twenty-foot drop. Midway down one rock is a red stain—a thread of sandstone I always mistake, irrationally, for blood. The tide is very low today. Hours away from the explosion. At the bottom, there's only a small tide pool. Walled off, unremarkable. Water laps gently at the mouth of the cavern. A strand of seaweed floats and twists beneath the surface. White spikes of barnacles breathe through tiny holes. It's peaceful. When I think of my parents dying, this is how I try to imagine it—like they were relaxing in a lagoon, sunbathing on a plastic float, and they simply slipped away.

Take a picture of Clara and me.

Sometimes I pretend my life is one of those movies where you find out at the end that everything was a dream. Or a time-travel movie, one where you go back and make different decisions. I could go back sixteen years, and I could tell my parents not to go for a walk that day. I could get out of bed faster, and we would reach the rock sooner, before the wave. I could keep my mouth shut. I could close my eyes.

Magical thinking, my therapists call it. It's dangerous to live in these fantasies, to convince yourself, even on the smallest level, that you might actually enter these other worlds.

But how do you live without the magical thinking? How can you bear to go on?

"Clara!"

The shout startles me. My right foot slips on the rock, but I get my balance and turn around. Teddy is standing at the edge of the woods in his running clothes, his hair raked back with sweat, his face ashen.

"Get away from there," he says.

"It won't go off for hours," I say, because it's like what my mom said that day, and saying the words makes me feel closer to her. She's speaking through me. I'm her vessel. But Teddy's right, obviously, and I'm already heading back toward him, treading a shallow ridge of granite like a balance beam. When I reach him, I hop off and spread my hands, ta-da. "See? I'm fine."

"Don't be a dick."

"I'm not!" I am. "You're out running? Did Jess come?"

"No."

I take a deep breath. "You know it's the anniversary."

"I know," he says curtly. Then he softens his voice and repeats, "I know."

Our eyes meet. We have the same eyes. Hazel spiked with gold. Heavy lids. When there was that trend going around to use TikTok filters to make a different gender version of yourself, I didn't bother. I could look right at Teddy any time I wanted.

"You want to sit for a sec?" Teddy asks in that tone that usually means a Serious Conversation is coming.

"Sure."

We find a flat spot a safe distance from the hole. The rock is cold from a night of fog and sea spray. Teddy props his elbows on his knees and stares out at the horizon, like he's figuring out what he wants to say. My unease grows. I try to think what he could be mad about.

"I'm sorry I didn't text you that I was coming here," I say tentatively.

He jerks his head sideways in a quick denial. "It's fine. I didn't plan anything, either."

No elaboration.

"Then what's wrong?" I ask, a little impatient. I think when you have a sex tape leaked, you should get at least a couple weeks off from your brother giving you a hard time.

Teddy sighs. He turns to give me a pointed look. "How's your hangover?"

I've been trying not to think too hard about my behavior yesterday evening, which has been easy, since I was busy thinking about our dead parents. I know I messed up, although I can't remember the details. Just a generalized cloud of shame. My new norm.

"I've had worse," I say.

"You almost told Conrad that you and Jess bribed your way out of a DUI."

"I did?" But this rings a bell.

"Do you know how damaging that could be? Not just for you. For Jess, too. That's a whole other news cycle right there. 'Candidate's wife covered up DUI.' 'Did Teddy Wieland help his wife break the law?' And so on. Right after all this mess with the video."

My cheeks heat. *After* implies the "mess" is over. And for Teddy, maybe it is. But my body is still out there, everywhere. It always will be.

"It was just Conrad," I point out. "He wouldn't tell anyone. He's your friend."

"It doesn't matter. You need to think about what you say before you say it. Even in front of my friends or your friends. Even in front of the campaign staff, like Phoebe or Mike."

That surprises me. "You tell Mike everything."

"No, I don't."

"You don't trust him?"

"I trust that our interests are aligned."

"That's depressing."

"It is what it is."

I pick at a piece of dried moss. The rock beneath us is dark with damp, but I can still see the colored flecks in the granite: pink, light orange, lavender, black. The whole island is like this, billions of mosaic pieces. Even after millennia, it's rough. Resilient. Granite is between a six and a seven on the Mohs scale; you can't scratch it with a knife. Teddy's like that. Strong and unbreakable. I want to be like that, too. Instead, I am sandstone. I am the part that washes away.

"I'm sorry," I say quietly. "I shouldn't have acted that way."

Teddy's posture softens. He angles his body more toward me.

"Are you doing okay? With—everything?" He sounds more patient than he sometimes does when he asks this kind of question. This time, he doesn't sound like he's looking for a specific answer.

This is my cue. I should tell him that I don't remember the video. I should tell him it might be fake. I should tell him last night I dreamed I was plunged into the sea. A shadow wrapped around my waist like a lasso, held me in place. Made me watch. There in the depths, I saw two bodies, preserved by salt, floating in the darkness. My parents, beckoning me.

"Clara?" he prods.

Slowly, I shake my head. "No. Nothing else is going on."

On the day of the funeral, after the Coast Guard brought Jess and me back and had their talk with Teddy, after the guests had departed and the caterers had cleaned up and left us with a house that looked exactly the same as before, except that it was overflowing with flowers, I went up to our parents' bedroom. I hadn't been in there since the accident. No one had, as far as I could tell. It still smelled like our parents—Mom's variety of Chanel perfumes, the weird tar shampoo our dad swore by. Had sworn by. Their bed was wide and neat, with decorative pillows stacked three deep against the headboard. Had Rosa made the bed before they died, or after? On the floor next to my dad's nightstand was a pile of ten or eleven books. He always read a stack of books at a time; he was probably halfway through all of them. And now he would never finish. I did a circuit of the room, touching the things my parents would have touched. The perfume bottle on my mother's vanity, the picture frame beside it, the window handle. Then I touched the things no one would normally touch. The wallpaper, the fringe on the curtains, the hinge on the door, the edges of their lives.

Their closet was the worst part. All I could see was the missing shape of my father's shoulders in his suits. My mother's evening dresses were tangles of straps; the only reason I could imagine them as garments was because I had seen her wear them before. Every item hung in a fluid line from its hanger, unobstructed by anything so casual as a body.

I pinched the sleeves of their blazers, toyed with the collars of their shirts. I rummaged through the pockets of my dad's trousers and jeans. I wasn't sure what I was looking for—something new, something I hadn't seen before. I wanted to still be able to learn things about them. But Rosa had cleaned all his clothes, of course, and there wasn't much to find. A tiny lump of lint. Some grains of sand. A crumpled gum wrapper that had gone through the laundry and melted down into a furry white pebble.

Celeste had already picked over the jewelry drawer. But one of the pieces she had left behind was a necklace I remembered my mom wearing sometimes, a triangular gold pendant with a four-carat yellow diamond at the center. It didn't have any particular meaning to me, but that was okay. I would will meaning upon it. I picked it up, hooked it around my neck. I studied myself wearing my mom's necklace in my mom's mirror. I decided I'd wear it forever.

"Clara? What are you doing?"

Teddy was in the doorway. I shrugged.

"Just looking around. How's Celeste?"

"Still sedated."

"Can we keep her like that forever?"

He let out a short laugh. I closed the jewelry drawer, then pulled out the shallow drawer where my dad had kept his belts. Each one was coiled like a snake in a nest. I ran my fingers over the leather's bonded edge. "Pierce said she's going to be my guardian."

"I guess so."

"Ugh."

"It won't be so bad. It's only until you're eighteen, and you'll be at Halpern most of the time."

"I know." I understood how it worked. We had been over this before. But already in these two weeks, I had noticed Teddy explaining things more and more, the three years between us stretching longer and longer. I didn't mind. It was nice to feel that there was still some-one else in charge.

I picked up a sweater and pressed it to my face. It blotted out all the light. All the everything. I smelled our dad, woven in those fibers, vanishing bit by bit each day. The wool itched against my face, sharp and feathery at the same time.

"Can you do it?" I said into the fabric.

"Go through their stuff?"

I moved the sweater away so he could hear me. "No. Be my guard-ian. It makes way more sense than Celeste."

"Does it?"

"She doesn't even want to live here. She hates it here. She wants to go back to London and drown her sorrows in absinthe and boy toys."

"I'll still be around. It's not like I disappear if I'm not your guardian."

"Come on. You'll just have to sign some things every now and then."

"I'm not a real adult."

"You're nineteen."

"I know that, thanks."

"And you're the most responsible nineteen-year-old ever," I added. His shoulders slumped slightly. I played my final card. "It's what Mom and Dad would have wanted."

"They're the ones who said Celeste," he said.

"Only because you weren't an adult the last time they revised the will."

A long silence.

It would sound better to say I didn't know what I was asking him to do, but I did. I knew the idea of taking responsibility for me weighed heavy on him, and I was glad. I wanted to weigh heavy on someone. I wanted someone to bear my weight with me. For me.

"Okay," he said. "I'll talk to Celeste."

I dropped the sweater and ran over to hug him. He wrapped his arms around me. The words rumbled through me along with his heartbeat. What a relief, the hug, the guardianship. Adulthood was a downpour into which I had briefly stepped, and now I could scurry back inside. Teddy was shaped like our dad, more or less. My body was shaped like no one: our mother had been smaller than me, tiny, ropy, thin. Hugging me was not like hugging her, and I remember feeling bad that Teddy could never get this simulation of hugging one of our parents. But I didn't feel bad enough to stop. I only leaned farther in.

When Teddy jogs away from the cliffs, back to his important meetings and world contributions, I tuck my legs up to my chest and rest my chin on my knees. Wind cuts my face. With the tide so low, the air is damp with the smell of seaweed: brine and rotten eggs. It's mistier than it was the day my parents died, but otherwise it's all the same. In the slapping of waves, I hear the scream, the thunk, the rush of greedy water. I can't escape them. It is monstrously unfair that my brain erases memories I need, but holds on so tightly to the worst moment of my life.

Tomorrow, I'll tell Teddy I don't remember the video. Just one more day.

Right.

Sure.

As I squint at the horizon, trying to make out the smaller islands in the distance, a shape dissolves from the fog. A boat, only a couple hundred feet away. I assume it's a lobster boat, or maybe a fisherman, because who else would be out in this visibility? But as it draws closer, I see that it's not a motorboat at all. It's a dinghy—no, too big to be a dinghy. An old wooden rowboat, low to the water, with several figures huddled inside. A few oars drag limply at the sides. No one is rowing.

I jump to my feet. The boat rocks over the waves. Somehow, the current has pulled them around the point toward me. They don't seem in distress, but if they don't start rowing again, they'll get caught in the crosscurrent and be pushed into the rocks. I wave my arms over my head. I mime rowing and point toward the harbor.

"*Row!*" I shout.

The boat keeps coming toward me. There are more people than I thought, maybe ten or twelve. I step closer to the edge and scream at the top of my lungs, but no one rows. My face is wet from the fog and wind, water running down into my eyes. The crosscurrent has caught the boat now, and it drags it inexorably forward, over the pounding waves. I have a horrible sense of déjà vu: out here on the rocks again, watching a tragedy strike, powerless to avert it. The boat is wide and flat, lined with planks of seats. A lifeboat. My voice goes up in pitch, burning my throat, a screech of desperation. Still no one moves. Then, just as the boat is about to splinter against the rock, it disappears.

My knees give out and I sit down hard, my tailbone colliding painfully with the granite.

I wipe the water from my eyes. In front of me is only the rock, the eddies, the empty froth. A stretch of blank sea.

The boat is gone.

No—it was never there.

Lacework mind, poorly stitched. Mostly holes.

I sit on the rocks for a long time, my fist pressed to my mouth, while the cold goes through my jeans and burrows down into my bones. In front of me, the waves hit the rocks over and over, each one as empty as the last.

In the end, I don't have another chance to come clean to Teddy.

Because the next day, another video comes out.

12

JESS

April 9

In the new video, Clara leans against an ornately carved door that appears to have last been painted sometime around Napoleon's reign. In the door's glass panes, you can see reflected the white circles of string lights, the dark shapes of people dancing in a crowd. Music blares. Clara looks nominally healthier. Beautiful, even. Her pale brown hair up off her shoulders, her makeup impeccable. She is wearing a high-necked cap-sleeved Naeem Khan dress that cost $10,400 before tax. I know the price because it's the dress she wore to be maid of honor at my wedding.

The video appears to have caught Clara mid-pontificating. She is holding a half-empty champagne flute, which she swings around as she speaks, to punctuate her ideas. Her other hand balances on the door's inside edge, index finger probing the hinge, and for the entire duration of the video, I expect the door to slam shut, crushing her fingernail into its bed, shattering the bone.

"Here's my message," Clara says to the person holding the camera. Her voice is mocking. "Hey, Teddy, sometimes you're a fucking dick. I bet someday you'll run for president so you can make everyone do exactly what you want. Even though you'd have to pander to the plebes, as you like to say, and you might choke on your own ego in the process."

"Stop! Come on, say something nice," a woman says from behind the camera. There's something familiar about her voice, but I can't quite place it.

Clara sighs. Her finger still worries the hinge. "Fine." She squares her shoulders and looks straight into the lens. "Congratulations, Teddy. I'm so fucking happy for you. You're a complete asshole but somehow you still get everything you want, so good for you."

The camera shakes as the person filming chokes down a laugh.

Clara swigs her champagne. When she finishes, she clicks her tongue with satisfaction and locks her eyes on the camera again. "Also, Jess only married you for the money."

The person behind the camera starts laughing fully. "No, Clara, you can't say that."

"Why not?" Clara challenges. "It's true, isn't it? Didn't you?"

"That's why you can't say it!"

"Then make sure you edit it out."

"Obviously."

The camera jerks then, like the video might be over, but then it flips around to show the person filming. And of course—it's me. Clara has the phone now, and I'm pressing my hands over my face, trying to stop laughing. On the fourth finger, my engagement ring winks in the light.

◈

"It's fake," Clara says when I accept her call. Then she adds, in a small voice: "Right?"

My jaw drops. "Of course it's fake."

"Okay."

I yank the steering wheel hard to the right, skidding close to the curb. "You'd never say those things. *I'd* never say those things."

"It's just—" She breaks off.

"What?"

"It's just a weird thing to fake."

She sounds pensive, like she wants to talk through the topic together for a while, and I'm not in the mood. My body feels hot and jittery. So I do something I never do. I end the call, pretending I lost service.

Teddy's campaign office is a squat one-story in Chaumont Harbor, where the cedar-shingled buildings hold a constant rotation of quirky stores. There's a seemingly endless supply of summer people who want to try their hand at selling artisanal cupcakes, maritime books, scrimshaw dog tags—until they inevitably run out of capital two years in and hand the lease off to the next aspiring whatever.

This time last year, the campaign office was a jewelry gallery, although you would never know it now. As soon as Teddy signed the lease, trucks started squeezing down the street to unload desks and task chairs, outdated computer monitors and landline phones and even a fax machine, in case they need to send any documents to 1999. Subarus spit out energetic staffers straight from law school and retired volunteers in crinkling ponchos. An earring display case became the snack table, the diamonds replaced with picked-over piles of fun-size Snickers and single-serving potato chip bags. Staffers took up residence at the jewelers' old workstations, filling the empty tool caddies with ballpoint pens.

Every time I've been in here the past few months, it buzzes with activity. Interns in Bowdoin sweatshirts ping around the room like clone invaders in a video game. Phones ring. Cold-callers hunch over chunky laptops all open to the same screen, a gray square bordered by colored buttons, which they click with the automatic reflexes of a teenager on a pinball machine. *Hi, is this Chantal? I'm Ashley calling with Mainers for Teddy Wieland. I'd love to talk to you today about . . .* CALL REFUSED. NEXT CALL. *Hi, can I talk to Stephen?*

Not today. I guess we were lucky that Clara's previous video broke in the evening, when we had private time to regroup. Today, Teddy's already at the office when I get the news, and I have to weave through a circle of confused staffers who stare open-mouthed as I pass. The phones are ringing, but no one's picking up.

I refuse to let myself be bothered. I'm not going to blow this out of proportion, the way Clara did. I'm going to take things in stride.

In the back room, Teddy and Mike are huddled next to a computer, pointing at the screen. When I enter, they look up in unison. Teddy's face is several degrees paler than it was when I last saw him two hours ago, when we finally had a quick, hard round of morning sex—one of his hands braced on the headboard, the other lifting my hips to the right angle.

Mike shuts the laptop and leaves the room without comment. I've never seen him preemptively give anyone privacy. Another sign that shit is about to hit the fan. The office walls are thin enough that when Mike closes the door behind him, the file cabinet rattles gently.

"The video's fake," I say when the rattling's done. "Obviously."

I expect Teddy to say *Of course.*

Or maybe *What a fucking mess.*

Instead, he says, "Fake?"

"A deepfake. CGI. You know, like, someone put my face on another person's body."

"I know what a deepfake is."

My stomach drops. "You can't seriously think I said those things about you."

He says nothing.

"*Teddy.*"

"Jess."

I'm almost speechless. I know the video is convincing. Before the camera turned around on me, I half believed it myself. It wouldn't be the first time Clara's said something intentionally shocking and later had to walk it back. But me—? I wouldn't say something like that.

"Did you watch the whole thing?" I ask.

"Yes," he says, his voice hard. "So I saw your face."

"It wasn't my face. I wasn't there."

He arches an eyebrow. "You weren't at our wedding?"

"You know what I mean."

"If it's a fake, it's awfully convincing."

"Okay," I say, "so it's awfully convincing."

My thighs are still sore from this morning, and the contrast between that ache and the coldness of Teddy's expression makes my stomach hurt. I've walked into the Twilight Zone. How do you convince someone something's not real? What do you use to prove it? I shouldn't have to prove it at all. He's my husband. He should believe me.

He starts pacing tight little circles on the industrial carpet, the way he does when he's thinking something through. "It just doesn't make sense. Why would someone drop a fake video of you and Clara talking crap about me, out of nowhere?"

I run my tongue along my teeth. "Well. It isn't exactly out of nowhere."

He stops. "What do you mean?"

"Clara told me the other day she doesn't remember the first video. She doesn't remember the room, the guy, the video—any of it. That's why she wouldn't tell us who the guy was. She didn't know." As Teddy stares at me in disbelief, I start speaking more quickly. "At first she thought the video was real and she had forgotten, because of her memory thing. I told her if she didn't remember, the video might be a fake. She said it wasn't, so I dropped it. But now there's this video of me, and I *know* that's not real. So hers might also be—"

Teddy cuts me off. "She told you this *when*?"

I wince. "A few days ago."

"And you didn't tell me?"

"She asked me not to."

He stares at me.

"I told her she should tell you," I say.

"But *you* should have told me."

"I didn't know it was going to come out like this."

"You mean you didn't know you were going to get caught."

"No, I mean I didn't know it would matter! I thought it was her business whether or not she wanted to tell you."

"There's no such thing as *her business*," he says. "Not between you and me. I mean, what if she was sick again and she asked you not to tell me? Would you tell me then?"

"Of course I would."

"Then why not tell me about this?"

"I don't know. It didn't seem dangerous. She asked me not to. She said she'd answer my texts. I didn't want to get in the middle." The more reasons I give, the less genuine I sound, but I can't seem to stop talking.

"So you picked her," he says.

"Don't say it like that!"

"Why not? It's what happened."

"Teddy."

"And now you expect me to just believe this video's fake?"

"Yes."

"Why should I believe you? You just told me you lied about Clara!"

"A lie of omission, maybe," I say.

"A lie is a lie."

I swallow hard. "Well, that doesn't mean I'm lying about the new video."

He doesn't have a response to that.

Out in the main office, the phones continue to ring.

My skin feels tight. My mind is a helpless buzz.

Teddy closes his eyes and inhales, like he's made up his mind. When he opens them, his gaze is clearer, a little softer. He takes a step forward. I figure he's coming to put his arms around me, and I prepare myself to be tucked into his body. My ear to his beating heart. Instead, he walks past me and flings open the door. Mike is right outside.

"Come in," Teddy tells him, adding with heavy sarcasm, "We have a *plot twist.*"

To my surprise, Mike believes me faster than Teddy did. When I say the video's a deepfake, he nods once and says, "Good."

His reaction seems to calm Teddy. So apparently my husband can believe me, as long as his campaign manager says it's okay.

"So now what?" I ask Mike. "We make a statement?"

"Once we figure out what it should say. I've already called a crisis management person, and they're flying in tonight."

I think about the threats Clara's been getting, the comments I'm sure are populating my own social media. "Shouldn't we tell people it's fake as soon as possible?"

"We need to get the words right. And we need to talk to Clara, too. Make sure the stories line up."

"It's not a story. It's the truth."

"The truth is a story, too. This is more complicated than Clara's sex tape. Your marriage is an integral part of the campaign, and this video throws that into question. Along with Teddy's character, which is even more important. Even if the video is a deepfake—"

"*It is.*"

"—people are going to have questions. Who would make a deepfake? Why? If Clara's sex tape is fake, too, then why didn't we say so earlier? Were we intentionally hiding something? I need to make some calls, get a focus group, get the temperature of things. We need to figure out the right angle."

I'm losing the tiny scrap of patience I had left. "We make some calls? That's the plan?"

"It's the next step to creating the plan."

"Oh, my god." I turn to Teddy, who's been quiet this whole time. "Teddy—"

But he makes a quick, suppressive gesture. "Slow down, Jess, okay? Christ. You sound like Clara."

My head snaps back. He's never talked to me like that before—this quelling, final tone. I've only ever heard him use it on Clara or, occasionally, an outside person who has really fucked things up.

I try to make eye contact with him, but he only looks at Mike expectantly.

"Give us half an hour to talk it over," Mike tells me. A clear dismissal.

Outside, the cluster of staffers has dissipated. Without them, the street is sleepy and quiet. Fog clings to the ground. Across the street, the hardware store's window display is in disarray, cardboard boxes piled in the corner, a naked mannequin leaning up against the wall. Joe Michaud changes the store stock every spring as he gets ready for the tourists, replacing the snow chains with Helly Hansen raincoats, the chisel sets with Cotopaxi backpacks. Seeing the window mid-change feels intimate, like I've walked past someone's dressing room.

I try calling Clara back. If Mike wants her story to line up with mine, then I better make sure it does. I don't want any of her hemming and hawing and *I don't remember* and *I'm not sure*. I want her to tell them, with great certainty, that the video is fake.

The line rings a few times, then goes to voicemail.

I type out a text: *Call me back ASAP.*

Then, even though it feels bizarre to send these words to Clara, I add: *I need your help.*

As I wait for her answer, I navigate back to the new video and press play. I squint my eyes, as if the issue is simply that it's out of focus, and with the correct prescription, it would all make sense. I watch Clara lean against the door, watch myself take the champagne glass from her hand. I wonder when in the night it's supposed to have happened. The band was already playing. Had we eaten cake? Had we done the toasts? The more I try to pinpoint the order of the night, the more it escapes me, a carousel spinning faster and faster. I remember a blur of tuxedos, chiffon, sparklers crackling, the soft collapse of the raspberry sponge, Teddy kissing the side of my neck, Clara's breath warm on my ear, confessing. Certainly the video would have been made before that, before the confession.

If the video were real. Which it's not.

I'm starting to understand why Clara wasn't sure about the first video. The minute you start to indulge the hypothesis, the theoretical possibility grows. You start pushing aside other memories, trying to make room for something that never fit in the first place.

My phone buzzes with a text message.

Clara: *Talk tonight*

My throat tightens. The day yawns open before me. Tonight's too far away. I try calling her again. She rejects the call after two rings. I type back quickly: *Can we please talk now? Really fast. It's important.*

After hesitating, I add: *Teddy's pissed off. He thinks the new video is real. It's a whole situation.*

There's a dot-dot-dot. It vanishes. Reappears.

After what feels like forever, a reply pops up.

Clara: *Sorry at work now*

I reread the message a couple times, bewildered. Clara went in to work? Since when does Clara care about work? Seeing her the other day, my impression was that she hadn't even been into the office all week. And what she does at WFCI isn't brain surgery. She could step away for a minute to call me back. How many times have I stepped away from something for her?

I take a deep breath, trying to calm down. I'm not being fair. Work is important, of course it is. It's good she's taking it seriously. It's a good sign.

A pickup truck rumbles past, then a sedan. I'm in public—how could I forget? In the apartment above the newsstand, a curtain ripples, as if newly dropped. Panicking, I start walking down the sidewalk with my chin tucked to my chest. A poor disguise. I walk all the way down to the end of Main Street, then back again, counting off the time remaining in my exile.

Across the road, the door of Pine Tree Market slides open to let someone out.

No, not just "someone."

Clara.

I stop in my tracks.

She has a brown paper bag in each hand, and the handles strain with the weight of her groceries, about to rip.

Clara never does her own grocery shopping. Stephanie's son does it for us, a weekly run to the Hannaford in Ellsworth. I'll still stop by the market for wine or snacks occasionally, but Clara avoids grocery stores at all costs. They trigger her. If she needs something urgently, she'll ask someone else to go get it, Stephanie or Paul or even me, in a pinch. It's a rule she created when she got back from Marien this last time, and I was so proud of her when she told me about it. I thought she was setting a boundary.

But now here she is.

Not at work.

Not busy.

In the grand scheme of things, it's a small lie.

The problem is, I know where her small lies lead. For years, she lied to me often and proficiently. She said she was nauseous, said she was full, said she had already eaten, said she couldn't make it until after dessert, said there was dinner at the other party, said she was taking portions home for a friend, said she had to pee, said she was too tired, said the weight loss was a side effect, she was seeing a doctor, she was seeing a different doctor, she was working on it, she was keeping her appointments, she was fine. Lies you wouldn't think to question. Small, small lies.

Even when I realized what was happening, I didn't know how to call her out on such little fabrications. Was I supposed to tell a grown woman she couldn't go to the bathroom alone? Was I supposed to stop the dinner party to ask for a rundown of everything she ate that day? Or save it for later, for private, and ask her then? I tried all options. They didn't work. At best, she got annoyed. At worst, she learned from the mistake. She started to lie more carefully. She improved her craft.

I tried another approach. The one where I let the lie slide. A big game of pretending. She pretended to have eaten and I pretended to believe her and together we pretended our way into the emergency room, where I watched from a shatterproof window as a nurse threaded needles into her tiny blue veins.

So I don't have to see into the grocery bags to know what's inside. Family-size sacks of jumbo marshmallows, Double Stuf Oreos, mini–candy bars. Bright, sugary things, with small shiny packaging she can shove down into the bottom of her trash can. She'll consume as much as she can in a single sitting, then vomit it up, starve herself for three days to atone, and do it all over again with whatever's left.

The one time I ask her for help, she's too busy hurting herself to bother.

You picked her, Teddy told me earlier. And Clara picked—what? Her illness. Herself.

I know what the pamphlets say: *Addiction isn't a choice. It's a disease.*

But it feels like a choice.

"Clara," I call out, before I've formed a plan. Just so she knows I see her.

She freezes and scans the road until she finds me. Guilt clouds her face. She hesitates. Looks toward her car, then back to me. Again toward her car. I see her calculate. She can get to the car faster than I can get to her. With one last apologetic smile, she takes off at a jog, leaving me behind.

13

JESS

Sixteen years ago

For the first couple years after Clara's parents died, we were closer than we had ever been. When she went back to boarding school, we talked almost every night on the phone or over instant messenger, typing so fast I used my overburdened modem as a foot warmer. We mostly talked about dumb things, our crushes or grudges or homework assignments, the kind of things any teenagers might talk about. My value to Clara had always been that I treated her like a normal person, or how she imagined normal people might be treated: I didn't harp on her money, I didn't gawk at her house. Now I tried to provide a similar service. I didn't treat her delicately or avoid mentioning her parents. Nor did I constantly give my condolences. I walked in the middle, right down the line.

When she came home on vacations, we spent every spare minute together. I had real summer jobs by that point, waitressing and working parks crews, but when I wasn't working, I'd be at Clara's house or stretched out next to her on the yellow chairs at the private swim club with a twenty-year waiting list. I slept over at Vantage Point, usually in her bed, curled into a comma on one side while she sprawled like an exclamation mark on the other. Sometimes I'd wake up sweating, wrapped in the covers I tended to hog, and I'd hear her breathing and I'd think: *Thank god.* That first time I visited her at Halpern, I had worried we were growing apart. What a relief, then, to find her next to me.

Being near Clara made me feel necessary, and occasionally bold. Most of the year, my life was a series of calculations. I did whatever I needed to do in order to get an A, in order to get a scholarship, in order to go to college, in order to never have to serve another tourist a double scoop of Moose Tracks in a waffle cone. In the summers, with Clara, I could set aside all of that. I could be thoughtless. I could be seventeen.

One time, one of those summers, I went with her to a house party. I was the one who lived on the island all year-round, but she was the one who had been invited. The party was dim and musky. There were so many bodies crammed into the room that the windows sweated. Everyone moved together, hip to hip to hip, a single organism with a thousand swaying arms. Clara was behind me, her hips pressed to my ass. Her hand went to my thigh, and I could feel how, under her touch, my thigh was bare and smooth. We were dancing. Just dancing. Her hand moved up, her fingers playing with the frayed hem of my shorts, which were in fact her shorts that I had borrowed. The crowd moved around us, around us, around us, and we kissed, her mouth sweet and dry from the tequila, and somewhere deep inside I felt—I felt—

Then someone jostled us, and we broke apart. We turned away from each other and kept dancing, as if it had never happened at all.

When we went to college, the differences in our situations became harder to ignore.

I went to U of M. Even with in-state tuition, it required taking on a sickening amount of debt. I had nightmares about interest rates chasing me down a mountain of loans, ugly boulders that would squash me flat if I slowed my pace. I chose courses I thought might be useful after college: nursing prerequisites, paralegal studies, accounting.

I spent summers back on the island, working waitressing and retail stints until, after graduation, I landed an uncoveted job in the mouse-breeding program at the Brenner, where I measured food pellets, packed live specimens for transport, and euthanized sick mice by sticking needles into their plump, hairy thighs.

Meanwhile, Clara attended a small liberal arts college where they gave no grades. She majored in cocaine comedowns. When school wasn't in session, she traveled, studied abroad, occasionally completed a cushy four-week internship at Teddy's insistence, then spent the rest of the time going to warehouse parties. At graduation, she was pulled across the finish line on the strength of her grandmother's timely two-million-dollar donation to the science center.

She moved to New York, where she claimed to be working on a hot yoga certification, although her life mostly seemed to consist of flinging herself around the globe to desert raves and yoga retreats. While her parents were alive, they had emphasized decorum and restraint; I was always overhearing her father talking about the "value of money," which to me was a stupid redundancy. Now that they were gone, and Clara had inherited half their estate, she let their money run through her like water. I tried not to resent it, but sometimes, the waste was all I could see. It became more and more difficult to stay in touch. Clara was always busy partying; I was always busy working. The gulf between us widened, bit by bit.

Then, when I was twenty-four, my mother and I had a terrible fight. The fight itself wasn't exactly a surprise. The truth was, we had never been close. I was ashamed of that. A hardworking single mother, her only daughter: we should have been the Gilmore Girls, us against the world. Instead, we had always been an awkward unit of two closed-off people, our love more a duty than an action.

My mother had recently met and married Dwayne, a guy who ran kayak tours of the bioluminescent bay in Castine. I had no problem with Dwayne, and I was happy my mother was happy. She and Dwayne had decided to move down to Florida, which had more bio-luminescent bays, which you could tour with glass-bottomed motor-boats, which was better for him because he had developed an issue with a ligament in his shoulder. Or something. I went over to their apartment to help her pack, and while I was there, my mother made a comment about how I could come visit them in Orlando for Christ-mas. This was in May. I said maybe; I'd have to see how long I could get off work, and what Clara was doing.

"You're choosing the Wielands over your own family?"

"Clara *is* my family," I said.

My mother had never liked my friendship with Clara. She had never explained why, which left open any number of explanations: she worried about an imbalance of power; she didn't want me to be in someone's debt; she envied that my friendship with the Wielands had given me opportunities she had never had; she thought it meant I didn't appreciate what she had given me. At various times, I had con-sidered all these explanations. At various times, they had probably all been true. In that particular moment, her resentment was simpler. I could see it in the way she paled at my words. She was jealous. She wanted me to be hers.

The argument unspooled from there. The details don't matter. We both said hurtful things, then pretended to apologize. The next day, she moved to Florida, with only a perfunctory hug goodbye.

I texted Clara about the argument with my mother, staying vague about the cause. To my surprise, given our waning communication, she called me back immediately. She sounded compassionate and invested. She must have been able to tell from my voice how upset I was, because she insisted on flying me to New York for a girls' weekend.

I didn't like visiting Clara in New York, or anywhere for that matter. I always seemed to end up in situations like the one at Halpern, embarrassing myself in front of people who thought I was pointless, or racking up credit card debt so they wouldn't think Clara was paying for me. But I agreed. I wanted to be with Clara. I wanted to tell her about how awful my job was, and how Daniel Spinelli had ghosted me right after we slept together. I would recount the entire sordid fight with my mother, even the parts that had to do with Clara, because that was how we were when we were near each other: honest, transparent as glass.

Or so I thought.

When Clara opened the door to her Manhattan apartment, I could tell right away that she was sick. Her eyes were shadowed. Her hair was matted. She looked like she hadn't bathed in days. I was stunned speechless. She hugged me, and she felt tiny in my arms. Then, as if she could hear my thoughts, she ushered me inside before I could inspect her too carefully.

I hadn't been to this new apartment yet, but I remembered the photos she had sent me when she moved in. So I knew that in the daytime, the living room windows would frame an elm tree's sturdy branches, a ledge lined with pigeon-repelling pins. Sunlight would fall in squares across the washed oak floor and cast the ivory walls in a soft, buttery glow.

At that moment, though, the windows were black rectangles. The walls looked bare. The whole apartment felt musty somehow, the air heavy and preserved. In the kitchen, she had arranged a spread of bagels and lox, enough to feed a family of six.

"So," she said, "what do you want to do? Did you eat? Are you hungry? Do you want a bagel? I was starving, so I just ate. There's a really good restaurant at the corner. We could order in. Also, a big bottle of wine and you can tell me what happened."

Her syntax wasn't quite right. Her voice was an octave too bright, a beat too fast. I wondered if she was high on something.

Her appearance was too extreme to be a new development. How long had it been since I had last seen her in person? Five months? On social media, red flags could be easily lowered by the right angle, a careful crop, the application of a tinted filter. In person, there were tricks, too. The last time I saw her, she had been draped in her classic old-money uniform, expensive oversize cashmere sweaters, vintage windbreakers, thick socks, knee-high rain boots—things too baggy to decipher much about the body beneath. Now she was wearing a tank top. I could see the thinness of her arms, the rooted bulge of her clavicle. Had she worn such a tiny shirt on purpose? Did she want me to look? Did she want me to be impressed?

"Let's go out," I said, desperate to see her in another context, as if different lighting might resolve the problem.

On our way out, she forgot to lock the door. I had to remind her. "Oh, duh," she said, slapping her forehead, but I had the feeling she often left it unlocked. Island habits died hard, if you could afford to replace anything that got robbed.

It was dawning on me that we wouldn't be able to discuss my mother this trip. We wouldn't be able to discuss anything that was bothering me, at least not in any way that would actually help. I would have to give Clara a few details, make her feel useful, but she was in no place to help me figure anything out.

"Stairs or elevator?" she asked. She lived on the top floor. I wanted to move, to get out of there.

"Stairs," I said.

She walked toward the elevator.

"Clara?"

"Oh. Sorry." She shook her head as if to clear it and turned toward the stairs.

She went down ahead of me, moving slowly. By the second flight, she was breathing hard.

"Clara?" I repeated, concerned.

"Hi," she replied. She kept going.

I paused, staring at the back of her head, trying to figure out what was going on. She only made it two more steps before her knees sagged. Her hand gripped the railing. The other hand went to her chest. She steadied herself momentarily, then swayed again. "Oh," she said, in a surprised voice. Her legs crumpled underneath her. I reached out to grab her, as she had caught me, all those years ago at her boarding school, but I was too late. She had already fallen head-first down the rest of the flight.

The paramedics took her to the nearest emergency room, where the doctors informed me that she was severely malnourished. I asked what could cause that, and they looked at me like I was stupid. "You've never noticed anything unusual about her eating?"

When I reached Clara's brother, who was in Germany on busi-ness, he sounded alarmed—but not surprised. I had always prided myself on being so observant. But everyone else had known what was going on, except me.

I explained that they wanted to admit her to the ICU to begin fluids and monitor her heart arrhythmia.

"There's a place I've researched," he said. "Marien. It's in Ver-mont. It's a rehab, but they have the best eating disorder clinic in the country. I'll go to the airport now. I should be able to get into JFK by morning, and then I can charter an ambulance to take us up."

Eating disorder. I mouthed the words, as if learning a new language. I cleared my throat. "I can go up with her. You can meet us there."

He paused. "You sure?"

"Of course."

The Marien Center for Wellness was five hours by car from New York. Clara slept the whole way, while the paramedics fidgeted with her IV. The side windows were frosted for privacy, so the only view I had was out the back windows, two small tinted squares that revealed monotonous highways receding behind us. When we got off I-83, the views got slightly better, but the ride got bouncier. Every time a pothole pitched me off the narrow folding seat, the same thought played in my head: *It's my fault, I made her take the stairs.* She was so, so thin. I didn't understand how I hadn't seen it before. It was so obvious, now that I knew what I was looking for.

Marien was beautiful. Colonial-era brick buildings with white trim; a lake that reflected thickets of trees. There were lounges and walking paths, a spa. It looked a lot like Clara's old boarding school, which turned out to be only forty-five minutes away, on the other side of the mountains. The biggest building at Marien was the Bartholomew Lekken Medical Center, the Lekken for short, but Clara later told me everyone called it the Leaky because if you went there you might end up on a drip. People who arrived in a bad state often stayed at the Leaky for a couple weeks, then moved into one of the pretty cottages named after trees. Maple, Sumac, Poplar. Clara was in a bad state; Clara was already on a drip. They gave her a room on the second floor of the Leaky. Even though she was stable, nurses were always rushing in and out to check her fluids, her vitals, scribble on her chart. It was difficult to determine whether this attention was because they were very worried about her, or because she had a yellow VIP label on her chart.

Teddy arrived a couple hours later, fresh from the plane. I was standing awkwardly in the corner of her room, which seemed to be the only place I wasn't in anyone's way. It had been many years since I had seen him anywhere other than the island, and when he strode in, with his broad shoulders and his confident gaze, I felt an odd leap in my stomach, which I attributed to relief.

I gave him and Clara some alone time and went downstairs to the main waiting room. It looked like a fancy hotel but smelled like a hospital. There was a tall plastic caddy lined with pamphlets. *A Loved One's Guide to Addiction. Twelve Steps or Twenty?: Alternatives to the AA Model. Self-Care for the Caregiver. Day Hikes and Local Attractions in the Vermont White Mountains.* Before today, I hadn't known private ambulances existed. I hadn't known rehabs treated eating disorders. I hadn't known a lot of things, it turned out.

Teddy came out while I was leafing through a brochure about sex addiction. I stuffed it back in its slot.

"How is she?" I asked.

His hazel eyes were shadowed. "Okay. She's awake, if you want to say goodbye before you head back."

I played with the strap of my purse. "Actually, if you don't mind . . . I was planning to stay nearby for a couple days. Just to see how she does."

"You don't have to. I'll stick around for a while." He cracked his spine, stretched his arms overhead. His rumpled suit jacket continued to rumple. "She won't be alone."

"Well, two's better than one, right?"

Perplexed, he dropped his arms. "You don't have work?"

"It isn't a big deal." It was a big deal. My boss would be mad. I had taken off a couple days for the New York trip, but starting Wednesday, my coworkers would have to cover for me. I would lose those hours, and my bank account was already overdrawn. Still, I couldn't imagine leaving Clara there, especially after I had missed all the signs. *I made her take the stairs.*

As if he could read my mind, he said, "It wasn't your fault, you know."

"I know."

"The doctors say she has Wernicke encephalopathy. It's caused by a severe thiamine deficiency. It affects coordination, memory, balance. It can make people confused and irritable."

I remembered the odd way she had loped down the hallway, and how she had asked me the same question several times. "That's why she fell?"

"That, or she fainted. They said it wasn't a stroke, so that's good news."

"Great," I said. Clara was twenty-four years old. Not having a stroke seemed like a low bar. "I do want to stay here for a couple days. If it won't bother you."

His eyebrows rose. "Of course not. I'm sure she'll be happy you're here." He checked his watch. "I need to stick around here for another hour to go over some documents with the staff. But I'm staying at the inn down the road—do you want me to get you a room?"

I knew from the *Local Attractions* brochure which inn he meant. It had three dollar signs after its name. I also knew, from the way he phrased the offer, that he meant he would pay.

Clara had paid for me plenty of times over the years. But we had long since agreed on an unspoken code of what felt okay for her to pay for (dinners, concert tickets) and what felt weird (clothing, coffee). We never needed to say any of that aloud. Teddy didn't know our code, and I would rather die than explain it to him. I wasn't sure whether I was more anxious about being a freeloader, or seeming like one.

I shook my head. "I'm going to stay at the Motel 6."

He looked slightly pained, the way Clara did whenever she had to talk about money. "The inn's my treat. I insist."

"Thanks, but the motel's fine."

Teddy studied me with renewed interest. I fidgeted under his appraisal. Having all of Teddy's attention was intense, like the sun opening up right over you.

"Okay," he said.

The motel room was small and worn. The bed was covered with a shiny quilt. I recognized the brand: I had tucked and smoothed it a million times as a kid, helping my mother when she had picked up some extra hours at another branch of the same motel.

As I showered, I wondered if I should have accepted Teddy's offer. The bathroom's grout was striped with mold. The light over the mirror flickered and buzzed. It made the solitude worse. My mother was mad at me. My closest friend was in a hospital bed. I felt deeply, extremely alone.

When I got out of the shower, I checked my phone and saw that I had a text from Teddy. *What's your room number?*

I told him. Twenty seconds later, there was a knock on my door. I checked the mirror. My hair was wet; my face was pink and shiny from the bad hotel soap. I pulled on my pajamas and went to open the door.

Teddy was standing on the walkway between rooms. He had a suitcase in one hand and a key card in the other.

"What happened to the inn?" I asked.

He shrugged. "This works."

It took me a moment to formulate a response. "You didn't have to do that."

He smiled. "Neither did you."

The smile sent prickles of awareness up my arms. I leaned on the doorjamb to hide the goosebumps. We looked at each other. His jaw was slightly stubbled. I was aware of his whole body.

He nodded down the hall. "I'm right there at the end if you need me."

When I got into bed, I tried to figure out what had just happened. I understood that he was staying at the motel for me, although I wasn't entirely sure why. He probably considered me his responsibility, because I was Clara's friend. Surprisingly, I didn't mind. I liked the idea that he was responsible for me. I liked that he was sleeping down the hall, in the same bed, under the same quilt. It was almost like he was sleeping next to me.

The next day, I woke at dawn. I hadn't closed the curtains all the way, and through the narrow gap, I had a straight view onto the motel parking lot. It looked strangely romantic, a pink-blue sky, a layer of mist. At the lot's edge, three white semitrucks fanned out like wings.

I hadn't brought many clothes to New York, but I did have running shorts, a sports bra, sneakers. I pulled those on, along with yesterday's shirt, and headed out for a jog. The motel was on a two-lane road that stretched in either direction. I picked a direction at random and ran along the shoulder. It was too cold out for what I was wearing. My breath made clouds in the air.

As I ran, I thought about Clara. The idea of an imbalance in our friendship kept nagging at the back of my mind. I didn't doubt that if I had been the sick one, she would have brought me to the hospital, too. But what good were counterfactuals? It had been many years since Clara was my protector. Somewhere along the way, I had become the more capable of us. The designation felt like a trick, a trophy I didn't want to win.

By the time I reached the motel again, the sun had risen fully in the sky. I saw another runner coming from the opposite direction, the first person I had seen all morning. His gait was smooth and even. It was Teddy. I waited for him by the MOTEL 6 sign, with its spurt of dandelions around the base.

"You run beautifully," I said as he drew closer.

He slowed. "What?"

Admittedly, it had been a weird thing to say. "Your gait. It's very elegant."

He laughed. "Thanks."

Of course he would be one of those people who looks good after a run. Tousled hair, a shine of sweat along the lines of his throat. When he lifted his shirt to mop his brow, his stomach was tan and flat, a muscle in his side twitching as he moved.

It was not news to me that Clara's brother was attractive. He had that height, that easy smile, the hair that flopped over his forehead just so. Having a crush on Teddy Wieland was a high school rite of passage. But I was older now. I thought I had become immune.

He dropped the shirt and smiled. He had caught me staring.

"I'm going over to see Clara at nine," he said. "If you want a ride."

Right—I didn't have a car. I had gotten to the motel by Marien's courtesy shuttle, which smelled like cigarette smoke and was driven by an old man who blasted German punk music the entire ride. I got the impression the shuttle didn't run very often. Most visitors to Marien could afford to rent a car.

"That would be great," I said.

When I got into his car thirty minutes later, I instantly regretted my decision. The car smelled much better than the shuttle, but being alone with him was more intimidating than I had expected. What could Teddy and I possibly have to talk about? The drive between Marien and the motel was ten minutes. I wasn't sure we had ever been alone together for that long.

Everything I knew about his life came from Clara. Through her filter, Teddy had seemed like a flat outline, a caricature of an over-bearing older brother. Now, in the car next to me, he was unavoidably 3D. His hair was damp at the temples. He smelled shower-fresh but somehow autumnal, woodsy and spicy, good enough to outweigh the new-car smell of his rental. His jeans were just tight enough that I could see his muscled thigh flex every time he pressed the gas. Of the many things in life that made me anxious, men weren't one of them. But I was nervous around Teddy. I couldn't think of anything to say.

After a few minutes of painful silence, he said, "What did your boss say about taking time off?"

"I haven't talked to him," I admitted. "I had already taken off

Monday and Tuesday to visit Clara. Wednesday I'll call out sick. Otherwise he'll ask too many questions." If I told one person on the island where Clara was, soon everyone would know. She wouldn't want that.

"Remind me where you work?" Teddy asked.

"The Brenner. In the mouse lab."

"I didn't know you were into science."

"I'm not really. I'm into health insurance and retirement benefits."

"Love a 401K," he agreed, as if he had ever worried about retirement, as if his whole life weren't already guaranteed.

A truck with several bales of hay in the bed was toddling down the road at twenty miles an hour. Teddy crossed the double line to zip around it.

"What about you? Was Germany angry that you had to go?" I asked.

He nodded solemnly. "Oh, yeah. The whole country was devastated."

"You were permanently disinvited from Oktoberfest."

"They revoked my beer steins. No, my bosses were a little annoyed, but it's fine. I can do the work from here."

"It's—finance law, right?"

"Mergers and acquisitions."

"Do you like it?"

"I do. I get to travel a lot, which is nice. I was in Barcelona for six months last year—I loved that. Amazing food, amazing people."

I imagined him walking through a European city, his stubble grown out, his shirt unbuttoned at the collar. In my mind, he sauntered across a plaza, across pale stones still warm from the day's sun, then looked back over his shoulder, a dimple creasing his cheek as he smiled.

The image made me sit up straight so fast that my seat belt jerked against my chest. I had been imagining myself in the scene with him. I had been imagining myself as the one who made him smile.

"So what were you and Clara going to do in New York this week-end?" Teddy asked, oblivious. "Before . . . all this."

"I don't know. Maybe go to a museum? Probably a club." I made a face.

"You don't like clubs?" he asked.

"No, I do." I didn't. "I mean, they're fine. Clara likes them more than me, I guess."

"I don't like them either. Too many people. Music's too loud."

I found myself smiling. "That's a real old-man complaint."

"You're the one who said you didn't like clubs!" he protested.

"I said they're fine."

"Well, your disdain was palpable."

"Don't backpedal. I get it. You hate fun."

His eyes slid over to me. "No, I know how to have fun."

His voice was a warm burr. I felt momentarily weightless, and I thought for a moment that we were sailing over a pothole, but no, it was just me, my insides opening up like Teddy had turned them with a key. I understood then that he was attracted to me, which didn't come as a particular surprise. Men often were. It was rarer for me to feel it in return. Rarer still for it to come on like this, so quickly, toward a person I had known for such a long time. It was as if at some point yesterday, Teddy had removed a barrier on his charm, and now it was coming at me full force. I didn't know why this change had happened.

"Well, it's nice of you to give up your love of raves and nightclubs to come up here," Teddy said.

He was joking, but also not, and the implied praise embarrassed me. "I only went to New York to see her. I didn't know it was going to turn out like this."

"Yeah." His voice turned solemn, too.

"But you did," I said. It came out slightly accusatory. "You knew about Marien, where to take her. So you knew she had been sick."

"I've tried to talk about it with her before. She wouldn't listen. So

I figured at least I could look into it and I would be prepared if . . ." He trailed off, because the *if* had already happened.

I pressed my finger to the rubber seam of the window, frowning. "When did it start?"

"Two years ago? Three?"

"I should have noticed."

"Don't blame yourself. Clara's good at hiding things."

"But I didn't think she was. I didn't think she liked lying at all."

He drummed his fingers against the steering wheel, as if deciding whether or not to say something. Finally he gave in.

"Sometimes I don't know if she thinks of it as lying. She justifies it in her head. She has her own sense of reality. Well—I guess we all do. But sometimes it scares me, how much she can be in denial. It's like she's living this performance of herself."

I knew what he meant. "She'll say something to shock you, but it's a diversion tactic."

He gave me an appreciative look. "Exactly."

I pushed my finger deeper into the gap. "She hasn't told me anything real in months. I thought we were just growing apart."

"Maybe that, too." There was no judgment in his tone. "You've been moving forward, growing up. Clara's been . . . stuck."

This part surprised me. It was the reverse of how I had always thought about us. I was the one still living on the island, after all. Clara was the one racing headlong around the world. I preferred Teddy's version. I wanted to see myself the way he saw me.

"Why do you think she's stuck?" I asked.

"A lot has happened to her," he said. "She has a hard time moving past it. I think she's afraid to grow up, because it means letting our parents go."

There had been a misunderstanding. I had meant my question as *What makes you say that?*—a defense of Clara—but it came out as *What made her that way?* I could have corrected myself. Insisted that she was more mature than he thought. I knew Clara sometimes dis-

liked Teddy's interpretations of her life, and the loyal thing to do, as
her friend, would have been to offer him evidence against it. But I had
no evidence to give. What he said struck me as insightful, and perhaps
more accurate than Clara's own versions of events. I also couldn't deny
that there was a pleasure in discussing Clara with someone who understood her. Teddy was maybe the only person in the world who
understood what loving Clara meant. And I was maybe the only person in the world who understood what it was to be a Wieland, without
being one myself.

"But she's lucky to have a friend like you," he said. "Someone who
isn't using her. Someone who wants to take care of her."

"I like taking care of people," I said.

He nodded. There was a long silence. Just when I thought the
conversation was over, he said, "But if you always take care of people—
who takes care of you?"

The question slammed into me. I jerked one shoulder up in a
shrug, trying to look casual, when actually I had the most embarrassing urge to cry. My only comfort was the way he asked the question, so
gently, like there was a simple answer. Any minute, the buzzer would
go off and someone would tell me what it was. Who took care of me?
I was desperate to know.

"Here we are," Teddy said. It took me a second to realize the car
had come to a stop, and outside was the front entrance to Marien,
with its brick facade and freshly squeegeed glass doors.

As I unbuckled my seat belt and moved to get out, Teddy spoke
again. "Jess?"

"Hm?"

He waited until I had turned toward him, until he could look me
in the eye.

He said, "I like taking care of people, too."

It was impossible to miss the low promise in his voice. The impli-
cation, coming on the heels of his earlier question. He was flirting

with me, except it wasn't really flirting, because it wasn't lighthearted. It was deeper, more determined. It vibrated the whole car.

All the blood in my body rushed down to my feet, back up again. I imagined him reaching over, placing his hand around the back of my neck, pulling me in. The imagination was as clear as a memory. My face went hot and probably patchy. I had to reply, but my mouth was too dry to speak.

Clara's brother, I told myself as we got out of the car. *Clara's brother,* as we rode the elevator up to the Critical Care floor. *Clara's brother, Clara's brother.*

But the more I repeated the words, the fainter they got. They lost their meaning. They became an arbitrary collection of sounds. By the time we reached Clara's room, where the sunlight spilled across what parts of her body she had not destroyed, the arches and angles I no longer recognized, and she smiled weakly from behind the machine, the words were already nearly empty. Closer to a rite than a reminder. Clara's brother. Clara's brother.

Clara's brother.

Deaths attributed to the Wieland curse

Vincent and Maria Wieland

On April 29, 1996, gun rights activist Vincent Wieland and his wife, Maria, were visiting cousins near the <u>Vantage Point estate</u> in coastal Maine. Late at night, while driving from <u>Locust Harbor</u> back to their rented house, they hit a <u>white-tailed deer</u> and spun off into a gully. Maria was killed on impact, her chest crushed into the dashboard. Vincent bled out waiting for the ambulance. The stag was euthanized at the scene.

14

CLARA

April 9

The Anchor is something between a tourist trap and a dive—a place tourists come to feel like they're in a dive. Hazy windows, neon signs, walls covered in old vanity license plates, hokey laminated menus. On summer nights it fills up quickly with cruise ship passengers and preppy college kids avoiding their families on vacation. The bartenders barely check faces or IDs. When Jess and I were teenagers, it was the only place on the island where we could reliably skate by with the fakes I bought from Halpern's skeevy assistant basketball coach. We'd drain tequila shots, request power ballads on the jukebox, shimmy together across the sticky linoleum floor. Back then, I measured my parents' deaths in weeks and months. Some days, my body felt like a hole that only those nights could fill.

Now that I'm older, I mostly avoid coming here if I can. I don't want to ruin my fond memories by confronting how dumb the whole place is. But I don't quite trust myself alone at my house right now, and the choices for bars are limited this time of year. The Anchor at least has bad lighting, which maximizes my chances of drinking in peace. I've tried Jess several times since we texted this morning. She hasn't picked up. Teddy isn't answering, either.

No one seems to notice me as I choose a seat at the shadowy far end of the bar, with my back to the rest of the room. I call out my order to the bartender, who starts preparing it without looking away from the baseball game on TV.

Just when I think I've made it undetected, I spot Conrad Gaffney sitting two seats down, his nose deep in a paperback. I start getting up, intending to slide farther away before he sees me, but the movement makes him glance up. We make eye contact. Shit.

He smiles. "Hey! Fancy meeting you here."

"Indeed," I say weakly.

He sets down his book. Not just sets it down. Puts a bookmark in it, and sets it down *closed*. Double shit.

"What brings you to this fine establishment?" he asks.

"Garden-variety alcoholism." As soon as the words leave my mouth, I realize Conrad might not understand it's a joke. *You need to think about what you say before you say it*, Teddy said. I feel my face heat. "What about you?"

Conrad gestures at the empty plate in front of him. "I ran out of food at my house, and this was the closest place that served dinner."

"Did you get the whale burger?"

He nods. "At first I thought it was whale meat. Turns out it's just really, really big."

I smile. "What are you reading?" He flips the book to face me.

Ernest Hemingway, A *Farewell to Arms*. "I didn't know people still read Hemingway for fun."

He shrugs. "I guess I'm old-school. Or uncreative."

"I'm basically illiterate. Did they do a movie adaptation yet?"

"I think in the '50s."

"So no Cate Blanchett."

"Probably not."

"Then I probably won't get around to it."

He laughs, and I start to relax. Despite however I acted the other night, and despite the new video, he seems actually happy to see me. I don't remember the last time anyone seemed happy to see me. Lately, the most I've been hoping for is total neutrality. Turns out all I needed was a lonely tourist.

The bartender delivers my vodka-cran. He must have grabbed the cocktail straws in a daze, because there are four stuck in the drink. I gather them together and take a big slug through all of them at once.

"Long day?" Conrad asks.

"You could say that."

"What happened?"

I snort, thinking he's joking, but when I look over at him, he's nonplussed. "Another video of me went viral."

His face falls. "Sorry. I didn't know. I haven't been on my phone much today."

This is the thing about the internet: you tumble down into this whole other parallel universe, it pummels and chews you into a nub of yourself, and then you go back to reality and people say they've never even heard of this thing that has eaten you alive. I don't know if his ignorance makes me feel better or worse.

"Do you want to talk about it?" he asks.

I haven't spoken to anyone about either video, other than Teddy and Jess and Mike, and I'm not sure what I'm allowed to say.

"Not really."

"Okay," he says easily. "Then can I ask you a random question?"

I brace myself for something invasive. *How much do you weigh these days? Do you still sleep with men?* "What?"

"I've been scoping out landmarks to feature in NatureEye—"

"NatureEye?"

His eyebrows lift. "My project? The one I brought to WFCI?"

Right. The reason he's here. I blush at my own self-absorption.

"Don't worry," he says, misreading my expression. "Teddy told me the other day that I didn't get the grant."

"I'm so sorry," I begin.

He shakes his head. "That isn't why I brought it up," he says with a tinge of embarrassment. "I'm still doing recordings for the project. I'm looking for landmarks, and I need to see some of them from the water, but I need to hire a second person to drive the boat. You know anyone who would do that?"

It takes me a second to realize this is his question. A normal, polite question. Compared to what I was imagining, it seems exceptionally pure.

"I'll drive you," I say. "We can use the *Transformation*."

He blinks. "You don't have to do that. That wasn't what I meant."

"I don't mind. Honestly, it would be nice to feel useful."

I poke my straw around in the ice of my drink. I'm somehow already almost done. The vodka is rushing in my head. My mouth dry, the saliva sucked clean. On the TV, the away team scores a home run. The grass on the diamond has been mowed into a checkerboard.

"I wish I knew when it would end," I say.

Conrad follows my gaze. "Looks like two more innings."

"No. I mean the online shit. About the videos. It's a lot. I don't know how to get ahead of it. First I was disgusting, or a slut. Now I'm an elitist cunt. And I just want to tell people I might not—"

Miraculously, I catch myself before I mention deepfakes. This must be how it happened the other night, when I almost told him about the almost-DUI. Secrets keep slipping out of me. It has more to do with the circumstances than anything about Conrad himself, although he is easy to talk to, in an unpushy way. A good listener, like Jess.

"Might not what?" he asks.

"I might not be as bad as they think," I finish smoothly.

Conrad spins the paper coaster, his expression thoughtful.

I point a finger at him. "Don't say I am. I can't take that right now."

He laughs. "No, sorry. I was just remembering FinSafe."

I know FinSafe is one of the failed start-ups Teddy told me about when we were first discussing Conrad's WFCI application, though I don't have a comprehensive recall of all the crypto platforms Conrad has run into the ground. If we start talking about blockchain and digital wallets, I might have to stab myself with one of these straws.

"After it went under," he continues, "that was a rough time. It was my baby. The remaining investors were upset. Some of them thought it was my fault. Then people wanted to make an example out of me. They said I had misled people or misrepresented it. There were tweets, posts, news articles, all the stuff you're dealing with now."

Ha. Probably not *all* the stuff.

Men love to tell women to grow a thick skin. Muscle through. Be less sensitive, don't take things so personally. They wouldn't survive an hour of being an average woman on the internet. People trying to check you, instruct you, puncture you, put you in *your place*, the one at the bottom of the heap, underneath them. People saying don't complain about being hurt. You don't have the right because you had the audacity to have an Instagram account, you wanted to connect or share or get some fucking compliments once in a while. How dare you. So sit back and take it. You're a slut, you're boring, you're too fat, you're too thin, you're disgusting, you used to be better, you'd be better *if* you got implants, you got lipo, you got a brain, you sucked more dick since that's all you're good for, but you should know all that already, you should know better, you should be ashamed, you should die.

Even with the blowback on the worst failed start-ups, has Conrad ever gotten any of those messages? Probably not. If he has, we'd know; he'd pull it out and hold it up like a flag and say *See? Look! The internet is hard for me, too!* But you know it's not, because he finds the insults remarkable. If you asked me to show you a sample death threat, I wouldn't know where to start. Pick at random from the swamp of my inbox, please, and take a few, because no single threat can ever convey what the whole mass conveys. What it feels like to have the avalanche be upon you, around you, snow dropping and crushing, and when you find a breathing hole at the last second it doesn't mean you're safe, you're never safe if you're a woman on the internet, the snow is always coming down the hill.

I don't say that, of course. I'm too tired from being buried alive.

Instead I say, "I'm really sorry you went through all that."

He looks down at his drink. "Thanks."

My phone lights up on the counter, and I check it reflexively. It's a notification for a coupon from a food delivery app I rarely use. Nothing from Teddy, nothing from Jess. I try not to think about them huddled together, discussing me, resolving me.

My drink is gone. So is Conrad's.

I point at his glass. "You want another?"

I call out to the bartender without waiting for Conrad's answer. I know he'll agree. That's the beauty of people who don't know you very well. They never tell you no.

Was I asking for the avalanche? It's true that I've often wanted to be seen. Wanted to turn myself inside out, reveal my softness and let it harden in the air.

I got the W tattoo when I was nineteen, to commemorate our parents. Like so many teenage tattoos, it seemed like a good idea at the time. I thought the family seal was an appropriate memorial; I didn't realize until later how it might come across, unironic and braggy. I went to a place my roommate had recommended, a dingy parlor a few miles off campus. It shared a parking lot with a Baskin-Robbins, and its glass door was fogged with scratches where bored teens had keyed it. When I entered, the door clanked shut behind me with a grimy thud, like chewing gum had gotten stuck in the hinge. The tattoo artist was conversational until he inspected my ID. His eyes first skipped down to the date of birth, then, pulled by a subconscious flicker of recognition, came back to rest on my name. His hand trembled as he gave back the card. He didn't say much after that, except, "You have a drawing?" and "Where do you want it?" In answer, I extended my arm. Over the phone, Jess had talked me out of getting it as a tramp stamp.

When the tattoo gun touched down, it hurt more than I expected. I had inadvertently chosen a very sensitive spot, where two large nerves ran below the skin. I was glad it hurt. What was inside me was worse and deeper. When this part was over, the other pain would rush back, stronger than ever. The needle stung, then stung again. Dots of black ink: rosary beads on someone else's arm. My loss scraped me from the outside in.

"All done," he said. He placed Saran Wrap on it, like I was a leftover steak. The letter shone up through the plastic, ghostly, drowned.

In the days that followed, as the skin around the tattoo scabbed and cracked, I began to have misgivings. The tattoo proved that my parents had lived, but also that they had died. I didn't want to need a reminder of my parents. I wanted them to be alive.

Still, I couldn't bring myself to regret the tattoo completely. Because for those two hours, at least, I got what I craved: pellucid, finite pain.

15

CLARA

April 9

The first time I purged, it only took a knuckle.

A single knuckle against the roof of my mouth. And bam, my stomach clenched and my lunch came rushing up like I had pushed an eject button.

From the stall over, some girl remarked, "Fuck. I wish I were still that fast."

Eating disorders were a dime a dozen at Halpern. We whispered weight-loss tips in health class while the teacher rewound the worn-out VHS of *Dying to Be Thin*. In the dining hall, we talked calorie counts over rice cakes with peanut butter, raw celery dripping water onto monogrammed plates, dry cereal shaped like hearts and stars. Purging was slightly more shameful—you could talk about it, but only if you did so with a twinge of humor.

"Must have been something I ate," I told the girl. Wink, wink.

For some people, it only gets easier. Every time, their touch gets more delicate, until finally they can hit the bulimics' holy grail: hands-free. Bend and purge, literally without lifting a finger. So easy and ladylike—until it wasn't. I knew girls whose gag reflex got so sensitive they couldn't brush their teeth unless they sprayed their throats with lidocaine first. For me, the more I threw up, the harder it got. I'd frantically wiggle my finger around in the back of my throat like a teenage boy looking for the G-spot. I tried a toothbrush, a straw. Once, desperate, I used a Pilot V5 pen and accidentally hit the retractable button and the ballpoint tip came out and scratched the inside of my throat, and for the next week, every time I purged, the stomach acid burned a hot line in the wound.

No one talked about any of that in the communal bathroom. No one told me that years later, I'd sometimes still have trouble throwing up when I have the stomach flu. Even if they had, I probably wouldn't have listened.

Death seems so distant, until it comes for you.

So when I crouch in the freezing cold outside the Anchor, trying to throw up, it takes a while to work. My stomach heaves, and my esophagus presses it back down. Up and down, until I'm cramped and sweating. People talk about your mind and your body being at war. But the real mindfuck is your body being at war with itself.

After what feels like an eternity of useless gagging, finally, finally, my throat releases a few pale strings of liquid. I spit into the grate. Through the buzz of relief in my ears, I hear footsteps approach. I duck my face and peek out through a curtain of hair to see who it is.

Teddy. Fuck.

He squats down next to me, and reaches around and gently gathers up my hair.

"It's not on purpose," I mutter. "I drank too much."

"Uh-huh."

He doesn't believe me, which I guess doesn't matter. I'm thirty-two years old. I'm too old to be throwing up in gutters for any reason.

I cough one last time. My eyes are fuzzy with stray tears. I blink a few times, until our shoes come back into focus. He's wearing one of his pairs of unscuffed hiking boots meant for looking outdoorsy in press photos. I sincerely hope we are not currently in a press photo. I exhale through my sour mouth and stand up, wiping my chin on the back of my hand.

Teddy holds my elbow. "Are you okay?"

"Better now," I lie. I do feel marginally less drunk, but vomiting has set off the usual post-purge emotions: pride at my accomplishment, and shame at my failure, and another bout of shame about feeling proud, and another bout of pride about feeling shame. The feelings don't care why I threw up. They're stored in my muscle memory, ready to be activated at the slightest gag.

Teddy guides me away from the gutter, toward the side of the building and the alley that leads to the parking lot. The alley is empty and dark. The single sconce has been burned out for years.

He leans me against the brick wall like I'm a rag doll. I tilt my face up to the fresh air. The bar was stuffier than I realized. All night long, it was slowly cooking me, like meat in a sous vide.

"What are you doing downtown, anyway?" he asks.

"Hanging out."

"With who?"

"Conrad."

"And he just left you like this?"

"No! He offered to give me a ride. Anyway, I don't need him to drive me home. I'm a—" I hiccup. "A feminist."

Teddy manages not to roll his eyes. "Please tell me you weren't planning to drive *yourself*."

"No. I was going to call someone."

"Who?"

"I don't know, a car! Jeez." Actually, I called Jess again, but she didn't pick up. "Where are *you* coming from?"

"I had dinner with Mike and a crisis management guy at the Bread Company. I was walking to my car and saw you. Anyone could have seen you," he adds, like he can't help himself.

"I'm sorry I didn't stop to think about appearances before throwing up," I say. I'm vaguely aware that there is some irony in this comeback, but too drunk to figure out exactly where. "Where have you been all day? I texted you earlier. A bunch of times. You didn't answer."

Teddy bristles. "Well, I've been a little busy."

Right—with the crisis management. The crisis being me. And now Jess, too, I guess. I'm no longer the only problem.

When I reach up to fidget with my hair, my hand grazes a tendril slick with bile. I drop it again. "Is Jess with you?"

"She's at home. She's very stressed," Teddy says, almost reprimanding, as if I don't understand better than anyone else what she's feeling. He places his hands in his pockets and rocks forward, then backward, an uncharacteristic hesitation. "She says today's video is fake."

"Oh?" My voice goes up at the end, an innocent falsetto.

He looks at me like I've failed a test. "She says the last video might be fake, too. You two talked about it last week, and you told her you didn't remember the guy at all. And you asked her not to tell me."

I'm not surprised Jess confessed. After today's video, she would have had to. Still, it hurts, like a light pressure on a day-old bruise. I guess we know who Jess chose.

I pull my coat sleeves over my hands. "It wasn't . . . we weren't trying to keep anything from you."

"Of course you were. That's what a secret is."

"You and Jess keep secrets from me."

"That's different. *She's my wife.*"

That's it, case closed. I search for a response that doesn't make me sound naive or petty. There isn't one. Marriage is the ultimate trump card.

Teddy crosses his arms. His earlier tenderness has faded now. His concern has sharp edges. "Why would you tell Jess and not me?" he demands.

"I was embarrassed about not remembering."

He scoffs. "Come on. There was already a sex tape. How is not remembering more embarrassing than that?"

My chest clenches. "I don't expect you to understand."

"Try me."

I worry the coat's lining between my fingernails, thinking of how to explain. "It's taken me so long to get back from that place. To feel like a person again. I thought if I told you I didn't remember, you'd see I was still broken. It would remind you how I used to be."

"I don't need to be reminded," he says. "I think about it every day."

I recoil. I look away before he can see my expression, but it's too late.

Teddy runs his hand through his hair. "Clara." His tone is exasperation wrapped in thin apology; the tone people use to say *Sorry, but* . . . How many times have I heard Teddy say my name in just that way?

"Come on," he says. "Don't act like that."

"I'm not acting like anything."

"You can't be so sensitive."

"I didn't say anything!"

"You were thinking it."

"Now I'm not allowed to *think* without telling you?"

He glares at me. I glare back. If Teddy's tired of apologizing, I'm tired of being apologized to—or not apologized to. Tired of him saying things that need apologies, or maybe just tired of being a person who appears to need them.

It's so quiet I can hear waves splashing in the harbor a block and a half away. A car engine turns over. A heating vent hisses. Around the corner, the bar door opens, releasing a warm rush of voices before it suctions shut again.

A couple rounds the corner, laughing. When they see us, they sober and hurry past, keeping their eyes on the ground.

"Shit," Teddy whispers when they're gone. He squeezes the back of his neck, embarrassed. Our parents taught us better than to argue in public. I'm used to not living up to what their standards would have been, but Teddy's not. He doesn't know what it's like to get carried away.

There's no way I can tell him what's been going on inside my brain. I can't tell him about the shadow, or the lifeboat, or this feeling I'm starting to have, like I'm walking through a field of marbles, just waiting for one to roll under my foot and send me sprawling to the ground. Teddy would never understand. Teddy would see a field of marbles and simply kick them away.

I admire that about him. I resent it, too.

Quick clicks bounce off the alley walls: heels on asphalt. I think it's the same couple coming back, and I spin around to snarl at them—but it's Jess, of all people. She's walking toward us, coming from the dark mouth of the parking lot, her head bowed as if she's deep in thought.

"Jess?" Teddy says, surprised.

She stops short. Her eyes flick between us, her expression wary. "Hi."

As always, her skin is unfairly luminous, even in the darkness of the grimy alley. I wipe my chin, checking again for stray vomit.

"I thought you were at home," Teddy says.

"Not currently." Her voice is a shade too pleasant.

"I can see that," he replies. "Were you looking for me?"

"No."

"Then what are you doing here?"

"Going out."

She takes a step forward, as if to move past us, but Teddy steps sideways, blocking her exit. "Going out *where*?"

It's a reasonable question. She's dressed up like she's heading to an event, her lips a red pout, her hair falling in neat waves around her shoulders. And it's nine at night, in the off-season; the only two places still open are already wiping down tables and stacking chairs.

But Jess takes it personally. "Why? Do I have to get your permission? Or maybe Mike's?"

"It wouldn't be a bad idea," Teddy says. "Under the circumstances."

"Right. The circumstances." She throws a dark look my way. Oh, yes. Me: the circumstance. "Nice to finally see you, Clara."

I remember her earlier text and wince. "I called you back," I say defensively.

"I saw," she says.

"I'm sorry I couldn't come earlier. I was busy."

"I saw," she says again, an extra bite in her voice. "Did you tell him?"

I glance at Teddy uneasily. "About the video being fake? You told him."

"No. The other thing."

"What other thing?" Teddy demands.

Jess jerks her chin at me. "Ask her."

I have no idea what she's talking about. The shadow? The lifeboat? But I didn't tell Jess about the lifeboat, either. Did I? The alcohol seems to have covered my brain in a smooth, chalky film.

"Clara?" Teddy asks.

I feel like I might cry. "I don't know what you mean."

Jess snorts. "Of course you don't."

"Jess," Teddy says in a soothing tone. The *be nice to Clara* tone. Even though two minutes ago, he was the one yelling at me. He reaches toward her, probably to take her arm, calm her down, but she flinches away.

"Not everything's about you," she spits, and he draws back his hand like he's been stung.

The silence reverberates. Jess blinks once, twice. Like she's as surprised as we are at the way the anger just—*broke* out of her. I guess I've always known that under her placid exterior, there's a thin ribbon of rage. But it's something I've only sensed, never seen, and the sight of it now makes me wonder if it's not a ribbon, but a whole layer, an invisible structure underpinning every smile.

I see her gathering herself, taking her bearings. Covering up the scaffold. When she speaks again, her tone is as cool as the air. "I'll see you at home."

Then she slips past us, around the corner and out of sight.

Together, Teddy and I stare down the alley. The street beyond is quiet again. Rows of streetlights in the fog: metal poles haloed in white. The heating vent rattles once, then goes back to hissing.

"Where is she going?" I ask. A rhetorical question.

"I don't know. Do you think she's drunk?"

"No." Drunk Jess is easy, loopy. Not cold and precise. "Just pissed off, I guess."

For the first time, I have the awful feeling that the videos have shifted something between us that I won't be able to put back into place.

Teddy turns to me slowly. "What was she talking about? She said 'the other thing.' Is there something else you need to tell me?"

"No. I don't know what she meant."

"Yeah. Right."

"I really don't!" It comes out like a squeal.

He tilts his chin up ever so slightly, as if he's bracing for a hit. I recognize the expression from my high school graduation. One of Halpern's many traditions was that the parents would walk the graduate across the stage to receive their diploma. With a last name starting with W, I was always near the end of any alphabetical line. I had to watch row after row of kids do the walk, some clinging proudly to their parents' arms, some wincing away with embarrassment as their father raised his camcorder. By the time my turn came, it felt like someone had filled my chest with bricks. Then there was Teddy at the end of my row, holding his hand out to me. Had he even turned twenty-one yet? He had a zit on his cheek. Everyone was staring. Still, Teddy walked me right across that stage. No hesitation, no trembling. The only way you would even know he was hurting was that little lift of his chin—a tiny, harmless tell.

"I don't know what she meant," I repeat more softly.

He pinches the bridge of his nose and counts to five. Silently, but somehow I can still feel each count, echoing through my chest. When he drops his hand, his face is calmer, though not by much.

"Come on," he says. "I'll drive you home."

"What about Jess?"

"I'll come back to make sure she's okay."

"I can help."

"You can't. You'll get in the way." He shoves his hands into his pockets and starts for the parking lot, his shoulders hunched, a sullen James Dean. "Don't forget to watch for deer."

The deer are always out this time of night, their heads primed to turn at the sound of an approaching car. Some of them will jump out right in front of you. People usually survive the crashes, but not always. The local police even do drivers' safety demonstrations downtown, carrying around the antlers of the stag that killed Vince Wieland. But these demonstrations are for tourists only; locals know the drill, and Teddy's instruction is so obvious it's insulting. Like he needs to remind me he's still in charge.

It's twenty minutes back to Vantage Point. The truck is warm and dark like a womb, broken only by the green glow of the dashboard. In the black night, the road looks the same from moment to moment, a strip of swirling fog in the headlights, like we're running in place on a large wheel. It would be so easy to let myself be lulled, rocked to sleep by the familiar bends in the road, my brother at the wheel, steadfast, carrying me home.

In the dense fog, I don't see the deer until we're almost upon it. Its eyes come first. Silver coins in the mist. I only have enough time to raise my arm and let out a sharp squawk before it settles its weight onto its back legs and lifts its spindly front legs over the guardrail—

Teddy veers. "Jesus Christ!"

He misses it, barely. I turn to watch out the rear window as the deer leaps through the red fog of our taillights and lands a few feet from our bumper.

"I thought you were watching!" Teddy exclaims.

My fingers dig into the side of my seat. "I was."

Far behind us now, the deer seems to split into two shapes. A man and a woman. I squint, trying to make out their faces, but we're moving away too quickly. They blur in the mist, and then are gone.

I settle uneasily back into my seat. The truck churns forward, devouring the road.

Deaths attributed to the Wieland curse

William Wieland Jenkins Porter-Smith

After receiving an insider tip that his venture capital firm was being investigated by the U.S. Securities and Exchange Commission, William Wieland Jenkins Porter-Smith moved to the famous Villa Piena in Taormina, Italy, in 1975, allegedly to avoid charges of fraud and tax evasion. On April 19, 1976, William and local craftsman Giorgio Puntanella died when the villa mysteriously went up in flames. Some hypothesize that the fire resulted from William leaving a lit cigar next to a wooden crate of Etna Rosso. Others believe the fire was set as punishment by the local Mafia after William called the don's wife an "ugly toad."

The Wieland family maintains that the fire was accidental. They later donated the insurance payment to establish the William Wieland Jenkins Porter-Smith Fund for Italian Sculpture at the Metropolitan Museum of Art.

16

JESS

April 10

In elementary school, Clara would host legendary sleepovers. She'd invite a dozen girls, and we'd line up sleeping bags in rows in their downstairs rec room to play light as a feather stiff as a board. Mafia. Truth or dare. We melted chocolate on popcorn, drank all the soda we could stomach, and rented pay-per-view movies we didn't even watch. The next morning, Mrs. Wieland would make us all breakfast using ingredients the housekeeper had chopped and measured the day before. It was perfect.

The first time I was invited to one of these sleepovers, a couple months after Clara and I became friends, I was the last to fall asleep.

Something was off. I couldn't figure out what it was. It was my first time sleeping away from home, but that wasn't it. We had drawn a Sharpie mustache on the first girl to fall asleep—but it wasn't that, either. I wasn't worried about being pranked. As Clara's best friend, I was protected by proximity. I should have slept like a baby.

Finally, somewhere near dawn, I realized what felt so unfamiliar. The silence. Our house in Kattinocket had had a loose pipe and creaking floors, plus my father, who made his own kind of noise. In our new apartment on the island, my mother and I had loud neighbors and single-paned windows that would shudder in their warped frames at the smallest breeze.

At Vantage Point, nothing needed repair. Everything was insulated. The windows were double-paned. The ocean was right there, and if you opened the windows you could hear the buoys ringing through the night, but with the windows closed, there was no sound except the gentle buffeting of central heating, the sticky snores of preteen girls.

Much later, when I moved in with Teddy and was sleeping here night after night, I started hearing tiny noises I had never noticed before. A tree scraping a window. A squirrel's fluttering footsteps. No house is completely isolated. It was only that my ear hadn't been attuned.

Today, I'm woken by the beeping of my alarm. I set it for seven thirty—decadent. Phoebe had me clear my calendar yesterday after the video dropped. I hit the off button and roll over to see if the sound woke Teddy up. He's not there. In fact, his side of the bed looks untouched. The pillow is a perfect oval. Teddy never makes the bed if he gets up first. Did he sleep in a guest room? Is he still that angry? I wipe the sleep out of my eyes and struggle onto my elbows. It isn't like him to go sleep somewhere else. He isn't one to retreat, even when he's mad. Especially when he's mad.

I check the whole house. The guest bedrooms, the living rooms, his office. It takes me thirty minutes. He's nowhere to be found.

Images leap into my mind: his truck in a ditch, his body splayed on the rocks.

I hear the silence again, for the first time in years. But it doesn't sound safe, like it used to. It sounds like something was here and now it's gone.

I put on a playlist called "Be Happy!" and try to obey.

Two hours later, I'm making strawberry muffins when the front door opens. I hear the familiar cadence of Teddy's voice mid-sentence and feel a pulse of relief. Then I hear Mike's voice, too, and my relief dissipates.

I'm really not in the mood.

By the time they get to the kitchen, I've turned down the music and have my expression under control. Teddy comes in first, and when he sees me, his shoulders tense and his face darkens.

Meanwhile, Mike claps his hands. "Jess!" Like it's a pleasant surprise to discover me in my own home.

I smile with narrowed eyes "Hey, Mike."

Teddy hangs back in the doorway and jams his hands into the pockets of his jeans. I want to hold up the cutting board and say, *Look! I'm making your favorite muffins!* But I get the feeling he won't be impressed.

"Sorry to barge in," Mike says, not sounding very sorry at all. "We had to get away from the campaign office to make some sensitive calls."

"Wow. You guys got an early start."

"We were working on a plan," Mike says.

"For the videos?"

"I'll fill you in." Without waiting for further invitation, Mike sits on one of the stools at the counter and opens his leather portfolio. "Shayna says hi, by the way."

It takes me a moment to remember that Shayna is Mike's wife.

I've only met her once, on a trip to D.C. early on in the campaign, one of those polite pretenses designed to solidify a working relationship. Teddy, Mike, Mike's wife and kids, and I all walked along the Washington Mall together, in a fog that was as thick and brisk as the fog in Maine, but without any of the atmosphere. The two men walked ahead, and she and I hung back with the kids and had a very earnest conversation about absolutely nothing.

That congresswoman Mike got elected in New York must have done a similar lap of the nation's monuments. I wonder if her husband stayed back to talk to the kids, or if he and Mike strode ahead, talking about important manly things, such as golf, while the congresswoman made nice with Mike's wife in a show of subservience. The women sticking together, to seem less threatening.

"Say hi back," I tell Mike, because I know he will anyway, and it might as well be true that I said it.

Teddy comes to the corner of the kitchen island, a small concession to manners. When I meet his eyes, he gives an almost infinitesimal shake of his head. *Not now.*

I try not to bristle.

"Here," Mike says, flipping to a spreadsheet scribbled with numbers and annotations. I wipe my hands on my apron and lean politely over the counter to look.

"We were able to run a quick poll yesterday, and it actually turned out better than expected." He runs his finger down one column, reading aloud. "Favorability metrics. Jess overall favorability, down fourteen. Health of your marriage, down ten. Teddy on women's issues, up six, because we hadn't polled that since Teddy's recent platform change. Teddy relatability, down nine. Teddy overall favorability, also down nine. Clara's numbers have dropped again, but they were already pretty low, and anyway, she doesn't matter as much as the two of you. Most importantly, likely to vote Teddy in primary was only down four, which is much better than expected, considering the other losses."

"Those numbers are good?" I try to wrap my brain around the idea that people like me fourteen percent less than they did two days ago. It feels so . . . concrete. "That's a lot to lose because of a dumb video."

"I think we're lucky there was only a four-point hit," Mike says reprovingly. "Relatability is important for Maine voters. The video reminded voters about Teddy's wealth and made you and Clara seem out of touch. The word 'plebes' was not good. The 'health of the marriage' rating also concerns me. It raises concerns about family values, to have a wife say she married her husband for money."

"Okay, but I didn't say that."

Mike waves his hand. "Or something like that."

"No, nothing like that. Because remember? The video's fake."

"Voters don't know that."

"They will when you tell them." A beat later, I catch on. Stupid Jess. "You're still not going to say the video's fake?"

Mike looks pained. "I told you yesterday, discussing deepfakes introduces a whole new set of issues. It changes the angle of the campaign too much. I'm not saying we won't get there. But Teddy and I agreed that if there's a simpler way, we should try that first."

I press my lips together. *Teddy and I agreed.* "What's the simpler way?"

"Just move past it. Address the underlying concerns. People think you and Teddy are on the rocks? We show them you're together, stronger than ever. People want to talk about your income disparity? Fine. It's a great opportunity to remind them Teddy's circle is diverse."

"I'm diverse?"

"Well, you have a different range of experiences than Teddy."

"Sure. A smaller one."

It was Teddy and Clara who accumulated all the experiences when we were younger, flying from continent to continent, going from ski chalet to yacht back to their fancy boarding school. I was stuck here, helping my mom clean the same hotel room over and over, washing blood and urine off her scrubs, paying off the same credit card for years and years, serving assholes, slaughtering mice. I'm sure there are many ways of being poor. But my way was only ever boring.

"We want to bring you front and center," Mike says. "Phoebe's drafting an initial statement now. We'll talk about your mom's job. Push the single-mother narrative. Oh, I wanted to check. Am I correct you were on SNAP for a while?"

"Uh, not very long."

"How long?"

"One year? Two?"

Mike scribbles a note. "That's fine. That's plenty of time."

"There's a minimum time you need to be on SNAP to count as poor?"

"I'd say probably six months if we're going to make it a talking point," he says, in all seriousness.

I flip open the carton of eggs and pick one up. I consider throwing it at Mike. Or even at Teddy, who is listening to this whole proposal with a solemn expression, as if it makes perfect sense.

But egging my husband probably wouldn't help the current situation, so instead I go to crack the egg against the bowl, right as Mike says, "Oh, and we'll schedule that appearance in Kattinocket."

The shell crushes into the yolk.

"Kattinocket?"

Mike's eyes track my mistake. The white bits of shell, the egg white coating my fingers. "Is that a problem? Teddy said it was fine."

Heat rises up my chest, over my throat and cheeks. I turn toward Teddy, who's watching me closely. Gauging my reaction. *This* is what they talked about last night. This is what they decided without me.

I take a deep breath. With quick, perfunctory movements, I rinse my hands and dry them on a dish towel. A smile strains the corners of my mouth. "Teddy, can I talk to you privately for a second?"

As soon as we step into the dining room, he puts his hands on his hips, already on the defense. In the morning light, his hazel eyes are bright and clear, like a hawk's. "I know you don't want to go, but that was before the new video. Now we have to show a united front."

"We *are* united," I say, even though right now it doesn't feel true. "And who would even notice if I don't go?"

"People will notice that you *do* go. That's what it's about. We want to create new narratives, to overwrite the existing one."

"'We' meaning you and Mike."

"And you. Assuming you still want me to win," he says, an edge in his voice.

I plant my hand on the back of one Queen Anne chair, trying to ground myself, but all that happens is I feel a nick in the wood under one fingertip. Another thing I'll have to get fixed. "I want whatever you want. And I'll do whatever you need. Within reason."

"And one appearance isn't within reason?"

"No, I didn't say that. But it's a big decision, at least from my point of view. I wish you would have asked me about it, instead of telling me."

His nostrils flare. "Well, I've asked you a lot of things lately," he snaps, "and I'm finding it hard to get answers."

I stare. "What answers do you want?"

"I want to know what other secrets you're keeping from me."

"I'm not keeping any other secrets from you."

"Yesterday, you said—"

"Can we please not hold anything I said yesterday against me?" I ask, almost shrill. "I was exhausted. And shocked."

"So was I," Teddy says unsympathetically, the subtext being, *and I managed to hold myself together.*

I hate arguing with Teddy. Not only because I hate arguing in general, but also because I'm bad at it and Teddy is good. It's the lawyer in him. Once he's committed to his side of the argument, he burrows himself deeper and deeper. There's no rethinking, no compromise.

It isn't hard to see what this Kattinocket thing is really about. Yesterday he saw a video of me telling Clara I married him for his money, and even if he knows it's fake, he can't unsee it. Kattinocket is a test of my loyalty. Or perhaps a punishment. A punishment and a test, all in one.

I run my tongue around my teeth. I don't like tests. But I'm good at passing them when they're put in front of me. In the grand scheme of things, what's one day in a place I hate? People get maimed, starve to death, survive wars. I can handle another stupid rally.

I squeeze the chair tighter, then release it. "Okay. I'll do it."

Teddy's surprised. "Just like that?"

"Yeah. You're right." This last part is a strategic addition, a cherry on top. Teddy loves to be right. "If it's important to the campaign, I should go."

He studies me skeptically for a second, then his shoulders loosen. His face unpinches. "Thank you," he says. Simple as that.

It's incredible how easy it is to end a fight, simply by giving up.

Back in the kitchen, there's a hole in the pile of strawberries, where Mike has obviously fished some out with his fingers to snack on. Teddy gives him a quick nod, telling him it's settled. Mike knowing I've caved is somehow more painful than actually caving.

"For Kattinocket," Mike says to me, picking up the conversation right where we left off, "it would be nice to brainstorm an anecdote. If you have a story tied to some particular location, we could plan a walk-through or a photo op."

A location. Sure. Like maybe the bar where my father spent most of his paychecks using his darts skills to pick up women. Or the consignment store where he pawned his wedding ring for cash on his way out of town, as my mother found out when she went in two weeks later to pawn her own. Maybe the elementary school playground where one kid asked me what I had done to make my daddy leave, or the church parking lot where another girl said maybe now that he was finally gone we could be friends, which her parents had previously forbidden because my father was such a bad influence.

In the mixing bowl, the crushed egg has slid farther down the well of flour. Gravity reveals a pinhole of red in the yolk, a trace of the mother's blood. I start teasing the shell fragments out of the yolk with a spoon.

"I'll think of a good story," I tell Mike.

"Let Phoebe know as soon as you can. We don't have a lot of time. We're looking at doing it the twentieth."

Thankfully, I'm not holding an egg this time. The sole external sign of my emotions is a quick spasm in my foot, behind the counter, where Teddy and Mike can't see it. The twentieth is barely over a week away.

"Got it."

Mike closes the portfolio. There's no relief in his expression, merely mild satisfaction, the kind I feel when I tick off an item on one of my checklists.

Across the counter, Teddy's eyes crinkle as he smiles. He looks hopeful again. He looks like my person again. Someone always wins an argument. Someone always submits.

I crack the next egg hard enough to split the shell all the way around.

17

CLARA

April 10

The morning after the second video comes out, I finally bite the bullet and google *deepfake experts.*

The idea of talking to yet another man about the video makes me want to die, so I scroll through the results until I find a listing for a woman: Dr. Donna Shallcross, a professor in machine learning at MIT. Her faculty profile picture shows a middle-aged woman with wire-rimmed glasses and hair dyed a dull, solid black. She's standing in front of an artfully blurred tree and appears to be wearing several cardigans at once. That's nice. I like cardigans. If I were in a better place mentally, I might even have a little crush on her, in a mommy-kink way.

I email her from my personal account, figuring my name will pique her interest. Sure enough, she responds within minutes. By mid-morning, we're on the phone.

"I took a quick look at the videos when I saw your email," she says after the customary greetings and the expected hints about her university's need for donations, "and I didn't find any obvious signs that they're synthetic. They pass many of our standard tests for fake detection. No issues with color, blending, lighting. Very little pixel feathering. Usually cheapfakes won't pass those tests."

My head is still fuzzy from last night's drinks. "Cheapfakes?"

"Cheap deepfakes, made by amateurs. Those involve more basic alterations, like pasting a face from one video onto another. But the videos you sent are much more advanced than that. If they're deepfakes, they're very, very good."

"So you can't tell if they're fake?"

"Not yet. But I can do a closer investigation with more advanced testing. It'll take me another couple days, and I'll have to consult some colleagues. And you'd have to send me some control videos of yourself—as close to the original as possible."

"You want me to make a real video of myself having sex?" I ask in disbelief.

"No!" She sounds embarrassed. "No, of course not. Just a video of yourself at some of those, ah, same angles, or making the same facial expressions or saying the same words . . . and then maybe if you have any other past candid videos of yourself speaking naturally. We need something to compare the muscle movements."

I tug my ponytail until my hair lifts from the scalp. I wish we were meeting in person, so I could read her expression. It's hard to trust a voice without a face. I pull up her faculty page again and look at her photo. The cardigans.

"Okay," I say. "I can do that."

Her voice gentles. "You know, whether or not the videos are synthetic, there are a lot of wonderful resources available for victims of these attacks. Have you made a police report yet?"

"No."

"Local police aren't always very helpful, but I have some contacts at the FBI who work on this kind of thing specifically. Or I can put you in touch with some counselors—there are some good therapy groups."

I've spent enough time in group therapy to last me a lifetime. Sometimes I still automatically give people snaps for sharing. Maybe it would make me feel better knowing that there are other people with fake porn videos floating around the internet, but mostly I think it would just make me sad.

"I'll think about it," I say.

After we hang up, I make the videos that Dr. Shallcross requested. I'm careful about what they include. I don't do the most explicit poses. I don't imitate the lewdest faces. I only say G-rated words. I don't repeat the insults about Teddy. The real videos are harmless and anodyne.

Still, I'm now acutely aware of how permanent everything is, every email, every text. When I finish the videos and hit send, I feel like I've freed a wild fish back into a stream, and some part of me is now flashing through the internet, vulnerable, about to be pierced by a hook or scooped by a net. Even once it reaches its destination, it won't be safe, not really. I should have asked what she meant by "a closer investigation." I imagine her going through the videos frame by frame. A cursor over my bare skin. A scalpel over the fish's spine.

My fridge contains a bag of wrinkled grapes, a gold-foiled end of butter, a tub of cut limes covered with a soft blanket of mold. It's been almost two weeks since Stephanie was last here to clean, and it's fascinating to watch the contents wilt and rot. I don't usually see old food; someone always cleans it up first. The decay has happened faster than I expected. I thought fridges would preserve things longer.

I poke at the grapes, rotate the container of limes. I've brushed my teeth several times since gagging into the gutter outside the Anchor last night, but I can't get rid of the grainy taste in my mouth. Same as I can't get rid of the memory of Teddy saying, *I think about it every day.*

Teddy and Jess had only been married a few months when he figured out that I was purging again. He argued with me about my eating and my behavior, told me I'd end up in the ER. For months, I proved him wrong. I wasn't in denial, exactly. I knew I had a problem; in some ways, I loved my problem, how special it felt, how urgent. His panic irritated me, and yet at the same time it brought me an unsayable satisfaction.

Then—that day. I was visiting Teddy and Jess for the weekend. We were about to sit down for lunch. My eyesight had been weird all day, brown spots coming and going at the edges. As I picked up the dish of shakshuka Jess had made, intending to carry it to the dining table, the world around me suddenly got flatter and slightly darker, with a black vignette around the edges. For a second, I thought someone had turned out a light. But there had been no lights on anyway. It was the middle of the day. The problem was on my end. I could no longer see out of my right eye.

I dropped the dish. Shakshuka went everywhere, tomato mush up the walls, glass shattering at my feet. Teddy and Jess heard my howl and came running.

"My eye—" I scrubbed at it furiously with my fist. It didn't help. "I can't see!"

Teddy and Jess said I needed to go to the hospital. They were always saying that, but this time I agreed. I thought I must have a brain tumor—something I considered a real emergency, unlike my eating, which I was sure I had completely under control.

At the ER, the blindness was attributed to malnutrition.

"It's an uncommon side effect, but thiamine deficiency will do pretty much anything," the doctor said to Teddy, as if I wasn't even in the room. "We call it the 'Great Imitator.'"

"Doesn't feel so great," I said, but no one laughed.

Off I went back to Marien. The best of the best. I had regained my vision by then, and I was ashamed to have caved for such a temporary setback. Shortly after I got settled—my room was almost identical to the one I had stayed in the first time around—Teddy came in and presented me with a slim sheaf of papers.

APPOINTMENT OF MEDICAL GUARDIAN, said the first page.

APPOINTMENT OF FINANCIAL CONSERVATOR, said the second.

"What's this?" I asked.

"The guardianship lets me help you make medical decisions," Teddy said. "And the conservatorship helps make sure important paperwork for the trusts doesn't slip through the cracks while you're recovering."

I didn't care about the financial part—I had never paid much attention to that anyway. I wouldn't miss signing tax documents or calling into board meetings. I wouldn't miss letting everyone down. The medical part made me more skeptical. I wasn't especially interested in recovering.

"Only really ill people would need something like that," I told Teddy.

He looked at me, at my body, at my bed.

"Yes," he said sadly.

So can I blame him for still worrying? Look at me now, foiled by a bag of grapes. Of course he still thinks about it every day. How could he not?

A thump comes from the backyard. I freeze, my hand still on the fridge door. The hairs on the back of my neck stand up. That was a big thump. Heavy and percussive. The woods are full of animals coming and going—foxes, deer, coyotes, bobcats, beavers, squirrels, birds—but nothing loud enough to make that noise.

People come and go, too, gardeners and landscapers, but they would park out front.

Relax, I tell myself. You're fine. You're alone.

A twig cracks. Another thump.

Slowly, I close the fridge door.

A black bear, maybe. There are a few on the island. The Goodwins caught one on their doorbell camera last year, rooting through their mailbox for the package of Christmas cookies it smelled inside. A moose is even more unlikely. Occasionally a brave one will swim over from the mainland to explore, but they usually grow bored quickly and leave.

The noise comes again. Louder. *Thump.*

My heart climbs up into my throat.

I edge my way down the hall to the useless little corner between the bathroom and the living room, where a small window overlooks the backyard. The wooden blinds are drawn. Sunlight enters in thin stripes.

I slide my fingers between the slats and press them open.

I nearly scream.

It's a bear.

Not just any bear. It's massive, maybe six feet high at the shoulder, twice as big as any bear I've ever seen outside a zoo. Its fur is pale brown. On its forehead is a white crest in the shape of a cross. Just above its shoulders, a rounded hump of fur. It's a grizzly bear, which isn't possible, because there are no grizzlies anywhere on the East Coast.

But here it is.

My yard isn't so much a yard as a neatly tended scramble of granite and moss. Despite the bear's size and its thick, silly limbs, it ambles gracefully across the rough terrain. When it reaches a ledge, it pushes itself up and over without hesitation. It keeps its nose to the ground. Sniffing. Hunting. Every time it picks up a paw, the light glints off its claws. Each one is as long as my finger. When the bear sets the paw down, it sounds like a sandbag being dropped from a great height.

I'm sweating now. This isn't possible.

Then, as if it senses me there, the bear swings its huge head around and looks straight at me. Its eyes are round black pits. I recoil, but I keep my fingers on the window slats, holding them open.

It cocks its head. It shifts its weight, and muscles ripple under its fur. It lifts its paw with impossible delicacy and stretches the paw out toward me, tender side down, the muted sunlight slick on those dagger nails. I can see it all. Each keratinous ridge, each torn layer of nail, the dirt dried on the claw.

We stare at each other for ten seconds, twenty, me and this impossible bear.

Then its mouth falls open, another black pit, a hole with teeth and a broad tongue.

It roars.

Instinct overrides logic. I drop to a crouch and scramble backward, my hands sliding on the hardwood floor. It's coming for me, the bear. Its paw is punching through the wall, the glass rips like tissue paper, it crawls through the wreckage, it hunts me, and it will find me any minute now. Any minute now. Any minute—

When I come back to myself, I'm curled behind a side table, forehead buried in my knees. I don't know how much time has passed. The wall is intact. The window is intact. I crawl to the window and get on my knees to peer over the sill. The yard is empty, of course. There is no bear.

What is happening to me? I press my hands to my face and they come away wet and trembling. I can't tell if I'm still crying. It was one thing to imagine a quick shadow, another to conjure a boat. And now yet another, to stare at an animal and *know* it is impossible, and still not be able to blink it away.

Everyone says an insane person doesn't know they're insane—but sometimes we do, and it's the worst feeling of all, to know you are wrong and to feel your mind push back against itself, one half of your brain against the other, grappling for control.

Maybe I'll die like this. Scared to death by my own imagination. A terrible way to die, but dying terribly is the Wieland specialty. We go out in a blaze of fear.

Matthew in the alley with the candlestick.

Gerald on the street with the falling marquee.

Elizabeth on the polo course, a horseshoe to the heart.

Beautiful, stupid Peanut Wieland. Did her bear charge her before she died? Did she see its jaws unhinge like a steel trap, like a claw in an arcade? When its teeth sank into her chest, did she see it as it happened? Which came first: the knowledge or the pain?

I straighten suddenly, my elbow knocking against the table.

The bear—Peanut Wieland. The deer in the fog—Vincent and Maria. The lifeboat—Delphine, on the *Titanic*. The shadow—my parents. Everything I've seen has been something that killed a Wieland.

Something brought by the curse.

I clamber hurriedly to my feet. I need to eat. Not in the sense that I'm supposed to eat something, but in the sense that I *need* to eat something, devour it, gorge. Sometimes I can't tell them apart: the impulse to care, the impulse to destroy.

In the kitchen, I open and close the cupboards with increasing panic, searching for the one thing that has ever made me feel in control. I find a half-empty can of Pringles, which I finish in a few generous bites, and a half gallon of Gatorade, which I drink straight from the bottle until my stomach sloshes uncomfortably. I work my way through a bag of dirt-streaked celery, six packs of fruit gummies, a sleeve of cookies, a cold can of beans.

I place my hands over my distended belly and feel the food pushing back at me, taunting me, and I lean over the sink and vomit as much as I can, which isn't much, but is more than nothing. The fruit gummies come out fully intact.

When I've done as much as I can, I turn my head to the side and lay my sweaty cheek against the ceramic lip of the sink. I regret what I've done, and also I am relieved, because the regret is enough to whittle the rest of my fear down to a manageable size. A triumph and a failure, all at once.

I thought the videos had hurtled me into the past. But the past has always been with me, latent in my blood. The videos only pulled it out from its hiding place. The videos only extracted it, with precise efficiency, from beneath its thin disguise.

I let my knees bend until somehow I've sunk down beside the cabinets onto the floor. A drawer handle digs into my temple. My throat muscles feel sore. My tongue burns with stomach acid. My mind has been waxed clean.

In that clean light, I inspect my theory anew.

Teddy and Jess would say the visions can't be the curse, because curses don't exist. They would say it's impossible.

But when it comes down to it, what is impossibility but improbability pushed to the max? And my whole life has been improbable, extreme fortune and terrible misfortunes, nothing in between. Blessed and cursed in equal measure. Tabloid headlines, cliffs with police tape, my mother's aborted scream. The shadow, undefinable, irrevocable.

A cursed girl is a haunted one. And wouldn't it be better to be haunted than insane?

Later, I go around the house and sweep everything even vaguely hallucinogenic into a trash bag. Sativa buds and my hand-carved wooden grinder, edibles and vape pods, leftover gin, a bottle of expensive wine, Drew's goodies. I tie the bag tight, until no air can escape, until the plastic strains at the edges of the jars and tins. Then I take it straight to the garbage can outside, for the groundskeeper to whisk away.

And still the bear comes to me again that night. It paws at the door. It rattles the windows in their frames. It paces my yard. It calls for me.

Come, Clara, it growls. *Come out and play.*

Deaths attributed to the Wieland curse

Jennette Wieland Jenkins Porter-Smith

Jennette, a fixture on the Manhattan social scene and close confidante of Truman Capote until the scandalous publication of "La Côte Basque 1965," was injured in a freak badminton accident in 1979, three years after her brother William's death. After receiving emergency surgery to treat a brain bleed, she began seeing unexpected flares of light in her peripheral vision and experiencing intense, debilitating headaches. Unable to cope with the pain, she threw herself in front of a southbound 6 train at the Lexington Ave / 59th Street Station on Easter Sunday, April 19, 1981. Traffic disruptions after the incident delayed the start of the city's Easter Parade by forty minutes.

18

CLARA

April 11

On Thursday, I get doxxed. Someone posts my number on the dark web, and the messages from unknown senders start pouring in.

Heard you were in the market for some big cock. Followed by a dick pic.

Lucky for you I like selfish whores. Followed by a dick pic.

Rich bitch scum I'm coming for u. No dick pic there. Just a little water gun emoji. Cute.

I need to get a new number, but my nerves are too jangled to trust the task to an assistant, and I can't make sense of the cell company's website. I've never seen a cell phone bill in my life.

I sleep badly, again. I see the lifeboat hit the rock, vanish, hit it again. I see disappointment on Teddy's face, and anger. I see the bear, and the deer, and the two people in the night fog. I see my face as pixels. I see my body as a line of code.

From the edge of the yard, a stag stares back at me. He has a full crown of antlers, shedding bloody velvet. Four months ahead of season. Another impossible thing. I feel the satin gloss of the floorboards under my feet and realize that I've come awake at some point. I don't know when.

On Friday, a box shows up on my porch. It's a bathroom scale. The packing slip says I ordered it three nights earlier. In bad periods of recovery, this was a daily habit, buying a scale, taking it out of the trash, putting it back in. To prevent myself from rescuing the scales, I started taking them to the dumpster behind the hardware store, until one time Joe Michaud caught me in the act, and then I started throwing them into the ocean. *Why do fish always know their weight? Because they have their own scales.* And at least a dozen of mine, if they hang out in the silt off the deep-water dock.

I text the groundskeeper to ask him to drop it by the Salvation Army on his way home. A few hours later, the package is gone.

When I was little, my dad took me fishing. Well, really, he took Teddy fishing, and I happened to be there. The three of us went out on the *Transformation* one morning, not even morning, night really, the sky pupil-black and the ocean more a smell than a sight. I cast the rod out as instructed, and waited patiently, as instructed. Teddy caught three fish right away, but the sun had come up by the time I felt a tug on the line. I handed the rod off to my dad to reel in. It was a decent-size fish, and it hung sputtering, flicking its body back and forth, eager to get free. The harbor stretched out around us like a puddle of glass. He showed me how to take the fish off the hook. He squeezed its white belly, fingers just shy of the sharp gills. Its eyes fluttered and glistened, circular, and blood crept from a wound in its mouth. My dad tossed it in our cooler and told me to cast the line out again. He was so proud. I cast it, half-heartedly, while in the cooler beside me, the fish suffocated on air. When we dropped anchor, my dad flayed the fish alive, right there on the boat, and cleaned it and cooked it on a camping stove for breakfast.

That's how I feel now: as if my consciousness has been skinned alive and set boiling over a rickety flame. Every day, another thing happens; the gas turns up, cooking me through.

On Saturday, I'm awake until 4:00 a.m., and then I sleep through an important WFCI video call with the leader of a wastewater treatment project in the Penobscot Reservoir who can only talk on weekends. I log on forty-five minutes late to discover that the meeting's over. Allan went ahead and led it without me. I email him to thank him and get back only a terse *You're welcome.*

Dick pics rain from the cloud like a summer storm.

In the afternoon, I run into Jess again, the first time I've seen her since we were in the alley. I'm pulling out of my driveway when I see her jogging up the road. I slow the car and roll down my window. She slows, too.

"Hey," I say.

"Hey."

Sweat has stuck some curls to her temples, pulled others free of her headband. Her cheeks are pink triangles.

It's annoying to keep running into Teddy and Jess while they're out exercising. I'm not allowed to run anymore; I've lost too much bone density in my shins. They fracture easily. When I see her like this, envy blossoms inside me: how quickly she can move, and move forward.

"I wanted to say sorry again," I say, "about the other day."

She bounces back and forth from leg to leg. She looks like she wants to say something, but she shakes her head.

"Forget about it," she says.

I can't tell from her voice whether it's a pardon or a barb.

On Sunday, I finally manage to change my phone number, but then I have to spend hours changing my contact information on all my important accounts. I'm trying to remember my bank password when I see a bright light flare in my backyard. A fire.

Flames lick the spruce trees. Blistering pops of sap and needles. The fire's edges roar pink and sharp. Its heart is white heat. Five seconds. Six.

My mind twists the world against me. My true self unzips my outer skin. My true self leaks from my pores. My true self infects, necrotizes, maligns.

I look again at the woods.

They are wet, brown, and unharmed.

On Monday, another scale arrives.

I pull off the packing foam and stare at it for a long time. My hands are shaking. It occurs that someone might be messing with me, the trolls taking things a step further—but when I log on to check my credit card statement, it's right there, ordered several nights ago.

I take the scale down to the dock and drop it over the edge. It sinks with a stream of bubbles.

It's gone now, I tell myself. And so I can pretend the problem is gone, too, the way I thought as a child that the mainland ceased to exist when the fog concealed it; back when I thought the only things that were real were the things I could see.

19

CLARA

April 16

The boat's wake is a pale ribbon, dividing the view in half. Starboard, the outlying islands roll up from the waves like seals sprawled on their bellies. Candy-stripe clouds and flat water. It's a perfect day to be out. Conrad keeps releasing big satisfied exhalations and saying things like, "That fresh air!"

I might enjoy the scene more if I had gotten any sleep last night. I feel like death warmed over. If driving Conrad around for his recordings had required anything of me other than a boat and a boating license, I probably would have bailed. But when he texted to ask where to meet me, he had the list of places ready to go. Even the clumsiest island kid could pilot a boat between Pike Cove and Little Plum with their eyes closed and one hand tied behind their back. If I doze off at the wheel, there's a fifty-fifty chance I'll still manage to navigate us home.

He mostly wants to photograph the major tourist stops featured on park service calendars: the picturesque lighthouse at Pike Cove, a white brick cylinder on a sandstone cliff, frequently featured on post-cards and park service calendars; the sleepy meadow inlet on Little Plum; the red-shingled building on the Tamford dock; the seals draped across the rocks at Shelter Ledge. This is just a preliminary trip, he assures me over and over. He'll come back in the summer for the real recordings, to capture the area at its peak. For two hours, I drive in circles while Conrad takes photos and waves around a laser measurement tool and chatters about triangulation and refraction angles. It's nice to be helpful, even though I'm almost dizzy with fatigue, and Conrad seems so eager to impress me that I worry he's gearing up for another funding ask.

We eat lunch in a cove in the sound, looping a line around the Coast Guard's gray buoy to hold us in place. It's high tide, when the water is clean as glass, all the algae and weeds tucked down out of sight. Neon-bright lobster buoys dot the waves. Conrad takes out the cooler he brought and proudly unpacks ham-and-cheese sandwiches wrapped in foil, barbecue chips, two cans of beer, a bag of gummy worms. All morning, the bad part of my brain was obsessing over what was in the cooler. Now that it's laid out in front of me, I can hardly look away. It would be suspicious not to eat anything, so I take a cola-flavored worm and nibble it one segment at a time.

"Where does the name *Transformation* come from?" Conrad asks.

"Kind of a long story."

He gestures at the blank water. "We've got time."

"When my dad was a kid, he and his dad made and collected ships-in-bottles. Some of them were from kits. But their masterpiece was this Dutch cargo fluyt they made from scratch. It was based on the *Mayflower*. It's huge." I make a two-foot span with my hands, the half-eaten gummy worm glistening in the sun. "All the materials they used came from somewhere on the property. Like, they made the steering wheel spokes out of pine cones and the sails out of handkerchiefs."

"Hence, the *Transformation*."

"Exactly. My grandfather died the year before my dad got this boat, so he decided to call this one *Transformation*, too. Even though he didn't make it himself, obviously. He just ordered it from a catalog."

I pat the seat fondly. Jim Hobart is under strict instructions to keep the boat looking exactly as it always has, down to the smallest button. When this cushion tore last year, he ordered vintage thread on eBay to repair it. Every season, when he brings it back from the shipyard freshly detailed, Teddy claps him on the shoulder and says, *You really brought it back to life!*

But it isn't really a resurrection, is it? It's more like an embalming.

A shiver goes up my spine. I stuff the rest of the worm into my mouth.

"Where's the other *Transformation* now?" Conrad asks. "The one your dad made with his dad."

"Teddy has it in his study. All the ships-in-bottles are there."

Conrad looks surprised. "All of them? You don't have any?"

"I'm sure I could take one if I wanted."

"And you don't want to?"

"No," I say, unsure.

He nods encouragingly, like he's stumbled onto a sensitive topic.

"There are other things I have from my parents that Teddy doesn't," I say quickly. I pull my necklace out from under my collar. "This was my mom's."

He admires it. "It's beautiful."

But he says it obediently, like I'm a kid doing show-and-tell. The thought that he's being delicate with me fills me with the ugly desire to hurt him back. Not a lot. Just enough to remind him he's vulnerable, too. A precision cut.

I don't know him well, but I know where to strike. "What happened with FinSafe?"

Conrad sits up straight, startled by the change in topic. "Huh?"

"At the Anchor, you told me people got pissed at you after it went under. But businesses go under all the time. Why were people so mad at you?"

He eyes me. "You don't know?"

"Not really." Here's how strung-out I am right now: I'm not even embarrassed to admit that I didn't do my research before his Nature-Eye presentation. "At least, I don't know why it would be a big story."

He sighs. "Why does anything become a big story?"

"In my experience? Usually because it involves money or death."

"Only the former, in this case." Conrad rubs his neck, then gives in. "I think the big problem was how visible it all was. I spent a lot of early money on public-facing things. Office space, logo design. I felt it was important to get our brand out there early."

"It backfired?"

"Turns out some things are more important than branding," he says wryly. "Payroll. Patents. Lawyers' fees. I was counting on a big influx of cash in the second funding round, so I put the other things off. The cash fell through, and we couldn't pay our bills. We filed for bankruptcy. Some investors were out a lot of money, and they got on Twitter saying I had mismanaged their money. They said I focused too much on appearances, that I made promises I couldn't keep. For a while, I thought I'd never work in Silicon Valley again."

"But now you are."

"Well. I'm trying to. You can't let one failure get you down, right?" he says with an ironic smile.

"I think I saw that motivational poster. The one with the kitten climbing a tree?"

"Puppy climbing a wall."

"There you go."

We share a smile. Then he tilts his head, squinting at me. "You really never heard of FinSafe?"

"I'm not exactly up on my financial news," I admit. "Does it make you feel better or worse?"

He considers. "I'm not sure."

I know what he means. Learning that some people are oblivious makes the public humiliation feel less total, but it's also weirdly embarrassing to realize that you're buckling under the weight of something smaller than you thought.

We sit in companionable silence for a minute, two fuckups trying to turn their lives around. Light glints off the water like tossed glitter. As we entered the sound, the radar depth measurement on the console rose swiftly. Thirty feet, sixty feet, a hundred, the bottom of the ocean falling out from under us as we skated across the surface. Right now, the display reads one hundred and fifty-three. I imagine the barren ocean floor, dark and cold, the pressure far above what any human body could withstand. Goosebumps flash across my skin.

"You know, I'm glad we got to reconnect," Conrad says. "We have more in common than I remembered."

I think about the past few days—the scales I've ordered without conscious thought, the bear clawing at my door, my mind splayed and broiling. Poor Conrad. I'm not the one anyone wants to have stuff in common with.

"Can I ask you a question?" he says.

"Sure."

"You used to live in New York, right? You seem like more of a city person. Why'd you move back here? Was it just to take over WFCI?"

I almost laugh. But of course, he probably doesn't know about me being at Marien, or how sick I was when I came back. Certainly he doesn't know about the conservatorship. He probably thinks I make all my own choices, like a normal adult. Moving somewhere for a job is a normal adult thing to do. "No. I moved back a few years ago to be close to Teddy and Jess. Teddy only asked me to take over WFCI when he decided to run for Senate. He's still on the board, of course."

"He likes to be in control." There's that tone again, the same one as when he mentioned the ships-in-bottles.

"Of some things," I say evenly.

Conrad doesn't seem to notice the chill in my voice. He nods thoughtfully, then picks up a bag of chips and squeezes it until the pressure punches it open. "You think you'll stay here on the island, if he wins? Or move somewhere else? Could the WFCI job be remote?"

I frown. "I don't know. I guess I haven't thought about it. I'll have to talk to Teddy."

Conrad starts to say something, then stops.

"What?" I ask.

He looks embarrassed. "Never mind."

"No, tell me."

"It's rude."

"That's fine. So am I, sometimes."

He takes off his baseball cap, scrubs his hand over the back of his head. "It's just—I mean, Teddy's my friend and everything. Nothing against him. But don't you want to make your own decisions? From watching you together, it seems like he has a lot of power over you."

Blood rushes to my cheeks. "That's a fucked-up thing to say."

"I told you it would be," he reminds me.

I take another gummy worm. Stretch it between my fingers. Blue hills rise and fall in the distance. Reflexively, I look across the sound, toward Vantage Point. This is its most innocent angle. No rocks, no cliffs, only a slant of green forest and the roof of the big house peeking over the tree line. Of course, there's no way to see if anyone is watching us.

"Teddy's a good person," I say.

"I know."

"He's done a lot for me."

"I know."

"You don't, actually." The worm snaps into gluey halves. I stuff them in my mouth, then check my watch. "We should probably get going."

With a worried frown, Conrad reaches out to touch my arm. "I'm sorry. I didn't mean to offend you. I just have—a different way of looking at him."

I can't bear the apology in his voice, or the weight of his hand on my arm, like he has some terrible news to impart. I stand up, a nicer way of shaking him off. "We should probably get going."

I untie us quickly, have the boat moving before Conrad's even finished packing up the cooler. I try to look indifferent as I guide the boat back through the Narrows. Inside, I seethe and rage.

A *different way of looking at him*—like it's a matter of interpretation, and we could both theoretically be right. Bullshit. There might be many ways to look at someone. But there's only one view that's accurate. One angle from which you see people as they really are.

Would I leave this place, if Teddy and Jess weren't here? I certainly would never have moved back, if it weren't for them. At one point, I intended to stay away forever. I rented hotel suites in Paris and London and Hong Kong and Dubai and Berlin. Cosmopolitan cities filled with writhing bodies. Jets and limos. I craved everything unnatural, larger than life. Strobe lights and smoke machines and imitations of phenomena, my mind a fun-house mirror, the world warping under my credit card's magnetic slide.

I thought that was my future, my real life. I thought I could leave Vantage Point behind.

But when you grow up somewhere like Vantage Point, it lives in you as much as you live in it. It isn't a place you can escape.

I've bled all over this property. In the kitchen when I was six and broke a glass. In the swimming pool when I cut my chin. On the bathroom tile during my first period. On the mattress in my childhood bedroom, when I lost my virginity on summer vacation from boarding school.

Even when everything's been scrubbed clean, there will always be those invisible stains in the center of a wood's grain, or in a microscopic crack of grout. My blood is in this place, and it's in my blood. An oath between us, holding me in thrall.

That evening, I flick mindlessly through the comments on my social media. Pierce's associate told me to keep a list of "credible threats," meaning the threats that include specific information or come from people I knew. Technically other threats *could* be credible threats, she said, and if I had only received one or two, then they might be able to investigate those; but because there are so many, we have to narrow it down. Since the second video came out, I've started checking Jess's comments, too, and it's simultaneously funny and depressing when I see the same ones copied and pasted across both our accounts. I imagine some random guy sprawled on his couch, rereading one of his misspelled grade-school insults and thinking proudly, *Pretty dope. Better send it to the other bitch, too.*

I've gotten pretty fast at the screening process—I read through and take screenshots, then transcribe the comments in batches, like I'm an assembly line—so I can do it while watching trash TV. Tonight's episode is a reunion show where a girl with bad lashes is complaining that she got an unfavorable edit. I start dozing off when a fellow contestant asks her why she was so surprised. It's a reality show. They all knew what they were signing up for.

The noise pulls me up out of a dream I can only remember as a color: a flat, grungy green, the color they paint helmets to help soldiers blend into the grass. It's the middle of the night. I'm still on the sofa, and I'm sweating everywhere except one arm, which fell out from under the blanket and feels ice cold in comparison. My other hand is cramped around my phone. The TV glows politely: *Are you still there?*

I shove off the blanket and sit up groggily, tucking my hand into my damp armpit to warm it up. I have the sense of being shaken awake, but my living room is empty. Shadows stretch over the furniture, turning the armchair into a hunched figure, the coatrack into a man with a gun. The noise must have been in my dream.

But right as I think that, it comes again. A screech, a roar. It's both animal and alien.

My heart starts to hammer. I press my hand over it, as if trying to push it back into its cage. I rise slowly and stagger over to the window, peer outside. It's too dark. I can't see anything.

Because you dreamed it, I tell myself. So there's nothing to see.

Even so—even so, I find myself sliding my phone into my pocket, walking to the front door, pulling it open.

A cold rush of wind whirls up the hill. When I look down the shallow slope of my driveway, the lights from my house fade into a black abyss. This must be what the bottom of the ocean looks like. A dark and seamless nothing, all the oxygen shoved out by an insurmountable pressure. A depth that hides all manner of monsters.

Don't you want to make your own decisions? Conrad asked earlier. Yes, probably—but when I step outside, it's not so much a decision as a compulsion. An invisible thread pulls me forward, onto the porch, the wood smooth and damp under my feet, then down the stairs and across the grass. In the driveway, gravel digs into the soles of my feet. I wrap my arms around myself until I can feel the ridges of my ribs along my back and move slowly down toward the road, squinting into the darkness.

I'm almost beyond the circle of light and onto the smoother road when I hear it.

Come, it says. *Come here.*

At first, the voice is deep, inhuman. *Come here, look, look.*

But as it continues, it changes. It goes up an octave, it becomes a voice I recognize. The open vowels. The slight fry. *Her* voice, hers.

"Mom?"

My knees are soft, I wobble. Tears spring to my eyes.

Clara. Come here, come here.

It's been so long since I heard her voice. It feels like a gift plucked from my dreams.

My arms fall to my sides. I walk faster, faster, until I'm jogging down the road toward the big house. My mom's voice, and at the same time, a rumbling purr beneath it, a growl. *Come here, come here.*

I run. I run even though I have no shoes or coat, even though I haven't run in forever because of my shins and my skin shrieks with cold and my lungs are dry. In my pocket, my phone slaps my thigh, over and over, hard enough to bruise, and I pull it out and carry it in my hand.

And as I run I seem to slide back inside the younger me, the me who could do anything, the me who hadn't yet tortured herself until she shed her bone. I am fast and free and unmarked. I am still innocent. I am good.

There's a bend in the road where it snakes around a patch of trees, and through the trees I see a light, so I take the shortcut. I plunge into the woods. The ground is covered with twigs and rocks and roots and it tears into the flesh of my bare feet. Sticks needle me; needles stick to me. I hop, hobble, whatever it takes.

Finally the forest tosses me back out onto the road, just before the turnoff to Teddy's house. There are two figures, running down into Teddy's front yard, slowing. They are brighter now, and I can see their shapes, shapes I have seen in my dreams more times than I can count, the tall man with the sloping shoulders, the long-necked woman with her graceful walk. My heart jams in my throat. Oh, how I've wanted this.

For sixteen years, I've craved the sight of them.

My parents.

I'm slowing now, too, with a cramp like a knife in my side, pain splintering up my shins.

"Wait, wait." I pant, too quietly. They don't hear me.

My father limps to a walk, then bends down to rest his hands on his knees and spits into the dirt. That's how he crossed the finish line in that island 5K where he finished third, a personal best. He beamed with sweat and pride that day. He hung the plastic medal around my neck and carried me on his shoulders and the crowd was small beneath us. Not that I remember it, exactly. I was only four. But it was caught on video.

On video! I remember the phone in my hand. Hobbling down the slope, I swipe my thumb wildly across the screen, opening the camera, hitting record, aiming it into the darkness.

The figures are moving across the lawn now. The one who stopped has started walking again, and I draw close enough to see their faces in profile. Their unmistakable faces. Dear, rare faces.

"Wait!" I cry out.

They stop. Their heads turn. My mother's brows come together in confusion. She is wearing turquoise pumps, and as she stops, she automatically brings the heel of her left foot in toward the arch of her right, arranging herself in her usual L-shaped stance, a remnant of ballet classes in childhood. Why is she running in pumps?

"Clara?" she says.

Now, finally, I'm close enough to treasure the details. The individual freckles scattered over my mother's cheeks. The flipped ends of her permed hair. Her favorite pearl bracelet gleaming on her wrist. The paler skin of her lip where the lipstick's worn off. The weave of my dad's favorite cashmere sweater. The line where his belly pushes against the waistband of his khakis. His stray eyebrow hairs. The puffs of fat under each eye and the way they crinkle when he sees me. The shape of his nose, Teddy's nose, my nose.

Days' worth of rationalization falls away. I don't care about the pain in my side or my feet or my legs, or what is possible or consistent. I'm not thinking about hallucinogens or bad weed or drunk nights out or my broken mind. I'm not thinking about curses or ghosts. The only thing I'm thinking is *They're here. They're here.* And so am I. Nearly naked, shivering, my barest self, trusting and desperate to believe, and all I have to do to be close to them is drop away the rest: the knowledge of their death, the impossibility of resurrection.

All I have to do is trust myself.

If I am insane, okay. If I am cursed, okay. If I am dead, okay. I will believe in whatever power has restored them to me.

I am walking toward them, breathing heavily, clutching at the cramp in my side, smiling in anticipation, when I hear a loud sucking noise. Water hollowing out.

Sense memory seizes my muscles a millisecond before the wall of water slams through the trees.

It is a bright, solid thing, this water, a hammer, a stone. Froth like white lace. It is as loud as a train. Branches crack. My parents turn, struck dumb, as the water stretches tall, and for a second seems to resist gravity, holding its arc high above their heads—and then tumbles forward.

I can't help it. I screw my eyes shut.

"No," I hear my mother say.

"Get back," I hear my father say.

And then I hear the water land.

A crunch. A scream.

My head to my chest to my knees, I curl like a snail. I curl until I am a pit of nothing. I can see nothing hear nothing feel nothing. I am nothing.

What happened on the rocks sixteen years ago was not the curse. Death is not the curse. This is the curse. Losing them again is the curse. The curse is that we dream and we wake up from the dream.

The curse is that we are left alive.

"Clara?"

Someone touches my arm. The insides of my eyelids grow brighter.

"Clara, can you hear me? It's Jess. It's me."

I open my eyes. A flashlight is shining in my face.

Jess pulls me into a sitting position. She's wearing a coat over pajamas. The shearling on her woolly slippers is spotted with mud, I think. It's hard to see. It's so dark out.

"Don't get up yet," she says.

"Go back inside," I croak.

Now Teddy's on my other side, crouching down. "Clara? Are you okay? What happened?"

I grab his sleeve. "Did you see them?"

"Who?" he asks.

"We were in bed," Jess says. "We heard you scream and ran downstairs."

Teddy puts his arm around my back, supporting me. "I don't understand. Who did you see?"

Even as I raise my head to look at the place where they stood, where the water took them again, I know what I will see: nothing. Only the lawn and the trees and the path lights along the driveway, dim fans of gold against the low ferns. The rest is a vortex, as black and empty as the bottom of the ocean, where air is swallowed whole.

"Mom and Dad," I whisper. "They were here."

20

JESS

Eight years ago

I stayed in the motel by Marien for eight days. When I say it aloud, it sounds like nothing. Eight days is spring vacation. Eight days is a stomach bug. But that's how time works. Intervals change shape. They stretch or shrink. Under the right circumstances, an eight topples over, becomes infinity. Those eight days changed my entire life.

Teddy and I quickly fell into a routine. In the mornings, we ran together. He was so much taller than me that our natural strides were completely different lengths, but over the course of several miles, we would slowly and unconsciously adjust, until by the end of the run our legs moved in perfect synchrony as we turned into the motel driveway. We would shower and change, then meet up again to drive to Marien. Teddy had charmed his way into using one of their administrative rooms as a de facto business center, and in the mornings he would take a string of conference calls while I hung out with Clara, which mostly involved making uncreative, wry commentary on reality show reruns while the nurses administered various medicines, or flipping through magazines while she drifted in and out of sleep.

For lunch, Teddy and I would eat at the restaurant of the inn where he had originally planned to stay. It was much, much nicer than the motel. It had monogrammed bread plates. The menus were tucked inside black leather sleeves. We would always sit at the same table by the window. Well, I would sit: Teddy lounged. An elbow here, a knee there. Casually taking up space.

After lunch, we switched stations. Not that we presented it that way, of course. Clara didn't know that when I left for lunch, it was always to eat with Teddy. She didn't know, I don't think, that I spent the afternoons in a plush armchair in the reception area downstairs, working my way through a pile of novels from the center's library while I waited for Teddy to drive me back to the motel.

If she had asked, I would have told her.

If she had asked what I did when I wasn't with her, or how I got to Marien, or if I ever crossed paths with Teddy, I would have said.

But she didn't ask.

After visiting hours, we would eat dinner at the local diner, or one time at Applebee's. Teddy had never been to an Applebee's before, and he experienced the Riblets Platter with the kind of wild excitement that, three months later, I'd feel when he flew me to London for the weekend—my first trip to Europe.

Aside from the time we each spent with Clara, we were together the entire day. Our conversations quickly shifted, became more personal. What song did we sing in the shower? Why didn't I talk much with my mother? When was the last time we'd cried? I asked him what the dating scene in Boston was like (digging for information, unsubtly; not quite admitting even to myself why I wanted to know).

"I think sometimes people have ulterior motives," he confessed. "It's hard to know whether someone's in it for the right reasons."

"I guess you really have to get to know someone."

He met my eyes. "Or have already known them for a very long time."

He asked me what my greatest fear was, and I said, "The circus."

"The *circus*?"

I shivered. "I hate all the tightrope stuff. The trapeze. It's like secondhand embarrassment, but worse. I'm always so scared they'll fall."

"But there's a net below them to catch them."

I knew that wasn't always true. Sometimes they fell straight to the floor. Sometimes they died. Surely Teddy, of all people, would know a freak accident could be fatal. But I came to understand that this was a sleight of hand that Teddy's mind performed. A bullish resistance to the possibility of fate, as long as he could be there to stop it. If he had been there that day on the rocks, he was sure nothing would have happened. He wouldn't have let his parents approach the edge. He would have caught his mother's arm before she fell. All else failing, he would have jumped down into the currents and saved them both, tossing his mother over his left shoulder and his father over his right, levitating out of the hole just as the water exploded beneath them, dazzling in the sun.

I became newly glad that we had started splitting up the time with Clara. No longer because I wanted to make sure she was occupied, but because what was inside me was too big to hide. Sometimes I would look at how his hair curled at the nape of his neck, or the dotted starts of stubble on his jaw, and a cavern of want would open up inside me, right there in the elevator or the sterile waiting room. I didn't want to bring that feeling into Clara's room, although looking

back, I don't know if I was trying to protect her from the thing between us, or protect the thing from her.

By the end of the week, I had called in sick to my job three days
in a row, plus the two vacation days I had already scheduled. We were
short-staffed and behind on a scheduled shipment of four hundred
live knockout mice to a university in western Texas. My boss had
made it clear if I wasn't back by Monday, I would lose my job.

Clara was stable. Nurses were always rushing in and out to check
her fluids, her vitals, scribble something on her chart. She was off the
drip and into a new hospital room. Not quite the cottages yet, but of
a lower priority than the wing where she had been. She had received a
provisional daily schedule printed in a pleasing green font. It read like
a menu of spa treatments: *individual medication consult, communal
discussion hour, personal growth seminar.* I was okay with the idea of
leaving Clara. She was in good hands, or at least well-formatted ones.

Leaving Teddy was another story. I had become attached to him
this week. I thought he had become attached to me, too, but I wasn't
sure, and I didn't want to find out one way or the other. I liked our
land of maybes, a territory of infinite potential.

Even after I got the warning text from my boss, I delayed telling
Teddy as long as I could. Only as we were walking back into Marien
from lunch on my last day did I say, as casually as possible, that I was
leaving tomorrow.

Teddy stopped short of the sliding doors. "Tomorrow tomorrow?"

"Tomorrow tomorrow."

He thought for a moment. His expression was inscrutable. My
stomach went into knots. Perhaps he didn't care about me leaving.
That would be a normal reaction. I was the one being dramatic. I did
not get close to people easily, which meant I was unpracticed at letting go. I often took it hard.

Then, finally, his mouth nudged up at the corner. That heart-
stopping dimple. "Will you go to dinner with me tonight?"

We went to dinner every night. We ate all meals together. He didn't need to ask. The unnecessariness made all my nerves stand to attention. Blood drummed in my ears.

I tried to sound nonchalant. "Sure."

That night, I shaved my legs and put on the dress I had brought in case Clara dragged me to a club. It was tight, cheap polyester. As soon as I put it on, I worried I had misunderstood the invitation. I thought how humiliating it would be if Teddy had meant something like McDonald's—if he hadn't meant it as a date at all. I was on the verge of taking it off again when he knocked on the door. I was relieved to see that he was wearing his suit jacket, which since the first day I had only ever seen him put on for video calls.

He kissed me on the cheek, which he had never done before. His skin was smooth and warm.

"Hi," he murmured.

"Hi."

The place he had chosen was not McDonald's. He drove us to a farm-to-table restaurant thirty minutes away. The type of place with its own herbarium, and chickens out back they kill themselves. We probably ate something like mushroom terrine or boiled fiddlehead ferns. I don't remember. I barely remember what we talked about, either, except for this one moment before our entrées arrived, when I asked him if he was looking forward to going back to Germany eventually.

Instead of answering right away, he looked down at the table. He placed one finger on the end of the fork and nudged it parallel to the spoon.

"I don't know if I'm going to go back," he said finally.

I put down my water glass. "They *fired* you?"

"No! No, I mean, I'll finish this project from here. After that, I think I'll resign."

I blinked. He had talked about his job plenty of times that week, and he hadn't given any hint of leaving. "Why?"

He adjusted the spoon now, and had to fix the fork to match. I wasn't sure I had ever seen him fidget before. "I think I'm going to move back to Vantage Point. Do something closer to home."

I had no words. The whole week, as whatever connected us wound tighter and tighter, I kept reminding myself that we were about to go our separate ways. Clara would be discharged eventually, and he would disappear back across the world. The knowledge had kept me in check. It had prevented me from veering too wildly around the turn. Now the brakes had been cut. He was saying he would be moving back to the island, *my* island. Why the change? *For you*, part of my brain said, even though I knew that couldn't be the real reason.

"But you love traveling." I must have sounded mildly hysterical. "You told me how much you love it. Why would you stop?"

His hand paused on the fork. He leaned in toward me, his eyes urgent.

"Look where we are," he said, and I looked around the room, as if he were talking about this particular restaurant. "With Clara, I mean. She's sick. She's *really* sick. I've talked to the doctors, I've read all the pamphlets. Even when she leaves here, she's not going to be magically fixed. She needs a support system. I can't help her if I'm swanning around Europe."

There was a self-loathing in his voice that I had never heard before. It seemed so out of character I thought I might be in a dream. "Why not move to New York?"

"She's hardly there anyway. You know her. She goes all over. She needs a home base. Somewhere stable she knows she can go to if she wants help."

"But giving up your whole career for her—she wouldn't want you to do that," I said, although the truth was I was no longer sure what Clara wanted. She had kept so much from me.

"I wasn't going to tell her. And if you don't mind, I'd rather you didn't, either. I don't want her to feel worse than she already does."

He was being too good. I felt a surge of protectiveness toward him. "That's a huge life change, Teddy."

"I like the island," he insisted. "There's things I can do to help out. Maybe take a more active role in the foundation my dad started. Run for mayor. I don't know. I just started thinking about it."

"Well, you should think about it some more," I said severely.

His mouth twitched up at the corner, flirtatious again. "You don't want me to move back?"

"No. Of course I—that's not what I meant." My cheeks warmed. "But you don't have to fall on a sword. I know you've had to take care of Clara before, but that doesn't have to be your whole life. You deserve to choose what makes you happy."

His smile vanished, and his eyes traveled over my face with strange solemnity, as if he were trying to divine some secret message from my expression. I knew I didn't have an expressive face. But at that moment, it seemed impossible that he couldn't see every thought that raced through my head. I felt like a live wire, translucent, fully charged.

"Thank you," he said at last. "I appreciate you saying that."

"I mean it."

"I know."

His knee brushed mine under the table. I didn't move my leg. He didn't move his. My whole body narrowed to that single point of contact, twill fabric against my bare knee, a coin-size circle of heat.

When he spoke, his voice was low and intimate. "You're a very good person, Jessica Pleyel."

And just like that, I knew how the night would end.

On some level, I had known all along. All week, we had quietly been setting a line of dominoes. The first one had already been tipped. All I had to do was fall.

Back at the motel, he let me precede him up the small flight of stairs and down the open hallway, with the parking lot on one side and the rooms on the other. Mine was before his. As we approached it, I looked back over my shoulder. Teddy smiled at me. He wasn't walking quickly, wasn't hurrying. He walked like he knew where he was going.

So I kept walking, too.

I hadn't been in his room before. It was the same as mine, but flipped the other way. Window on the left, chair on the left. Bed on the right. The air smelled expensive. Cedarwood and sage. When Teddy turned on the bedside lamp, the light flickered orange.

"Nice room," I said.

He smiled. "There's a cute neighbor."

He took off his watch and set it on the nightstand. He loosened the collar of his shirt. These were normal things a person did when they got home. They didn't mean anything.

Except they did.

I watched his fingers on the buttons of his shirt. "Should we talk?"

"Sure," he said.

"About this."

His mouth quirked. "I figured."

He seemed completely unfazed. In a world of flakes and ghosts, his straightforwardness was bizarre, addictive, a little frightening. It was like he had never heard of any dating rules. Or did not think they applied to him.

He took a step toward me. Then another. My heart hammered, hammered.

"It can't be casual," I warned.

"I don't want it to be."

"You might change your mind. It's been one week."

"And fifteen years."

"Fourteen and a half," I said, like I was catching him in a lie.

He was very close to me now. He took my face in his hands. "Jess. If you don't want to do this, we won't. But don't make it about me." His eyes were tender. "I've already thought about it. I've decided."

I had been sure he would falter. Now I saw how stupid that had been. Teddy Wieland did not falter. He had made up his mind. For whatever lucky, unknowable reason, he had chosen me.

I was struck by a wave of dizziness, a rush of oxygen, as if I had been diving and had come up too quickly. So I did not so much fall in love with Teddy as I surfaced into it, gasping, shaking for air. Dizzy from the decompression. Loving him was a relief, a pressure removed.

I reached up to touch his face. I knew it so well by sight but had never touched it. To touch someone's face is rare and intimate. I ran my fingers along his jaw, with the bone beneath, and the rough cat's-tongue feel of his stubble starting. His ear, the whorl of his cartilage. It reddened under my finger: I could affect him, too. I touched his throat. He swallowed, the muscles working. I threaded my fingers through his hair, which felt like Clara's hair, and also not like hers at all, and brought his mouth down to mine.

In bed, time dripped away from me like hot wax. Teddy peeled off his shirt, then my dress. He kissed the shallow indent between the two halves of my rib cage, the place unprotected by bone, and I had the wild thought that he might reach into that space and wrap his fingers around my heart. I would have let him do it; that was how badly I wanted him inside me.

We undressed each other quickly, and then the rest was slow. His big hands against my back, my hips, easing me into whatever place he wanted me, any position. I went like water. And yet there was no fear. I sensed he was choosing what would be good for both of us. I did not have to worry about my own pleasure anymore.

When he was finally inside me, he was sweating and shaking, shivering almost, as if lost in a fever. For my part, I felt that I had gone exquisitely still, the world narrowing and quieting around me, its balance restored. Who had I been before him? How could I ever be that person again? I placed my palms on his cheeks, the way he had placed his on mine—*I've decided*—and I made him look at me, his hazel eyes gone black. In our lives there are so few times when we can look at someone that fully; when we can see one another, just as we are.

Yes? he thought.

Yes, I answered.

And he ran me over the edge.

Afterward, Teddy trailed his finger along my collarbone. "Jess," he whispered, as if suddenly now we should care about noise, "what should we tell her?"

I was surprised that he asked it as a question. It seemed like the kind of thing on which he would already have an opinion. And when Teddy had an opinion, you would know about it. Now he sounded genuinely uncertain. Which made sense. There was no good way to spin it. Clara was in a hospital bed a few miles away. We were here, naked, upending her life. As soon as we told her, things would change, in ways I could foresee but didn't want to, ways I could explain but would pretend I couldn't.

The truth was, I wanted Teddy to myself a little longer. Had I ever had something Clara hadn't?

"Nothing," I whispered back. "Not yet."

21

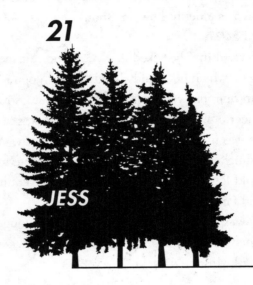

JESS

April 16

For the first half hour after we find Clara screaming in the fetal position on our front lawn, she says almost nothing. Which is not to say she resists. She lets us peel her up from the grass and carry her inside. She lets us lay her down on the sofa and cover her with a blanket. Her feet are a mess—the soles black with dirt, smeared with blood and seedlings and fragments of dried pine needles. She lets me do what little I still remember from my emergency wilderness training: I rinse and sanitize the cuts, wrap them with gauze and medical tape, test for signs of sprain. She watches it all with detached curiosity, barely wincing even when I pull a thick thorn from her heel. My own hand trembles as I drop it into a tissue.

When I finally close and latch the first-aid kit, Teddy takes my spot on the edge of the sofa. "What happened?" he asks for the third or fourth time.

Clara stares at her hands. The adrenaline has crashed out of her, leaving her limbs limp and her eyes heavy. "I told you. I saw them."

"I mean before your dream."

"But I wasn't—" She seems like she's about to say something else, but she stops, recalibrates. She adjusts her feet on the pillow. They still look terrible. There's dirt in the ridges of her toes and a crest of dried blood at her ankle, and her skin stands out raw and pink against the bandages. Just seeing them makes my own feet ache. But with Clara, I'm used to taking on a pain that's not mine.

"What don't you think?" Teddy prods.

She swallows. "I wasn't dreaming."

He doesn't like that answer at all. "You were. You were sleep-walking."

"I saw Mom and Dad."

"It was a dream."

"They were right outside."

"Mom and Dad are dead," Teddy says, his voice hard.

Clara doesn't wince the way I expect her to. The way I think Teddy almost did, just saying the words. Instead, she says miserably, "I know."

"So you have to have been dreaming," he says, like a math professor solving an equation.

"Or—" She stops.

"Or what?"

Clara looks over at me. She has the same pleading expression she had last week, when she told me she had seen the shadow. And suddenly I know how she was going to finish the sentence. *Or maybe it was the curse.*

But that isn't how Teddy and I are finishing the sentence in our minds. That isn't how any reasonable person would finish it. There are only two real possibilities. Either Clara was dreaming, or she was hallucinating.

"Clara," Teddy says, his patience wearing thin, "we want to help you. We can get Dr. Lanzerman involved, or call Dr. Carmody. Or a sleep specialist, if you were dreaming. But you have to talk to us. Tell us the truth about what's going on."

She knots her fingers into the blanket. The clock on the mantel ticks loudly in the silence, the mechanism clicking, clicking, clicking as the pendulum swings. I want to rip out the gears and throw them across the room. *Just say it*, I think furiously. Just say you were dreaming. Everyone has nightmares.

"I'm tired," she says in a small voice. "Can you drive me home?"

I convince her to stay the night, which is easier than I expect. She's timid, deferential. This is how she was when she first moved back to the island three years ago: tiptoeing everywhere like she was a hermit crab, carrying her body around in a shell. I put her in her childhood bedroom and go to get her a bathrobe and a change of clothes. When I return, she's standing at the window, worrying her hair between her fingers as she stares out into the darkness.

"I'll leave these here," I say, like the maid in a period drama.

"Okay," she says to the window.

Because no noblewoman thanks her maid. I grit my teeth and start to pull the door shut behind me.

"Jess?"

"Yeah?"

She still doesn't turn around. "I really did see them."

I have the sudden, horrifying urge to sink a knife between the cold knobs of her spine.

———————

In our bedroom, Teddy is stripping off the sweatshirt he threw on earlier. His movements are jerky, frustrated. It's nearly two in the morning. We have to be up in four hours.

"How is she?" he asks, his voice more hard than soft.

"Okay, I think."

"Did she say anything else?"

"She said she wasn't dreaming. Again."

"So what's her other explanation?" Teddy flings the sweatshirt on the floor with unnecessary force. "That she's crazy?"

"Shh!"

"She can't hear us."

He's probably right. Clara's room is on the other side of the house, down miles of sound-absorbing rugs, past the white noise of heating vents chugging through a chilly spring night. I wouldn't even have heard her scream earlier, if I hadn't already been awake. Through the insulated windows, it sounded soft, like a fox's cry. Only when it went up an octave did I register that it was human.

"Still," I say.

I pick up the sweatshirt and fold it into a neat square. Whatever energy left Clara seems to have fled straight into me, and my whole body is twitching. I want to give in to what Teddy's feeling—the frustration, the rage—but one of us has to be kind to her. You can hardly be angry at someone when they're in such a bad way, right? Even if they're throwing everything into chaos. Even if they've been a terrible friend.

So as Teddy and I crawl into bed, I say, "Should we cancel the events tomorrow?"

He looks bewildered. "Cancel on *them*?"

We've had plenty of cancellations this week, but not coming from our side. The fallout from the new video has been harder to manage than the first one, and this week has been a slog, all the exhaustion of the previous week with none of the good poll numbers. Canceled events, lost endorsements, tense meetings. I have yet to see Mike's brilliant "plan" reap any rewards. I'm starting to suspect that him not wanting to announce the video is a deepfake has less to do with his strategy's viability and more to do with him not wanting to admit he's lost control of the campaign.

"We can't cancel. People are counting on us," Teddy says.

"I know, but—" I turn toward him. "If Clara wasn't dreaming, she was hallucinating. We need to figure out how to get her help."

The bedside lamp casts shadows across his face, exaggerating his cheekbones, lengthening his patrician nose. My toes are cold, and I want to press them against his legs to warm them up, but the mood is wrong.

He tilts his head back against the headboard and closes his eyes. "This is exactly like three years ago," he says. I can't tell if he's talking to himself or to me. "And four years and five years and my entire fucking adult life. Convincing Clara she needs help. Figuring out how to get it for her. Signing things for her and making excuses for her and making decisions for her. Then she gets better and she swears she doesn't need our help, swears she can take care of herself. At some point, maybe I should let her. Some families have this thing called boundaries."

"We're not exactly a normal family."

He opens his eyes and looks at me, unamused.

I steel myself. "I think maybe the campaign isn't good for her."

"So, what, I should drop out?"

"No, I'm not saying that, but . . ." I trail off. That was exactly what I was saying. "Maybe tomorrow I could stay home, and you could go."

"It's a tour of a women's center. You have to be there."

And after the women's center, there's a luncheon, and after the luncheon, there's a rally, and after the rally we go to the next place and we do it over and over again until June and then, if we're lucky, until November. I'm not sure what makes me feel worse: the idea of all that, or the idea of stopping it all for Clara. The campaign isn't my dream—more like my nightmare, if I'm being honest with myself— but being forced to give it up feels as bad as being forced into it in the first place.

Still, I remember Clara on the ground, screaming.

"I don't think anyone will notice if I miss one day," I say.

"Mike says we're stronger together."

"Teddy, it's *Clara*."

His mouth pinches a little, but he seems otherwise unmoved. I've never seen Teddy give up on Clara before. I'm trying to make sense of the change. I want to know what straw broke the camel's back, so I can avoid breaking it myself.

"I'll talk to her tomorrow as soon as she gets up," I continue, trying to keep my voice steady, "when she's rested. I'll make sure she's okay, and we'll call the doctor together. Then I'll come join you the day after. If she still refuses to get help, then at least we can say we've tried."

"I can already say I've tried. I've tried a lot. For years." His eyes are shadowed, difficult to read. "You do whatever you want tomorrow. But I can't anymore. I'm done."

With that, he reaches over and turns out his light. The room clicks into darkness. Teddy rolls over onto his side, away from me. The mattress is so expensive that my side barely moves. The stillness makes it difficult to stay attuned to him, difficult to sense what he might be thinking.

He can't simply *be done* with Clara. Right? And if he is, then must I be done, too? What does *being done* even mean? What does it look like?

Out of nowhere, he says, "Are you sure you aren't just trying to get out of going to Kattinocket?"

Startled, I glance over, remembering too late I can't see him and he can't see me. "What?"

"Staying home an extra day. Are you trying to get out of Kattinocket? I know you don't want to go."

I squint in his direction, trying to make out his expression, but it's too dark, and anyway I don't think he's rolled back toward me.

"This has nothing to do with that," I say quietly. "That's not until Saturday. I'll be there."

"Because you agreed."

"I said, I'll be there."

There's a hard edge in my voice. And an even harder one in his when he says:

"You better."

I stiffen. For long moments, his retort hovers in the air. The cruelty grows between us, bigger and bigger, until it feels like another person in the bed. I keep my ears pricked in the darkness. He's going to apologize, surely. *Say something*, I think toward him. *Say something*, I think to myself. Neither of us does. I wait and wait. The room is so quiet. At last, I hear a soft intake of breath, followed by a gentle whistle through the nose.

He's snoring.

I turn onto my side, pressing my hands together in a prayer on the pillow, so I can feel the hard square of my engagement ring pressing into my cheek. My sheets are all the way up over my shoulders, my beautiful Frette linens, and even under four thousand dollars' worth of Egyptian cotton, I still feel cold.

22

CLARA

April 17

Three years ago, when I was discharged from Marien for the second time, Teddy drove me back to Vantage Point on the same highway our parents used to take to ferry us back and forth from school. It was January, a new year, and the air was clean and blue and the snow on the sides of the road was still white, except where it was pecked with pine cones and animal tracks.

We stopped for gas at the service plaza in West Gardiner, which was one of those places arranged like a rotunda, so you could stand in the middle of the circle and have your pick of sins: Burger King,

Starbucks, Popeyes. There was even an oculus at the top, like in the Pantheon in Rome.

The men's and women's restrooms were on opposite sides of the circle, and Teddy started to split off before he turned back to me.

"Are you okay by yourself?" he asked. "In the bathroom?"

"Are you saying you want to come with?"

He rolled his eyes. "Never mind."

He disappeared behind the partition. I stared around the rotunda at the food, and the people eating it. The plastic laminate of the Dunkin' sign. The wide squat Starbucks city mugs with their orange and blue doodles of moose, Mount Katahdin, a whale mid-breach.

A woman pushing a stroller gave me a weird look as she passed, and I realized I was blocking foot traffic. I started walking slowly around the rotunda. It was like touring the reptile cage at the zoo: no sudden movements, don't want to startle the beasts. A teenage girl sat down at one of the sad gray tables and unrolled a greasy paper bag. She pulled out a cardboard box of chicken nuggets and another one of fries. My pulse accelerated. How had she decided on those? And there were sauces grabbed from self-serve: wrinkled packets of ketchup and mayonnaise, cells of salt and pepper. How had she known which ones to take, and how many?

There were so many questions to consider, so many decisions to make every day. At Marien, it was all determined for us. Our schedules were full, or if they were empty, they were supposed to be empty, a time blocked out for meditation and reflection. The first time I left Marien, I'd flown to an Ayurvedic retreat in Bali, and then went straight back to partying and, soon, to purging. I had it under control, I thought. I wouldn't end up back there again. Now look at me. Little fool.

"Clara?" Teddy had returned. "Did you already go to the bathroom?"

"Um. No."

He followed my gaze to the food court. "I'm going to get something," he said casually. "Do you want anything?"

I was hungry. And I had to get something, didn't I, to show him I was better, to show him I was trying? But the options, the choices.

I feigned indifference. "Yeah. Whatever. You decide."

Back on the road, I cradled in my lap our fast-food burritos, which had come in warm, leaky aluminum pockets. Red juice, blood I guessed, was already seeping into the seams of the plastic bag.

I noticed for the first time that Teddy drove the same way our dad did, with his left arm braced against the window and his right hand on the bottom of the steering wheel, third finger flickering over the cruise control. Had he always driven like that? Or was I only noticing it now because I felt like a little kid being shuttled back home for winter break?

"So the conservator thing," I said.

"Uh-huh?"

"Should we call Pierce about the paperwork to end it? Or does it end automatically?"

Teddy was quiet for a moment. "You want to end it?"

"At some point I'll probably want to be able to vote."

"I mean, do you want to end it *right now* or do you want a few months to adjust?"

Adjust to what? I had been at Marien for six months. I didn't know anything about what came next.

"I don't know," I said.

"You don't have to rush anything."

It was something our dad used to say. *No need to rush into a decision.* I could parrot his lessons, but I couldn't state them with assurance, like Teddy could. He had internalized them, developed experience. I thought about everything he had been doing these past six months. Managing the island, running WFCI, sitting on nonprofit boards, managing investments—and taking care of all of my stuff, too. Meanwhile, I had been getting remedial lessons on how to eat.

I put the burritos on the floor and pulled my knees up to my chest and stretched the seat belt over them to hold them there. It gave me a nice feeling, like I was being hugged tight.

"Thanks for picking me up," I said for the fifteenth time.

"Of course." Teddy glanced over and smiled at me, and for a moment he felt like my brother again, not a parent or a guardian. "So you'll stay at the big house with us for a while, if that's okay. There's an issue with the wiring at the guesthouse."

The lie was blatant. The cottage had been rewired a few years earlier. I thought about saying I knew what he was doing, and he didn't have to worry, it was okay to leave me alone. I wasn't going to hurt myself. Instead, I leaned my head against the window. The glass pressed against the part in my hair, a cold line down my scalp. The truth was, I would rather be thought weak than be alone.

I remember that day when I wake up in my childhood bedroom, age thirty-two, under the same tie-dye bedspread I've had since I was a teenager, next to the Lisa Frank alarm clock my dad gave me for my twelfth birthday. On the wall, Orlando Bloom stares moodily out from behind a sticky windswept mullet. It's the same view that greeted me every day those first couple weeks I got back from Marien. I'd wake up here, the way I used to, and at breakfast Teddy would read the newspaper with his ankle propped on his knee, the way my dad used to, and Jess would drink her coffee looking out at the backyard, the way my mom used to, and it was all like a weird awful parallel universe in which everyone else had grown up and I had stayed the same.

I struggle onto my elbows. Last night comes to me in flashes. My parents. The wall of water. Teddy and Jess carrying me inside. It all seems so far away, like it wasn't really me who lived it. I remember saying, *I wasn't dreaming*, but I don't remember what made me so sure. In the morning light, all of yesterday feels like a nightmare. I guess it's always hard to tell the difference between memories and dreams. They feel the same. Sleep blurs them out, pushes them both away from the present moment.

I swing my legs over the side of the bed. My joints feel rusty, my muscles ache. The soles of my feet hurt when they brush against the floor. I grab hold of my left foot and tilt it to see the damage. I've lost one of the bandages Jess put on. The cuts underneath are already fringed with a subtle pink that means either healing or infection. There are more scratches on my calves and hands.

That's the difference between dreams and yesterdays. Yesterdays have consequences. Your body brings home party favors.

I fumble my phone off the nightstand. The screen is cracked from where I dropped it last night. The battery is at thirteen percent.

The top notification is a message from Jess: *I'm downstairs, let me know when you're up.*

A planned intervention. Great.

That look on her face last night, when I was about to say the word *curse*—her eyes blazing at me, like she was willing me to suck the words back down. Which I did. Because the thing is, I know what I saw, and I also know it wasn't possible. I know Teddy and Jess won't believe me about a curse, and I know that they're probably right. The simplest answer is that I was sleepwalking. The most likely answer is that I hallucinated. Either way, Occam's razor says: I'm fucked up.

So what next? An intervention, to tell me what I already know? Or do I do the grown-up thing and get myself help? There's nothing mysterious about how to do it. I have all the doctors' phone numbers, same as Teddy does. I can make things easier on everyone. I can show them that I've changed.

Again, it comes down to weak or alone.

I look at the clock, then back at my phone. They both say 7:20. In the end, that's what makes up my mind: the fact that for three years, while I've been eating my three square meals and taking leadership of WFCI and getting better, I swear, *being* better—someone has been keeping the unicorn clock in my childhood bedroom on track, waiting for me to need it again.

I haven't snuck out of this house often in my life. So maybe there's a better route out of the house than the one I take, down the old servants' stairs and out the north side door. When I finally reach the door, I realize that I made a miscalculation: I'm barefoot, and the mudroom where we keep rain boots is on the other side of the house. I check the nearest closets until I find one with out-of-season beach gear, including a collection of water shoes. I grab a pair and slip them on. They're men's, so big that I don't even need to stretch the elastic to get them around my ankles. Close enough.

I flop around to the front of the house, picking my way along the woods on the far side of the front yard, back toward the road. The route takes me close to where I saw my parents last night, and even though I mean to get out of view fast, I find myself coming to a halt.

Right there.

I saw them *right there.*

Mom.

Dad.

At the end of the driveway, the road climbs toward my house like a fat gray snake. No movement in the thick, brutal forest. There's a buzzing in my ears: the sound of total silence. The quiet so quiet I can hear it. Time is crawling around me, circling for a meal. It senses the gash inside me, reopened, spilling blood.

I notice a small black shape in the grass maybe ten feet ahead of me. It looks like a wounded animal, perhaps a dead crow.

When I get closer, I realize it isn't an animal at all. It's an object.

I scoop it up from the ground and stare at it uncomprehendingly. It's a strip of black silicone, with seven black lenses embedded in it and a weighted square box at each end. One box is covered with a grille of holes—a speaker. I pry up a silicone flap on the other box and discover a charging port that matches the one on my cell phone. Next to the port is a series of small raised letters, embossed in the plastic: PATENT PENDING.

It's a projector. The same kind Conrad brandished at his failed presentation for NatureEye.

But it's out here, in Teddy's yard.

I feel like I've been clinging to the very end of a rope, and now the last strands slip through my fingers. Now I'm falling through air.

I turn in a circle, looking from the place where I was standing last night, to the place where I saw my parents and the wave, to the projection strip in my hand. Searching, rearranging. Remembering.

And I see it then. Finally, I see where I went wrong.

23

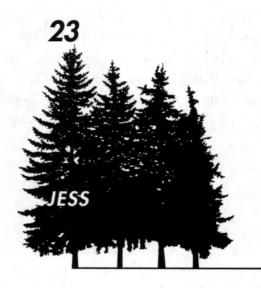

JESS

April 17

Teddy leaves at the crack of dawn. I spend the next two hours planning out my conversation with Clara. I research hallucinations, delusions, schizophrenia, stress-induced psychosis, post-traumatic stress disorder, the connections to memory loss, the connections to eating disorders. I'll start by making her coffee, sitting down with her in the front living room, formal enough to make it official, informal enough that she's not on the defensive. I'll tell her gently that I know she's bingeing. I'll tell her I'm worried. I'll pretend that everything is fine on my end, that I'm not mad, that I haven't spent the last few days waiting in vain for an apology. Because she's the sick one, and I'm the well one, so I'm supposed to be able to contain my emotions. I'm supposed to forgive her, and be patient, and move on.

While I wait, I tidy. Admittedly, there's not much to do: Stephanie came yesterday. I smooth down a throw blanket that was already smooth. I fluff some pillows that were already fluffed. I'm straightening a straight picture when I happen to glance outside and see Clara walking in tight circles at the edge of the lawn.

Her hair is a tangled mess on one side, flat against her ear on the other. She's wearing a white bathrobe and what looks like Teddy's water shoes on her feet. She's holding a clump of black wires, and periodically in her circles, she lifts it up at various angles.

She looks crazy. A person you'd move away from if you passed her on the street.

I try to remember the steps of the plan. My checklist. I had a checklist. Make her coffee, sit her down—but that was when I thought she would be coming down the stairs the way she was last night, penitent and docile. Now she's outside, wild-eyed.

As I'm trying to construct a new plan, Clara pries a piece off the wires, drops it in the grass, and starts toward the front door.

I start walking, too, parallel to her, watching her through the windows, hurrying to beat her. I don't quite make it. I pull the door open at the same time she starts to push it, so she ends up off-balance and stumbles into the foyer. The momentum causes one of the water shoes to fly off her foot. It hits a small painting of Thomas Wieland Sr., which drops onto the console table and then flips onto the floor.

Clara barely notices.

"Jess," she says, out of breath. "I have to talk to you."

I press my lips together. I pick up the painting, dust off the front. I hang it back on its hook. My throat feels tight, like I might cry.

"What were you doing outside?" I try to sound neutral. I don't think I succeed.

"Walking home," Clara says. "But look what I found."

She uncurls her hands and holds the wires out to me like an offering.

I don't look at them. "I was waiting for you to come down. I sent you a text."

"I know. I got it." She's not really listening to me. Her whole energy is heightened.

"So you were—sneaking out?"

Impatiently, she shakes her outstretched hands. The wires click and rattle. "Look. It's a projection strip."

I try to focus. "A what?"

"Remember Conrad's project, the one WFCI denied? NatureEye."

"Not really." I'm not involved with WFCI. "Something about VR?"

"The whole idea was these projection strips, which they could ship out so people could project super realistic holograms of different national parks in their living room. And I found this *outside*," she says meaningfully. "Just sitting there in the grass."

I feel like I'm reading a book that's missing every other page. "So?"

"So," she says slowly, as if speaking to a child, "what I saw last night? It was a hologram."

"A hologram," I repeat.

"Yes." Her words start coming faster. "And it wasn't the first time. The other day, I saw a bunch of people in a lifeboat out by the rocks—then it disappeared. I told you about the shadow on my lawn, right? And I saw a grizzly bear, too. There are no grizzlies here. Everything—"

"Slow down."

"—has been related to the curse. So I thought maybe it was the curse. But that was the whole point. He's been trying to scare me, trying to make me think I'm cursed, or haunted, or whatever, when actually he's the one—"

"Who's 'he'?"

"Conrad." She clutches the wires to her chest, thinking out loud.

"It must be. He doesn't have a big team, and he made such a big deal about the strips being patent pending. He said they weren't ready for demonstration . . . but that must have been a lie. And of course, he's here. Why is he still here? No one stays this long in April."

She finishes with a triumphant smile. Like *Ta-da!*

Memories tumble through me, all the years compressing: her startled gasp as she tumbled down the stairs; the crash of glass when she dropped the casserole dish and pressed her hands to her eye. *I can't see.* The grocery bags in her hands.

Just once, I'd like my friend to be stable enough that being pissed off at her doesn't make me a bitch.

"Don't worry," she says, misreading my expression, "I left the part with the camera and sensor outside. So he can't see us right now."

I press my fingers to my temples. "You think Conrad Gaffney, a person you barely know, has taken time off work to come to the island to sneak around projecting holograms of lifeboats and bears to scare you."

"Yes! And I bet he made the deepfake videos, too!"

We're talking about Conrad, a milquetoast rich kid whose greatest claim to fame is that he's sort of friends with Teddy Wieland. Worse, we're talking about *holograms.* Last night wasn't the only hallucination. Neither was the shadow. This has been going on for weeks.

Stay calm, I tell myself. You have to stay calm. Get more information. Get the scope of it. Don't contradict her.

"Why do you think he would do all that?" I ask in the gentlest voice I can manage.

She falters. "Well . . . I don't know yet. Something to do with WFCI? I'll figure it out," she adds, recovering her bravado. "But it has to be him. Programming fake versions of national parks can't be that different from programming fake versions of me and you."

"Okay," I say, though I'm not sure since when Clara knows anything about computer programming.

"It being holograms explains why the things disappear so fast," she says. "He just turns them off. He probably planted this one when he came for drinks that one time, and controls them wirelessly. Or—maybe Bluetooth. Maybe he comes onto the property, too, to get in range. The gates aren't closed."

Yes, I think, we leave them open so people can come simulate your dead parents.

"That's interesting," I say.

Her smile drops an inch.

"You don't believe me," she says, almost wonderingly.

"I'm a little worried about you," I allow.

Again, she lifts the thing she's calling a projection strip and shoves it toward me, like it's some incontrovertible fact, and not just a collection of silicone and wires that looks exactly like the tangle of cables behind our media cabinet. "*Look.*"

I do look. I really do. I look at her wild hair, her bathrobe slipping open, her single mesh shoe. Her cheeks are flushed with victory and frustration, like she has it all figured out and I'm the only one in her way.

A whole week of icing her out, and she hasn't even noticed.

"This is a projection strip," she says again, as if I might have misheard.

"Okay," I say. So what if it is? Conrad could have dropped it when he came over for drinks. Clara could even have taken it from him, and put it outside herself. Having a projection strip on the lawn doesn't prove anything. I don't say any of this, because I'm not supposed to, although I'm starting to vibrate from the effort of holding everything in.

"Don't do that. Don't just say 'okay' and pretend like you agree and secretly you're thinking I'm crazy."

"I didn't say you were crazy."

"You don't have to. I can tell what you're thinking."

"No, you can't," I say. "Not always."

She waits, tapping her foot.

"I just—want to help you find someone to talk to," I say.

"I know a million people to talk to. I know enough shrinks to fill a football stadium."

"Then let's call one of them."

She actually stamps her foot in frustration. It's the foot with the water shoe still on it, and the hard rubber smacks comically against the floor. "What will it take for you to believe me?"

"About *holograms?*"

"Yes!"

"I don't know. Proof."

"Proof," she repeats. Her brow clears. "Wait! My phone. I forgot. I took a video." She tucks the wires under her arm and digs in the robe's pocket. When she pulls out the phone, the screen is cracked, mud still smeared across it. For some reason, the crack irritates me. I know it's because she dropped it in the throes of panic, but it feels like a slap in the face. She's always so careless with her possessions. She thinks anything can be replaced.

She scrolls to the end of her photos. "Here! See?"

She angles the phone toward me and presses play. The screen stays dark but the phone lets out a keening sound. I realize after a moment that it's her, mid-scream. A few seconds in, the darkness brightens: the porch lights coming on, revealing the lawn in a blurry wash. Teddy's and my panicked voices overtake the sound of her crying. Then there's a thump and the image goes black again, and the video ends.

Clara stares at the screen in horror.

"I thought I hit record earlier," she whispers.

I sink down on the entry bench. "Clara."

She shoves the phone back in her pocket. "Okay, I messed up the video. Never mind that. Can you please just trust me?"

"Why should I?"

"Why shouldn't you?"

I gape at her.

"No, really," she says. "Tell me. Explain why you shouldn't trust me. And don't use things from years ago, or the fact that you think I'm having hallucinations. What have I done, *recently*, to make you not trust me?"

My whole body flushes hot—my face, my toes, but also my insides: my lungs, my veins, fury searing through each cell wall. "Hm. Let me think." I count the reasons on my fingers, starting with my thumb. "You didn't tell me you didn't remember the first video." I put up my index finger. "You promised me you'd tell Teddy, and you didn't." A third finger. "You promised you'd text, and you didn't." A fourth. "And then, the day the second video came out."

Clara blinks. "What about it?"

"You said you were at work, so you couldn't talk."

She looks confused. "I *was* at work. I was in a meeting about expanding the South Pond reservoir. I called you back later."

"No. You were at the grocery store."

"I never go to the grocery store."

My last thread of patience snaps. "Well, you went to the grocery store, and you bought all your fucking junk food shit, and then you went home and spent the day eating and throwing up and eating and throwing up because I know what you do, and it's sick and disgusting and that's what was more important to you than calling me back, and okay, fine, you're sick, I'm supposed to let it slide, but you can't get away with it one minute and the next pretend like you're totally fine." The words tumble out of me. They seethe and foam. I'm not used to it, this anger, and now that it's rushing out of me it feels hard to put it back inside. "It's exhausting. You're so much *work*."

Clara stares at me, astonished.

I press my hand to the top of my chest, my finger and thumb making a V around the indentation between my collarbones. I make myself be calm.

"Jess," she says slowly. "I promise you. I was not at the grocery store that day."

"Clara, I *saw* you!"

The blood drains from her cheeks. "Oh, my god. Oh, my god. Jess—"

"And you didn't even apologize." My voice cracks, and it's so embarrassing that this is the thing that does it, this one missing apology. "You never even said sorry you weren't there."

Clara bends down and traps my hands between hers. Her fingers are freezing. There's something new on her face, almost joyful, like a puzzle piece has slid into place.

"Please listen to me," she says earnestly. "I did apologize."

I twist out of her grip. She leans forward, trying to grab my hands again, and I slide sideways off the bench, out of reach. I back a few feet down the hall, putting distance between us.

"I know what happened," she says. "The holograms—"

"Clara, I don't want to hear about the fucking holograms!"

She pursues me. "What about the Anchor?"

"What about it?"

"Were you in the alley behind the Anchor last week?"

I shake my head, trying to follow her chain of thought. But why do I think there's a chain at all? Why do I assume anything she does is logical?

"I haven't been to the Anchor in months," I say.

She hisses, a low sound of satisfaction. I have no idea what's going on in her mind. The whole conversation has swerved so far away from what I intended. I try to remember my research, my checklist, what I'm supposed to do next—but it's all been wiped away.

So many times, I've picked up the pieces. I've put her first. I don't know if all the chances we've given her have been infinite or insufficient or both. *I'm done*, Teddy said last night. Incredible to think you could end it, just like that. Sever the debt. Be free.

"Let's call Dr. Lanzerman," I say.

"What?" Distractedly, she drops her hands, shrugs the bathrobe up her shoulders. "No. That's not what I—" She turns to the left, then the right, as if she's lost track of where the door is. She spots the discarded shoe and snatches it up, shoving it on her foot. "I have to go."

"Clara, if you leave, I'm not coming after—"

But she's out the door before I can even say *you*.

Deaths attributed to the Wieland curse

Warning!

The truthfulness of this article has been questioned. It discusses a **superstitious belief** and relies heavily on **anecdote** and **apocryphal sources**. Please help us improve the page by adding reliable, independent sources and including information on possible **alternative explanations** of the phenomenon.

24

CLARA

April 17

I limp back along the road to my house, bathrobe and water shoes
and all, the projection strip dangling from my hand. Other than the
loud slapping of the shoes, the forest is silent. My brain feels like a
snow globe: picked up, shaken, and set down again.

Jess thought she saw me at the grocery store and therefore that I
was lying, which is why she didn't return my calls that day. I thought
she was avoiding me, which was one reason why I got drunk. Teddy
and I thought we saw her in the alley behind the Anchor. But didn't
I think, after the Anchor, that Jess wasn't acting like herself? I was

right, literally: that wasn't her at all. Conrad has been making holograms of us, too. Probably having AI generate responses, to make it seem like a conversation.

This explanation makes no sense, and at the same time it's the only explanation that makes any sense at all. It's the only possibility that explains all these different events. The videos, the ghosts, the tension. Why they all started at the same time. I attributed all these disparate things to coincidence or to the curse, but in fact what they had in common was something else entirely: a basic fucking dude.

How many times this month have I thought I saw someone and I was actually seeing a hologram? Every time Teddy and Jess acted weird? Every time someone from town crossed the street to avoid me? Certainly the time I apologized to Jess the other day, because she doesn't remember that, and her memory isn't fucked up like mine. Our argument just now can't have been fake, because I touched her, I grabbed her hands and felt her pulse thrumming against my fingers, fast and fragile as a butterfly. But anything where I didn't physically touch or hug someone: it's all suspect.

Conrad must have more than one device hidden across the property, to have created all the visions he did. One at the rocks, one in my yard, one by the road. Maybe more. Spread over a hundred acres, it would take days to find every single one, even if I called in the gardeners to help. And what would I do once I found them? I wouldn't have proof he had done anything. I'd only have a pile of ugly cords, and Conrad would know that I was on to him. He'd be able to run.

By the time I reach my house, my calves are red and bumped with cold. I kick the stupid water shoes into the bushes by the porch. My toes are red, too. Everything inside the cottage is where I left it last night, but so much has changed since then that it feels like a museum, hushed and esoteric. Yesterday, I thought I might be going insane but no one else knew. Today, Teddy and Jess think I'm insane but I'm not.

Probably.

It's hard to know for sure.

I shove Conrad's device in the freezer, like they do on spy shows to block wavelengths or whatever. Upstairs, my bathtub drain has a thin ring of black mold I don't know how to clean. A downside of Stephanie's absence. I sit on the edge of the tub, turning the faucet halfway between hot and cold. I test the water against my wrist: lukewarm. Still, when I submerge my feet, it feels like I'm sticking them in a bag of hot coals. Only a few bandages survived the walk, and in the water their loose ends detach and drift upward. I peel them off and lay them one after another on the side of the bathtub. A graveyard of beige.

The thing I don't understand is: I must be Conrad's primary target. I'm the only one in both videos; I'm the only one he's made think was hallucinating. The fake-me that Jess saw going into the grocery store must have been intended to drive a wedge between me and Jess, and the fake-Jess that Teddy and I saw must have been intended to drive a wedge between Teddy and me. Is that why he warned me against Teddy when we were on the boat? To separate me from the pack, bring me down for the kill?

I prod one of the cuts. But why would Conrad target *me*? He's only ever been close with Teddy. I barely even remember him from when we were younger. I try to imagine him at his computer, choosing the shadows under my ribs, the color of my nipples, the bruising on my arms. The first video came out the day after the WFCI presentation, before he even knew the funding had been rejected.

It doesn't make sense. There's some bigger picture I'm not understanding. Maybe when we were kids, I did something that I (irony of ironies) really have forgotten: a rejection, a mean joke, an ill-timed laugh.

You don't think about other people, Jess said.

Her voice shaking with anger. Her lips tight and pale.

I slide a finger into the cut and press until I feel the strike of pain.

Deep down, I know it's my fault she didn't believe me. A story is only as good as its teller, and I don't have a great track record with the truth.

On the other hand—

I'm not the only one who's lied.

The winter after my first stay at Marien, I agreed to spend Christmas at Vantage Point. I didn't usually like going back to the house for the holidays, but Teddy had moved back from Germany and was spending more time on the island. Entering his hermit era, I guessed. He had been asking me to come up all autumn, and I was running out of excuses.

"This way you can spend Christmas with Jess, too," he said. I thought it was nice of him to think about including my friend.

When I arrived, I went straight to my parents' old room. Better to do it early, or I'd spend the rest of the trip thinking about it.

I was surprised to find an open suitcase on the bench at the foot of the bed. Teddy's Yale Law hoodie was tossed over a chair. It felt like a violation. In the nearly eight years since their deaths, the only time either of us had slept in their room was when I fell asleep in there crying the night of their funeral.

I opened the closet and discovered that our parents' clothes had been pushed to the back. Fresh shirts, Teddy's shirts, hung neatly in the empty space.

I found him in the kitchen. "You're sleeping in Mom and Dad's room?"

"For the king-size bed. Is that okay?"

He asked like he assumed the answer was yes. I guessed it was supposed to be yes. "You don't want to just order a new bed for your old room?"

"Why?"

"I don't know." He opened the fridge door between us. I played with my cuticle. "Someone emptied the closet."

"I asked Rosa to move some of it. I didn't get rid of anything."

"So where is it?"

He leaned back from the fridge to give me a strange look. "You sure you're okay with me staying in there?"

"Yes," I said.

"Because you should let me know if you aren't."

Now there was no way I could protest.

Christmas dinner was only the three of us: me, Teddy, and Jess. I was glad to see her, mostly. I was still a little embarrassed that she had seen me so ill. That she had been the one to take me to the hospital.

The dinner was delicious. Rosa had found us a beautiful turkey. I still remember the glint of the carving knife, which was freshly sharpened, and pronged at the end like a serpent's tongue. The bird's skin was crispy and bubbled, and it popped apart with only the slightest pressure from the blade. Teddy divided the meat into light and dark. The long white muscle fibers, pulled out like taffy. All the meat was tender. The cranberry sauce was tart enough to burn your tongue.

As I cut into the cherry pie, Jess got a text.

"My mom says she's home," she announced.

"Already?" I asked.

"She can't stay up too late these days."

"Why not?"

She glanced at Teddy. At first I thought it was because she didn't want to talk about it in front of him, she wanted to tell me when it was just the two of us. But then he gave a tiny nod and I realized she was *checking with him.*

"She had pneumonia last month. She's still recovering."

"Oh my god," I said. Teddy didn't say anything. He didn't seem surprised by the news.

"It's okay. She's fine now, just gets tired easily. I'm sorry—I thought I told you."

"No, of course. I understand." But I didn't. How had Teddy known and I hadn't?

I spent the rest of dinner stewing over this question. I scrolled back through recent text threads in my mind, wondering if I had missed any clues about Jess's mom or about Teddy and Jess. Were they friends now, on their own? He said he was spending more time on the island. Naturally, that would mean they saw each other in passing. But were they actually hanging out? I was strangely unsettled by the idea of them interacting without me there.

After dinner, Teddy went to start a fire in our dad's study. I went to the bathroom. I was probably in there for five or ten minutes. When I came out, jazz notes filtered softly through the house. As I approached the study, the music grew louder, and I heard Jess laugh, the deep three-beat laugh that only came out when she was genuinely entertained. I stopped and watched through the crack in the door.

Teddy was crouched in front of the fireplace, feeding twists of kindling into a weak fire. Jess was watching him from the sofa, where she had leaned back against the rolled arm and tucked her socked feet up into the space between the cushions. She was drinking whiskey from a crystal glass, orange diamonds in the flaring light. They looked like a couple in an ad.

"That's the best you can do?" she was saying. "I thought you were an Eagle Scout."

"I was not."

"You seem Eagle Scout-y."

He sat back on his heels and smiled. I had never seen him smile like that before. "What does that mean?"

"You know." She waved her glass in a small circle. "Outdoorsy. Do-gooder. Ambitious."

"Capable?" he asked meaningfully.

She laughed. "Not like that," she said in a way that meant *definitely like that*.

That was when I knew. Not from the words themselves, but from the tone. The anticipation, the sense that they still had something more to say.

Teddy reached out and wrapped his hand around her ankle, tugging her slender foot out from the cushions. He pinched it playfully. She squeaked and pretended to try to shake him off. He kept his hand around her foot, his thumb massaging the arch. She glanced up at the door, but I was hidden behind the door, and she couldn't see me.

"Stop," she whispered to Teddy, smiling. He kissed the top of her foot, then released her.

I turned my head away. I rewound the past year in my head. Jess taking me to Marien, Teddy meeting us there. The days there bled together in my head, especially the first couple weeks. I had been so preoccupied with figuring out a way out of there that I had barely even considered what Teddy and Jess might be doing when they weren't with me. Had they been spending all that time with one another? Over the summer, when I called from Bali, Jess had mentioned she was seeing someone, though she wouldn't tell me anything about him. Now that I thought about it, that had been around the time Teddy's trips to the island became more frequent.

I felt drunk. Well, I *was* drunk, but I felt more drunk than I was, dizzy, trying to sort through the mess of emotions clogging my throat.

On one hand: Teddy and Jess were happy. That was good.

But also: they were each supposed to be mine.

When I entered the room, the air changed. The conversation skipped. Somehow, without actually moving a muscle, they moved farther apart.

There had been a moment there where I thought I might address it. Tell them what I had seen. Now, I discarded the idea. I understood in that invisible flinch that whatever conversation happened next, it would be them against me, Teddy and Jess explaining, justifying, begging. I didn't want them to put into words what they had done. My emotions were liquid in my throat, water in my mouth, and I couldn't speak without them spilling out.

"I have to get more kindling," Teddy said, getting to his feet. As he passed me, he paused and squinted. He seemed suspicious. "What's wrong with your eye?"

I walked over to the mantelpiece, where a weathered mercury mirror sat next to a Spanish cutter in a bottle. When I looked in the mirror, I saw that the white part of my left eye was now a bright, vicious red. I had spent most of those five minutes in the bathroom on my knees. I had purged so hard I burst a blood vessel.

"I don't know," I said. I prodded the space under it as if curious. As if oblivious. "I hope it goes away."

The thing is, Teddy and I have always looked so much alike. And I wonder sometimes which of us was Jess's original love, and which was the one she picked for the resemblance.

25

JESS

April 18

I join the campaign on Thursday as promised, ready to hit the ground running, right back into our usual fourteen-hour days of appearances and podcast interviews and meetings with local politicians and conspicuous visits to children's hospitals. It's nothing we haven't done before, and it should go smoothly. But we keep running into roadblocks. The hospital cancels the visit with an hour's notice. A normally easygoing talk radio host presses Teddy hard to release information on his investment portfolio. A candidate for state assembly refuses a photo op.

The real sign of trouble comes at the Orono rally on Friday, when several college students stand up in the middle of Teddy's speech and start shouting *"EAT THE RICH!"* A security guard at the venue tries to escort them out, but he can't corral all of them at once, and the whole thing unfolds like a Marx Brothers skit, one pasty-faced kid ducking away while the guard ushers the others out, the guard spinning around to catch the first kid and the other kids slipping away in the process. It takes several minutes for the commotion to die down, and by the time Teddy can resume his speech, he's lost the crowd. He hurries through ten more minutes, accidentally calling Orono by another town's name, and exits to tepid applause.

"It's a fluke," Mike says soothingly that night, as Teddy paces on the cheap carpet in our hotel suite. I'm standing by the window, trying not to get involved.

"It's humiliating," Teddy replies.

"We knew the video was going to have consequences. We're in the eye of the storm."

"I thought the eye of the storm was supposed to be last week."

"Sometimes it takes a little time for things to build?" Mike's voice lifts at the end involuntarily, which makes his reassurance sound like a question. My eyebrows shoot up. Things must be really bad if they've punctured Mike's bravado.

"I wasn't even *in* the video," Teddy says. "It was Clara and Jess."

Not actually us, I want to remind him, but I hold my tongue. Things are still tense between Teddy and me. I hate this sharpness between us. It should be solvable. If Mike weren't here, I would go to Teddy and put my arms around his waist from behind, interlacing my fingers so the palms of my hands pressed flat against his stomach. I would lay my cheek against the hard plane of his shoulder. Close like that, I could absorb his weariness into me, and he could absorb mine. We could pass it back and forth, and it would lessen in the passing, the way water cools when you pour it between cups.

But Mike's here, so.

I nudge aside the blackout curtain and peek out the window. It's full night, and the parking lot's single floodlight casts the rows of cars in a horrible white glow. It reminds me of the motel near Marien. That might be the last time I had a room with such a shitty view. I wonder if the room assignments are another sign of campaign troubles.

I wonder what Clara's doing now, back on the island. Normally I'd worry that I haven't heard a peep from her since our argument. But I'm done now, and as a person who is *done* with someone, I must push all that worry away, back behind the boundary I've so lovingly erected. If I'm not going to do anything, then I certainly have no right to worry. No right to wonder if Clara's tried to convince anyone else that she's been seeing holograms, or if she's checked herself into a psych ward, or if she's sprawled dead in her foyer. The most I know for sure is that nothing has happened on social media, because then I would have heard about it.

But again, I'd only think about that if I were worrying about her, which I'm not.

Teddy says to Mike, "You said if we put Jess more front and center, it would blow over. You said if we rejigged our message, we'd avoid the consequences."

"We don't know that's not working."

"I saw the poll numbers."

"Polls go up and down."

"You only say that when they're going down."

Mike sidesteps the question. "We'll get back on track. Let's see how tomorrow's events go before we get too excited. We have the seal pup photo, the DAR brunch, and the meeting with that alderman."

I turn back to them. "And Kattinocket."

Teddy and Mike look over at me in unison. They forgot I was here.

"We're going to Kattinocket in the afternoon," I say.

A few weeks earlier, if I'd said the word *Kattinocket*, Teddy would have reacted. His eyes would have softened. He would have reached out to touch my shoulder. He would have gathered me into a hug.

Now, he blinks and turns back to Mike. "Seal pup, DAR brunch, alderman, Kattinocket," he recites, as if the events are all equally unremarkable.

Mike nods, and the conversation moves on.

To a neutral observer, Kattinocket Elementary looks a lot like Brunswick High. It also looks a lot like a hundred other schools whose cinderblock innards I've seen over the last few months. Of course, there are always little differences. Sometimes the rally is in an auditorium and sometimes it's in a gym. Sometimes the greenroom is a counselor's office, and sometimes it's the music room, with silent cymbals collecting dust. Sometimes the venue is near the ocean, and sometimes it's in a town I swore I'd never set foot in again.

While they get today's auditorium ready, they put us in a kindergarten classroom. It has colorful mats rolled up against the walls and a bulletin board edged with wavy cardboard cutouts. An illustrated poster lists vowel combinations that make the same sound: *ai* in *bait* goes with *ay* in *May*, *oi* in *coin* goes with *oy* in *toy*. The image for *bait* is an anchor hooked through a struggling worm. The image for *toy* is a kite drifting away.

Teddy has disappeared somewhere with Mike, accompanied by the two new bodyguards who quietly joined the entourage today. Phoebe is sitting at a child-size desk in the corner, banging out press releases. The social media intern has sprawled on the floor to caption a video. A solitary PTA volunteer monitors us with a stony expression, like she thinks we might steal a box of coloring books if given half a chance.

I've been permitted to ditch the skirt-suits for a sweaterdress, part of the relatability push. It's itchy and too warm. My shoes have already given me a blister. Louboutins, but the stylist painted the soles black so no one would know. I want to sit down, but I don't want to mess up my dress, so I lean against a pile of stacked kids' chairs. I was up at five to get hair and makeup. Blowout, curling iron, hairspray, concealer, foundation, more concealer, eyeshadow, blush, contour, highlighter, setting spray, eyeliner, mascara, lip liner, lipstick.

It's just a rally, I remind myself. A rally like any other rally. All those other rallies ended, so this one will end, too, soon enough. Soon enough, I'll drive away.

"Jess?" It's Phoebe, apologetic. "Sorry, but we're about to start."

The room has emptied out, without me even noticing. I straighten. "Okay."

She's standing between me and the door. I wait for her to move aside, but she doesn't. Her smile grows more apologetic.

"Can you—?" She twirls her finger.

"Oh! Sorry." I turn around so she can check my panty line.

When I walk onto the stage, the first thing I notice is the audience. Namely, how small it is. At least half of the chairs are empty. This happens sometimes at rallies. Sometimes they book a space that's too large, sometimes there's a basketball game people don't want to miss. I scan the rows for faces I know, but I'm a little dizzy and they are all too far away. All I see are lines of identical pink ovals. My stomach feels like a black hole. Still, if all the different weird parts of my life have taught me one lesson, it is how to move through panic and come out the other side with no one knowing.

That's one thing being poor and being rich have in common. They both teach you how to smile when you don't mean it.

So I take the microphone off the stand and turn it on as if I have been doing it all my life, and I smile so widely I can feel the lipstick stretching on my lips, and I read my speech off the teleprompter without even registering the words.

"—my husband, Teddy Wieland!"

The applause alerts me that I'm done. Teddy walks out, waving. The room comes a little more to life, responding to his charm. I hand him the microphone. I recede.

When Mike said I'd be a good surrogate, I thought he meant they wanted a stand-in, someone to be where Teddy could not. That isn't really what they want. They don't want me to vanish entirely. They want me to vanish selectively, maintaining the parts any particular audience needs at any given time. Reduce myself to a word or two. Every other quality can bleed away. At a Planned Parenthood fundraiser, I am a woman. At a DAR luncheon, I am a wife. In a mill town, I am poor white trash, and I can make even a man like Teddy Wieland seem poor by association. Not too poor. Just the right amount. I am the human equivalent of a TV-ready quarter-zip, an outline someone else can fill in.

Now that I'm not talking, I examine the crowd more carefully. It's even smaller than I realized. There are big empty spaces at the sides and back of the auditorium. The whole point of me coming here was to bring people out. Come gawk at the local girl made good. All the nights I've spent stressing about this moment add up to, what, fifty extra bodies in a room?

Teddy's speech starts as usual. Even better than usual, actually. He sounds at ease, genuinely at home. He talks about how beautiful the town is, how wonderful it is to see everyone. We are all here for the same reason, he says: because we all believe in a greater vision for America. He starts in on the stump speech, threading the talking points on like beads on a string. The mill closing, the need for more jobs, coming together to battle climate change.

He is well into the section on the opioid crisis when I realize why the speech sounds more natural. The change is subtle; it would be easy to miss if you don't know his voice like I do, if you haven't felt that voice strumming all along your body, all temperatures, all times of day. Even though Teddy and Clara grew up on the island, they have always spoken with the clear tones of the modern New England upper crust. Boarding school and college smoothed their voices even more, until you would be hard-pressed to say they have any accent but money. Now Teddy's voice has shifted. His *r*'s have softened. The final *g*'s on his words have slid away. He's speaking in a midcoast Maine accent. My accent.

I stare at him in earnest, not merely as a matter of blocking, but out of genuine surprise. Does he know he's doing that? Is it unconscious?

"I will protect you," he says, and I snap to attention. He's at the end of his speech. The part where he vows to make changes. He leans forward into the lights and he tells the crowd, with total conviction, "If you send me to Washington, I won't take no for an answer. I will get you everything you deserve."

He ends with a final pound of his fist against the podium, then steps back toward me for our usual wave. A victory gesture. I forgot this move was coming, and when he seizes my hand and raises it high in the air with his own, my head tilts back automatically, watching our hands rise without any effort from me. My nails are shiny pastel mirrors, reflecting the camera flashes popping in the background. My cuticles are wrangled, my skin soft and smooth. Teddy's hand grips mine tightly, at once familiar and strange.

When all is said and done and donated, we congregate outside by the back door and wait for the cars to be brought around. The sky has started to darken. The parking lot looks north up Bates Street, toward Mount Katahdin in the distance, a looming slab, a giant turned on its side. Its sides are streaked blue with valleys and fog. The pure white ridge seems to extend forever, creating its own horizon.

For years, I've been terrified by the thought of this place. For days, I've been dreading my return. And yet now that I'm here, now that it's done, the dread hasn't left. My muscles won't release. I still feel tense, tight, jittery. I'm not thinking about my mom or my dad or the people in this town. I'm thinking about Teddy's long vowels, and Clara's scream, and how thin it seems now, the world I made for myself, or rather, the world they made for me.

The top of that ridge on Katahdin is so narrow they call it the Knife Edge. Every year, the Knife Edge takes a few lives—overconfident tourists in bad gear, perhaps a few skilled hikers who have an unlucky day. I thought I was born with my fear of heights, but now I wonder if it comes from growing up with this mountain towering over me, peaceful and deadly, news of bodies draped like broken dolls over implacable granite. It's good for fear to have a reason, right? It makes it more noble.

"Fuck!" Teddy shouts.

I spin around to see my husband staring down at his sweater. Across the front, just to the side of the flag pin, is a huge glob of white foam. Spit.

The guy the spit belongs to is standing right across from him, grinning with satisfaction. He's maybe six-six, burly and bald. Teddy usually has a way of seeming taller than everyone in his vicinity, no matter their height, but next to this guy he looks surprisingly small and embarrassingly kempt. It's like a magic act gone wrong; one where the handkerchief has slipped too early, and the schtick has been revealed.

Teddy takes a step forward. His voice drops low. "You mother-fucking—"

But the bodyguards are already between him and the man, pushing the man away, holding Teddy back. Everyone is looking now, the staffers and interns and drivers, and a few people on the sidewalk who have stopped to watch the commotion. Quickly, Mike puts his arm around Teddy's shoulders and steers him back into the school.

"What happened?" I ask Phoebe. She shrugs helplessly.

A staffer leans in. "Phoebe, I think that girl might have filmed it."

The girl in question is a teenager in leggings who slides her phone back into the pocket of her puffer jacket. Phoebe immediately starts walking toward her. The girl sees her coming and scurries down the sidewalk. Phoebe pursues. Another bystander whips out another phone and films the chase.

The staffer steers me into a car so I'm not in the middle of the mayhem. I hike up my skirt and sit sideways, my feet dangling out the open passenger door. I have a feeling no one will notice any wrinkles now.

The school is still illuminated, so I can see straight down the hallway. The wall is decorated with projects from a mishmash of holidays: green pipe-cleaner trees, cotton-ball lambs of God. Teddy walks into view, mopping at the wet front of his sweater with a paper towel. His face is a growl. Mike pulls him over to the side. They start talking intensely. Teddy makes a violent slashing gesture. He motions to his sweater, obviously talking about the spit. Mike responds firmly. Presses a hand to his shoulder. Calming him, which used to be my job. Which I thought was still my job.

Teddy shrugs him off, and Mike raises his hands in surrender and walks away. Teddy rakes his hand through his hair and turns toward the window. His mouth is a flat line. I wave, as if to say *I'm here*, but there's no way he can see me; I'm too far away, and he's the one in the light.

Again down I-95, 395, 1A. Again through Ellsworth, and Trenton, and over the causeway. I'm so sick of this drive. Teddy was supposed to make more calls to donors, but he doesn't touch his phone. He barely speaks for the entire two hours. His sweater is pilled with remnants of the paper towel he used to rub at the spit.

When we cross onto the island, I reach over to rest my hand on his thigh. His muscle tenses under my hand, as if he would flinch away, if there were anywhere to go.

"You okay?" I ask.

"I'm fine."

I try to lighten the mood. "Good thing you have ten more of that sweater."

"It isn't about the sweater," Teddy says.

Obviously. I retract my hand.

We look out our respective windows. We're on an anonymous stretch of road, a spindly guardrail with darkness beyond. A meadow or a lake. At night, they're indistinguishable from one another, or from coves or mountains or yards. It bothers me that I can't figure out where we are. I know every inch of this island, this road. I crane my neck, trying to see farther down the road for a street sign, a familiar bend.

"I'm going to tighten the May Day party," Teddy says.

I turn away from my window, even though it's too dark to see much of anything about his face. "Tighten it how? It's only three hours. That's not so long."

"I mean tighten the guest list. Maybe fifty people."

"What? That makes no sense."

"It's smart, actually," he says, getting excited. "Mike has been wanting us to do an event at the house. So we'll make it a campaign event. May Day, but smaller."

I shake my head. "May Day is public. You can't just uninvite people."

"Why not? It's my property."

"It's a tradition."

"Yes, my family's tradition."

Our family, I think. Out of the corner of my eye, I see a low brown fence. The Hubert property. I'm okay. I know where we are.

"The party's only a few days away. It's too late to cancel," I tell Teddy.

"Well, if people want to come ogle my house, maybe they shouldn't spit on me."

"*They* didn't spit on you. One person spit on you."

"It's a safety consideration," he says.

I decide to play along. "So how are you going to limit the guest list? Who are you going to keep versus disinvite?"

"We'll invite politicians, people with influence. People who understand our situation." He bares his teeth. Or perhaps it's a smile. "People who matter."

"You sound like an asshole."

"No, I sound like someone trying to keep his family safe."

"Safe from what? Spit?" It's the wrong thing for me to say, which I know even as I say it, and I'm not surprised when Teddy glowers. "We host this party every year. Why don't you just have a security check at the gate if you're so concerned?"

"Why are you arguing with me about this?" he asks.

"How can you not see the problem? Everyone's already calling you an elitist. Canceling a public event *for the island* so you can invite a bunch of millionaires to eat canapés is only going to make it worse."

"No one even knows about May Day outside of the island."

I'm used to Teddy being stubborn, but not stupid. "Islanders know about it. That's who we have to live with after your campaign is over."

"So you don't think I'll win."

"I didn't say that."

We've reached Vantage Point. The private road is a black tunnel fringed with fog.

"It's safer like this. If something bad happens at the party," Teddy says, "it's on my head. I'm a Wieland."

"So am I."

He pauses. "Right."

I try to tell myself the pause doesn't mean anything. It's just a pause, a gap. A hole in the road. There could be anything behind it.

But I recognize Teddy the same way I recognize the road. Even in the dark, I know what the pauses mean.

26

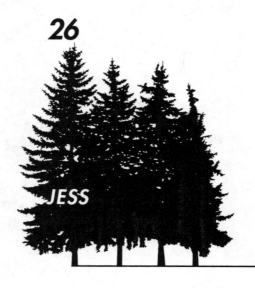

JESS

Five years ago

When our wedding was over, Teddy and I were not yet married. It was a logistical thing. We had decided to have the ceremony in Aix-en-Provence, because in Teddy's circle you can simply spin a globe and invite people to wherever your finger lands, and they'll come. After we sent the save-the-dates, we discovered that getting married in France involved thirty days of residency and an insane amount of paperwork. We intended to get our license beforehand, but then there was a delay with the prenup, and eventually Teddy suggested we wait until after the honeymoon. No need to tell our guests.

Sure, I said. What was three weeks, in the context of a lifetime? I didn't expect the formality to bother me. I didn't expect it to follow me, as it did, all along our honeymoon. The formality stalked me through the lavender fields of Provence and up the hills of Portofino. It swam alongside our yacht, slippery and playful, rejoicing in the waves. It oozed cherry-red from the layers of each congratulatory cake.

The last leg of our trip was at the Hôtel de Paris in Monaco. Our suite was named after a princess who had died young, after marrying into a cursed family. I considered asking to switch rooms, but it would have meant downgrading.

The room was beautiful. Everything in it was shades of white or tan. Cream, ecru, eggshell, biscuit. The fancy kinds of beige. The air duct emitted a gentle hum: even the noise was white.

Teddy rounded the marble coffee table, big as a tomb, dropping his wallet on it as he went. He headed for the French doors that led onto the balcony and threw them open. The sunlight rushed in, along with the muted sounds of traffic down in the casino's court-yard. The air smelled like the ocean, but from the week we had spent on the yacht, and the two nights in Portofino, I knew this ocean was not the same as the one I had grown up on. This ocean was clean, warm, predictable. You could see through it. You could see every-thing it held.

"Well!" He stuffed his hands into the pockets of his linen pants and slouched like an Armani model, surveying the view. "We made it!"

"We made it," I agreed.

He didn't seem to have noticed the room, which was par for the course. He was accustomed to French linens and silk carpets and hand-dipped candles. I was starting to grow accustomed, too. I felt mildly guilty about it, but only mildly. After all, it's human nature. Your brain learns your surroundings, so you can notice the aberrations.

While Teddy gazed out at the city, I wandered toward the rest of the colorless suite, which had a dining room and two bedrooms and

walk-in closets. It was bigger than any apartment I had lived in growing up. It was obscene and stunning.

The bathroom was more of the same. Veined white marble floors
and sinks and walls, a white bathtub, a white chair, white soap dis-
penser, and white towels. On two white satin hangers hung two white
robes with discreet white embroidery on the front pocket. *ETW* on
one, for Teddy. The other one said *JPW*, and it took me a moment to
realize that meant me.

Jessica Pleyel Wieland.

I touched the soft embroidery. My hand lingered on the W.
Wieland, not yet my name. Did the hotel people know it was a lie? I
had turned my passport over to them at the front desk. It said *Jessica
Pleyel*. Then again, changing a passport would take time, wouldn't it?
A normal newlywed wouldn't have a new passport, either. Right?

"Okay?" Teddy had come back from the balcony without me noticing. Now he wrapped his arms around my waist, pulled me back
against him. "I'm sure there are plain ones, too, to wear to the spa."

Of course he thought I was concerned that it was conspicuous,
gaudy. That was what a Wieland would worry about. I made a note in
my mind.

"My first monogram," I said. "Those are my initials now."

I said it like that as a challenge, I think. Daring him to argue,
testing to see if he believed it, if he had been thinking about the formality, too.

"Jessica Pleyel Wieland," he agreed, pleased, kissing the skin below my ear.

I relaxed a little, but not enough. He sensed my stiffness. His lips
moved against my neck: "Hey. Are you okay?"

I wanted to tell him what I was feeling. But how could I explain it,
without it sounding like an accusation? I was not worried—not
really—that he was going to change his mind. Teddy never changed
his mind. He never changed; that was what made him so special. He
was solid, stable, unyielding.

"I'm good," I said, turning in his arms. "I'm perfect."

I moved my hands to his shoulders, the nape of his neck. Warm, living creature; my creature. I ran my nails down the length of his back, the soft material of his shirt. His hands skimmed over my ass. Then clenched, lightly, pulling up the hem of my dress, working it over my hips. He took the robe from the hanger and laid it down on the marble floor, and then laid me down on top of it, and we made love in the sunlight, to the gentle sounds of cars and waves, as down in the casino, martinis were poured, cards were dealt, fortunes were traded back and forth.

Afterward, as he dozed, I put the bathrobe on and tied it tight. It didn't help my mood. All this time, I had been yearning for the formality of marriage. Only now did it occur to me that a formality wasn't a guarantee. Formalities could be reversed. The monogram pretended to make my claim to the Wieland name permanent, but in fact it only reminded me that it wasn't. After all, a monogram can be removed so easily: the stitches unpicked, the thread discarded. The fabric pile pressed flat again, blank, as if the letters had never been there at all.

27

CLARA

April 18

Every hour I used to spend reading message board posts about what a disgusting slut I am, I now dedicate to finding out as much information about Conrad as I can. He's a computer guy, so he's better at covering up the address and mortgage-status stuff that normal people forget about erasing, but he isn't invulnerable. From the internet stalker's perspective, he's made two cardinal errors: having a memorable name, and creating a LinkedIn account.

Here is what I cobble together:

Conrad Gaffney was born in Potomac, Maryland, to two bankers who met on the job (their wedding announcement was in *The New*

York Times). He went to Choate, where he ran track and field but never made it past junior varsity (all the team's past records are still public). He went to Harvard, as I already knew. He graduated without distinction, interned at his dad's bank, and then worked a succession of unimpressive jobs at underperforming startups (truly, LinkedIn keeps no secrets).

He stopped updating the LinkedIn about four years ago, which I assume is when he started FinSafe. He's scrubbed any mention of it from his own accounts, but I find a smattering of articles explaining that the company was supposed to use machine learning to produce better forecasts and trades. When I go looking for the blowback he keeps whining about, all I find is a few interviews with people who lost their money when the company tanked, a few threads that call him dumb and selfish. One person says he ran his business like he was taking guidelines from *Start-Ups for Dummies.*

What a terrible insult.

Amazing that he even survived.

A few days into my research, my phone rings. Not many people have my new number, and I hope it's Jess, apologizing, saying come back, let me hear you out. But the caller ID says Donna Shallcross.

"Hello, Clara." Her voice is patient and academic. Going through her inbox after her weekly Zumba session, no doubt. A normal person's morning. "How are you doing?"

"Um." I look at my browser window, open to a news story about a digital artist who exhibited a hologram of a dead pig. "Fine."

"You said to call as soon as I had news. My colleague and I were able to confirm the videos are synthetic. I'm forwarding the full report to you now."

I turn away from my computer, trying to focus. With everything that's happened the past couple days, I honestly forgot she still hadn't officially confirmed that the videos were fake. So I'm surprised by how relieved I feel to have this piece of outside validation. "How could you tell? When you couldn't before."

"Eye movement. That's Dr. Xu's specialty, which is why I looped him in. We compared the control videos you sent—thank you for those—to the sample videos using a program he created that analyzes eye movement patterns. Synthetic videos generally struggle to reproduce blinking rates anyway because they pull from a corpus of photographs in which eyes are generally open, because people usually don't post photos with their eyes closed. Both test videos get quite close to an acceptable range, but they don't match your particular patterns. You're a very rapid blinker," she adds. I think it's supposed to be a compliment.

"Can you tell who made the videos?" I ask.

"That's not my area, unfortunately. All I can say is that the videos are very advanced, so someone must have gone through some trouble." She hesitates. "There is one thing in the report that might be relevant, though."

"What's that?"

"In the paragraph on background imaging, we note that the results of those tests were inconclusive. Meaning we couldn't determine whether the background portions of the videos were genuine or synthetic. For a variety of reasons, the processes we use to decipher human expressions are more advanced than the processes we use to analyze background images. The primary way we test for synthetic static content is to look for deviations from a norm. If there are absolutely no deviations, we still technically call the results inconclusive, because we can't guarantee someone hasn't come up with a better algorithm than us. For example, last year we received a synthetic video from CHG that showed no deviations in our tests, but because we knew ahead of time that it was synthetic, we were able to—"

"Sorry," I interrupt, "but what does that have to do with who made these videos?"

"Oh." She sounds a little affronted to have been cut off. "Well, my point is, even though we can't say this part with any legal certainty, my personal opinion is that these backgrounds are taken from genuine videos. For the first video, that doesn't mean much, because it's just a hotel room. But it's my understanding that the second video took place at your brother's wedding. So whoever made these deep-fakes probably had access to some real video footage from that event."

Teddy and Jess's wedding was enormous. There were literally hundreds of people there, all with cell phones. Conrad was one of them.

But *why*?

"Ms. Wieland?"

"Sorry. I'm . . . processing." I think through the timeline. "How long do the videos take to make?"

"The algorithm and assets would have taken some time to perfect. But once someone has those, they could probably make new videos in a few minutes."

"A few *minutes*?"

"Maybe a couple hours, if the videos needed additional editing," she allows. "But they might not have, with a good algorithm."

"So this person can just keep making them forever."

Dr. Shallcross is tactfully silent. I think not only about the videos, but the holograms, too, a lifetime of fake-mes running around, online and off, convincing people I'm someone other than I am.

"I know it's a lot to take in," she says gently. "Again, if you want me to connect you to that victim support group, I'd be happy to send you that information."

It's depressing to be offered the same solution as before, but before I can get sidetracked by the futility of it all, something clicks in my brain.

"CHG," I say.

"I'm sorry?"

"You mentioned CHG just now. What's that?"

"Oh. It's one of the Silicon Valley start-ups using GANs to develop more advanced deepfakes. I've probably mentioned them to you before. There are a few similar companies."

"What does CHG stand for?"

"I have no idea," she says, baffled. "I think it's someone's initials."

Like—Conrad H. Gaffney.

I say urgently, "Can you compare the videos I sent you to the video you got from them? See if the same person made it?"

"I can try." She sounds doubtful. "But the whole purpose of using GANs is that they're perpetually refining the code and datasets. The video I have from CHG is at least a year old. Their code has probably changed a lot since then. Besides, it's just a small start-up. I don't think many people would have access to their back end."

"But you can try."

"I can try," she agrees.

We hang up, and I check my email. Sure enough, she's already forwarded the full report. It's two pages long, with some detailed paragraphs about testing protocols and methodologies that I don't understand. The valuable thing is what's on the last page of the document: her signature, over an electronic version of the MIT watermark. Bona fides.

She, unlike me, is a reliable source.

My phone beeps with my usual reminder to take my Prilosec. That means it's already five and I haven't eaten anything today. My instinct is that I should either keep going with the starving or eat three boxes of macaroni and cheese in a row, but my instincts are bad. So I drag myself to the kitchen to go through my usual stupid ritual of feeding myself in a normal human way.

There were other anorexics at Marien who now claim they lead completely normal lives. They have whole days where they forget they were ever sick, ever had any food issues at all. Whether or not they're telling the truth, I'm not like that. The only way I can get recovery to stick is the same mental trick that got me in there in the first place: distancing myself from my exterior. I still think of my body as a thing apart from myself. Only now it's a resource I have to maintain to go on living, an animal to feed, a plant to water.

So I do the same boring pattern as always. I open the fridge. I inspect its contents top to bottom, bottom to top. I look at a deli container of potato salad I bought yesterday. I leave it there and take out a box of eggs and some leftover broccoli. I close the fridge. I boil water and put in one single egg. I think about the potato salad. I arrange the broccoli in a crescent on my plate. I spread peanut butter across a rice cake and put it next to it. I'm still thinking about the potato salad. I look at my plate. I open the fridge again. I take out the potato salad and scoop some salad onto my plate. My egg is done. I eat it all standing up, swallowing it as quickly as I can. By the end, I'm emotionally drained.

Jess is right. I am a lot of work.

Later that night, I set up camp on the window seat in my bedroom. I wrap my duvet tightly around myself as I wait, my breath clouding the cold glass. The stars scatter like salt flakes. The moon is round and bright, half-hidden behind a thin cloud. An eyeball with a cataract.

I'm worried nothing will happen. That's what happened last night, and the night before, when I sat up waiting for hours and saw only darkness. Possibly Conrad realized I caught him, and he's decided to stop, which would be a good thing. Except that I need my proof.

Teddy and Jess are still away at campaign events, and I haven't heard from either of them. I sent Teddy a few tentative *how are you* texts, trying to suss out whose side he's on about the holograms, but he didn't reply, which I guess means he's on hers. They've closed ranks.

There's this one moment from their wedding I keep thinking

about. After a dinner I didn't eat, after the dancing had begun, as I sat alone at a table, dissecting a slice of cake, Celeste eased herself into a chair next to me. She was wearing an orange caftan and a sapphire necklace that covered most of her sternum.

"Beautiful couple," she said, which for her was the highest compliment. She nodded to where Teddy was whirling Jess around the dance floor. Jess had changed for the reception, into a silvery fringed dress that sparkled under the lights and exposed her tan back. "Though the first ones never last."

"Celeste!"

"What? Think of your father."

My father had been married before my mother, to a woman named Sharon who had quickly vanished into a sea of alimony. I had never met Sharon and I didn't know much about her other than that in the divorce she had gotten the Aspen house my dad really liked, and he was so bitter about it he never skied Aspen again.

"Jess isn't Sharon," I said. "Look at them. They're so in love."

Celeste was unmoved. "We'll see."

I put down my fork. "You know she's my best friend, right?"

"Not anymore," Celeste said, as Teddy dipped Jess backward over his arm. "Now she's your brother's wife."

I'm snapped out of the memory by a blur of movement in my peripheral vision, through the glass. I turn toward the window—and there they are, standing right in the middle of my lawn.

My parents.

I prepared myself for this moment. I thought I was ready. I thought knowing they were fake would make it easier to stand the sight of them. But if it does, the alleviation is so slight that the difference is barely noticeable. I've still maxed out my heartache. I am all pressure, all hurt, every organ squeezed flat by longing.

My mom raises her hands to her mouth like a megaphone.

"Clara!" she calls toward the house. "Clara, come here."

I want to. I want to go to them. At the sound of their voices, my muscles contract, ready to fling me through the window onto the lawn. It takes everything I have to stay seated, but I do. The only movement comes from my arm as I point my phone toward the lawn and press record.

My dad, more sternly. "Clara! Come here."

Now that I know what I'm looking for, I can see that some things don't make sense. Their shapes are a little too bright for the darkness. The coat my mom's wearing is the same one she was wearing in that famous video of them walking a friend's dog in Beacon Hill, but she hated that coat and never wore it much. It's not what I would associate with her. And my dad would never get impatient in this particular way. When he was angry, he would get quiet for a while, then he would burst out with it, out of nowhere, like he had been saving it up inside.

Or am I splitting hairs? If this were real, and my mom wore that coat, I wouldn't question her. If my dad started shouting louder, I would think maybe he had had a bad day.

There *is* something off about these versions of my parents, but who of us is ever perfectly consistent?

They could be real.

I want them to be real.

I'm crying now, silent gulps while the camera records, and their figures go in and out of focus through the film of my tears.

What does it feel like, to have an illusion broken? It feels like something giving way. Not all at once, not evenly. It's a flood, a burst pipe filling a room. The truth rises. It pushes at the walls from the inside. And, denying, I push back, plugging my fingers into the cracks until my fingers are bruised, then turning and holding the wall with all my weight.

I listen to my parents calling for me, asking me to come.

Clara.

Clara.

Clara: an omen of an easy life.

Finally, they stop shouting.

They lower their hands from their mouths and stare up at the house. Or seem to stare. Because they're only puppets moved by strings of code: lift chin forty degrees, run package "slight squint" on eye area.

And even knowing that, I feel that my parents are staring right at me, through darkness and a pane of glass and sixteen years. Across the plane of death.

On my arm, my tattoo throbs.

They turn to go, and I hear myself whisper, "Wait," because for one instant I don't care if they're real, I want to look at them longer, just a little longer.

But that isn't how any of this works. Fires catch, gravity pulls, animals bite, tides funnel in and smash you to the wall. And my parents disappear the way they've always disappeared: before I'm ready.

They walk away from me. The forest parts for them. They enter. The trees close behind them, like a curtain falling shut across a stage.

My heart is beating out of my chest, but I force myself to watch the video. Yes, I've caught it. There they are. I zoom in and out, play it and pause it. When I'm sure the video's good, I run to the bathroom and throw up. Then I wash my face with cold water until I can't tell clean from tears.

It takes a long time for my grief to reassume its usual shape. The devil I know.

As I dry my chin, I catch sight of myself in the mirror. I lower the washcloth. I look horrific. The parts of my face that should be full are hollow. The parts that should be flat are puffy. My eyes are bloodshot. It's me, but doesn't look like me, as opposed to the visions of my parents, which looked like them but weren't.

I reach toward this other self carefully, my fingers outstretched, as if tempting a wild animal. I don't know what I think will happen. That my reflection won't move with me? That through the mirror I'll find a pulsing body, the hideous suede of human skin? Both. Neither. The border between what's real and what's fake feels so blurry now. Anything could cross over at any time.

When my knuckles bump the glass, I yank away like I've been burned.

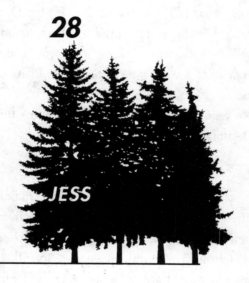

28

JESS

April 22

I agree to do the uninviting for the May Day party. Not because I think it's a good idea, but because Teddy has been acting so strangely that I'm terrified of how he might choose to break the news. *Sorry, we've deemed you unimportant. Apologies, you are too poor.* I wait an entire day to do it, hoping that he'll come to his senses, or that Mike and Phoebe will be able to talk him out of it— they agree with me that it's a terrible look. But no: once again, Teddy has made up his mind. With the help of a condolences template I find in one of my old etiquette books, I draft a disinvitation for the YMCA coordinator to send to the community listserv. I sign my and Teddy's names and I hit send. By the following afternoon, everyone seems to know.

The reaction is more or less what I expected. Lucas Fiorini sends me a message that reads: *I've attended the May Day celebrations for over twenty-five years and am disappointed in your selfishness.* I can't bring myself to feel bad for Mr. Fiorini, who I know to be a bad tipper and handsy with waitstaff. A message from sweet Dana Reynolds hurts a little more. *Is it true about May Day? I was so looking forward to the dahlias. Please let me know if I might visit them another time, as they were Jack's favorite flower before he passed and Paul does excellent work with yours.*

Most people send me no message at all. I know this place well enough to understand that this is the most damning.

The campaign continues to deteriorate. Several major donors politely decline invitations to the new May Day fundraiser. The string of postponements and cancellations unspools. I'm scheduled to host a journalist from a women's magazine, to talk to her about what's in my handbag, and at the last minute she claims she has a burst eardrum and can't fly. A new poll comes out: the health of our marriage is up five, but general opinion of Teddy is down three. Mike grimly fires two staffers. Phoebe is a tumbleweed of anxious energy.

Teddy himself is a nightmare. He communicates—if it can be called communicating—through grunts and sighs, clipped answers, nonanswers. There is no variety, no reprieve. He is a record player stuck repeating the song "Teddy's Worst Mood," and no one can figure out how to lift the needle. The spitting and the heckling and the downward-trending have gotten under his skin more than they should have. More than I thought they would have.

His problem is, he's never had people dislike him before. Not en masse. Not that he knew about. He has never felt himself to be hated, and he doesn't know what to do with it, how to survive it.

That's the only explanation I have for why, the day after we get back from Kattinocket, before his spit-soaked sweater has even been to the dry cleaner, three black cargo vans pull up in the driveway. They park bumper to bumper, like a funeral cortege. Each one has the same small, tasteful gold decal on its front passenger door: DIAMOND SECURITY SYSTEMS. The vans disgorge a collection of beefy men in matching black polo shirts, who somberly install throughout the house what I can only imagine is their entire catalog of products. Cameras upstairs, downstairs, outside. Emergency alert system. Motion sensors. When they're done, the foreman shows me how it all works, where all the cameras are. For the rest of the day, every time I walk into a room with a camera, my eyes go straight to its hiding spot. To someone watching the footage, it would look like one of those fake-documentary sitcoms where the characters keep breaking the fourth wall.

The foreman doesn't say who has access to the footage. I decide it's better not to ask.

On Monday morning, Teddy comes into the kitchen as I'm going through my list of local caterers. It isn't easy to transform a casual party with no invite list into a dinner party for eighty rich snobs on short notice. The usual May Day arrangements were straightforward: tents in case of weather, a sound system, heat lamps, the bar, cleanup. Now we need an actual caterer, and different tents, and better tables and chairs. We need people to stand at the gates and check the guest list.

Most importantly, we need things to look nice, which is easier said than done. The azalea gardens are known for their summer blossoms. Delphiniums, coneflowers, bee balm, sage. But in late April, after a hard winter, the gardens are still underwhelming. Perennials have been pruned to piles of dried sticks. Stems are pebbled with mysterious buds and knobs.

Islanders wouldn't have been surprised by any of this. They know what spring entails. They would have had realistic expectations. But Washington politicians are going to want more than rented tables arranged awkwardly in a barren clearing. I can picture their expressions, the lifted chins, the lips bowed in pity, and it makes me sick to my stomach.

"I'm going to close up the front gates," Teddy announces when he enters.

"Huh?"

"For our safety."

"But we just got the cameras."

"Those are deterrents. This is a barrier," he says with the great authority of someone who has recently fallen down an internet wormhole. I wonder if Mike approves of this use of time.

"Is this about the guy in Kattinocket?" I ask. "Or the hecklers?"

"Someone's been following me," he says.

I frown. "Who? Since when?"

"This short guy with glasses. I don't recognize him. I saw him last week, and again just now, in Axe Harbor."

"And you're sure he's following you?" I ask doubtfully.

"Yes."

"Did you call the police?"

"Yes."

"Without telling me?"

He raises an eyebrow. "I wasn't trying to keep anything from you," he says, in a perfect imitation of me. "Also, I had them put up a camera facing Clara's house. On one of the trees."

"I thought you were done with her," I say.

"I still want to know if she's alive."

"Well, is she?" It's been strange, being home and not seeing her. We've never had such a long fight. Or any fight.

"So far," Teddy says.

The next day, I stop by the campaign office to run catering options by Phoebe, which takes an unexpectedly long time because she's dealing with the unhappy news that the Teamsters have announced they're backing another candidate. They don't think Teddy's a man of the people.

I guess the accent needs some work.

As I'm walking back to my car, someone calls my name. I turn to see Joe Michaud's daughter Sadie jogging down the sidewalk toward me.

Sadie was in my class all through middle and high school, and we waitressed together for two seasons at a hotel restaurant, back in the day. Like a lot of our coworkers, she would sometimes forget I was in earshot and make snide comments about the Wielands, then get nervous when she remembered I was there. I was never going to tell Clara anything they said, of course, but I still hated overhearing. It felt like being handed a document censored with a failing marker, where I could still make out the words I wasn't supposed to know. It was only when I married Teddy that I finally stopped hearing the other side of anything, like they had realized the mistake and gone back over the document a second time. It was such a relief, not to have the temptation to read.

As Sadie slows, I see that her brows are drawn together in a scowl. This is going to be about May Day, I assume. I face her square on.

"Hi, Sadie."

"I heard—" she begins, and I draw myself up tall, a bird under threat. "—about the cameras."

I deflate slightly. "Cameras?" Maybe she means the videos.

"The security cameras you installed at Vantage Point."

I'm not understanding. "We've had some safety issues—"

"My dad's been asking to install a system for you for months," she interrupts. "You promised he could have the job. You didn't even let him *bid* on it."

I shake my head. "That wasn't me. I didn't arrange that."

"Do you know what the install rate on a system like that would be?"

"Like I said, I didn't arrange it."

"For that size property? Ten thousand, easy."

It takes me a beat to realize that the number is supposed to impress me. It doesn't. A few years ago, ten thousand dollars would have seemed like a huge amount to me, too. Enough to pay off a credit card, trade in my car, look for a new job. Now it's a handbag. A coat. Now it's I don't even know what. I haven't seen a credit card bill in years. I'm so used to thinking about the price of things, noticing it even when Teddy and Clara don't, but it turns out over time, I too have grown immune.

Sadie misreads the surprise on my face. "Yeah. It's a lot."

I hitch my bag higher on my shoulder. "I'm sorry, Sadie. Things have been really hectic lately. I didn't think about it."

"Exactly."

I start to regret apologizing. "What do you want me to do? The system's already installed. I can't take it down. Do you want me to apologize to your dad directly?"

"He doesn't want your apology."

"Right. Just my money."

"You mean your husband's money," she says.

There it is. It's always been here, of course. Under every interaction, every polite and impolite exchange. Mike thinks people always like to see upward mobility. But they don't, not always. Not if they think you didn't work for it. Not if they think it should have been them.

"I think you should talk to Clara and Teddy about this," I say.

"I don't need to talk to them. I get why the Wielands don't think about us. They never have. They've never had to. They've always been this way, they've always had all these things. But you have. *You* should think about these things."

I narrow my eyes. "You're saying they should get a pass because they were born with money, but I shouldn't, because I wasn't? How is that fair?"

Sadie shrugs, unmoved.

Back to the house, fuming. I'm turning onto the private road when a large shape looms up in front of me. I slam on the brakes. The force tosses me forward like a rag doll; the seat belt locks against my chest, knocking the breath out of my lungs. The car squeals to a stop a few inches from iron bars.

The gates are closed.

Rubbing my sternum where the seat belt cut into it, I lean over the steering wheel and peer up through the windshield. There's a chain and motor on each gate. Behind me, a keypad with an intercom sticks up on a pole from the ground.

Right. I put my car into reverse and back up to the keypad. I try a couple possible combinations: Teddy's birthdate, Clara's, mine. None of them works, so I press the intercom button. There's a squawk of static, then silence. What happens if no one's there to answer? Do I have to drive back to the campaign office, beg my husband for the codes to get into my own house?

I notice for the first time that there's a design wrought in the iron. I've never seen it before, because I've never seen the gates closed. Now it's obvious. At the seam where the gates meet, the curlicues form a large, intricate W. The family seal. A perfect match to Clara's tattoo.

"Jess!"

I shriek. My foot comes off the brake, and the car jolts forward. I brake again and put the car in park. Clara is standing just inside the gates, waving at me. She's holding a Popsicle, of all things, as if it isn't fifty-five degrees and cloudy.

I haven't seen her since Teddy and I got back from Kattinocket. It is neither accidental nor intentional. I didn't want to seek her out until I was calm, and I haven't been calm.

I roll down my window.

"What's the code?" I ask. "For the gate."

She shakes her head. "I forget."

"Clara."

She shrugs. "Looks like you forgot, too."

There's something off about her. Then again, there's always something off about her. I grit my teeth. "There's probably a motion sensor on that side. Can you go wave your arms around so it'll open?"

She tilts her head. Licks the Popsicle. "What'll you give me?"

"What will I *give* you?"

I feel like I'm arguing with a child. Maybe it's the Popsicle.

"I'm not going to give you anything," I say. "Let me in."

A mournful sigh. "Teddy's right. You're so demanding."

With that, she turns and walks away. Not down the road, where the motion might open the gate, but into the woods, her shining hair disappearing into the pines.

"Clara!" I shout. I lean half out my window. "Come back! I need to get in!"

I jam the intercom button once, twice. *Demanding.* Surely she made that up. Teddy can't have said it. I never make any demands. But now she's put the idea in my mind, made it something I need to consider and reject.

Finally, a staticky voice comes on. "Hello?" Stephanie, I think.

"It's Jess. Can you buzz me in?"

When I get to the house, I jump out of the car and slam the door hard enough to echo off the trees. As I storm up the front path, a splotch of purple catches my eye. Crocuses, a clump of six or seven, near the steps. I stop to stare at them. They must have been growing for a while: green stems jackknifing up through rain-swollen dirt, white roots slithering down into the soil. But this is the first time I've noticed them, and to me it seems like they've popped out of the ground fully formed.

I reach down and pluck the biggest one. The stem doesn't snap easily. I have to pull and twist and wring its neck until it rips free from the cluster and lies in my palm. The stem is bruised a darker green where my fingers strangled it. Otherwise, it's perfect. The plummy petals. The secret, soft orange heart. I'll put it in water, and it will be beautiful for days. If you take care of it right, even a dead thing can look alive.

29

CLARA

April 23

The lobby of the Brenner is busy. Technicians slap their key cards against the turnstile to get to the labs. An administrator puts up a poster for an upcoming talk on the desalination of the Northern Atlantic. A school group meanders across an elaborate floor mosaic of whales and dolphins. One dolphin's tail has a W inlaid in mother-of-pearl, a tribute to my father, who commissioned the mosaic twenty years ago.

I wait for the elevator with three scientists in matching wire-rimmed glasses. Their eyes dart around: toward me, away, toward each other. I can't tell if it's the usual stares (*a Wieland, in the flesh*) or a result of the first video (*that poor slut*) or the second (*elitist bitch*) or some other catastrophe I have yet to learn about. I haven't been keeping abreast of all my public failures. I've been too busy with other things, like bluffing my way through scientific papers about hologram refraction angles and googling Conrad until my fingers bleed, trying to piece together when he must have started this, and why he decided to target me. Somewhere around the fortieth page of search results, it occurred to me that his original application for WFCI funds might contain more information. I couldn't find a copy anywhere on my computer, but the grant applications are all archived on the WFCI shared drive.

On the building's fifth floor, the WFCI offices are mostly empty. The receptionist's chair springs upright as soon as I beep myself in.

"Hi," she says quickly, dropping her nail file. A soapy teen drama plays on her computer monitor. "Sorry, it's been a slow day—"

"It's fine." I shrug off my coat, trying to figure out what feels different about the room. "Is the heat still acting up?"

"On and off."

"Let me guess: on when I'm here, off when I'm not."

The receptionist looks guilty. I don't think she's responsible for the heating crises, but I bet she's put in a few calls to facilities herself the past few days, begging for a pardon. *I'm an innocent bystander! Your problem is with Clara, and she hasn't been in for days!*

My office is the same as I left it, simultaneously cluttered and impersonal. I sweep some manila folders off my desk and sit down at my computer, jiggling the mouse to wake the screen.

I find the backup drive quickly. It's well organized—Allan's doing, of course, not my own. The folder *Grant Applications* is further divided by funding round and then by applicant. I scroll until I get to the Ns. *Native Plant Restoration Project, New England Lobstermen's Fund* . . . Nothing about NatureEye. I scroll back up, looking for CHG. Nothing there, either. I go back to the top and read every single folder title, clicking into anything that sounds even vaguely related (*Parks*

Sightseeing Tours, Community Whale Watching). Nothing. I start running searches for *NatureEye, CHG, Conrad, holograms, projections,* but those turn up no results at all.

I lean back in my chair. There should be *some* information there. At the very least, the original packet, as unhelpful as it was. So someone must have gone through and deleted it, but hardly anyone else has access to those files. The receptionist, and Allan, and Teddy.

Allan is in his office, hunched over his computer with what looks like a lengthy journal article pulled up on the screen. The binders on the shelves over his desk are neatly labeled. He has exactly one family photo. I knock, and he pivots his knees slowly toward the door as he finishes reading the paragraph.

When he finally looks up, his face shifts from concentration to surprise. "Hi, Clara. I didn't know you were in today."

"Just briefly. I had a question for you."

He looks relieved. "About the May Day party?"

"No." I frown. "Why? Is something wrong?"

"Well, usually I help the library run a donation table at the event," he says awkwardly, "but now that no one's invited, we don't know how it'll work. Are you not going to have the table at all?"

"What do you mean, 'now that no one's invited'?"

"We got an email saying the event was canceled for a scheduling conflict."

"Who's 'we'?"

"Everyone. The whole town." He blinks. "You didn't know?"

"I haven't been very involved in the planning this year," I say uneasily. "Can you show me the email?"

He does. It's short and formal. The signature reads *With best wishes, The Wieland Family.* The return address is no-reply@wfci.org. It's well within Conrad's capabilities to send a fake email. But something about the wording strikes me. The distant phrasing. The *With* before *best wishes.* The capitalized *T.* It sounds a lot like Jess.

"Annie Schumacher says Jess booked a tent rental for that night,"

Allan says, watching my face. "For a campaign event instead? Maybe we could put the table for the library there? They really need the money to upgrade their catalog system."

"I'll talk to Teddy about it," I promise.

He nods, though he still looks worried. "What was your question?"

I hook two fingers onto the doorframe, channeling my tension there, and try to sound casual. "I was looking for something in the old grant applications folder, and I can't find it. Have you done anything in that folder?"

"No. But it's organized by the organization's name."

"I know. The organization isn't listed."

He tucks his chin. "Did you try alternate names?"

"Yes. You didn't delete anything?"

"I would never," he says stuffily. "What are you looking for?"

"The application from NatureEye. The VR system for the national parks. They use holograms to make people think they're in nature."

"I don't remember that one."

"You weren't at the presentation, it was just Teddy and me."

With a sigh, Allan turns back to his computer, gesturing for me to join him. His first contribution is to type NatureEye into the search bar. God, people must really think I'm an idiot.

"It's not here," he concludes. "Maybe there's a copy in the physical filing cabinet?"

"I checked there."

"And you're sure it was called NatureEye?"

"I'm sure."

"I just feel like I would have remembered seeing the word *holograms*," he says. "That's not the type of proposal we usually get."

I can explain the files going missing from the hard drive—Conrad might have hacked it. I can explain them going missing from the filing cabinet—Conrad could have cloned a key card and snuck in, maybe messed with the building's security cameras. But Allan not remembering it is weird. Allan is always on top of everything. He reads all the grant applications carefully, even if he can't attend the presentation, and he has a great memory. He would probably be running this place himself, if he had my last name.

Out in the parking lot, the air has the clean smell of fog shifting into rain. The lot is spidered with frost heaves, hilly ruptures where winter ice has swelled the soil beneath the asphalt and cracked it open like an egg. Spring comes, the ice melts back into the earth, the lines remain. Nature's stretch marks. There are a decent number of cars here today, and it seems to take me forever to reach mine. Inside, I turn the heat up to high.

The only other person who I know saw the application was Teddy. My copy came from him. So either Teddy went into the drive and deleted the files, or he never put them there in the first place. Both are weird. Suspicious, even.

On the boat, Conrad said *I was counting on a big influx of cash.* I thought he meant he was overconfident. But maybe there was a reason he was counting on it.

Maybe he trusted someone in particular to follow through.

My stomach turns.

I scroll through my contacts until I reach "Business Manager Rebecca." Rebecca has worked for us for a decade, but I've met her maybe five times. Our relationship is conducted almost entirely by FedEx. She sends me things, I sign them.

When she picks up, her surprise is evident. "Clara. Is everything okay?"

"Everything's fine. I had one quick question. Kind of random." I clear my throat. It feels like I've swallowed a bag of sawdust. "Could you tell me if Teddy ever considered investing with a company called FinSafe?"

A long pause. "I'm so sorry, but that's confidential information. I can't tell you anything about Teddy's personal investments."

"Even just whether or not he discussed it?"

"No. I'm sorry."

I rub my throat, trying to dislodge the powdery feeling. This was a dumb idea. Why would I think I could figure this whole thing out on my own? Everyone is obviously shocked to discover I have any individual brain cells at all.

"Okay," I say, defeated. "Thanks."

I move to hang up, but Rebecca stops me, her voice hopeful, eager to help. "Do you want me to send you *your* records on FinSafe?"

My finger stops just shy of the button. "*My* records?"

"Yes, regarding your potential investment."

I lean closer to the speaker, thinking I've misheard. "I invested in FinSafe?"

"You were considering it, back when Teddy was signing things for you. You decided not to move ahead. Those records are in your name, so those would be fine for me to send over."

Undoing an illusion is like peeling off your own skin. Logic says you shouldn't. It will hurt when it's removed. It will have consequences.

But I was born with tragic curiosity. The irrepressible desire to pick at a hangnail, pull at the skin, see where it ends, see where the pain will lead. That's human, isn't it? We want to know what happened. We want to know why.

"Sure." My voice is faint. "Yes. Please send them along."

Forum Discussion: Politics & Current Events

New Teddy Wieland video

@PoliMath72: Have you guys seen this?

TRENDING NEWS FOR APRIL 24: New video appears to show Senate candidate using hard drugs, burning $100 for fun

> *Teddy Wieland's beleaguered senatorial campaign has encountered a new obstacle with yet another controversial video. Unlike the past two videos that have made headlines, this one features Mr. Wieland himself and apparently dates to his college days at Harvard University. In the video, he can be seen snorting white powder with the assistance of a hundred-dollar bill, which he then lights on fire.*
>
> *"This behavior is entirely out of keeping with the Harvard ethos," said Anthony Milhurst Daiman, the current Harvard University president.*
>
> *"Of course I think this will affect Wieland's campaign," said pollster Karina Trowbridge. "Maine is a blue-collar state with a significant opioid problem. Voters are not going to respond well to reckless drug use, and certainly not to the cavalier treatment of money. Plus, we've gotten three leaked videos in three weeks. I'm starting to think this is just the tip of the iceberg."*

Thoughts?

> **@Mundoutin:** Personally, I've always thought Teddy Wieland seemed like a sack of shit. I'm glad we finally have proof.

30

CLARA

April 24

It's going to be one of those days where the fog sticks like Velcro. When I park in Teddy's driveway around noon, the light is still milky and thin. Mist hovers low over the ground. Moss glows with water. It's a setting out of a fairy tale, but not the kind with a happy ending.

I haven't even raised my hand to knock when the door opens, and there's my brother, a big looming shape in the doorway. I've been following the headlines online—*Wieland Heir Tumbles in Polls, Discord in Wieland Senate Campaign*, and then the new video this morning, cocaine scandal for breakfast!—but it's been a week since I saw him in person. It feels like much longer, long enough that the news clips I've been watching seem more real than he does. Like he was brought to life from the computer screen, rather than the other way around.

"Hi, Clara," he says flatly. He braces one hand on the doorframe and keeps the other on the door handle, filling the gap, as if he doesn't want to let me in. I register the lack of surprise on his face, then the new security camera mounted over the doorway. That's why he was already at the door. He saw I was here and came to intercept me.

I wasn't necessarily expecting a warm welcome—he hasn't responded to my texts in days—and I figured whatever happens next might get unpleasant, anyway. Still, I wasn't prepared for the stony expression on his face. I expected him to be wary or dismissive, not outright angry. But that's the danger with these holograms, isn't it? He probably thinks I've done something I haven't.

I tuck my manila folder tighter under my arm and lift my chin. "I want to talk to you."

He starts to step forward, I think to herd me back onto the porch. I come forward, too, and block him, pressing my hand against his chest. It's solid. He looks down in surprise, like the hero does in a movie when he discovers he's been stabbed.

"Inside," I add.

He glances out at the yard and does some internal calculation before he finally steps back, letting me in.

The house is very quiet. He leads me through it like I've never been there. Like we didn't skid down this hallway in our socks as kids, or shake hands with sharklike mourners in the dining room. I watch the nape of his neck, his freshly clipped hair. This is my brother. This is my brother.

It's harder to tell from behind.

He leads me past the kitchen and two living rooms and the nook with the red armchair, places where we've talked many times before—places that belong to us both, in memory and in name. He's making a statement, setting a boundary. Except the boundary goes straight through our shared territory; so is it a boundary or a chasm?

He leads me to the study, which looks the same as it did when our dad was alive. Same wood paneling, tinted faintly orange with age. Same mediocre landscape of Linnet Pond, done by our dad's third cousin Jennette before she turned herself into subway goop. The same oxblood leather sofa, crackled pink at the corners. Walls still lined with Dad's ships-in-bottles. Some are a foot long, some are only a few inches tall. The *Transformation* in its glass case, right by the door.

I guess this is an embalming, too.

There is one new addition I haven't seen before: a big TV, mounted in the corner and turned so you can see it from Teddy's desk. I focus on it, because it has no memories attached. "When did you get that?"

Teddy barely glances at it. "Recently." He crosses to sit behind our dad's desk. No, Teddy's desk. Leather creaks as he drops into the chair. He gestures for me to sit in one of the green velvet armchairs across from him. Like I'm a guest, a penitent. It doesn't feel good to do his bidding. But why would I resist this, so small in the scheme of things? I sit on the very edge of the chair. I press on my knee to stop it from shaking.

"I heard you uninvited the town from the May Day event," I say.

"Not everyone. Only the excess."

Excess. I hate that word. I've heard it so much. Excessive calories. Excessive thinking. Clara, you're doing too much. Too little.

"Isn't everyone excess?" I counter. "No one is *essential*."

"How philosophical."

Teddy seems intent on riling me up, and he's succeeding. I'm ready to brawl. My strings pulled, my buttons pressed. I make myself rein it in.

"I thought," I say slowly, "the point was that we open the doors to people who don't usually get to come in."

"'We'?" he repeats. "When was the last time you planned any of it?"

I ignore that. "The library is supposed to be raising money for a new catalog system. Who's going to run the table if no one's invited?"

"There's not going to be a library table."

"Why not?"

"It'll distract the campaign donors."

"You think people aren't going to donate money to your Senate campaign because they're going to spend it all on the Chaumont Harbor library?"

"It's about messaging. We can't have a separate fundraiser at a campaign event."

"Teddy, you can't turn May Day into a campaign event just because you feel like it."

He shrugs. Meaning: *It's already done.*

His coldness is deliberate and unrelenting. This doesn't seem like Teddy, but I touched him, so it must be him. The light is better in here, and I notice the lines around the corners of his eyes. Laugh lines, but he isn't laughing. This was supposed to be the easy part of the conversation.

"That's not going to look good in the press," I say.

He lifts an eyebrow. "Do you know a lot about what looks good in the press?"

"I know a lot about what looks bad."

Footsteps in the hallway, quick, running. Jess appears in the door, a little out of breath. "Teddy, I heard the door sensor and I think Clara's—"

"Here," he interrupts. "She's right here."

She blinks. I give a dry little wave. Her lips tighten.

It hurts to see her, to a degree I didn't anticipate. *You're so much work.* Her hair is done, the curls loose and shiny around her shoulders, and she's in full makeup, poreless and contoured. She's wearing a weird outfit, sweater and pearls on top, but sweatpants on bottom. A Zoom interview, I guess, something where she only had to look perfect from the waist up. On one foot she has a blue sock and on the other foot she has a white one with stripes. Mismatched socks are very unlike Jess.

I get up from the chair, walk over to her. She rears back slightly, like she thinks I might hurt her. Normally if I wanted to touch her, I'd hug her, or nudge her with my elbow, or loop her arm through mine. None of those seem right, under the circumstances. I brush my hand over her shoulder, just enough to feel the cashmere of her sweater graze my palm. It comes with a static shock. The hairs on my arm go up, and I drop my hand.

"What are you doing?" she asks, confused.

"Clara came to yell at us about May Day," Teddy tells Jess.

I pull myself together. "No, that isn't why I came." I set the folder down on his desk with a flourish. "I want to talk to you about the deepfake videos. I have proof that they're deepfakes. I talked to a professor at MIT and she ran tests on them."

I open the folder and take out the report from Dr. Shallcross. I place it face up on the desk in front of Teddy. Exhibit A.

Reluctantly, Teddy leans forward to read it. Jess comes to look over his shoulder.

I explain about the algorithms, the tests they ran, the blinking rates. I'm proud of myself. My voice shakes, but not as badly as I thought it would. I only use a few *ums* and *likes*. Not that it matters. I don't think Teddy's really listening to me. His eyes skim the letter. He flips it over and keeps reading before I'm done talking about the first page, so I stop talking altogether and wait for him to finish.

As he reads, he rolls a fountain pen back and forth across the desk. *Click-roll-click* as the clip hits the wood. *Click-roll-click.*

The wait makes me jittery. The nearest bookshelf still holds all our dad's most prized books—his first editions, his signed copies—as well as some trinkets with sentimental value. I run my finger over the cold curve of a trophy shaped like a globe. The latitude and longitude lines are etched into the jade marble, and I trail my finger along the Atlantic Ocean until I find where we are.

"Stop that," Teddy says.

I snatch back my hand, then am annoyed at myself for doing so. The globe belongs to me as much as Teddy.

Tucking my hand into my pocket, I nod toward the letter. "You can release that to the press. She said that's fine. You can include it if you make a statement saying the videos are deepfakes. Which I assume you're going to do now, with the new video out."

I don't need Shallcross to test that one to know it's fake, too. Teddy might have done coke a couple times in college, but he wouldn't light money on fire. He'd be too aware of how it would be perceived.

Which is why this whole May Day thing is so confusing.

"We already have a press release planned," Teddy says. "But fine."

I wait for more. *Thank you. Great work.* But he only slides the letter over to the side, then goes back to rolling the pen. *Click.* And back. *Click.* I want to rip it out of his hand and hurl it through the window.

"There's something else," I say steadily. "And I do know it sounds crazy, so hear me out. It's about the holograms."

"What holograms?" Teddy asks.

I look at Jess. Jess looks at Teddy.

She didn't tell him.

I was sure she would have told him. I don't know what it means that she didn't.

I say, "The other night, when I said I saw Mom and Dad outside, I wasn't going crazy. I wasn't dreaming. What I saw were holograms. Like those deepfakes"—I gesture toward the letter—"but in 3D. It's the same VR technology Conrad was talking about, in his presentation for WFCI."

Teddy covers his eyes. "Clara . . ."

"I have proof!" I add quickly. "I didn't come without proof." I open the folder again and take out the next page. "This is a screenshot from a video I took the other night. Look. See?" I point at the figures. Our dad's face, then our mom's. It isn't the clearest image. It didn't film well, being night, being through a window and across a distance, and the graininess and the odd wavering quality of filming a hologram made the whole thing look strange. But you can tell it's our parents, and that's the important part.

Behind Teddy, Jess straightens. Teddy hasn't even fully lifted his hand from his face.

"I have the whole video—" I take out my phone, hurrying to load it. I press play and turn the phone toward him. Together, we hear the crinkle of my blanket, the murmur of voices.

Teddy barely glances at the phone. "And how am I supposed to know that's real? Since you're so obsessed with deepfakes now."

I start to laugh. Then I realize he's not joking. The laugh dies with a creak. "Of course I didn't fake it. I mean . . . come on. I wouldn't do that."

There's a charged silence, like someone's hit pause on an interrogation tape. I glance over at Jess. She's watching the phone, chewing her lip, but she doesn't say anything.

My face heats. I should have anticipated this. Obviously I know how easily videos can be faked. I just didn't expect that Teddy and Jess would think *I* would fake one.

In my most measured voice, I say, "This is me—Clara. Standing in front of you. I'm telling you this is what I saw the other night. I filmed it in my backyard."

"Okay," Teddy says, the way you agree with a child to get them to shut up.

My chest is tight and hot. I did this in the wrong order. I should have started with the information about Conrad. I wanted to tell everything in the order I learned it, I thought that would make it more convincing. I was sure that if I could organize it correctly, and say it correctly, and if I had evidence, good evidence, then they would believe me. I thought that would be enough to outweigh my track record.

The video is still playing. My parents' voices call out from the tiny speaker. *Clara, Clara*—

"Clara," Jess murmurs. I wish they would stop doing that. Stop saying my name like it's a reprimand.

I pause the video. I keep talking, even though my voice wobbles a little. "And he's been making holograms of me and Jess and probably you, too, making us think we see each other doing things."

"Oh fucking hell," Teddy says.

"I'm serious! Remember that night at the Anchor? In the alley? Jess told me the other day she hasn't been to the Anchor in months. She said she saw me buying binge foods, but I haven't been to the grocery store in months." I glance at Jess for confirmation. She looks dumbfounded and a little angry. Definitely not like she's rushing to my defense. So I barrel on, "Anything out of character you've seen me do the past few weeks, it *wasn't me*."

Teddy says, "You mean like running onto our lawn screaming that you saw Mom and Dad?"

"Well—no. That was me," I admit. His mouth is a flat line. I'm losing control of the situation. If I ever had it. "You remember Conrad's presentation, right?"

"*I* don't have any memory problems," Teddy says.

"Those projection strips? I found one on the front lawn. I showed it to Jess right after I found it, she can tell you."

Teddy swivels his chair slightly toward Jess. She pales.

"I didn't—" she begins, then breaks off. She gives me a pleading look like *Stop talking*.

"You wanted to know why Conrad would do it," I remind her. "Well, look." I scramble for the last printout in the folder, the notes

Rebecca sent me after our conversation, and slide it toward Teddy. "I talked to Rebecca about FinSafe. She told me that when I was at Marien last time, when you had control over my money, you were planning to invest in FinSafe on my behalf. You promised Conrad you'd—*we'd*—partner with him." I point at one line in the notes. "You agreed to make a cash investment. You even planned the disbursement. But the money never left the account. You pulled out. You were the reason his company went under."

Jess whips her head toward Teddy.

He's no longer rolling the pen.

"If he'd had more cushion," he says after a long pause, "it wouldn't have been an issue."

"Well, that's not how he sees it. He thinks that investment is why the company went under, and he thinks it's my fault. Because you did it all under my name. You told him it was all my decision, didn't you?"

Teddy's face has gone very slightly pink. "He was my friend. You didn't have a personal connection."

"Tell me exactly what happened."

He rubs the bridge of his nose. "He had shown me some early projections, some plans, and I said we'd invest. It seemed like he had a good plan, and crypto was doing well. Then he started spending money on stupid stuff. He was doing everything out of order. I lost confidence in him." He sighs. "They had a deadline to repay a bank loan. We had already agreed you'd transfer the funds the first week of April. I told him you refused to finalize any investment in April. You wanted to wait until later, because you were superstitious about the family curse."

The curse. I feel a trickle of understanding.

"If he had been more responsible with his credit line," Teddy adds, "a delay wouldn't have been an issue."

"You only gave him four days' warning!"

"He should have had other money in place," Teddy says staunchly.

"If you think he sucks so much, why'd you even invite him to pitch to WFCI?"

He sighs. "I didn't plan for us to actually invest. I didn't even send the materials to Allan. But I knew Conrad got raked over the coals after FinSafe fell through, and I thought it might help smooth things over. The campaign . . . I didn't want the FinSafe stuff coming back on me."

"You mean on me," I say. "Because it was my money. My name."

A shadow of guilt passes over Teddy's face—or maybe I'm imagining it. Because when he speaks again, his voice is hard. "I'm very sorry that I took care of things for you for so many years. I can see how upsetting that must be, to have someone protect you."

"You didn't protect me. You exposed me." I'm speaking too loudly now, almost at a shout. "Don't you get what I'm saying? Conrad's behind this!" I slam my hand down on the still of our parents, wavy and pixelated, unnaturally lit. "He's behind the deepfakes and everything! To get back at me because of something horrible *you* did!"

He shoves himself up from his desk. "Something horrible? Where do you think our money comes from? Saving baby deer? You think we have what we have because we act nice? You want me to stop investing in big pharma, or housing bonds? You want your name off defense contracts? What about diamond mines? Please, Clara, tell me more about these ethics that you've suddenly discovered."

I start to answer, then realize I have nothing to say. He's right. I know nothing about our money or where it comes from. I've chosen not to know.

I'd probably admit that, if he gave me a second. But he surges on: "Do you know what I've sacrificed for you? For this family? After our parents died, I took care of you. I was nineteen and I became your guardian! Do you know what that's like, as a college freshman, to become someone's legal guardian? Do you understand? My friends were playing flip cup and I was signing fucking travel waivers for you to go to a soccer game—"

"Oh, I think you played a little flip cup, too," I say dryly.

"—and then you turned eighteen and I thought maybe you would grow up and I wouldn't have to take care of you anymore, but no, you kept winding up sick again, and again, almost killing yourself, and I dropped everything to help you. I have spent *years* of my life worrying about you. Managing you. Making decisions for you."

My stomach sinks. "I didn't ask you to do that."

"What choice did I have? Let you die? You've always expected me to help. I always have. And I'm done now, Clara!" He makes a sharp cutting motion. "You're talking about random investments from years ago and making up stories about how everything bad you've done is a hologram. You're blaming it on Conrad fucking Gaffney, who can't start a successful business for the life of him, who couldn't get his name in the social register if he wrote it there himself. FinSafe was a business transaction. It doesn't have anything to do with sex tapes. It certainly doesn't have anything to do with your hallucinations."

"You're only saying that because you don't want it to be your fault."

"Want *what* to be my fault? Your conspiracy theory? I'm in the middle of a Senate campaign. I have real problems to worry about."

"Poll numbers aren't real problems!"

His face twists with anger. "My campaign is *important*. I stand to make a difference."

"Sure. But a good one?"

He braces his knuckles on the desk, wrinkling the printouts. "If that's how you feel, then maybe you shouldn't come to May Day after all."

I let out an incredulous laugh. Turns out I'm excess, too. Unnecessary after all.

"I *live* here. And the party's in honor of our parents."

"Who you *killed* with your fucking"—he makes a fluttering motion in front of his head—"visions!"

I suck in a breath. Jess has been slouching back, gradually, toward the window, out of the range of fire. Now she stops and swings her head around to stare at Teddy. I expect her to say something. *That's too far. That's cruel.*

She doesn't.

The silence is unfathomably long.

Teddy doesn't correct himself, the way he did the other night. He doesn't apologize. He stares right back at me, unforgiving.

We look so similar. It's like looking into a mirror. No, even more familiar, because mirrors have lied to me in the past, shown me something other than what others see. Teddy's face has always been static to me, the solid standard by which I know my own, and to have it turned on me now, its lip curled in anger, cuts deeper than any of the times I've looked at myself with the same expression. His face belongs to me more than my own does.

I lean in closer. "You know what, Teddy? You keep saying you sacrifice so much. But you choose to do that, so you can control people!" I don't realize until the words are out of my mouth that they're basically Conrad's. They feel oily in my mouth, but not untrue. "You *liked* making decisions for me. Then you knew I wouldn't fuck anything up, and you could arrange things exactly how you want them. Just like you've arranged Jess exactly how you want her."

In the background, Jess does a double take. "Excuse me?"

My tears have burned out, but my cheeks are still wet. I am pressing so hard on the table that the tips of my fingers have gone white. I have been this hurt before, but I have never been this angry. It boils inside me like a cauldron of ore. One mistake in the factory and the whole vat could tip, burning me alive. "You've changed since you got with Teddy," I tell her. "You don't see it, but I do. You aren't the same as you used to be. You do whatever he says, whatever you think will make you the perfect Wieland wife."

"That's not fair."

"The old you would have argued with him about what he just said. You would have called him on it."

She looks stricken, then pissed. "You don't know what I would have done."

"I've known you since we were nine!"

"And people change."

She's right, of course. People change. I'm changing. I can feel it in me, something working its way up, darkness or brightness, I don't know which, tunneling toward air.

I look down at my hands on the desk like I'm seeing them for the first time. When we were little, I always hid in this room for hide-and-seek or sardines. Teddy wouldn't come in here because it was off-limits. Our dad said we'd break something horsing around. When Teddy was searching, he'd check every other possible place in the house before he dared cross the threshold. I spent so many hours crouched smugly under this very desk. Snickering to myself, running my hands over the carpet's bristles. *Shhh, Clara. You'll give us all away.*

I used to go places Teddy wouldn't. I used to do things he wouldn't do, and I thought myself clever for it. I used to trust that I would choose wisely, and that I could be on my own. Then a shadow raced across my sight, and everything changed.

But now.

I know what I've seen, the past few weeks.

I know what Conrad's done.

I know more than Teddy does, more than he'll admit to himself, more than he'll believe. It might be the first time in our lives I've *let* myself know more. And therefore it's the first time in our lives that I have to be the one to fix things. Not halfway. Not for show.

This time, I have to make it stick.

I yank back my printouts and gather them into my folder.

"Fine," I tell them. "Be that way." There's a high pressure in my voice, but that's only how I sound. Inside, my mind is cold and hard, my heart a steady thump of blood.

I'm almost to the door when Teddy calls after me, "You need help, Clara."

But that's where he's wrong.

31

JESS

April 24

Clara has barely disappeared through the doorway when Teddy turns on the new TV, installed yesterday so he could see the whole security feed at once, arrayed in a grid. Together, we watch her go down the hallway, through the kitchen, into the foyer, her image hopping from one screen to the next as she moves through the house. As she leaves, the feed switches over to the driveway camera and we watch her march to her car. Her hair blows against her face and she pushes it away. I can't tell if she's crying. She looks very small in the fish-eye lens.

When her car pulls out of the driveway—a messy K-turn that al-

most takes out a landscaping light, but that's always how she drives—
Teddy swivels his chair toward me.

"Holograms," he says. "She thinks she's seeing holograms."

"Apparently." A laugh bubbles in my throat, panicked, hysterical.
My head is swimming. Conrad, FinSafe, the deepfakes. I try to put it
all in some logical order, and figure out what to consider first, but
things keep slipping out of place. The morning has already been a
disaster—the coke-snorting-money-burning video dropped at eight,
and after an hour of Teddy shouting down the phone, Mike and
Phoebe started putting together a press release saying the videos are
deepfakes. I guess Teddy being faked warrants a real response.

"And she told you about it?" Teddy asks. His voice is still sharp,
which at first I attribute to shock, or to residual anger. I'm getting
Clara's remainders. Picking up the pieces, again. "She showed you
the projection strip?"

I nod absently. I'm staring at the empty desk, thinking about the
printout with the photograph of her parents. I wish she had left the
papers behind. Without them, the conversation feels like a dream. I
should have asked to look at them more carefully. Clara is hardly a
Photoshop expert. I would have been able to see that they had been
doctored, and then I wouldn't have this little voice in the back of my
mind saying, *She did what I asked. She brought me proof.*

"And you didn't *tell me?*" Teddy demands.

His anger breaks over me, a storm I should have seen coming. I
snap to attention. "It wasn't—she didn't tell that part about thinking
we were holograms. She never said that. And she didn't have any
proof, except the strip. Which I had never seen. She wasn't organized,
the way she is now. She was rambling. I thought it was nonsense."

"In that case, you *definitely* should have told me."

I'm confused. "You told me you were done with her. I thought you
didn't want to know."

"And I thought you weren't going to keep secrets from me anymore," he says.

"It didn't seem like much of a secret. It seemed like—the same way she had been the night before."

"No," he says. "It's completely different."

I furrow my brow. "Are you saying—you believe her?"

"Are you *kidding* me? No!" He throws up his hands. "Do *you*?"

"No," I say, less confidently.

"Because she's *paranoid*. She's insane."

Actually, this time, she wasn't. She was so calm. Teddy's the one who's been staring at security feeds for days, who pissed off a whole town because one guy a hundred miles away spit in his direction. I've seen Clara in so many moods before, in her head and out of it, lying and not lying, but I've never seen her so prepared, so determined, so slow to take the bait. When she was ranting to me about projection strips, I saw a version of Clara I could understand as her extreme. Delusional, self-absorbed. Today's version, I don't recognize.

I remember the strip of black lenses she found in the yard. The grainy photo; the video; the letter with the professor's signature. Would she really have faked all that?

Then there was the other day, when I saw her standing by the gates with the Popsicle. That was strange, wasn't it? Even for Clara? And the day after the second video came out, Teddy was so angry with me. I thought it was because of our fight at the campaign office. But maybe it was this thing Clara says happened at the Anchor.

I say slowly, "Is she right about Conrad's technology? Could it do those things? Did it look realistic when he showed it to you?"

"He didn't show it to us!" Teddy cries. "Jesus Christ, it doesn't even work."

Or Conrad could have simply pretended it didn't work. If Teddy screwed over Conrad, the WFCI presentation was probably in bad faith anyway. If the technology *does* work, then what Clara's saying is improbable, but not impossible. She isn't claiming that aliens are tracking her via computer chip, or that the CIA has commandeered her brain.

"She needs to go back into treatment. I thought you were going to try to get her to see a doctor," he says.

"I did try."

"Obviously not successfully."

"Obviously." I remind myself not to clench my teeth.

"I'm going to look into hospitals," Teddy says.

"She's not going to agree."

"She doesn't have to. If she's a danger."

He can't mean what I think he means. "Teddy. Come on."

"It would keep her—" he begins, and I think he's going to say *safe*, but instead what comes out of his mouth is, "under control."

"She is under control. She's not being erratic."

He points to the seat Clara vacated. "I call that pretty fucking erratic."

"I mean that she's not talking about hurting herself."

"You're splitting hairs."

"Not really," I say. "That's the criteria for people getting admitted involuntarily. If they're a harm to themselves or others."

He knows this as well as I do—we've looked it up before—but he scoffs. "You're arguing just to argue."

This is the stupidest accusation I've ever heard. I never argue just to argue. I hate arguing. Anyway, if I were going to pick a fight on purpose, it wouldn't be over something as serious as putting Clara in a psych ward. I would choose a small, manageable argument, one where losing wouldn't hurt.

You've arranged Jess exactly how you want her. I hate Clara for saying that, and I hate that I understand what she meant. She took a knife to me, flicked the gristle away from my bone. The way only your best friend can do. The downside of being known is—being known.

"I'm just saying we should think this over," I say, emphasis on *we*. Us together. A team.

But Teddy's never been on a team where he wasn't the captain.

"I will think it over," he says, emphasis on the *I*. "Unless you think I'm a hologram, too."

I press my lips together.

"Of course I don't," I say.

I don't want to be on the side I know will lose.

Later that night, I walk past Teddy's office. Dinner's been ready for two hours, and I've been waiting for him to finish work. He said he was making calls. But when I go to his office to check on him, he's sitting ramrod straight on the sofa, watching the security feed: an unchanging grid of night-vision squares, trees with gray trunks, white leaves flapping blindly in the breeze.

32

CLARA

April 24

In my quest to destroy Conrad, I begin with the car.

A few hours after leaving Teddy's house, I'm at a shitty off-brand rental place outside Bangor, a glorified driveway with an inflatable-tube man bending and twisting behind a stack of tires. The clerk wears her hair in a slicked-back ponytail that accentuates the pointed shape of her head. I ask her for the most forgettable car they have, which confuses her.

"So economy? Or midsize?"

This is more decisions than I expected to be making. "Sure."

"Which one?"

"I don't know, like that one." I point at a shiny red car. "But less shiny and less red."

"Oo-kay." She types on her wide keyboard. Tells me a type of car that I recognize as a type of car. "I just need your credit card and driver's license."

"Why do you need my driver's license?"

She stops typing and peers around her monitor at me. "Because," she says slowly, "we're renting you a car."

My face warms. I've never actually rented a car myself before. Usually if I'm traveling I order a car service, or I have the travel concierge make the arrangements. This is only the first step in my plan and I'm already useless.

I give her the credit card and license. In return, she gives me a sheaf of papers and tells me to sign here, here, here. My last signature is faint and sloppy, a last gasp from a dying pen. I think about the forms Teddy pushed in front of me back at Marien. Authorizing him to take over my board seats, make my decisions, speak in my name. There was a space of several years where my signature was almost meaningless. Why didn't that bother me? I guess because I never put that much stock in my signature anyway. I never gave much thought to what it meant.

I flip back to the first page. This time, I read what I've signed.

When everything's done, the clerk gives me the keys to a blue hatchback that smells like tennis balls. The keys come on a key chain made of laminated paper, the plastic bubbled and peeling, its edges sharp.

On my drive back to the island, I worry my mom's necklace between my fingers. I keep thinking about the conversation with Teddy and Jess. What he said. What she didn't say. I've always been afraid that Teddy blamed me for our parents' deaths. I was sure that if I ever heard him say so aloud, it would crush me, because it would prove to me that my worst fears were true. It did crush me, but not for the reason I thought. When he said I had killed our parents, I could hear the hyperbole in a way I never have when the words are coming from inside my own mind. I could hear that he was wrong.

No, what crushed me was the fact that he would say it in the first place. That he would pull the words out and crack them like a whip. That he would see them hit me, and he would smile.

All my life, I've had an image of Teddy in my mind. I've never considered the image very closely. I've never had to. He was always Teddy, and always there. He's an extension of me, a force upon me. But the things that have happened the last few weeks, the things I've learned about what he's done—they're messing with the image. I didn't think he was someone who would sacrifice me for himself. Now I find myself replaying the past, rearranging. When he got together with Jess: Did he think I would be happy, or did he know it would hurt? When he chartered that ambulance to Marien: Was he trying to save me, or trying to contain me?

I close my fingers around the pendant's sharp point and squeeze.

None of this would have happened if it weren't for Conrad, the videos, the holograms. He played us like fiddles. He pulled us apart. And the version of Teddy he made, or unearthed, is a temporary portrait, like the projections of Jess, like the projections of me. And when I stuff Conrad back into whatever sick little box he sprang out of, things will return to normal. There will be a time when I'll have forgotten what Teddy said yesterday. But it won't happen until Conrad's out of the equation, and there are no holograms to worry about, no videos, nothing left except our real selves.

It won't be easy to punish a person like Conrad, with the tools he has. He could release deepfakes of me that might land me in jail, and maybe this time Shallcross wouldn't be able to prove they were wrong. He could use the projections to show me committing a crime and invent eyewitnesses. He can frame any bystander, create any alibi.

I need evidence he can't transmute. I need something final, and the element of surprise.

By the time I get back to the island, the tide is out, and the bridge has become a causeway. Water laps at the bared rocks. Ahead, the skyline is a zigzag of pine trees. I've seen this view a million times before, so I'm not sure why I notice it now, or why I have the sudden thought that I might never see it again. Maybe paranoia, maybe a premonition. Sometimes I hear these stories about people who didn't get on a plane because they had this gut feeling they shouldn't, and then the plane crashes. Their instinct saved them. But I don't know how they can feel so certain. My gut is always crying wolf.

Conrad's staying in one of the Victorians on Ledgelawn, not far from the town green, down the street from the Holy Redeemer. Over the next few days, I get to know the street very well. The polite little sidewalk on each side, the matching front porches with matching railings. The church is a hulking thing, its thick granite blocks forced into turrets and arches, dotted along the sides with faded red and yellow paint. I stay parked across the street from it, because I figure that's where a forgettable car is most likely to be forgotten. People are always coming and going, in and out like a drive-through. Commuting to their confessions. They walk in as sinners and out as lambs. Sometimes I watch them, trying to spot the change.

But mostly I watch Conrad.

His schedule isn't interesting or varied. He's usually home. He leaves in the morning between ten and noon, for a walk at Shell Beach, and after that he might stop at the deli for a coffee and sandwich. Or at the grocery store to buy a bottle of wine. Then he goes home, stays there most of the day, the blinds drawn. Working, I guess: on NatureEye, on making deepfakes, on ruining other people's lives. I don't know. I follow him each time. I spend hours staked out on his street, day into night, watching the glowing gaps at the edges of the windows.

I learn his routine, if it's really his routine, if it's even really him leaving the house, and not a projection. Maybe he saw me watching him and now he's tricking me. Sometimes in my vigil, when my ass is numb and my eyes are dry and hopelessness is a maw inside me, I start to wonder if there's anything that can constrain someone like him.

Forum Discussion: Politics & Current Events

Re: New Teddy Wieland video

@PoliMath72: EDITED TO ADD: Wieland campaign just released a statement saying that the cocaine video is a deepfake, and so are the other two videos that came out this month.

> **@EatMyPopTarts:** Eh, I don't buy it. If the other videos were fake, they should have said so as soon as they came out.

> **@DearPippin:** My wife's friend is friends with Mike D'Onocchio's wife, and she said it was a strategic decision. Obviously, it backfired.

> **@SnowDaddy:** The statement says the findings are supported by an expert at MIT.

>> **@EatMyPopTarts:** The Wielands definitely have enough money to pay off an expert.

> **@BallWizard9000:** Wait, the video of Clara Wieland is fake, too? You mean I've been jacking off to a fake pussy??

>> **@ComicJohn:** YOU JACKED OFF TO THAT??

>> **@BallWizard9000:** What can I say. I like seeing women get put in their place.

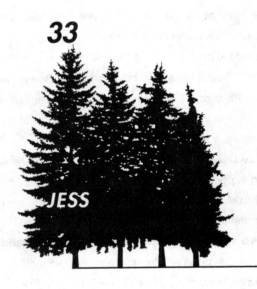

33

JESS

April 25

When I worked at the Brenner, we would house one male mouse with a couple female mice until one of them got pregnant. Then we would give the lucky girl her own nursery cage, her own personal clear plastic shoebox filled with fresh nesting material, until she gave birth to the pink, blind, struggling pups. After they were weaned, we would move her back to a harem cage, sometimes with the same mice that were there before, sometimes with others. I never liked that second part. The mama mouse would resist at first, until I trapped her gently against the wall of her cage, and then she would go limp in my hands, that small exhausted body. I could feel her warmth through my latex gloves. Her tail flickering through the air. I didn't know if she expected me to kill her or to save her; I didn't know if expectation was even something mice could feel. Still, it felt like a betrayal when I did neither, when I simply put her back in an identical cage, ready to do the whole thing over again.

When Mike releases the statement that the videos were deepfakes, I'm elated for a whole day, sure the announcement will make things better. Teddy's campaign will get back on track, and he and I will, too. He'll stop watching his security feed, stop thinking everyone's out to get him. He'll sleep through the night and not pace our bedroom like he's looking for a fight.

But then the day passes, and everything is still the same. Despite Mike's announcement, the deepfakes have teeth. It's hard to forget something you're being told to forget. Hard to unbelieve something you once believed. Endorsements continue to vanish. Pundits continue to pun. One day I receive five different versions of an itinerary for our Chicago trip, followed by an update that the trip has been indefinitely postponed. Teddy's still brittle, unpredictable. We are all on edge.

That poor mouse, when I set her back down on the wood shavings. *Free*, she must have thought for a moment. And then, when she saw where she was: *Not quite.*

April 28

"What a perfect night," coos the wife of a hedge fund president, an hour into the May Day party. They flew up from Boston on a private jet this morning. "And these gardens! They're incredible!"

I give a modest nod. The gardens do look good. The tent is clean and sturdy, if a little large for the smaller gathering. Panels of fake parquet have been unfolded into a shiny dance floor. The catering staff circulates with polenta bites. We have a cover band and heat lamps and a three-course meal featuring Wagyu beef and lobster bisque.

We even have flowers. I had just about resigned myself to the spring mud when yesterday, at the last possible minute, I got an idea. I called up a massive greenhouse near Brunswick, the kind where florists get supplies, and offered to buy up all the plants they had in bloom.

The guy on the other end almost choked on his own tongue. He said it would cost a lot—*cahst a laht*, and I could hear the stretched vowels in a way I never used to, before Teddy's imitation. I said the money didn't matter. He named a price in the tens of thousands. I said the money didn't matter. He said I couldn't be serious. I told him my name. Then he believed me.

This morning, two massive trucks rumbled down the lane and unloaded potted versions of all the same shrubs that were already here, plus some extras. All improbably, impossibly, simultaneously in bloom. Rhododendron and marsh marigold and snow azaleas and mountain laurel, geraniums and chrysanthemums and dahlias, their flowers bright and vapid. The maintenance guys did a beautiful job arranging them. In the torchlight, it's almost impossible to see the empty plots behind them, where their real counterparts lurk, unbloomed, like jealous stepsisters.

And even after all that hard work, I walked into the party on the arm of a husband who will barely talk to me. I'm wearing a dress I hate, because I was told it looks good in photographs. My shoes hurt, again.

Free.

Not quite.

"I told Bill we should summer near here," the hedge fund wife continues. "We usually do the Vineyard, but I've been looking for a change. I don't know how you live here all year-round, though. It seems very isolated."

"I guess I'm used to it."

She laughs like this is a joke and touches my arm with one ringed hand. "Well, anyway, soon you'll be in D.C.!"

This is the kind of confident prediction I heard a lot a month ago. Lately, though, not so often. I can't tell if this woman is genuinely oblivious to the campaign's problems, or if she's saying what she thinks I want to hear. Regardless, D.C. feels a long way off.

"Fingers crossed," I say.

She laughs again, touches me again. She wants people to see us laughing and think we're friends. Perhaps she thinks an intimate gesture will create actual intimacy. But I keep remembering Clara brushing my shoulder with her hand, testing to see if it's really me, and the touch feels unbearable. I'm subtly shifting away when my gaze snags on a blond head across the tent.

Conrad.

My stomach drops. He's dressed well enough, in a gray suit. The color is a little light for this time of year. He's drinking a glass of champagne and talking to a state legislator. As she talks, he scans the party, looking for someone. Teddy? Me?

Why is he even here? He wasn't on the invite list. If there is even the slightest chance he's the one who made the videos—and this, holograms debate aside, seems perfectly plausible—I don't want him anywhere near us.

Excusing myself, I make my way through the sparse crowd toward Teddy. The response to the new batch of invitations wasn't as enthusiastic as he expected, but the people who did come seem to be having a good time. Politicians and regulators and developers and city council members greet each other with delicate quarter-hugs and loud laughs. Deals are being made, or planned, or alluded to. No one is talking about the money-burning video. These aren't the people who would be offended by it.

Teddy is dressed impeccably, of course. His tie is just narrow enough to seem youthful, just wide enough to be taken seriously, and his cuff links are gold flags—his father's, if anyone asks. With the heat lamps' orange glow shimmering off his hair, he looks a little like he did on our wedding day, under the fairy lights.

But when I slide in next to him, the similarity falls away. There's something dispassionate in the way Teddy looks at me tonight, not unappreciative, exactly, but utilitarian. Like how an actor might look at a prop he's rehearsed with before.

He touches my waist and introduces me to the man he's speaking to, an oil executive. "Dave grew up like you," Teddy says.

"Like me?"

"With a single mother," Dave explains.

I don't know how to reply to this bizarre introduction. Congratulations? Condolences? I'm so distracted by Conrad's presence that I forget my list of preapproved conversation starters.

"Wow," I say. "Great." I raise myself on my tiptoes to whisper in Teddy's ear. "Did you invite Conrad?"

Still smiling at Dave, he gives a brief shake of his head. *No.*

"Because he's here," I say.

Teddy sips his drink while he glances around. His eyes settle on Conrad. "That's fine," he says.

"How did he get in?"

"That's fine," he repeats, a little more loudly, making an apologetic expression toward Dave. "We can talk about it later."

I angle myself to watch Conrad. He gestures with his champagne as he speaks to the legislator. Someone who's spent less time trying to fit into this crowd might not notice the performative straightness of his shoulders, or that he's holding the flute too high on its stem. But I've spent years studying these people, and I know effort when I see it. He's trying, which is something the Wielands never need to do.

The born Wielands, I mean.

I try to imagine him making the videos. Dreaming up the things Clara says she saw, the bear, the boat. Me, in the alley. Clara, at the gates. I can almost picture it.

"You have an incredible story," Dave says to me. I jerk back to attention.

"Sorry?"

"I told him about where you come from," Teddy says. "And about your mom, how she worked three jobs to put you through college."

I force my mouth into a small smile. My mom usually worked two jobs, not three, and she didn't put me through college. I took out loans. I can tell from the compassionate look on Dave's face that Teddy probably embroidered other details, too. An ended lease turned into an eviction. A summer job made more grueling. Little changes, to make me sympathetic.

I reconciled myself to being the white-trash wife for the sake of Teddy's campaign, but now that the campaign seems doomed, the gambit feels worse, pointless, like I let myself be sold out for no reason. And I'm wondering, for the first time, why Teddy tells these stories at all, why they jump so quickly to his mind when he thinks of me.

"And look at you now," Dave says.

"I'm very lucky," I say. As I always say.

A lucky, lucky girl.

I tell them I'm going to grab another drink before we sit down for dinner. Teddy says, "No, I'll get it." He only says it to look chivalrous in front of Dave. I insist, laying a hand on his arm, smiling sweetly up at him, which is what he wants me to do.

You've arranged Jess exactly how you want her.

I slip out a back entrance. On the other side of the hedges, a thin railing divides the gardens from the steep tumble of rocks into the cove. During Prohibition, smugglers stashed crates of rum in those crevices. Tonight would have been a bad night for it: the moon is a perfect disk, and the water is dark silver in its light. Without the fake parquet underneath, my heels sink into the soil.

For years, I double-checked the guest towels, memorized the family tree, learned about wine. I bent to Teddy, and I told myself that bending required a kind of courage, too. I tricked myself into thinking I was an active participant in my life. As if enough small contributions could add up to a big one. As if I could checklist myself into equality.

As if I could agree myself out of the cage.

There are things about the way our life is set up. Take FinSafe, for example. The investment report Rebecca sent Clara—I've never even seen one of those. I don't know anything about our finances. It even feels strange to call them *ours*. It's true that my name is on a joint bank account with an obscene balance, and I carry several heavy credit cards without limits, and I have access to a never-ending flow of cash. But it's not mine, exactly. The flow could be stopped with the twist of a spigot.

The wind shifts, and I hear the melancholy echo of a buoy ringing on the other side of the point. My shoes hurt, hurt, hurt. I lean down to wrench them off, but I pull too hard, and one of the narrow ankle straps breaks. Shit. I hobble over to a bench and sit, holding the shoe up to the light, squinting to see where the fabric snapped.

I'll have to get someone to run up to the house and get a new pair, but I don't want to go back into the party wearing only one shoe. I sit there for three minutes, four, five, staring at the strap. Willing it to fuse itself back together. "It's not a big deal," I whisper to myself, out loud. But it feels like a big deal. It feels like my only job was to look pretty and I can't even do that right.

A noise comes from somewhere nearby. Rustling leaves or sticks. The hairs rise on the back of my neck, and I turn to look behind me, peering into the darkness.

"Hello?"

No response. What flashes into my mind is Clara's story about the grizzly bear in her backyard, and immediately I feel like an idiot, because of course there was no bear. Whether it was a hallucination or a hologram or *whatever*, there was never an actual bear. Still, I start to sweat.

"Hello?" I repeat, more loudly.

A shape moves in the shadows. I get up, keeping my weight on the foot still wearing a shoe. The shape takes form. A man.

"Hi," Conrad says, turning my blood cold. "Sorry. Didn't know you were out here."

I don't believe him. As if he can read my mind, he raises his hands, revealing a cigarette pack, which he holds out to me.

"You want one?"

"No, thanks."

He extracts one cigarette, and lights it without asking permission.

"I didn't know you were going to be here tonight," I say.

"Last-minute decision."

"I didn't see your name on the list."

"Teddy walked me in," he says, unbothered.

I stare at him. I know that's not true. Teddy couldn't have walked him in. Teddy and I got ready at the same time, drove down together. The guest list was being checked at the main gates, a twenty-minute walk from here. I feel a dull, thudding sensation in my throat. I realize it's my pulse.

Conrad removes the cigarette from his lips. "How's Clara doing?"

His eyes glitter. No, it's the light. The moonlight, reflecting. Why would he ask about Clara, right now?

"She's fine," I say unsteadily.

He taps ash onto the ground. "That's good. I know she's been struggling."

I'm trying to figure out how to respond when I hear Teddy shouting.

I shove my shoe back on by its one remaining strap and scramble to the path, hobbling, running toward the voices. I don't check to see if Conrad's following me. My run is awkward, chickenlike, my knees constrained by the cut of the tight dress. I take a wrong turn, nearly crash into a bust on a pedestal, have to turn around. Finally I round a hedge and am back in the main garden. The heat from the lamps swallows me up, a shock to the system after the cold sea air. Everything is bright and loud, and it swirls before me in a nauseating blur.

Disoriented, I almost bump into a server carrying a tray of empty glasses out of the tent; I take a step backward, and a thorn on the hedge snags on my dress. I turn in a circle until I catch sight of Teddy at the side of the gardens, just over the line of shadow.

He's shouting at Mike, who keeps reaching out, trying to calm him. There's something on Teddy's front—a thick pink liquid, down his shirt and suit. A girl in a white jacket stands to the side. One of the servers. Her head's bowed, her ponytail draped down her back in a straight line. Next to her is the caterer, a polite woman I hired last minute. She doesn't look polite now.

Furious, Teddy twists out of Mike's grasp and jabs a finger at the girl. "We pay you to serve the soup, not spill it on people. Or did someone send you? Did someone tell you to embarrass me?"

The girl lifts her face, and now I recognize Lisa Cicero, who served us on Cicero's opening day. This must be her side job. Her fingers thread nervously together, apart, together, apart. "I wasn't coming after you," she says in a quavering voice. "It's just soup."

"Just soup? Look at me! I'm a fucking mess."

He gestures at his front. Lisa winces.

"It was an accident," the caterer says. "If you want, I can send someone back up to the house to get a change of clothes—"

"Oh, so you can get inside our home? Is that part of your plan?"

"Plan?" Lisa repeats.

"Teddy," Mike says gently, coming to stand in front of him, "it was an accident. It won't happen again."

"It certainly won't. She's leaving."

The caterer says, "I can move her to cleanup, but if I send her—"

"*I want her off my property!*" Teddy shouts.

Everyone freezes. Mike, Lisa, the caterer. Me, though I wasn't doing anything helpful anyway. The only movement is in my peripheral vision, and when I glance over, I see a dozen people standing in the archway to the gardens. Politicians, moguls, tycoons, all staring wide-eyed through the gap.

Dave is at the front. He coughs unevenly. "Ted—"

Teddy turns and sees them all. A series of emotions pass across his face in quick succession. Anger, recognition, shame, denial, back to shame. I see it in the muscle that ticks in his jaw, the slash of his eyebrows.

Then he does the worst thing he could do: he summons his calm.

When he speaks again, his voice is collected, his face is smooth and his smile pleasant. As if nothing ever happened. And even this crowd of accomplished pretenders seems perturbed by the speed of the transition, the ease with which he discards such ferocious anger.

"Go on with dinner," he tells the caterer. "I'm going to go change my clothes."

He strides out of the circle, toward the road that leads back to the house. For a long moment, we all stare after him; then, as if a spell has been broken, the onlookers turn toward one another. Their whispers sound like hissing cicadas. I recover myself and run after Teddy, limping in my tight dress. My broken shoe slaps against my heel. He's almost to the road when I reach him and grab the sleeve of his jacket.

He turns to me sharply, and I lay my hands on his chest. His heart pounds beneath my fingers.

"It's me," I say.

I expect his face to soften in relief. But it twists further, into another kind of rage, something cold and permanent. It's worse even than how he looked at Clara the other day.

"Let me go."

I drop my hands like I've been burned. "Teddy—"

But he's already turning away, marching alone up the dark wedge of the hill. He doesn't turn back, no matter how many times I call his name.

34

JESS

April 29

When I jog past the gardens at eleven the next morning, almost all evidence of the fundraiser is gone. There are only a few trucks left, their trailers filled with rows of chairs and tables collapsed like butter-flies. The flowers are still there, but they look garish in the daylight. I need to figure out what to do with them next, move them or donate them or . . . the prospect of deciding fills me with exhaustion. Maybe I'll let them rot.

I run and run and run, past the shrub where Teddy yelled and the railing where I talked to Conrad and the tumble of roots where Clara and I used to leave tokens for forest fairies when we were children.

Each time my foot strikes, my whole body shakes, like I've never run a day in my life. It's a hangover, I tell myself, because a hangover is temporary, a hangover will disappear.

After Teddy stormed off last night, I tried to get us back on track. I sat in my seat and drank the expensive wine and cut my knife into the cold pats of butter formed in the shape of the Wieland seal. I saw the covert glances, the people who had seen the meltdown whispering to the people who hadn't. I could see the news traveling across the party, the ripples left in its wake. A few politicians made obligatory clucking noises of sympathy for Lisa Cicero, who had been quietly sent home, but most people seemed uninterested in the fate of a clumsy server. But they were titillated by the crack in Teddy's demeanor, the intimation of violence, the unexpected breach of good manners. And from a Wieland!

Still, the show went on. Teddy returned in a fresh suit. Everything happened as scheduled, the speech, the dancing, and I stayed through it all, like I was supposed to.

Or—like I'm now supposed to. Because of course originally, which is to say back before I started dating Teddy, I wasn't supposed to host this party at all. I was Lisa Cicero. I was the girl with the serving platter, the girl who made the mistakes. All us servers had a story like Lisa has now. Once, I spilled wine on a woman, white wine at that, and she screeched like a howler monkey. She didn't yell at me, she didn't speak to me at all; I wasn't worth that. When I tried to apologize, she turned her face away.

"Must be nice," Sadie said afterward, "to be so rich you can pretend people don't even exist."

At the time, I laughed. Privately, I thought she was probably right. It probably *was* nice to be that rich. When someone upset me, I didn't send them away. I couldn't afford to. Wouldn't it be nice for my forgiveness to be a sign of moral righteousness, rather than a necessity for survival?

I didn't think through the flip side of this equation. Because if you're powerful enough that your tolerance means goodness, then your intolerance can only mean you're cruel. I have no more excuses. I've built my life around Teddy. I am his decisions. His lapse is my own moral failing.

I run my usual loop once, twice, three times. The twisting in my chest doesn't go away. When I get back to the house, sweat sticks my hair to my forehead, and my lungs ache from the cold air. I check my phone and see a series of texts, all from Mike.

Did you see it?

New video

Need to discuss in person

At campaign office

REMEMBER: NO COMMENT!

My chest twists in a different direction, panic wringing me dry. Another deepfake. It's too soon. They're coming too fast. I remember Conrad in the dark, his eyes glittering at me. Like he already had something planned.

I search *new Wieland video.* My hands are shaking. The video could show anything. It could be terrible. With a deepfake, the sky's the limit: BDSM, water sports, bestiality. Oh god—pedophilia. I feel sick.

Then the results load, and my brain stops short. The calculations vanish.

The thumbnail for the top video is dark and grainy, but I can tell right away what it is. Teddy is clearly visible, towering over Lisa Cicero, soup down his front, his mouth open in a shout, his finger in her face. A crowd gathers in the background, surrounded by bright flowers.

The video title reads: TEDDY WIELAND'S TRUE SELF—REVEALED.

The campaign office's blinds have been drawn, and the remnants of the jewelry store's window decals stand out in stark relief. ENUIN GEM-STO ES. A single photographer waits at the corner of the building and raises his camera as I approach. I try to keep my mouth neutral, not a smile, not a frown. I'm not even sure that's the right reaction. Mike didn't say what comment my face should make.

Inside, it's silent. The only sound is the door creaking as it falls shut behind me. For a moment, I think maybe I read Mike's text wrong, and they're somewhere other than the campaign office; but as my eyes adjust to the dim light, I see that a half dozen people are circled up in the far corner, away from the windows. My eyes go to Teddy first, at the center of the circle, and I try to telegraph something like *It's okay* or *I've got you*—some platitude. But his face goes tight as soon as he sees me, his brows coming together in an expression of anger I've gotten to know well the past few days.

I freeze.

"Jess." Mike steps out of the circle, looking relieved. At least someone's happy to see me. "Hi."

The rest of the circle is made up of a couple senior staffers and a couple other people I don't know. The room smells like stale coffee and stress. As I pass the desks, I realize why the silence is so total: there aren't any phones ringing. Someone has taken every landline off its hook.

Teddy turns back to the others, boxing me out. "I don't think the story is going to stick," he says. "It's not that big a deal."

Mike says, "*The New York Times* already wrote about it. *The Washington Post.* There's a trending hashtag. The primary is a month away, and our polls were already dropping. We've always known class was going to be one of the main issues of the campaign."

"This isn't about class! I didn't get mad because she was a waitress. I got mad because she was a klutz."

"Your response made you look paranoid."

"*Paranoid?*"

"And cruel."

"So I should just let her spill on me and do nothing?"

"Well," Mike says, "yes."

"I refuse to believe my entire campaign goes up in smoke because I yell at one person."

"I don't care if you believe it. The fact is that we are in serious trouble."

Teddy's nostrils flare. "Just tell everyone it's another deepfake."

"But it's not."

"Say it is."

"I'm not going to put my reputation on the line covering for you," Mike says. There's a hardness in his eyes I've seen before, turned toward interns, staffers, even me—but never toward Teddy.

That's when I understand that Teddy's campaign is over. It might not end right at this moment. It might take weeks to convince him to give up. Possibly, he might make it past the primary. Possibly. But then what? Teddy has always been underqualified. What he had going for him was that he was the golden child. The videos have taken that away. Now, he's tarnished.

Perhaps Teddy realizes this, too, on some subconscious level, because he rubs his throat like he's having difficulty swallowing. He looks around the circle wildly, waiting for someone to agree with him.

When no one does, he throws his arms up and storms across the room, heading for the back door. He slams it open and walks out into the parking lot.

Back to silence. The staffers look at each other, then down at the floor.

"What should we do?" a staffer asks. He looks about fourteen. "Should we put out a statement?"

Mike shakes his head. "We need Teddy to sign off on it."

"Where's Phoebe?" I ask.

"She quit," Mike says.

"I'm in charge of communications now," the pubescent staffer says, with a mix of pride and dread.

"If last night's video was real," a guy in a Yale baseball cap says, "does that mean the coke video was, too? Did we lie about that?"

Mike ignores him. "Can you go get Teddy?" he asks me. "Get him to come back."

Of course that's my job. Collect Teddy, soothe Teddy.

The back of the campaign building isn't much to look at. A utility pole, a couple parking spots occupied by Teddy's truck and Mike's BMW. There's some grass still overgrown from last summer, brown and patchy. Teddy's doing his pacing thing, around and around the concrete pad, running his hand over his mouth.

When I step outside, there's a moment where I look at him and he seems to shrink a little, and I see that his skin is soft and his body like any other body, penetrable, and his mind like any other mind, wrong about some things, big things, limited in its own ways. However long I know him, however long we're married, I will never be able to see things the way he sees them. I will never really know what he's thinking. I suppose I never truly wanted to, before.

I try to bring out my platitudes again, but they won't come. On his next circuit, he glances up and snarls, "Go away, Jess. You're the last person I want to see right now."

I let out a startled laugh. "The *last* person?"

"This whole thing is your fault."

"How is it my fault?"

"Don't play dumb, okay?" His hand trembles as he runs it through his hair, yanks at the ends. "I saw you and Clara together, last night! In the gardens."

"Huh?"

"I saw you—" The words come out of him in a rush, twisted and pained, the *saw* rising in the middle and snapping, breaking into two syllables. He nearly can't finish the sentence, which is so unlike him that I understand in a flash what he means, even before he says, "I saw you *together*."

I remember Conrad's face across the crowd, and how calm he looked. And then what he said to me behind the hedges. *Teddy walked me in.* A projection strip at the entrance, another in the gardens . . .

The false image comes to me in pieces. Clara and me in the shadows. Hungry mouths and pressing hands. Our breath uneven in the night. Perhaps I kissed the tender space below her ear. Or perhaps her fingers were on the hem of my dress, brushing over my knee. Or perhaps I was kneeling before her, her thigh on my shoulder, her skirt hiked around her waist.

The specifics don't matter, I suppose. Teddy saw what he saw.

"You're why I was upset," he says. "If I hadn't had to see that, I wouldn't have yelled at anyone. I wouldn't have gotten angry."

I recognize on some level that this would be an unfair reaction no matter what, but I'm too shocked to argue that point. I step into his path, blocking him. "Teddy, I wasn't with Clara last night. I haven't seen her since your study the other day. If you saw us together, she must be right—it must have been a hologram."

He rolls his eyes. "Not you now, too."

I place my hands on his arms. He still smells like himself. The cedar, the sage. "Teddy, I *promise*. Please trust me."

Clara said the same thing when she found the projection strip. *Trust me.* What a joke, I thought then. If you were telling the truth, you would have evidence; you wouldn't need my trust. Demanding trust is a last resort. A desperate measure. The moment you ask for it, you've already failed.

I understand now that when you're doing the asking, it doesn't feel like a last resort. It feels like the most basic possible request. The fundamental thing. Yes, it's obscene, what I'm demanding. Asking him to trust me more than he trusts his own sight. But—shouldn't he? Isn't that what being a partner means? I have played by his rules and done what he wanted and been the person he needed me to be. I pushed myself. I gave myself blisters for him. I sucked up to horrible people for him. I played golf for him. Hasn't he seen that? Haven't I banked some currency by now?

I press my fingers more tightly into his forearms. "Please. I know today has been awful. But think for a second. You know me. I wouldn't do that to you. At a campaign event? Out in public?"

"I *saw* you," he replies.

"That's what Clara said, too. When she saw your parents, which we know wasn't possible."

"Yes, but that was Clara."

"And this is *me*. Your wife."

I widen my eyes and relax my mouth—trying to make myself look earnest, open, although the harder I try, the less honest I probably appear. One second passes, then two, and I feel him slipping out of reach. What else has Conrad showed him, to make him doubt me?

"You have to believe me," I say more urgently.

He shakes me off. His shoulders are broad and tense. "I don't have to do anything I don't want to do."

When I get back to Vantage Point, there's another photographer waiting outside the gates. His car is parked only a few inches from the property line. I didn't think to bring sunglasses or a hat, and my windows aren't tinted. As I wait for the gates to open, I swear I can feel him taking photos. Snap, snap, snap. Breaking off pieces of me.

I drive past our house, straight to Clara's. Her car isn't in the driveway, and her windows are dark. I ring the bell anyway. I knock and knock. No response.

I sink down onto the porch swing. Its paint is chipping, and I fiddle with it, peeling the edge up with my fingernail. Overhead, drops of rainwater dot the eave like a string of pearls.

All this time, I thought love and knowledge were overlapping circles. The people who know me best are the people who love me the most; the people I love most are the people I truly know. Now I think I had it all wrong. Because this is the best I have ever known Teddy, and the least I have ever loved him. Is love just willful blindness?

Seeing the truth flutter in your peripheral vision, the reality of who that person is, and deciding to turn away.

It's not that I didn't see what Teddy was doing. How he asks questions and doesn't wait for the answer. How he switches off the bedside lamp as soon as he's done saying what he wants to say. How he always has to be the one to drive. I saw those things, and I turned away. Now I'm looking, and it doesn't feel good.

In our wedding vows, Teddy and I promised we would always make each other's lives easier. I thought that was so romantic. The problem is, I never thought about how he and I were starting from such different places. Making my life easier required so little work from Teddy. He only needed to give me what he already had, to share what was limitless. Making his life easier was less simple. It required things I didn't already have. It required contortions.

I want us to have sacrificed the same amount for each other. But I don't know how to judge a sacrifice. Is it about how much it helps them, or how much it hurts you?

I sit on the swing for a very long time before I hear an engine. A blue Nissan Versa with a dent in its front bumper turns into Clara's driveway. To my surprise, the driver is Clara herself. She throws open the door and tumbles out. Her smile is a mile wide. She's glistening, red-cheeked. Thrilled.

"I did it," she announces. "I fixed it. It's over."

35

CLARA

April 29, earlier

On my last day of stalking Conrad, I get to my usual spot at seven thirty with a thermos of coffee and a silicone container that female truckers allegedly use to pee in while they're on the road. I'm taking no chances. I was up half the night worrying that I might miss my opportunity—that today might be the day Conrad deviates from his routine, that he might take his morning walk before I arrive. Or not take it at all. In that case, I'd have to choose between talking to him on his own territory, or delaying my plans another day, which seems both unbearable and unwise.

After the past few days of stakeouts, the car is a mess. Empty plastic cups and straw wrappers are everywhere. Mountains of chewed gum. Yesterday I went to a souvenir store and bought a small beanbag in the shape of a puffin's head. It slumps on my dashboard, crocheted eyes downcast.

When Conrad finally emerges from his house at 10:16, the relief nearly flattens me. I slouch low in my seat as he pulls out of his driveway, and as soon as he's rounded the corner, I start the car and do a U-turn that makes the tires squeal.

In the winter, Shell Beach is a blanket of snow rushing down to the sea. Frost crystals form between the grains of sand, and the tide line becomes an iridescent stripe. In the summer, it's the busiest beach on the island. The water is sprinkled with a confetti of swimmers in bright suits, and the sand is tunneled through with moats and castles. There are lifeguards on duty and lines for the public restrooms.

Today, the beach is neither. It's in an awkward phase. Somber. A little dirty-looking. Under the white sky, the ocean is gray on gray on gray. When I reach the bottom of the stairs from the parking lot, I pause to get my bearings. Not many people are out. A man in a bucket hat walks along the flat beach path. Alicia Samuels throws a stick for her dog.

And down by the water, a blond man strolls along the waves.

Adrenaline swoops in. For a moment, it gives me a stunning sense of clarity, like the whole scene has been rendered in higher resolution. Everything is sharp and crisp and perfect.

I hurry down the beach, cutting close to Alicia as her dog gallops back, the stick clamped between its sand-wet jaws. I make a point of saying hi. This seems to confuse Alicia, who I've only met tangentially, but she nods back and I gesture down the beach to Conrad, even though she didn't ask. *I'm here for him.*

There's a ripe, jammy taste in my mouth. Bloodthirst.

The dog whines.

I stumble through the soft sand like a drunk astronaut. Ahead of me, Conrad stops to inspect a shell. This motherfucker. How dare he be whimsical, after everything he's done.

I pick my way over the tide line, with its dark feathers of seaweed, and the rounded pink rocks that cross the beach like a fresh scar. On the firmer sand, I can move more quickly, and even though a few seconds don't matter, I break into a jog.

"Conrad!"

He stands, turns, looking for the voice. I wave and smile. His returning smile is wide, a row of fucking pearls.

"Clara! Hey!"

I come to a stop a few feet from him.

"Out for a walk?" he asks.

"Actually, I was looking for you." I can feel that my cheeks are flushed from the adrenaline, but maybe that's good. Maybe it'll read as fear. "I need your help."

Conrad looks surprised.

I crane my neck, checking behind him, then behind me. Then I tilt my head down the beach. "Can we walk?"

There's a slight pause. I don't think he likes taking my direction. "Sure," he says.

We start plodding. I hug myself tightly, fingers gripping the shoulders of my parka, and let the weight bow me forward. I make myself small. I've had plenty of practice doing that, over the years.

For a good twenty feet, I don't say anything at all. I let the silence build. I can't drive the conversation too aggressively. I need to let him feel like he's in charge, like he's pulling something out of me.

Sure enough, when he finally speaks, his voice is filled with gentle pity. "What is it? Are you okay?"

I huddle tighter into myself. One second. Two. I can't overplay it.

And yet it's hard not to lean into the performance, with my blood thrilling like this, whispering *You're so close.* But first, the stoicism. The quiver of uncertainty as I say slowly, "Your NatureEye technology . . . the projection strip you showed us in the conference room. Does it work? Can you make holograms? Are they convincing?"

He stiffens slightly. He turns the questions over in his mind. I can feel him wondering if I'm on to him, deciding whether he should play dumb. He isn't as good an actor as I thought, now that I know what to look for.

"It works," he says. "And they are."

"You could make holograms of things other than nature, right? You could do objects? Animals? People?"

Another beat. "Yeah." His voice is guarded. "Why?"

I let out a shaky exhale. "I think someone's been using your technology to make me think I'm going crazy."

Conrad stops in his tracks. "What?"

"I know it sounds insane," I say, as I'm used to saying now, and before he can protest, I launch into the same spiel I gave Jess and Teddy. I tell him about the lifeboat, and the bear, and the woods on fire, and the tidal wave, and how at first I thought they were hallucinations and then I thought they were ghosts and now I know the truth. I don't get into the holograms of me or Jess, but I tell him the videos of me were deepfakes, I say I'm sure it's all related. I let myself ramble, let my words come out so fast they're almost garbled. I let myself act the way I knew I couldn't act when I wanted to be taken seriously. I let my voice tremble. I let my eyes fill with tears. "I can't believe he would do this to me."

Through this whole narration, Conrad has been the picture of compassion, his head ducked as he nods along solemnly. Now he glances up, thrown. "*He?*"

"Teddy."

"What makes you think *Teddy* did any of it?"

I feel a smile slipping out, and I break eye contact before Conrad can see it. I hunch my shoulders and resume walking against the wind. Conrad jogs after me.

"You must know I went to rehab a couple times," I say. "For my eating disorder. The first time I was only there for a month or two, but the second time was longer. Six months. That second time, I signed some papers. I gave Teddy a medical guardianship and a financial conservatorship. Do you know how those work? He had control of my medical decisions, my legal decisions, et cetera. My finances."

I peek over to see if he's figured out where this is going. He still looks slightly slack-jawed, so I continue, "That was three years ago. Right around the time you were getting investments for FinSafe. I didn't know anything about what was going on with my money. Before that, I hadn't paid much attention, but I still had to sign off on things, approve things. When we did the conservatorship, it all went straight to Teddy. I trusted him. I didn't know I was investing in Fin-Safe. On the boat, when you told me about the person who canceled the deposit and fucked everything up? I had no idea you were talking about me."

"Well, I got *that*," Conrad says. "I thought you forgot because it was so inconsequential."

I reach out to squeeze his arm. "You must have thought I was such a terrible person," I lament.

He grunts. It doesn't sound apologetic, so I push on. "Anyway, once I knew he had done that, it all fell into place. Clearly I hadn't really known him at all."

"But what does that have to do with the holograms?"

"Well, you showed us both the technology, and then they started right after. He must have stolen one of your projection strips, and figured out how to make it work." I widen my eyes, a picture of innocence. This is my big gamble: Conrad's weakness is his ego. He won't be able to stand the idea of someone else getting credit for his idea, especially Teddy. "I'm just so relieved you believe me. I thought as soon as I said the word *holograms*, I'd—"

"Teddy doesn't even know anything about tech!" Conrad bursts out.

"He's really smart, though," I say. "He can figure out pretty much anything. If there's anyone who could do something like that, it would be him."

Conrad lowers his head, swearing under his breath. I'm sure I've overplayed it. The ploy feels so *obvious*. Too heavy on the ditz, too cliché. He can't possibly believe I'd learn about the holograms and not suspect him first.

But after weeks of successfully torturing me, Conrad's opinion of my intelligence is at an all-time low. After only a few more steps—the gulls cawing around us, the ocean thundering—he flicks his head, like a dog shaking off water, and puts out his hand to stop me.

"Show me your phone," he says.

"My phone?"

He holds out his hand. When I place the phone in his palm, he inspects it to make sure I'm not recording. He glances up at me, a little wary, and I arrange my expression into the right combination of earnestness and pathetic desperation. This is where years of lying pays off.

"Who would believe you anyway?" he murmurs.

"But you just said—"

His hand tightens on my phone. "Clara, it was me. *I* made the deepfakes. *I* made the holograms."

"W-what are you talking about?"

"Teddy could *never* do something like that. He doesn't under-stand the technology. He doesn't understand *anything*. He's always had everything handed to him. Both of you have."

"But you barely know me. Why would you want to do that to me?"

"Because of FinSafe! Like you said." Frustrated, he kicks a shell, splintering it. "In college, everyone knew me as Teddy Wieland's roommate. People would only invite me places on the off chance I'd bring him. It was probably the same with your friends—I bet you didn't even notice how their whole lives revolved around you. When I got FinSafe together, and you and Teddy agreed to be part of it, I knew it would be the same thing again. As soon as I could tell investors the Wielands were behind it, all these doors would open up. I had an ace in my pocket. You were a sure thing. Then you pulled out, and my whole life went to shit."

"But I didn't know we pulled out. I didn't know we were ever even involved."

"I got myself together," he says, ignoring me. "I figured out the NatureEye technology. I reached out to Teddy to ask about pitching to WFCI. I knew having you attached would help, just as it would have helped FinSafe, and I wanted to show you what you could do. Do you know how hard it is to come up with one blockbuster tech idea, let alone two? In such a short amount of time? I'm *good* at what I do."

I resist saying that however impressive the projection strip is, calling a crypto platform "blockbuster tech" seems like a stretch, not to mention that the NatureEye concept hasn't even gotten off the ground. It's done a great job scaring me shitless, but that's hardly a profitable endeavor.

"So you knew you were going to make the deepfakes even before you got here?" I ask. "Is that why you planned to stay so long?"

"It's my island, too. I visited here growing up. I have memories here, too. I needed time to gather recordings. And I thought—well, sure, I thought the longer I stayed, the more time I'd have to see you guys. For you guys to see me. How far I've come."

"But when did you fix the technology?" I say, still playing dumb.

"It was never broken! I was going to show it to you. I was going to dazzle you. Then I started the presentation and you weren't focused on me at all. You were whispering to each other. And *you* seemed to have forgotten me entirely. Like FinSafe didn't mean anything to you. You had ruined my whole plan, and you didn't even remember."

"Because I didn't know about it," I remind him.

He isn't listening. "You were treating me like a joke. I wasn't going to beg for your approval. I'd done some work with deepfakes before. Making the first one was easy. I wanted you to see how it felt to be humiliated. I didn't expect you to think it was real—I thought you'd announce it was a fake and move on. I didn't understand why you hadn't until I went over to Teddy's house that day, and I saw how it was affecting you. And how it was affecting Teddy and Jess, too. I saw all the strain between the three of you. It was so obvious." His lip curls as he remembers. "Teddy told me you rejected the funding, and I decided to see how far I could push you two apart. With the videos, but also—you didn't even put this together, did you?—with the holograms. I made deepfake holograms of *you* three. That time in the alley outside the Anchor? When you and Teddy argued with Jess? That wasn't really her. And you had no idea!" he crows gleefully. "There were other times, too. I made Teddy think he had a stalker. I made him think everyone was turning against him. I showed Jess a hologram of you just the other day, made her think you wouldn't even open the gates to the property for her. That kind of thing. I *got* you."

By my feet, a bubble of sand pops: a clam, breathing.

"Why Jess?" I ask. "She didn't have anything to do with FinSafe or NatureEye."

He shrugs. "I wanted to hurt you and Teddy. She was the fastest way to both of you."

"So she was collateral damage?"

"Don't say that like she's innocent," he warns. "I'm tired of you women acting so smart, acting like you're above it all. I mean, you're the ones who fell for it. You can't blame me for wanting to see how far I could push it. I wasn't about to stop right when it got interesting."

I wait for him to continue. But he's done.

That's all.

That's his whole motive.

He spread a fake sex video of me because it was *interesting*. He made me think I was going insane because he had nothing better to do. He thought I lost him some money once, so he faked holograms of my dead parents and made me watch them die again, in vivid color. All for fun. Because he could.

Interesting is what you call a logic problem. An art exhibit. An experimental film. My life destroyed, my trauma displayed, my relationships shattered.

But what kind of motive *would* satisfy me? What reason would justify his actions? And if they were justified, would they hurt less? I was being naive to think that his explanation would make sense to me, help me understand. Torture's only objective is pain.

The wind picks up, slaps the collar of my parka against my cheek. The sky has started spitting intermittently.

"So what's the next step?" I can't help it: my voice turns high-pitched, accusatory. "Attack me? Slit my throat? What else do you have planned?"

"I would never hurt you," Conrad says self-righteously.

"People online have been threatening to *kill* me."

He raises his hands like a soccer player to a referee. *Look, no hands.* "I didn't do that."

I gape. "You made the videos. You caused it."

"I'm not responsible for what those people say."

Of course. He's not responsible for anything.

Rage slams into me again, and sucks away, a riptide of hopelessness. I'm going to leave unsatisfied. Half the reason I came down here was to understand why he did it, and now I have to settle for this non-explanation.

All my life I've believed in the stupid Golden Rule—that I could avoid being seriously hurt by never seriously hurting anyone else. I thought, in my little journey of self-improvement, that if I understood what I had done to Conrad, then I could avoid ever doing it again. But now look. Conrad gave me what he thought I deserved, and it doesn't matter that it isn't the same as what I think I deserve. An eye for an eye, they say, but that requires both people to agree on what constitutes an eye: the retina, the lash, the full ball dripping in its socket?

We're back at the start of the beach. A few feet away, the sea churns. I glance up at the path. The man in the bucket hat is gone now. Alicia Samuels has left, too. The beach is empty. I could reach out for Conrad so easily right now. Catch him off guard. I could push him down the slope, into the water. He isn't so much taller than me, and I have rage and the element of surprise on my side. I can picture him stumbling through the water, tripping on the rocks, falling forward. I can picture myself holding him down. He would struggle and flail. I could move fast. I would slam him down into the water. I would grab his face and press my thumbs to his eyelids. I would push down, down, down until I heard the squelch of blood.

"I hope you're not waiting for an apology," Conrad says. He's frowning now, dissatisfied with my reaction. He wanted more from me. He wanted fear and awe. He wanted the counterattack, the proof he had boiled me down to nothing.

I shake my head once, slowly. "No. You've given me everything I need."

Back in my car, I pick up the puffin beanbag, toss it between my hands.

What it feels like, to have an illusion broken: It feels like a magic trick gone wrong. A rabbit on a tray. The magician drops a white napkin down over it and waves his hand. Abracadabra! The rabbit is supposed to disappear. But the napkin keeps moving. Out from under the neat hem, the rabbit pushes its quivering nose. Its beady black eyes, bulging, panicked. It doesn't want to leave the napkin behind. The napkin has become the rabbit's home, its protection. It has kept the rabbit warm for many years. Without it, the rabbit is only one rabbit among many, a vulnerable mammal with spillable blood and a heart that will stop if you stomp on it. People are hungry, and a rabbit can be skinned. It has muscles, which will be tender to eat, and a layer of fat, which will melt in their mouths, and blood that will become juice on their tongues.

So why would it give up its disguise, unless it had to? Why would it ever let itself be revealed?

On the count of three, I raise the beanbag and smash it into my eye.

I'm in town for another two hours, which is a little longer than I thought it would take. It's raining in earnest by the time I'm done with what I came to do, and I didn't think to bring an umbrella. I wring my hair out on the hem of my sweater before starting the car.

Back to Ledgelawn, the church. The street is just how I left it this morning. Conrad's car is back in his driveway. I park in front of the house next to his. Closer than I've parked on my other stakeouts. This time, there's no point in hiding.

Again I wait.

I drum my fingers against the steering wheel, start picking at a thread in the leather. I eat a granola bar, 210 calories, and I'm so strung out on suspense that I only barely feel the weight in my stomach. I flip down the shitty rental car's shitty mirror and assess my eye. The beanbag left a bad bruise. The whole area is fuchsia, already turning to indigo, the color of a broken mood ring.

Fear and joy fizz together inside me, baking soda in vinegar.

Finally, two matching SUVs crawl down the street. They're powder-blue and freshly waxed. Unlike my rental, they aren't forgettable. Their front bumpers are labeled in white: MAINE STATE POLICE.

They stop in front of Conrad's house. Four troopers in black vests get out. I sink low in my seat and roll down my window. Over the edge of the dashboard, I watch two of them walk up the sidewalk. Kavanik and Rooney. The ones I talked to an hour ago, as I sobbed dramatically into my hands. The other two stand by Conrad's car.

Kavanik rings the doorbell. They wait twenty seconds, thirty. Rooney reaches out to ring again when the door opens. Conrad.

Same outfit he was wearing this morning. Same dumb face. Rooney hikes up his shirt to expose his gun in its holster.

"Conrad Gaffney?"

"Yes."

Kavanik holds out a piece of paper. "We have a warrant to search your car and home."

Conrad puffs out his chest. "For what?"

"It's listed on the warrant," Kavanik says. "We'll start with the car."

Conrad grabs the paper, reads. He doesn't get far before he looks up, shaking his head. "I don't even know what this is."

"Open the car, sir."

One of the other troopers tries the car handle. It's unlocked, again. I noticed that, during my stakeouts. Conrad's so desperate to seem a part of island life that he's stopped locking his car. But we're coming up on tourist season now. You should always lock your car. You never know what someone might take.

Or put inside.

It doesn't take them long to find it. I chose a good hiding place. The pocket behind the driver's seat, which you never check inside unless you're looking for something lost. Rooney sticks his arm down it and pulls out a golden chain. He turns to the others, holding it aloft.

"Think I got it."

Conrad is so shocked that when Kavanik prods him to turn around, he does so without resisting, only craning his head over his shoulder to stare at my mother's necklace.

I did my research. The penalties for deepfakes are unimpressive. But there are things that are worth more to the law than my shame. In Maine, theft of an object worth more than ten thousand dollars is a Class B felony. Causing bodily harm during the robbery elevates it to Class A.

So revenge porn will get you a fine. But if, for example, someone were to punch someone in the eye and steal a twenty-thousand-dollar necklace, that's another story. For that, the maximum punishment is thirty years.

Conrad might not get the maximum. But the evidence is against him. The item was in his car—I put it there before I joined him, while his car was in the beach parking lot—and Alicia Samuels will testify that she saw us on the beach, in the middle of an intense discussion. When I said hi to her, my face wasn't bruised.

I wanted his explanation, but I also wanted an eyewitness.

Sometimes the fake is easier to prove.

Kavanik herds Conrad to the car. As he reads him his rights, Conrad's still looking over his shoulder, at his car, at the evidence bag, then scanning the shrubs, the windows of nearby houses. Looking for me.

Just before they put him into the back of the cruiser, his gaze lands on my little rental car.

His eyes narrow.

I wiggle my fingers and wave.

36

CLARA

April 29

On the drive home, adrenaline kaleidoscopes my thoughts, splitting them into conflicting fragments. I did it. I did it, I did it. He's gone. *It was interesting.* I beat him. *Collateral damage.* I was right. I'm a genius and a star.

Jess is sitting on my porch swing when I pull up. I flail out of the car, overcome. "I did it. I fixed it. It's over," I say, almost laughing. I can hardly believe it.

"Over?" she repeats, confused. "What's over?"

Just short of the porch, I finally get a good look at her. I stop in my tracks. The weird not-quite laugh dies in my throat. She looks terrible.

Her face is sallow, and her forehead has a cluster of stress pimples. Her lips are pale and dry. In the rain, her hair frizzes around her head like a halo.

The kaleidoscope turns again. Teddy's study. Jess hanging back, silent. My joy starts to fade.

She's staring at me, too. "What happened to your eye?"

I forgot about the shiner. It didn't even hurt, the whole drive. As soon as she mentions it, the dull throb returns.

"It's fine," I say dismissively. "What are you doing here?"

Instead of answering, she steps forward. She reaches up, her palm flat, and brushes it over my shoulder, down my arm. The nylon of my parka rustles under her fingertips. When she reaches the end of my sleeve, she plays with the snap on the cuff, then lets her hand drop back to her side.

Surprise thickens my throat.

She's testing me, the way I tested her in Teddy's office. She's making sure I'm real.

"You were right about the holograms," she says.

"I know." I don't say it to be mean, but the words have a rough edge. I thought not being believed was bad, but being believed belatedly only feels like a different strain of betrayal. "What changed your mind?"

She chews her lip. "Did you see the video that came out this morning?"

"I've been a little busy."

"It's of Teddy."

"More cash bonfires?"

"It's not a deepfake. It's a real video."

The back of my neck tightens. "Something bad?"

She glances around, nervously skimming the woods. "Can I come inside?"

I have the childish temptation to say no—to seal her out, just so she can see how it feels. But it only lasts a second. She looks so crumpled and insubstantial. And she believes me now. Is willing to say she be-lieves me.

Rain drips from the roof.

I dig my keys out of my pocket. "Of course. Come on in."

The first thing Jess says when we get inside is "Do you have alcohol?"

I blink. The only time I've ever seen Jess drink before 4:00 p.m. was at Felicity's bridal shower, when she didn't realize there was vodka in the strawberry punch. "Um—yes."

When I come back from the kitchen with two glasses of single malt and an ice pack tucked under one arm, she's still standing in the middle of the living room, wringing her hands and rotating uselessly from side to side, like a robot vacuum that got stuck in a corner. It's so unlike her usual poise that I feel the last pieces of my anger slide away.

"Sit down," I say gently.

She obeys.

A few weeks ago, I was the one on the sofa, and she was the one getting me a drink. A few years ago, she was the one watching me like a hawk as I took my heart medicine, my vitamins, my antidepressants. It's weird to be the one doing the monitoring. I feel like I'm violating her privacy somehow.

"Take a sip," I say.

She obeys that, too.

I hold the ice pack to my battered eye, wincing when it stings. "Now, start at the beginning."

Even with my coaching, it takes Jess ten full minutes to spit out the events of the last twenty-four hours—about talking to Conrad at the party, Lisa spilling soup on Teddy, Teddy thinking he saw us together—and when she finally rambles to a close, she turns to me with a desper-ate, expectant expression I've only ever seen in the mirror.

I don't know how to respond. What to feel. Shock is for someone who's had a different day, a different month. A different life. Bafflement? Maybe bafflement.

Weirdly, the hardest thing to process is the fact that during our whole conversation on the beach, Conrad knew all of this. He knew what he had made Teddy see. I tricked him, but he still knew something I didn't. It's like finding a bite on your arm from a spider you've already killed.

I sip my whiskey. Peat and brine. When I swallow, my throat is a line of fire. "Conrad's in police custody," I say.

"For the deepfakes?"

"Not exactly." I can't decide whether to tell her what I did. She'll report it to Teddy as soon as they make up, and I don't want him to know yet. On the other hand, it feels wrong not to confide in her. In the past, when I've lied to her, it's always been to cover up something I'm ashamed of, not something I did right. "I framed him. I told the police he stole my mother's necklace. They arrested him for theft and battery. It's better that way—the sentence is higher than it would be for the deepfakes."

"Battery?" She stares at the ice pack still pressed to my face. "He gave you the black eye?"

"I gave it to myself."

Her face is a mix of horror and awe. "Clara, filing a false police report is a crime."

"Then I hope you don't tell them it's false."

"No, of course I'm not going to—but—" She shakes her head. "Damn."

"I met with him this morning, too. Before I reported it. I wanted him to tell me why he did everything."

"Did he?"

My chest tightens at the memory. "Sort of. He said he did it because it was fun."

Jess looks as disgusted as I feel. Her hands have stopped trembling, though. "Can't he just get out of the charges? He could make new videos or—holograms." Even now, she hesitates before the word, like she can't believe she's saying it aloud. "A video showing you putting the necklace in his car."

"I doubt he can do that from jail, and he would need images of his rental car, the house in the background, the necklace . . . And if he did somehow make a video, Dr. Shallcross could disprove it." I try to sound confident, because Jess needs me to be, and mostly I am. But a little part of me remembers Shallcross saying: *We can't guarantee someone hasn't come up with a better algorithm than us.* She could disprove this video, but can she disprove *any* video? And even if she did, would the jury care? Or would they believe what they had already seen?

I shove this thought aside and say firmly, "So it's okay. What he did last night was awful. But he can't hurt us anymore."

Jess stares down into her glass. "I should have believed you."

"It's okay."

"I didn't think you were lying, exactly. I thought you were mistaken."

I smile around the ice pack. "Well—you thought I was lying at least a *little*."

Her mouth twitches at the corner. "Maybe a little." She sobers. "But I'm sorry for thinking that. And sorry for not standing up for you."

It's so different than the apologies I'm used to getting—but *I'm sorry* is somehow worlds away from *I'm sorry, but.*

"I put you in a bad position," I say. "I'm sorry, too."

"Going forward, no more secrets."

"No more secrets," I agree.

We sit there silently for almost a minute. Jess rolls her glass between her hands, like she's looking for the answers on the liquid's surface. "Do you think—the way Teddy's been lately. Is that how he's always been, and we didn't see it?"

"I don't know. He's never yelled at me like that before. But I've never talked to him like that, either." I feel a whisper of unease, a

sense that I'm not going to like whatever she says next. "I mean—
we've all been dealing with a lot . . ."

She lifts her head to search my face. Finally, she says, "He used
to make me feel safe. That's why I fell in love with him. He doesn't
make me feel safe anymore."

Cold water drips from the ice pack down my arm. Slowly, I re-
move the pack from my face and set it on the coffee table. "What are
you saying?"

Instead of answering, she reaches over to slide a coaster under the
dripping ice pack.

"Jess."

She nudges the coaster parallel with the table's edge, not meeting
my eyes. "But you and I would still be friends, right? If I . . ."

My stomach churns. "If you what?"

"If I left him."

I stop breathing.

Jess without Teddy, Teddy without Jess.

I've thought about the possibility before. All their marriage, I've
secretly hoped that someday my place in Jess's order of precedence
would change again, I would move back to the front of the line. Once
again, I'd be her best friend before I'd be her husband's sister. In my
imagination, it was always a rewinding. Back to the way things used
to be—not five years ago, but fifteen, even twenty, back before my life
deformed into something I don't recognize.

But that was always a fantasy. It deflates immediately under the
word *divorce*. The practicalities. Jess would move out, maybe off the
island altogether. The legal system. A month ago, I would have said
Teddy would be mature about it. Now I'm not so sure. Pierce made
her sign a prenup, but does that mean it's easy? I need to google *prenups*. Or would googling *prenups* mean I've already picked sides?

"But it's only been the last couple weeks that he's been so bad," I
say, feeling a little hysterical. "The person he's been lately, that's not
the real Teddy."

"It was. I touched him."

My hands are clammy. I try to wipe them on my jeans, then remember my jeans are still wet. "Okay, yes, it's Teddy. A part of Teddy we didn't see before. But it only came out because of Conrad. And Conrad's gone now, so things will go back the way they were."

"Back the way they were," Jess repeats. "You mean like how they were when he threw you under the bus with FinSafe?"

"Well, no. Not like that. Better."

Her brow puckers. "Can you forget he did that? Can you forget about everything he said to you?"

At first, I think she means it as a challenge—like *No way you could possibly forget*—but her expression is sincere and curious. Like I could teach her the limits of what's possible.

"I'm going to try," I say, then feel a pulse of uncertainty, like I've buzzed in with the wrong answer. "I mean, I have to. He's my brother."

Outside, the rain picks up again, a quick drumming at the window. Jess doesn't seem to notice. She squints at me, like she's trying to make out my face from a long distance.

"You didn't answer my question," she says.

"What question?" I know what question.

"Would we still be friends?"

A rattle of wind. The kaleidoscope turns, and turns, and turns.

"Always," I say, looking at the rain.

There's another moment from Teddy and Jess's wedding that I try not to think about, and mostly I succeed.

It was toward the end of the night. After my conversation with Celeste. The music had shifted to 1990s R&B deep cuts. The dance moves were devolving from spins and flourishes into a contented zombie shuffling. Women had kicked off their heels, men had torn off their ties. A general deshabille. Teddy was off at one end of the patio having cigars with some of our male cousins, and the photographer was capturing images that would later make us laugh with their resemblance to *Vogue* ensemble fashion shoots. Handsome men in tuxedo shirtsleeves, clapping each other on the back as smoke swirled around them. Conrad might have been among them. I don't remember.

Jess was just inside the villa, drunk on champagne and happiness. She had a little plate of wedding cake, which she was eating with focused attention as she swayed on her feet, sometimes bumping against the stone wall of the villa when she lost her balance. She had for some reason decided to eat the cake with a spoon instead of a fork, and every bite took her a few tries to get it right. The spoon glinted silver as she stabbed it again and again into the sponge.

"How you doing?" I asked. I wasn't in much better shape.

"Great," she slurred. "Best night."

"You look beautiful." I had already said it one million times.

She got some of the cake on her spoon and lifted it triumphantly. "You too."

The music pounded. I leaned on the wall next to her. The door was blue and ornate. You could see the reflections of the dancers in the window.

By this time in my life, I was familiar with self-destruction. It always started the same way, in my belly, and rose like flooding water seeking an outlet. It tried my heart, my lungs, my skull, it went down to my littlest toenail and out to the pads of my fingertips, and when it failed, it went the trusty route, up my throat and out my mouth. There was no stopping it. If I let it out, it would kill me, but if I held it in, I would drown.

I looked over at her. "Jess. I have to tell you a secret."

She licked the spoon with her pink tongue. Her eyes were wide. "Okay."

There it was, the flooding water rising.

I wove my fingers through her hair and drew her head to me until my right temple was pressed against her left, skull to skull, and I could smell the sugary scent of the cake, her perfume, her. Her breath was hot against my ear, and mine must have been hot against hers.

"I love you," I said.

She froze. Then laughed. "I know, bitch. That's not a secret."

"No?"

She bumped her hip to mine. "I love you, too."

Choices unfolded. Possible interpretations. Forked paths, taken or not taken. They blurred in my mind. I was drunk, I was desperate. I was running on intuition and Chandon.

Mostly, I didn't want to be forgotten.

Always, I didn't want to be alone.

I brushed my fingers along her neck. Her skin melted and shone. She gave way to me, as she had started giving way to Teddy. It was true I didn't mind as much when it was for me. I cradled her neck, her soft neck, and she turned her head and pressed her mouth to mine.

We stood there, breathing. A second elapsed. Enough for it to pass from a mistake into a fact.

Then I turned away. You'd think she would be the one to turn, but it was me. My throat went sour and strange. I felt that I had been cheated somehow, though I couldn't have articulated how, or of what, or by whom.

"Sorry," Jess said. She flapped her hands once, twice, as if searching for words. Finally, she gave up and hurried away.

That was the moment I truly feared someone had captured, when I saw that there was a video from the wedding. Not very much could have been made, externally, from a one-second kiss. But it would have been much worse to me, because it was real.

37

JESS

April 30

Our closet is as I left it yesterday. Teddy's side: suit jackets on wooden hangers, wing-tip shoes paired on the shelves. Stiff jeans, pressed trousers, a new set of quarter-zips. On my side, dresses arranged according to length and then color. A rainbow Missoni peeking out at one end. Sweaters stacked by color, rotated with the seasons. My Chanel jackets in pastel tweeds. Handbags stuffed with tissue paper. I walk over to the shirts and run my hand over the fabrics. Silk charmeuse and French linen and crepe and dupioni and georgette and faille. Navy and white and periwinkle and green. I want to press my face into the fabrics and warm them with my tears. "Such beautiful shirts," Daisy told Gatsby, weeping, wishing they were hers. These are mine, and still I want to cry.

I change out of the top I borrowed from Clara and into a plain sweater and jeans. I'm looking for a hair elastic when I hear the faint sound of a door closing downstairs. My heart stutters.

Teddy's home.

I find him in his study, rooting through the drawers of his desk. The TV is playing the camera feed. The shots are so motionless that they might as well be photos.

"What are you looking for?" I ask.

He startles, but spares me only a glance before he goes back to his rummaging, slamming a drawer shut so he can move on to the next.

"Where's that paper Clara brought?" he demands.

"Which one?"

Staples and paper clips go flying. "The one from the deepfake expert."

"Clara took it with her. But we can find out the name of the—"

"I don't want the name, I want the paper!" He slams this drawer, too, punctuating his words.

His face is flushed, his hair falling over his forehead. He is a mess. I've never seen him like this before. What other lies has Conrad shown him, these past few weeks, to make him act like this? Or was he always like this, and I just wasn't paying attention? When I moved into this house, I started hearing things I wouldn't have noticed before. Perhaps the same thing has happened now that I've gotten used to Teddy. My senses have adjusted. The cracks are starting to show.

"What do you want the paper for?" I ask.

"I need to see how it's formatted. So I can—" He breaks off, but I already understand.

"Teddy, the video of you isn't fake. You can't lie and say it is."

He slaps the desk, exasperated. "Will you shut up and help me look?"

"Please don't talk to me like that."

He straightens fully and inspects me, head to toe, as if he's never seen me before.

"Where did you stay last night?" he asks.

"Clara's house." There's a beat, and I see where he's going with this. "Because she's my *friend*. She's your sister! What would you rather I do, go to a hotel? Like you want more bad press? I told you already. We didn't do anything. Clara wasn't even there that night. You have to trust me."

"Trust you over my own eyes?"

"Well, yes! If you want to make this work—"

"Make what work?"

"This." I move my finger between us. "Us."

The air changes. An electric cord dropped in a bathtub, the water coursing with invisible danger.

"What are you saying? You want a divorce?"

"Of course I don't *want* one! But I can't be with you if you don't trust me."

He shakes his head once, abruptly. "We can't split up. The campaign needs us together."

"*That's* your main concern?"

He isn't listening. "I'd think very carefully before you say something you regret. A divorce won't end well for you."

"What's that supposed to mean?"

His face contorts until it looks like a mask of itself. A flatter, harder version of my favorite face. "Be realistic. You cheated on me!"

"I didn't!"

"*And* you signed a prenup." He takes a step toward me, glittering with anger. "Whatever you want, you won't get it." His finger is pointed at me, straight at my heart. "I will *bury* you."

And just like that, I'm sent back to that time I don't like to think about, in Kattinocket, before my mother brought me here to be reborn. Hiding under the table from the screaming. Hands over my ears. *I'll kill you, Denise*—his fist smashing through plaster—her cowering by the fridge, a stack of plates, and the *crash crash crash* as she threw them one by one. *You just try.* Waiting for the sound of the front door closing and his car engine starting, which would mean finally I could unwind myself from my ball, lift the hem of the tablecloth onto the scene of destruction, and go to comfort my mother as she sobbed.

Eight years I've been with Teddy. That's a long time. I thought I knew him like the back of my hand. I worked at it. I worked at knowing him. Still, until the past few days, I had never seen this part of him before. He kept it a secret, perhaps even from himself: this boiling heat, this rage. A man on the verge.

"You won't get anything," he's saying. "I won't let you. You leave me and you leave all this behind. Every penny. You start over again."

I feel myself shutting down. He's so large and broad, and when he first held me, it made me feel like I was safe: but now, as the muscles in his shoulders tighten, I see that his strength is dangerous, too—that he might not be the safety net. He might be the wind knocking me off the wire.

"Say something," he spits.

I can't. My tongue is frozen in my mouth. I'm a deer in headlights, all panic and instinct.

He grabs me by the arms, shakes me. His eyes are wild and bright. "Say something!"

I struggle in his grip. He holds me tight. His fingers dig into my skin. I go limp, and the change in momentum throws him off-balance. His full weight comes against me, a sweet embrace—

And then we're both stumbling backward, and my back crashes into the glass case for the *Transformation*, shattering it. Fragments rain down. I'm still plowing backward. There's a sharp pain across my neck, and another in the middle of my back. I gasp, and it comes out all wrong. Something warm and wet trickles down my chest. I clap my hand to my neck and feel a jagged shape. Teddy and I stare at each other, shocked. And then my knees go out from under me, and I crumple to the floor.

38

CLARA

April 30

My great-great-grandfather commissioned every carriage road that slithers through the park—the ones that connect Brooks Mountain to Lafitte Hill, Tallis Pond to Falcon Lake and beyond. Seventy miles of carriage roads. The roads were controversial at first. Ambrose's rival said he was destroying the forest. Ambrose said he was making it accessible, allowing others to experience nature's transformative potential. He liked to quote John Muir: "Between every two pine trees there is a door leading to a new way of life."

"My work," Ambrose would explain, "is to open the door."

It was just a coincidence that the first carriage road led from Vantage Point directly to his mistress's home.

On the last day of this cursed month, I find myself walking that carriage road. It was my parents' other favorite walk—the one we could have taken, sixteen years ago, and spared ourselves. The weather is typical April, cold and misty, so there's no view to speak of. Only the gray sky and the gray road and the gray stones that separate the gray road from the wet gray trees. Thanks to yesterday's rain, a coat of mud slicks the ground where the gravel was thinned by snowmelt over the winter. Every step I take echoes in the quiet: a squelch as my feet hit the mud, a crunch as the remaining gravel gives way.

Secretly, I thought today might dawn warm and sunny, as if Conrad's arrest could fix everything, even the weather. And some things *have* improved. The news about the arrest will probably be picked up by the major outlets by the end of the day. Conrad's bail hearing is scheduled for tomorrow, and the district attorney thinks he'll be able to get Conrad remanded until trial.

It might help, he says, if I can be there, too. My face is good evidence.

Still, my euphoria has faded. Overnight, my eye has swollen almost shut. It looks like I'm keeping a golf ball tucked under my eyelid. Jess hasn't made a decision about Teddy, as far as I know, but she went back to the main house to pack some clothes, which can't be a good sign.

And this morning, I've already received six offensive DMs and two rape threats. It's sinking in that even if Conrad gets the maximum sentence, the last few weeks aren't magically going away. Not for me. Teddy's video will probably blow over by next year. Men recover from scandals in dog years. For every year a man spends in "reflection and healing," a woman has to spend seven. They'll be talking about my sex tape for the rest of my life.

All in all, it's not exactly what I imagined.

I come to one of the huge stone bridges that dot the carriage roads—also commissioned by Ambrose. The creek below is full to-day, a rush of mud and dead leaves. Winter shedding its final skin.

When Jess said she was going to pack a bag, she didn't say if she was going to bring the bag back to my place or find a hotel. I didn't ask, because then I'd have to respond.

Jess or Teddy. Teddy or Jess. I can feel the choice coming, a train rattling the tracks.

I remember that day coming back from Marien, the rest area with the Starbucks, the abundance of options. This time, no one's coming to give me the answer.

Across the gorge, aspen trees tilt in the wind. Tall white rods. The branches are dotted with fluffy catkins and new leaves.

The trees all look identical, which is no coincidence. In fifth grade, we learned that aspens clone themselves. What looks like a grove of many aspens is actually one big tree connected underground. It's dangerous, though, to be so similar. If a virus gets into one, it can kill the whole plant, working its way through the grove, tree by tree, clone by clone.

Some of my classmates were shocked by this revelation. It didn't faze me at all. It made sense to me that a family of trees might be doomed together. That a resemblance could signal power and death at the same time.

I can piece together which parts of the last few weeks were fake. But the original shadow, the one from sixteen years ago—that one, I'll never be able to explain. I'll never know whether it was the curse or a trick of light or a figment of my imagination.

I only know the consequences have been real.

The wind picks up, and the leaves on the aspens tremble in uni-son, like a curtain of coins. With the gust comes a horrible feeling, like the one I felt the other day driving back onto the island, but stronger. Undeniable. It's more than a cry in my gut. It's a scream, a howl.

It shoves me away from the bridge, back down the road the way I came. Faster now, my feet slapping water up onto my legs.

Jess, I think. *Teddy*.

Although I'm not sure, exactly. Maybe I think their names the other way around.

The big house looks the same as it always does, the same as it has my whole life. There's no reason for me to feel strange about the blank front of the house, the sky reflected in the polished, darkened glass. It's drizzling again, a patter of water on moss. Jess's and Teddy's cars are both outside, which sends another frisson of nerves up my arms. That's also silly: they both live here. Of course they're both home. They could have made up. Everything could be fine.

The door is unlocked, and the entrance hall is dark and quiet.

"Teddy?" I call out. "Jess?"

No one answers.

I feel stupid for the quiver in my voice. When I find them both chatting and laughing, Teddy's going to make so much fun of me for being scared.

Then I remember Teddy and I are a long way from teasing, right now.

The front sitting room is empty. So are the kitchen and the living room. I peek into the mudroom, the rows of galoshes, raincoats, sports equipment. Nothing. Rain scratches the windows. A door slams nearby, and I jump a mile, nearly knocking a tennis racket off its peg. I listen, trying to figure out which door it was, but I can't tell. I laugh at myself, high-pitched. A laugh for posterity. Stupid Clara.

I'm halfway down the back hallway when I hear it. A thud. A muffled, garbled noise. I call out again, and again no one answers. I hurry down the hall, checking another sitting room, a nook, a bathroom—still nothing—until I get to Teddy's study, which is where the horror begins.

My brain registers the objects first. The computer tipped on its side. The *Transformation* ship-in-the-bottle smashed to pieces. Oh no, someone broke in. My brain slows and dizzies. I see the rug, now red, and I think, Someone broke in and changed the rug. Then I think, No, they broke in and spilled wine everywhere. And: That will be hard to clean.

Then I see Jess. She's been there the whole time, right in front of me, right in my line of sight, but it's like my brain wouldn't let me see her, my brain wished her away. Even now, when I see her lying there—her body sprawled out, face down, legs at strange angles, arms flopped to the side in a widening circle of red—my first thought is *Jess fell asleep and the burglar spilled wine on her.* My mind refuses, but my legs push me forward until I fall to my knees next to her and everything comes into focus in a sick, spinning rush.

I reach out to touch her. Please. Please let it be an illusion. Please let Conrad have escaped, and have planted this image. Please let my hand pass through air.

Her shirt is solid, and slick with blood.

Instinctively, I pull back. I hold my shaking hands a few inches above her, hovering them the length of her body, like a fucking Reiki healer trying to align chakras. Really I'm just trying to figure out where to start. The blood keeps coming. I don't know from where. A piece of glass the size of my hand protrudes from her neck. That'll do it. My head lightens like a balloon. More glass glitters on her shirt. A small brown stick pokes out from the middle of her back.

"Jess?" I whisper.

It's hard to get my phone out of my pocket; my hand is wet, everything is slippery. It takes me three tries to dial 911 correctly, then several stammering seconds to explain that someone is hurt. As the dispatcher says they're sending an ambulance, Jess's arm twitches. She makes a small sound. A whimper or a wheeze. Startled, I drop the phone. It lands on Jess with an awkward splat. Her body jerks in response.

"Te—?" she whispers.

I jump up and over to her other side, closer to her face where it's pressed against the floor. "What? What is it?"

"Ted . . ."

"I'll call him. I'll get him. Don't worry."

I see where the blood is coming from now, not only her neck and back, but also somewhere under her torso. I reach one hand under her side, feeling for the wound, and my fingers slip inside her. Just . . . slip inside. Through a gash, through wet flesh. I pull my sweater over my head and ball it up and press it under the wound as best I can, trying to stop the flow of blood.

"Ma'am?" comes the dispatcher's voice from the phone. It's still lying on Jess's back, the case now smeared with blood. "Ma'am, are you there with me?"

"She's alive," I say. "I think—can they hurry? Are they here yet?"

"They're on their way." The dispatcher keeps asking me questions, my name, Jess's name, what room am I in, what happened. I try to answer, I think I answer, but I'm looking around the room. I'm seeing things now, more things. The trail of blood between Jess and the broken ship. Oh Jesus fuck. The stick in her back is the ship's mast. There's a handprint on the edge of the desk, like someone tripped and caught themselves. It couldn't have been Jess. It's too far away. There's a red shape near it, an oval crossed with wavy lines: a large footprint, a shoe's tread.

"Ted," she says again, fainter now.

A pressure builds inside me: a truth, trying to dawn.

"Teddy's fine. Stay with me," I tell her. "Okay? Stay the fuck alive."

Minutes pass like years. Like being held down. Like fighting to swallow.

At last, a stampede of footsteps. "In here!" I shout, and the paramedics are there, pushing me away. Jess twitches and moans. I step back, my hands lifted as if in surrender. It's incredible how quickly the paramedics move, how quickly they make you redundant. But then

Jess would know this: we've been here before, many years ago, our roles reversed, her standing over my body, at the bottom of a flight of stairs.

I can't watch them work on her anymore so I look away. Out the window. I try to focus on the water, the yard, anything. Then I catch sight of movement down on the dock, next to the *Transformation*.

My heart stops. No, no, no, no.

I take a step toward the door. Then another.

"Please sit down," one of the paramedics tells me, "please stay here," but they can't stop me, they're busy rolling her onto a stretcher, muttering jargon into their radios. I'm out the door. I'm in the hallway. The stairwell. The living room. I don't know what I'm doing. More sirens in the distance: the police.

I run for the back door, tracking blood.

39

CLARA

April 30

With the wind coming from the south, the water on the sound is choppy and gray. Waves rise with pale shadows, crash back down onto themselves in white lines. Pain splits through my shins as I run down the sloped path. By the time I reach the platform above the dock, the *Transformation* is halfway to launched. Teddy is a dot of nylon on the prow, pulling in the bowline.

"Teddy!" I scream. The wind carries it away, or he chooses not to hear.

The bridge down to the dock is a steep curve, nailed intermittently with nonslip tracks. The wood in between is already wet, the railings open, and I have to move slowly to keep from falling onto the rocks far below. When I'm halfway over, a wave crests beneath the dock and the bridge sways beneath me. I lose my balance and slide the last few feet on my ass.

Teddy has moved on to the rain covers. He unhooks them methodically, like he's peeling an orange. Through the mesh of the windshield cover, his shape is beige and blurred.

I scramble to my feet. My injured eye throbs. "Teddy!"

He looks over the boat's roof, and his face darkens. "Go away!"

There's a flash of fabric as he finishes unbuttoning the cover and hops off the gunwale onto the boat's deck, the cover bunched in his hands, just as the boat bounces on a wave. He lands on his feet, but it seems like a near miss.

"Jess is hurt," I say, but even as I say it, I'm registering the sight of him. He's covered in blood. It's streaked down the side of his neck, pooled in the crease of his ear. It circles his wrists like handcuffs. Diluted by the mist and sea spray, it drips pinkly off his chin.

"She's hurt," I repeat quietly. Unnecessarily.

Teddy jerks his head to the side, a denial. "She'll be fine."

"No. The paramedics are with her now. Did you—" I can't say it. Can barely think it.

Teddy comes off the boat onto the dock, unloops the stern line, and tosses it on board. When he reaches for the last cleat, I try to block him, but he elbows me aside, crouching down to grapple with the wet rope.

"What happened?" I demand. "What are you doing?"

"What does it look like I'm doing?"

"Taking the boat out."

"Correct." He gets the spring line free.

"But you can't leave. Jess needs you. She needs us. You can't leave."

He stands up, so much taller than me. "Fuck off, Clara!"

He leaps back onto the boat before I can come up with a response.

As I stand there, frozen, he turns on the navigation system and lowers the engine into the water. This is all out of order. He should have done all that before dropping the dock lines, because now the boat is moving with the waves and he has no power underneath him. The fact that he's made this stupid mistake tells me he's panicking. I've never seen him panic before, certainly not to the point of incompetence, and I find myself staring at him like he's a circus spectacle.

He hits the gas, and the engine whirs to life. But in his panic, he forgot to take the spring line with him when he jumped back on, and it's still looped around the cleat, holding the boat a few feet from the dock. When Teddy sees what's happened, he lets out an agonized noise I barely hear over the engine and the waves.

Together, we look back up the hill to the house. The rain is getting heavier, and the house blurs into the surrounding woods. Two people are tripping down the slope. Police.

"Get the line!" he shouts to me, one of his usual commands, but there's a pleading note in his voice I've never heard. He's never asked me for help.

If there are no packages, the local mail boat doesn't dock during its runs: when it reaches an island, it comes close to the dock, and the boy jumps off with the mail and dashes down the planks, drops the mail inside the box, and runs back to jump on the boat before it moves past the dock's other end. If he's left behind, he's left behind.

I would have been left behind, too, in another life, if Teddy hadn't slowed to wait. If he hadn't always hauled me aboard and carried me along. You couldn't have called me ballast: at least ballast has purpose. I was dead weight. Even then, he brought me with.

I untie the line and leap across the gap.

I barely make it. With the line untethered, the boat starts moving before I even land on the gunwale. I hit it with my knees and hook my arm over the rail. Teddy looks over his shoulder again, to make sure he's clear of the dock, and he sees me clinging to the rail. He glares at me. He didn't realize I had jumped on. But it's too late now. He turns away, pressing the handle forward, forward, forward, faster and faster, until we're cutting over the waves, every swell jostling my bones.

I use the rail to pull myself onto the deck and collapse on the closest seat, pushing my wet hair back from my good eye. Teddy doesn't spare me another glance. We're still in the wake zone, but he's going full speed, the boat slamming down over the waves, tilting from side to side as he dodges the lobster buoys that dot the water in pink and green and yellow stripes. On a clear day, we'd be able to see Vantage Point in the distance, the calm curve of the backyard; now the only thing I can see are the lights of the ambulance and cop cars, red and blue pinpricks in the fog, and within seconds, even those are gone. I turn back toward the front just as red metal rises suddenly out of the fog: a channel marker, tipping back and forth frantically, rocked by the swells.

Teddy tugs the wheel, and the boat veers right, tilting sharply. I slide several feet down the wet seat. We miss the buoy by a hair.

"Teddy!" My wail is high and sharp, and it vanishes into the wind.

Teddy cuts across the sound at an angle, perpendicular to the waves, headed for the far end of the narrows and the open sea. The cold air slaps my cheeks. The fog is dense and all-consuming. Everything is noise: the sound of the buoys at the mouth of the harbor clanging loudly, the chugging roar of the engine, the windshield wipers shrieking back and forth, the waves slapping one another as they crash down.

Teddy's wet hair sticks to the sides of his face. He's under the hardtop now, protected from the rain, and water courses off him, carrying blood, dripping pink onto the floor. The puddle grows and grows, and then slides with gravity, a tiny river running straight toward me.

Hysteria swamps me. I scramble up the deck, over the river of blood, closer to Teddy.

"We have to go back," I tell him, trying and failing to control my voice. "It looks bad for you to be running. You get that, right?"

"I didn't do anything wrong."

"I didn't say you did, but—"

"She tripped."

"We have to go back," I say.

He won't look at me. His hands, white with cold, tighten on the wheel. He swerves around another fluorescent buoy.

"Mike quit," he says.

"No one gives a fuck about Mike."

"It's over. It's all over."

"Teddy, it's just a campaign."

"Jess betrayed me. You betrayed me."

"We didn't." I grab his arm and try not to notice how the red comes off on my hand. "I swear on our parents' graves. You didn't see Jess and me together. *The holograms are real.*"

He turns to me then, and the expression on his face, fearful and unsure, makes me tighten my grip on his arm. Our eyes meet. Again I have that feeling of looking into a mirror. *Okay, good. We're turning around—*

But then there's a loud screech. With a mechanical huff, the engine cuts out, yanking the boat to a halt. I fall back, hitting the deck hard, and slide toward the stern as the boat tilts. Black smoke puffs up from the engine as it tries to turn.

"Turn it off!" I shout to Teddy.

He does. The engine stops, and the boat slaps down hard on the next wave. "What the—?"

I crawl on my hands and knees to the back of the boat and look over the edge. A thick white rope is wrapped through the motor. A piece of neon-pink Styrofoam flashes in and out of view as the motor dips in and out of the water.

"You hit a buoy!"

Teddy comes down to the stern and elbows me out of the way. I retreat under the hardtop, trying to balance the weight of the boat. He reaches over the back, yanking at the lobster buoy's rope, yanking harder. He's dangling almost halfway over the boat now. His hands in the motor. If it turned on suddenly, it would take off his hands, maybe more.

Under normal circumstances, getting tangled with a buoy is a pain. Right now, it's a disaster. The water is too rough for a boat this size, even when it's cutting through the waves. Without any power, we've already been twisted parallel with the waves, and each swell slams the boat side to side. Rain pelts us. The air is thick with salt, and I think of how the study smelled when I walked in, the metallic tang of blood.

Teddy tugs again at the rope, but it won't move. "FUCK!" he screams.

The boat rocks. Clinging to the seats for balance, my fingers slipping on the wet leather, I struggle up the deck to the cockpit and reach for the radio.

"What are you doing?" Teddy shouts. He's hauled himself up from the motor and has his legs braced against the swells.

"Calling for help."

Terror crosses his face. "We'll be fine! Put it down."

"We need help!"

He shoves his hands through his wet hair. Blood is a dark smear across his pants. His whole body is shaking. "You can't call them." His voice is shaking, too. "They'll want to know why I left her there."

Jesus Christ. "Then maybe you shouldn't have left her there!" I press the distress button and raise the radio to my lips. "Mayday, mayday, mayday, this is the *Transformation*, mayday—"

With an inhuman roar, Teddy lunges up the deck toward me and grabs the back of my shirt, pulling me out of the cockpit and shoving me across the deck. I slide down the length of the boat and crash into the bench seat where the life preservers are stored. I try to stand up, but he's on me again, my brother, heavy, his hands wet around my throat as he holds me down.

"Don't call!"

"You're hurting me!"

Teddy starts shaking me again. He's much stronger than me, I can't fight back. I don't know if he knows what he's doing. The sky weaves gray above me. My head knocks against the seat. Teddy's hands tighten on my neck, a circle of pain.

So *this* is what it feels like, to have an illusion broken.

It feels like losing everything.

Spots gather in my vision. But some final instinct boils inside me and I give one huge shove, and then the weight is off me, and the boat is tipping again.

A strangled shout.

As I struggle to sit up, I see Teddy as if in slow motion. His feet scrabble for purchase on the deck. His arms windmill. His mouth falls open in shock. His balance is off. Another wave shoves us. His feet slide from under him, and he falls backward over the side of the boat.

"Teddy!" I scream.

I run to the side and look over. Teddy bursts up for air, flailing. I wrench open the seats with the life vests and throw one toward him, but it's flaccid and light, and the wind catches it and carries it twenty feet away. It bobs bright orange in the gray-green waves.

I go back to the seat and find the life preserver, which I haul up and throw over the edge. This time is better. It lands just a few feet from Teddy.

"Grab it! Teddy, grab it!"

He grasps for the preserver once. Twice. The waves are huge. Finally he hooks an arm through it. I sob in relief and grab the rope and start to haul him in. He's so heavy, and I am pulling against the current, and my feet keep sliding on the slippery surface of the deck. The boat keeps rocking on the swells, and I think for sure the hull will crash into him, hit him in the head, but then somehow he's there, at the side of the boat, and I reach over and he grabs my forearm, and I hold his arm harder than I've ever held anything in my life.

Then I feel myself slipping. He's too heavy. He's pulling me overboard. He grabs at my shirt, trying to pull himself up, and with his hand dragging at my torso I can't pull back.

"No, Teddy, no—"

The boat rocks again, and he's back in the water and I'm half overboard, holding myself on to the boat with one hand on the tie-out and my toes hooked under the lip of the open storage container. Teddy's hand latches at my collar. I push at him, and he falls, but he doesn't let go of my collar, and suddenly I am overboard with him, the water like ice through my veins. I break through the surface, gasping for air, and try to take a stroke toward the boat, but he's already there with me, reaching for me, his hand closing around my wrist.

"Stop!" I cry.

I yank my arm. His grip tightens. He won't let me go. He's trying to save me—I think—but it feels like drowning. I can swim well enough on my own, but he's weighing me down.

His mouth moves. I can't hear him. My ears are underwater. In the lull of a wave, I push up to the top and hear him shout.

"I've got you—!" he shouts.

"You're making it worse!" I scream.

He tries to get a better grip on me. I inhale salt water, a burn up my nose, down my throat. The waves push me into him, then pull us apart, and he still has my arm trapped. I turn my head, searching the water for the life preserver. I see the orange dot in the distance and I try to take a stroke, but I can't, Teddy's still gripping me.

"Let me go," I try to say, but I swallow water. Our faces are so close, almost pressed together, and his eyes, my same eyes, are wild with determination.

He will kill me with his helping.

He loops an arm around my shoulders, and his weight pushes me down into the dark water. No matter how hard I kick my legs, I can't push us both up. So instead I go down: out of his grasp, deeper, sliding my head out from the crook of his elbow.

I kick. I kick wildly, and then, miraculously, the water splits and I am back in the world.

I spit and cough and choke and flail my arms through the water. Another flash of orange in my vision. I swim toward it. My progress is both frantic and slow. A wave carries me forward, the riptide pulls me back.

I kick and pull and kick and pull. It goes on forever. My arms are burning. I remember suddenly—I haven't thought of this in years—when I was learning to swim, and how Teddy would help my parents teach me. We would go to the swim club, and in the pool's shining aqua light, my dad would hold me gently by the waist and Teddy would swim backward a couple feet in front of me. He was such a good big brother. He was always smiling. The goggles pinched his eyes. *Come, Clara, come.* I would always follow.

Rope under my hand, and a slick surface. The preserver. I summon all the energy I have left to throw my arms over it and pull myself a few inches out of the water. Waves crash onto me, over and over, spinning me like a top. I wipe my hair from my face and wheel around, sucking in air, searching for Teddy.

For a while, all I see is fog and water. The waves pounding me with every breath, pushing me into the water and back out. The cliffs on the side of the sound are gray shadows. Down below us, the invisible abyss, a dark crack through the bottom of the ocean floor. The *Transformation* is blurred by a curtain of mist. Far off, cutting through the fog, a bright siren. Squeamish lights. The Coast Guard.

But they're too late. I kick again, spinning the rest of the circle, and finally I see Teddy, only twenty feet away, a tan blotch. He hangs in the water like a cross. His head tipped forward, his arms flung out to his sides. His hair plastered to his skull. His arms are moving, and for a moment it looks like he's paddling, but when the next wave lifts me up, I see that I'm wrong. He's sinking into the water, lower, lower still. When a person drowns, the waves will push their arms for them. Up, down, up, down. The aftermath of death: the illusion of swimming.

40

JESS

May 1

"That's good, Jess," Marcela says. "That's really good."

Marcela is my speech therapist. She congratulates me on the stupidest things. I've been working with her almost a year now, so I know when she says *That's good* what she means is *Not quite*. If she wants to tell you something is good, she'll say *That's amazing*. If something is very bad, she says *Let's try again tomorrow*. It took me a while to figure out the code. For weeks, I was garbling gibberish and thinking, thanks to Marcela, that I made perfect sense.

On the clock behind her, the minute hand moves.

"I better get going," I say in my new rusty voice, which still sometimes surprises me with its sound. "I don't want to be late."

"Of course. You have a lot to get done!" She closes the workbook and stands up. "And next time I see you, it'll be online."

"You aren't coming tonight?"

Her constant smile falters. "I have another obligation, unfortunately. But I'm sure it'll be wonderful." There's something in her tone—a stiffness, a self-awareness—that tells me she's part of the boycott.

"Thanks." I was sure she would come. My face reddens, but only barely. These days, it's harder to be surprised.

A year ago, I opened my eyes to a gridded ceiling. Big white tiles interspersed with fluorescent rectangles of light. There was something up my nose and something else down my throat. I tried to turn my head, and a strange feeling split through my neck. I thought it was pain, but it didn't hurt. Everything was muffled except the machines, which beeped mercilessly.

"Welcome back," someone said. "Don't worry. Don't try to move. You're okay. You're safe now."

The speaker came into my field of vision. He was tall, or at least he looked tall from this angle. He was wearing scrubs decorated with cartoon pictures of dogs.

"My name is Will," he said, "and you're in the hospital. You have a breathing tube, so don't try to talk. Okay? I'm going to get the doctor, and he'll explain."

He left. Another face came in. For a moment I thought that person was a stranger, too. I didn't recognize her, with the bandages on one half of her face, the other half swollen and bruised. Then she pressed her hands to her cheeks, as if overcome by the sight of me, and I saw the tattoo on her arm.

Clara, I tried to say. *What happened?* It came out garbled. I choked on the tube.

"Don't try to talk," she said. Then she burst into tears. "Oh my god. Oh my god."

My ears were adjusting. I could hear past the beeps of my machines, to the hospital's other sounds, carts squeaking down the hallway, moans of pain from the room next door, rubber-soled clogs clomping on linoleum, two nurses talking about the action movie they were going to see this weekend. I could hear Clara's sobs.

The doctor came in, in a white robe. Behind him, the nurse, and another nurse, and a man I slowly recognized as a member of the island police. There was no Teddy. The tube kept me from asking where he was. I didn't know about the boat chase yet, or the struggle in the water.

But I looked at Clara, and in response to the question I didn't know to ask, she shook her head. That was how I learned that he was gone.

For several weeks, I lay in the hospital bed and veered between extremes. Sometimes I wanted to die. Sometimes I felt I already had. Sometimes I wanted to change my name. I wanted to peel myself away from my entire life and vanish like a ghost. I felt chained in place. I felt like I was finally free.

For those first few weeks, I couldn't bear to look at Clara. She had told me everything that had happened, and I believed her story. The death had been ruled an accidental drowning. Even so. She looked too similar to Teddy. She had been present for too much. It sent me into memories I remembered—our first kiss, our last fight—and memories I didn't. Ones I made up all on my own: his skin gray from the ocean, water streaming from his mouth. If I had had my way, I wouldn't have seen her at all.

But I didn't have my way. I couldn't talk. The glass had struck me through my neck, and I needed a breathing tube and seemingly endless surgeries to get my throat working correctly again. Another piece of glass had sliced my lip down almost to the chin, and the stitches made it difficult to move my mouth at all.

The medical team was amazed. The glass had stopped just shy of the jugular. The mast had stopped just shy of my lungs.

Lucky girl, the doctor said.

Lucky, lucky girl.

Because I couldn't speak, the most I could do to get Clara out was jab my index finger toward the door, which she ignored. I finger-spelled GET OUT to her, and she ignored that, too.

At first, I had other visitors. Acquaintances from college, or from the island. Phoebe, of all people. They came so they could say they had come. I lay in my bed, silent, a witness to their witnessing. My mother came for three days, then had to get back to Florida. The bioluminescent tours must go on. They were thinking of expanding their services to another lagoon.

When everyone else forgot about me, Clara kept coming back, day after day. She watched soap operas with me and read books aloud to me and painted my toenails. She did all the things I had done for her, a long time ago, and I finally saw that it wasn't better on this side of it. Not at all.

In fact, perhaps that logic had been our problem. We were so certain someone had to have it better—one of us had to be wealthier or stronger, happier or more beloved—that our love had become inseparable from envy or self-doubt.

I did sometimes want to burn it all down, start over. But could I really bear to let Clara go? No one else would understand what we had been through. What we had been through was a part of me now. Sometimes it felt like it was all of me.

By the time they took out the tube permanently, and I could open my mouth for the lisping guttural sounds that Marcela would later have to help me correct, I had begun finger-spelling THANK YOU and

LOVE YOU and, when Clara told a bad joke, THAT'S FUNNY. We had to be generous to each other. We had no other option. Clara and I were tied together forever.

Just as we had promised, when we were kids.

I used to be able to go unrecognized if I was off the island and out of context, but those days are gone. The events were splashed all over the national news. Everyone was in a fever about it. My photo was everywhere, along with Clara's and Teddy's. Someone at the police station leaked the security footage of Teddy shoving me into the glass case, and that went viral, too.

His security system did catch a crime in progress, in the end.

I didn't know murder tourists existed until we became their destination. They arrived quickly, over the next few months, eager to absorb the tragedy, marinate in our loss. Many of them had seen the video of Teddy pushing me, and it had lodged in their minds so fully that they occasionally forgot I had lived to tell the tale. Sometimes if I ran into one in town, they stared at me like they had seen a ghost.

Conrad was convicted of assault and felony robbery and sentenced to fifteen years in prison, thanks mostly to a DA whose reelection campaign we agreed to sponsor. Another quarter million went to private lawyers.

So justice prevails.

Clara and I never told anyone that Conrad had made the deepfake videos, and we never mentioned the holograms publicly. We agreed it would only add to the media circus, which might redirect attention to the circumstances of Conrad's arrest. Rumor had it that Conrad had been trying to pitch his lawyer on a defense involving holograms, but the lawyer refused.

Come up with a story someone might actually believe, he said.

I went to visit Conrad in prison once. With no product, his hair was flat. Without the Burberry trench, his shoulders seemed smaller. There had never been anything remarkable about him, and now there was even less. If the guard hadn't brought him straight to me, I might not even have known it was him.

We sat across the glass from each other. I thought perhaps I would get an apology. I believed he had been telling Clara the truth when he said that he had never planned to hurt anyone, that he hadn't realized how far things would spiral. Remorse seemed the natural next step. I intentionally took the bandage off my neck before I went, so he could see the raised purple line of stitches. His eyes kept drifting to it as we talked, and I thought I saw a shadow of compunction. But then there was a turn, toward the end, when I said he owed me, and the shadow slid away.

He wasn't to blame, he insisted. We had driven him to it. We had made him do it all.

In the end, the only way he would give me what I wanted was if I wrote a letter to the parole board on his behalf, begging for early release, on the grounds that he was a changed man. I promised I would.

We'll see. We have several years before that day comes. Promises get forgotten all the time.

With Teddy gone, Vantage Point passed into Clara's name. We agreed together that we couldn't bear to live there anymore, but nor could we bear to tear it down. Instead, Clara had the idea to turn it into a clinic dedicated to recovery from eating disorders. To be honest, I thought this would be another big idea she never carried out, but instead she pulled it all together faster than I relearned how to say the letter r. She went back to Marien to see how they ran the ED program, see what she wanted to take and what she wanted to change. She hired a director, several doctors, several counselors. She did the nonprofit paperwork and the insurance paperwork.

The clinic will open in a few months. Overall, I have a good feeling about it, if we can get the murder tourists to stop taking pictures of patients as they come and go.

Meanwhile, Clara and I have decided to start fresh. She handed WFCI off to Allan, who was the only person ever qualified to run it anyway. We leave in a few days for London, where we'll be for a few months, then maybe Paris, Tokyo, Shanghai. I want busy cities, cities where I can pass mostly undetected, where I can't be left alone with the quiet of my own mind.

Tonight is the last May Day we'll host before the clinic takes over the space. Last year's event was an obvious disaster, and we want to end the tradition on a good note. At first, I wasn't sure anyone would want to come. Many of the islanders are still distant. Sadie Michaud doesn't acknowledge me when we pass each other in the street. I'm not even offended. It's hard to care about things like that anymore; the grief takes up too much room. Anyway, after having so much written about me—*battered wife, playing the victim, gold digger gets her payout, bitch drove him to it, how dare she mourn someone who tried to kill her*—Sadie's type of anger comes as a relief. At least she hates me for me.

So I prepared mentally for a poor turnout for May Day. Then, two weeks ago, I was told all the hotel rooms in town had been booked up. An hour ago, I learned that cars are already lining up outside the gates. Many of them will be murder tourists, I'm sure. But maybe some of them will be islanders, too, who want a last chance to ogle, or gloat, or judge, or admire. Type E: the Entertained.

Clara meets me in the gardens five minutes before the gates are due to open. I have the security app pulled up on my phone. She's in a sweatshirt. I'm in a farm coat. I gave away most of my clothes when I gave away Teddy's. I mostly wear jeans and T-shirts now. The coat is maybe unnecessary. Spring came so early this year. By the beginning of March, the last traces of snow had melted and the deer had started to push antlers forth from their narrow skulls.

"Not looking their best," Clara says cheerfully about the gardens. The thaw has made a couple shrubs bloom early, but the rest are still muddy sticks. "Maybe you should have rented a bunch of flowers again."

"Eh. Too much work. And you said no more secrets."

She snorts. "I don't think anyone was really fooled by the flowers."

She wraps me in a hug. She's cut her hair short now. The edges brush my chin. Pale brown strands. I'm wearing her boots. She smells like my shampoo.

She releases me and looks me in the eye. "You okay?"

"All right. You?"

"As I'll ever be."

She drops her hand to mine and squeezes.

Together, we let them in.

No more secrets, except one.

A while back, Clara told me she still had the NatureEye projector that she picked up from the yard—one of the many that Conrad must have used, although we never found the others; he must have collected them when he was here for May Day. It had been in her freezer this whole time. Classic Clara, she had forgotten it was there. She was planning to throw it in the ocean, because it gave her the creeps to have it around. I told her I'd take care of it.

The next week I went to visit Conrad in prison, as I've described. But I wasn't there to gloat. When he and I made our trade, I didn't want an apology.

I wanted an algorithm.

So here's my secret: many nights, after Clara's gone to sleep, I go to a room far away and lock the door. I take out the projector. I turn it on.

And then he's there—

Teddy, as I remember him. The way I want to remember him: at Marien, that first time, his eyes locked on mine. *I've decided.* At our wedding, dipping me on the dance floor, his hand tensing against my spine as he took my weight. On our honeymoon, diving off the yacht and resurfacing, swimming back, shaking the water from his hair.

We talk for hours. Into the computer, I fed in things I thought he might say. Things I wanted him to say. Not the bad parts, not the parts that broke us. I taught the machine his language, his accent, his expressions. I filled it with enough photos and videos and words that it could think on its own.

Now, I just let it run.

Clara doesn't know. She wouldn't understand. I told her the idea once. I mentioned it in passing, as if it was a casual thought, and not something I had been mulling over for months. I phrased it as a hypothetical. *Are you ever tempted to make the projector show you your parents again, or—?*

"No," she said sharply. "Absolutely not. Last time I saw them like that, it only made it worse. I don't want to be tricked."

"But you'd only be tricking yourself."

"I don't think I can trick myself like that anymore." She shivered. "I would know it wasn't really them."

I dropped the subject. I understood it made her feel better to think that she would know. And yes, when I turn the projector on, I know what I'm doing. I'm aware that technically, it isn't really him.

But then he's there in front of me. He looks and sounds like Teddy. The length of his arms, the shape of his nose. The small dimple in his cheek. His eyes crinkle when he looks at me, as if he's the lucky one. He tells me I'm beautiful. He tells me I'm safe. And for that window of time, there's no reason for grief. Time's been wound back. Fate's been undone. The only way I would know he wasn't real would be if I tried to touch him.

So I don't try.

That's all there is to it. I suspend my disbelief. I choose not to see.

You do it, too. We're wired to believe. A soul is invisible, after all. Everything important is unprovable. So of course we are happy to go along with the imitation. The video, the photograph, the reel. The book.

Take me, for example. You think I'm Jess, and Clara is Clara. We told you so. But we could be imitating each other, for all you know. We could be Conrad, or Teddy, or a stranger. Someone behind us telling our story, speaking for us, pulling our strings. When it comes down to it, have you ever touched us? Have you ever held us and felt our beating pulse, the oxygen pushing at our lungs?

Of course you think this voice is mine.

But what proof do you have?

How could you ever really know?

ACKNOWLEDGMENTS

I love thanking people but hate coming up with synonyms for the word *thank*. So let me get right to the good part. Immense, joyous, radiant thanks to—

Daphne Durham: greatest, most supportive OG editor of all time. Believed in me and this book even when she really, really shouldn't have. Worked patiently through many terrible drafts. 10/10. No notes.

Katie Liptak: greatest, most supportive adoptive editor of all time. Treated this novel with such care and energy, from the line level to the get-it-in-front-of-people level.

Danya Kukafka and Michelle Brower: greatest, most supportive agents of all time. These are people you want in the trenches with you.

Allison Malecha: same, in a foreign language.

Allison Warren and Kayla Grogan: same again, in Technicolor.

The whole team at MCD; Farrar, Straus and Giroux; and Macmillan— Abby Kagan, Nina Frieman, Claire Tobin, Christopher Lin, Chandra Wohleber, and Nancy Elgin—for making the book readable, then beautiful, then talk-about-able.

Especially Brianna Fairman and Lydia Zoells: who helped this book in many ways I know about, and probably many more I don't.

And also especially superstar Sean McDonald: for being a rad publisher, and for carrying this book across the finish line.

Amy Jo Burns, Julia Fine, and Katie Gutierrez: the most caring and brilliant writing group. Not sure how I conned my way into your ranks but I appreciate you all falling for the ruse. This book would be a serious garbage pile without your comments, and I would be a garbage pile without your friendship.

Subject experts Anjie Zheng and Seguin Strohmeier. Plot-talkers-through Joan Flores-Villalobos, Honora Talbott, and Paige Safyer. Robin Wasserman, for a sharp read and comments that unlocked so much for me.

Jamie Rosengard, Stacy Greenberg, et secret alia: your belief in *Take Me Apart* buoyed me at a time when I (and therefore *Vantage Point*) really needed it. Extra credit to Jamie for some premium plot-hole-plugging work.

Anne: brain-fixer extraordinaire. I really don't know who I would be today without you.

Nancy Ruttenberg: who introduced me to Charles Brockden Brown's 1798 novel *Wieland* in a grad seminar, never knowing what she would set in motion. Nancy's *Democratic Personality: Popular Voice and the Trial of American Authorship* and Christopher Looby's *Voicing America: Language, Literary Form, and the Origins of the United States* are both excellent books with chapters on *Wieland* that helped shape my understanding of that novel's political themes.

Carrie Goldberg: for her book *Nobody's Victim: Fighting Psychos, Stalkers, Pervs, and Trolls*, which was enormously helpful and disturbing when I was researching revenge porn.

Nina Schick: for her book *Deepfakes: The Coming Infocalypse*, which was an invaluable resource on deepfakes, which continue to become more terrifyingly convincing every day.

Of the deepfake technology in this book, much less is invented than you would probably like to believe. I started planning this book in 2016, when deepfakes were a niche phenomenon, and they've only gotten scarier. At the time of writing these acknowledgments, a number of bills related to deepfakes are working their way through legislatures in the United States and abroad. While I hope this book publishes into an environment with more legal oversight of deepfakes (and harsher repercussions for spreading revenge porn), I am sure that even in the best-case scenario, there will be plenty of work left to do.

I took many, many liberties when creating this fictional island. But I am still enormously grateful to the people and institutions of Mount Desert Island and Acadia National Park, especially Rosemary Matchak and Charlie Stephenson, Jay and Alicia Scribner, and the Northeast Harbor Public Library. I would say there's no way to express how much this area of Maine means to me, but I guess I wrote a book about it.

My colleagues and students at USC: for helping me stay passionate about books every day. Also for providing me with a regular paycheck.

My writing community, especially in Los Angeles: I am convinced this is the best city in which to be a novelist.

I can't name every friend who helped return me to solidity when working on this book turned me into a puddle, but special thank-yous to Aku Ammah-Tagoe, Batia Snir, Bree Barton, Catherine Down, Cordelia Loots-Gollin, Honora Talbott, and Joan Flores-Villalobos. And to Elizabeth Della Zazzera, who first taught me the word *deepfake* back in 2016.

My parents, Steve and Mary, and my siblings, Laura and Chris: your love and support mean everything.

Wilkie: for a potato, you wore that dog costume very well. You were by my side through every page of this book. Drafts upon drafts were written to the music of your snores, the warmth of your weight on my lap. I miss you so much. Thanks for being my pal.

And, of course, readers and booksellers. You are the real ones.

A Note About the Author

Sara Sligar is an assistant professor of English and creative writing at the University of Southern California. Her first novel, *Take Me Apart*, was published by MCD in 2020. It was a *Kirkus Reviews* Best Book of the Year and was short-listed for the Ned Kelly Award for Best International Crime Fiction. She holds a doctoral degree in English from the University of Pennsylvania and a master's of philosophy in modern European history from the University of Cambridge.

l